MINE THE DARKNESS

JACK GARRETY

FOR'SAIL PTY LTD

MINE THE DARKNESS

JACK GARRETY

FOR'SAIL PTY LTD

To Annie
for being my light that dispels the darkness

PROLOGUE

Melbourne:

Jessica heard footsteps behind her. Heard them nested within the patter of the rain.

Even.

Steady.

Matching hers.

It could be anyone.

The cross street was a shortcut—hundreds of workers and shoppers used it every day.

But not this late.

The footsteps sounded closer. She walked a little faster, the guitar case bumping an urgent rhythm against her leg.

Red traffic lights at the far end of the alley; she was close enough to make out the cars hissing to a stop, cautious in the misty rain—too far away to help. Turning to look over her shoulder, she saw nothing and everything, her second sight spiking with frenzied imaginings.

He's coming for you. White noise whooshed in her ears like indistinct voices trapped between frequencies. She increased her pace, craving the safety of the cars at the end of the alley.

The lights turned green.

She ran, high heels making it harder. One shoe slipped, slewing sideways, sending her foot deep into a water-filled pothole.

Lurching.

Cursing.

The strap of the guitar case slipped from her shoulder—she lost more ground hauling it back up.

The heel of her right shoe was gone, lost in the pothole. Hop-hobbling, Jess managed a limping run.

She could definitely hear him now; his footfalls pounding and heavy behind her.

Catching up.

Then... the first clutching touch. Jerking away from it, she screamed, words lost, realizing in the yawning space between ragged breaths that she could not outrun him. Instead she turned to face him, the fear swept aside by something primal and molten that surged from her core.

Angry, scared—already scarred—Jess used the weight of her body to swing the guitar case in a wide arc. It struck him on the side of his head with a dull thunk, the displaced energy jolting along her arm. He grunted and doubled over, clutching his head. Red leaked, then ran between his sausage-shaped fingers.

He was a big man, dressed in black.

The white noise grew louder, and she knew what she had to do.

Raising her arms to steady herself, she drew her leg back, arching her dancer's foot before driving it into his balls. With an outrush of air he fell to one knee, torso folding over instinctively. She kicked him again; he fell back, his face caught briefly in the backwash of spilled light from the end of the alley.

Leaving behind her useless shoes, she ran again, bare feet splashing lightly through the puddles toward the amber light beckoning from the main road. Behind her, shambling steps followed, but by then she'd rounded the corner.

IT WAS ten o'clock in a place that didn't keep time.

Ten missed calls.

Their persistence must have finally drawn her back from where the white noise had dumped her.

The ringing began again. Caller ID: Blocked, same as the others.

Whoever it was seemed desperate to get through. Mum, probably. If ever there was a blocked number, it was hers. Yet Jess was unwilling to reach out and connect, to take a chance that it wouldn't be the man who'd attacked her. She didn't want to imagine that he might know where she lived.

The ringing stopped abruptly once more. She waited. There was no reassuring beep to say a message had been left, and Jess remembered: Mum hated voicemail.

The ringing began again. She considered turning the phone off.

But that would mean he'd won.

The memory from the alley barged through unannounced. The man's energy had felt red and dangerous, but she'd matched it with her own, surprising herself.

Perhaps her ex-everything, Martin, had been wrong after all. She wasn't weak and helpless, certainly not without him. Yet something yielding and even more terrifying remained, and now she remembered what it was. When she'd hit him with the guitar case, one flap of his long black coat had gaped open. In that frozen moment she'd seen what in hindsight looked like a long, shiny metal axe strapped to the side of his body and knew it had been meant for her. Not just attempted rape then, but annihilation as well. She imagined herself mutilated and bloodied, sprawled in the alleyway. Another human headline: Next Hacker Victim.

A cracking noise startled her.

Did I lock all the doors and windows?

It cracked again, and Jessica relaxed, recognizing it—the fridge's auto-defrost kicking some icy butt. She laughed and shook her head.

10:03.

She needed to bring her anxiety levels down before the white noise returned. Leaning back, she closed her eyes, breathing deeply, regularly, but her mind refused to release. Yesterday the sound from the fridge would hardly have registered—just another urban night noise. Now, ten floors up in a locked apartment building, the compulsion was there to check all the doors and windows—twice, the taste of horror still fresh.

Perhaps she could try to use it? So few actors experienced real terror. Martin would say it was a blessing, "another layer of experience to be mined, Jess." But Martin was obsessed. Always and all ways: with the theatre, her, but mostly with himself.

This wasn't helping; already she could detect a thin high-pitched whine at the far reaches of her consciousness, faint but definitely there, like a distant train whistle, warning but defiant.

The white noise express.

Write it out.

Get it down.

She fumbled in the desk drawer for her diary, opened it to a new page, and wrote:

Rape is such an ugly word; it doesn't even have to happen to happen.

Seeing the words angling across the page, their letters jagged and angry, brought the feeling of helplessness back. She felt like a small skiff caught without oars on an out-flowing tide.

The phone rang again. She jumped.

It had to be Mum; something must be wrong.

Reaching for the handset, Jess noticed that her fingers were wet and stained with blue, the jagged remnants of the fountain pen adrift on the diary.

'Hello?'

No one spoke from the other end, though she could hear sounds, someone breathing.

'Hello? Who's there?'

When the voice came it was reluctant and aspirated, as if unused to making words.

'I've got your guitar.'

ONE

Milt stirred, felt sleep leaking away.

He groaned. The headache was already intense. It beat against his skull, trying to find a way out while something hard and sharp pushed against his right cheek.

Opening his eyes, he blinked. The room was blurry, too bright—and on its side.

He tried to focus, his thick eyebrows bunching together as if conferring with each other—"the chatting caterpillars," the guys used to call them—but the squint served to shift his perspective and he realized he was sprawled across the carpet of the lounge room, his cheek heavy against his hand. When he tugged it free, something unfamiliar dragged against the overnight bristles—a chunky gold ring inset with a large polished stone jammed onto his thick pinky finger.

Where the hell did that come from?

He sat up, trying to pull the ring off, but it was stuck. His knuckles had always been too big for rings. They'd go on all right but getting them back off again.... *Why can't I remember?* He looked around for something to prompt his memory. Two empty packets of cigarettes mocked him from the side table.

Bloody smokes. Again.

He'd quit them along with the force two years before. Then, only last month, he'd found a crumpled pack in the pocket of his leather jacket. Even then he would have put that down to picking up someone else's—it wouldn't have been the first time—but inside had been a disposable lighter wedged upside down between the remaining smokes. His habit; his smokes.

Since then, there'd been other instances. A myriad of hows and whys that he couldn't quite recall; black splotches in his memory, without continuity between when and then, like now—waking up in a set of clothes he didn't remember changing into, his fingernails rimed with grime, some split and broken. Now here was this blasted ring.

Lumbering to his feet, he felt water squish inside his shoes. He swore and bent down to tug them off. The sudden movement threw him off-balance. He hopped, then lurched against the side of the three-seater. Using it for support, he cautiously eased off the shoes and saturated socks, tossing them into a soggy heap on the carpet. The white skin of his toes was puckered as if he'd stayed too long in a bath. He rubbed the soles of his feet against the thick carpet, noticing the dried clay-like mud in a filthy trail from the front door. It matched what was on his shoes. *Did it rain when I went out to get the smokes?*

Doggedly he shuffled through ragged remnants of yesterday: first had been the gym, then afterwards a lazy breakfast down at that cafe on the corner. What then? *Yes, I came back up here to the apartment.* He recalled that the sun had been streaming in at about the same brightness and intensity as now. Automatically, he glanced over at the round chrome clock on the kitchen wall.

11:30.

He nodded. Good, that would be about right. Now he had a time frame. He'd gone straight through to shower before settling down to paint. He glanced over at the easel in the corner, at the dark glaring slashes of crimson and black. Then, something had happened. He vaguely recalled the feeling of being both irritated at whatever the interruption had been and pleased for the excuse to leave the disturbing flow the painting had taken him on. A phone call? Yes, that had been it, but from who?

The gaps in his memory were becoming wider and more frequent. The only clues were the increasingly violent style that had crept into his art, as if he was trying to tell himself something.

It was the uncertainty he found the hardest. What if he'd done something? All his life there had been one thing he'd been sure of: himself. Yet here was incontestable proof that he could no longer trust his particular worldview. If that wasn't nailed down, then what else might be coming loose?

He shook the feeling away.

Stick with what I know. What are the facts?

He was wearing a ring. He brought that up for a closer look. Definitely not new, so logically it had been someone's. The thick metal was dulled, abraded by a multitude of miniscule scratches in a way that only eighteen-plus carat could be. So it was probably valuable. Yet the stone was plain. Grey and smooth—waxy. It reminded him of stones he'd fossicked for at Lightning Ridge looking for opals. The same coloring and feel... pre-opal. Potch. That's what it was called. Why would anyone set a hunk of that worthless stuff into a ring, much less one that required this much gold?

More important, though, the ring felt too tight. He needed to get it off. It would be a race between easing the pounding of his head or finding something to grease the ring over his misshapen knuckle.

He staggered into the kitchen, pausing in front of a hall mirror to examine the cause of the pain. The ugly gash on the side of his head had broken open. Streaks of dried blood led from it. No other new wounds though, that was something, but his eyes looked like pissholes in the snow.

Jesus. Where was I last night?

He fumbled through the medical kit, found aspirin, dropped two —then a third—into a tumbler of water, and lifted it to his mouth, gulping down the contents before they'd fully dissolved.

Phew, what's that stink?

Putting the glass down, Milt tentatively sniffed his fingers. He recoiled, nose crinkling.

Whoa. Where have they been?

He filled the big metal sink with warm soapy water and thoroughly washed his hand with the kitchen wipe. Once the smell had lessened, he worked the liquid soap under the ring on his left hand and tried to drag it off. It still wouldn't budge.

What else?

The feeling of tightness around his finger squeezed out a latent memory of himself at seven, his arm stuck between the front seats of a rusted-out ute his father kept "for parts." His mother had slathered his arm with butter to get him out. He recalled the slimy feel when his arm finally slipped free. She'd made him eat his toast dry for a month afterward.

Butter? Why not? He quickly dried his hands, opened the fridge, and gagged.

The same putrid smell that had been on his fingers wafted out of the fridge, only much stronger. Something had gone horribly off in there. He bent down, examining each shelf until he reached the meat drawer. He'd never used this section, yet he could see something through the translucent plastic.

Something motley green.

Milt sucked in a lungful of fresh air, holding it in as he slid the drawer open.

It was a hand, severed at the wrist, partway through decomposition. Hot gorge rose in his throat, sour and burning. Choking it back only sucked up even more of the stink, and he vomited in an explosive stream over the tiled white floor.

AFTER CLEANING UP, he turned back to the fridge. The door was still open, water beading on the inside of the crisper drawer. He eased it open and peered inside.

It was a left hand, he could tell that much from the thumb. The fingers were swollen and bloated as if they'd been overfilled, the yellowed nails resembling claws. All fingers were intact save the third—the ring finger. That lay in two pieces at the side of the crisper. Milt's guts churned again, and he spun away, hands moving to hold his head, traitorous fingers still heavy with the stink—or maybe the smell was trapped in his sinuses.

Jesus, what is going on here? What have I done?

Finally, he forced himself to stride over to the island bench and pull out a shopping bag from the cupboard beneath the sink. Slipping his hand inside the plastic bag, he picked up the rotting flesh. It felt squishy and overripe.

Hastily he pulled the bag inside out and tied it off with a double knot. More fingers came loose and slid around the bottom of the bag.

Now what?

He'd obviously dug some poor dead bastard up and must have broken the finger to get at the ring. There was no telling who would have seen him, so he wouldn't risk ringing the police. Not just yet. Not until he found out what had happened.

On impulse, he put the bag into the freezer. That at least would stop the decomposition until he decided what to do with it.

The stink remained, stuck deep. He found a tissue and tried to blow his sinuses clear, deciding belatedly the smell must be still coming from the meat drawer.

Turning back, he bent down and gripped the drawer, ready to pull it out and take it over to the sink.

Something else was in there.

Tentatively, Milt reached for it. A business card, scrunched with damp. He turned it over. It was one of his. His own scratchy scrawl angled across it:

Moncrieff Restaurant

An address was written below.

The card had soaked up some of the condensation, and the final line of text had run. He held it up to the light.

Wilmott. Dinner, Monday 18th—730.

He glanced over at the calendar on the wall. That was tonight.

TWO

'Good evening, sir.'

The maître d's practiced eye swept him, estimating his worth. Milt doggedly stared him out. The guy looked like his old grandpop; he even had the same pasted-down hairstyle.

'There's a table booked for—er...' Milt glanced at the card in his hand. 'Wilmott.'

The maître d's face brightened immediately.

'Ah, Dr. Wilmott. Of course, of course. Please to come. This way.'

Milt followed the man through the restaurant. He hadn't been to this joint before—it was a restored Victorian and everything from the waiters' long aprons to the tablecloths was starched white. There were no other diners. Bloody joint was full of wait staff, all old farts — waiting. He grinned.

The maître d' paused at a square table angled for privacy and warmth beside a gray marble fireplace. He pulled out one of the high-backed chairs and waved toward it. 'There was a message. Dr. Wilmott will join with you shortly.'

Milt settled cautiously onto the chair. It creaked but held. The maître d' snapped open a starched white napkin and draped it across

Milt's lap before reverently presenting a massive menu bound in burgundy leather.

'May I be getting you a pre-dinner drink, sir?'

'Champagne. Mumms, if you have it,' Milt said. Whoever Dr. Wilmott turned out to be, he'd better have his credit card charged up. The maître d' made a half bow and backed away.

Bloody wanker.

'Excellent choice, Milt. I would have gone for Veuve myself. They have an excellent '69 in their cellar.'

Milt started. A woman was sitting in the chair opposite.

Where the hell had she come from?

He made an attempt at recovery. 'I've been known to drink anything, but a '69 might be getting on a bit now, even for me,' he said, eyebrows bunching.

'I like to think of time as a relative concept. It all depends on where you start from, wouldn't you agree?' The woman smiled, her face brightening as she reached across the table. 'Aggie Wilmott. Sorry I wasn't here when you arrived, Milt. Can I call you Milt?' Her vowels were clipped and well enunciated.

Milt nodded, enveloping her small hand inside his. Her grip was deceptively firm. She was one of those little women who appeared large. With makeup she could probably squeak in under fifty, however, the thatch of gray at either temple pushed her age out considerably, as if she didn't care. Normally, he would have found that refreshing.

'Confused, Milt?'

He reached inside his jacket and flicked the crumpled business card across the table. It lay face up, bent and smeared where the condensation had spread the ink.

'Only about this—and an extra hand that I found alongside it in my fridge.'

She glanced at it and then quietly met his fierce glare. "The policeman's stare," his daughter used to call it.

The champagne arrived, and Aggie held up her hand, placing

Milt on pause. He waited while the *sommelier*, a key hanging from a silver chain at his belt, quietly presented the wine. Aggie nodded, and the man deftly dismantled the restraining cage around the cork before expertly turning and drawing the base of the bottle away. The cork released with a discreet pop into his other hand. Aggie sampled the champagne. This guy looked even older than the maître d'. *What sort of retirement joint was this?*

When the *sommelier* left, Milt leaned across the table and pointed a stubby finger at the card.

'Give me one reason why I shouldn't just call the police?'

'And say what, Milt? Can I give you a hand?' She chuckled. 'No, it seems that you're the one with the dilemma.' Aggie picked up the card as if it were a dubious fish fillet. 'Even this card, which you seem fixated about, appears to be one of yours, and I daresay this might even be your handwriting? Am I right?'

She offered it to him, and after a moment he snatched it back, returning it to his jacket pocket. 'The trouble is, I don't remember writing it. So I'm figuring you must have set this up. Even this weird-looking joint....' He opened his hands to include the restaurant as if that said it all.

'Set up what?' she asked, innocence in her eyes.

Milt settled back against the chair's plush velvet upholstery and folded his arms, nodding. 'So that's it, is it? You've got the body belonging to the hand stashed somewhere and I'm linked to it. Well, if this is a shakedown, you're shit out of luck because there is no money behind this handsome mug—'

She snorted, bringing the back of her hand to her mouth, suppressing laughter. 'Oh, I am sorry, Milt. Believe me that's the very last thing— But I can see why you may think that.' Her expression settled, and she leaned forward. 'If I can be frank with you, it was simply time for us to talk.'

'Talk?'

'Yes. You see, I do know what's been happening to you, Milt. The gaps in your memory—the blackness, the white noise, all that. In a way, I am a little bit responsible for it.' She sighed, her gaze sliding away from him to look down at the table. 'You're right about the body too. There is one, but be assured, you didn't kill her.'

Milt was surprised to feel a weight dissolve from between his shoulder blades.

'So who did? You?'

She shook her head. 'But I do know who she was.'

'Who?'

'Angelique Watson. She was a member of our, er, group.'

The name meant nothing to Milt, and he shrugged. 'Then you really should be talking to the police. I don't see what any of this has to do with me. This is your bloody mystery, not mine.'

She picked up her champagne flute and tilted it toward him. 'Here's to mysteries, then. This is fine wine; we really shouldn't let it go to waste.'

He picked up his glass, ignoring her invitation to clink glasses, and sipped. She was right. The champagne was excellent. He swallowed, feeling the cold effervescence trace down his throat, into his stomach. He drained the glass and set it down, sliding the silver cutlery into a cluttered pile at his elbow. Each piece was engraved with a crest, a small *M* nestled within it.

'I'm starving,' she said, picking up one of the oversized menus.

After a moment, Milt did the same. What she was doing was a technique, he knew that, designed to unsettle him. Well, two could play in that mud puddle. Besides, he had to eat somewhere, and as she was paying....

The menu was all in French, but he managed to find the steaks.

When he looked up, one of the ancient waiters was standing beside the table.

'Tournedos Rossini,' Milt said, handing back the large menu, '*bleu*.'

Aggie ordered something in French. It sounded far too long to just be food. The waiter allowed himself the ghost of a smile, looking briefly at Milt before drifting away like so much smoke.

'I told him you were my toy boy and you needed to keep your strength up. Sometimes the steaks here are a little on the small size.'

A log collapsed in the fireplace, releasing a rush of warmth, and with it Milt found his face creasing into an unaccustomed smile.

It was as if he were watching himself as he said, 'Some toy boy—I'm playing the back nine of forty. Just a burnt-out ex-cop with a story he sold, but I'm guessing you know all that.'

'Yes, Milt. Yes, I do.' Her eyes softened, and he felt uncomfortably sure she knew all of it. Everything. He shook the feeling away and gulped at the champagne, his mouth running dry almost immediately. Aggie refilled his glass. The frustration returned, settling dark and heavy around him.

'You still haven't told me how this concerns me,' he said. 'If I had nothing to do with the death, then why was her rotting hand in my fridge?'

'I didn't say it had nothing to do with you.' She pointed at his fingers drumming beside the piled cutlery. 'Take that ring, for example. Have you had it long?'

'No. Why?' He resisted the urge to move his hand onto his lap.

She reached over and lifted his little finger, angling it so that the ring caught the firelight. The touch of her skin was cool, but not pleasantly so.

'It's Angelique's,' Aggie said, releasing it.

'The dead woman?'

'Quite. The ring's design is quite distinctive; I'd know it anywhere. I'm not sure it... suits you, though. Do you remember how you came by it?'

'No,' he mumbled. 'It was there when I woke up this morning. I can't get the damned thing off.'

'You won't be able to. Not until it's ready.'

'Not until *it's* ready?' he asked, his voice mocking. 'What's it waiting for? A bloody bus?'

'No. Its new owner.'

'Now I know you're nuts. I'm leaving.'

Aggie dipped her index finger in her champagne and ran the moistened tip lightly around the rim of the crystal flute. It began to sing, the crystal resonating beneath her touch.

When Milt tried to stand, he found he couldn't.

'What have you done? What's happening to me?' His voice rose. 'I can't get out of the damned chair.'

'Everyone needs a little help to bring out their song, Milt. Just relax. The more you struggle, the more difficult this will be.'

Milt pushed his feet against the floor, straining, but couldn't raise himself off the chair. He was stuck.

'The more you struggle....' She allowed her voice to trail off.

His nickname in the force had been "the bear." Thanks to the gym, he was even stronger now but neither the chair nor the table would budge. Clenching his teeth, he tried again. It was as if they were screwed into the floor, yet he'd felt the table move beneath his arm earlier when he'd sat down.

Without taking her eyes from him, she increased the speed of her finger around the rim of the glass.

'What the hell do you want?'

The high-pitched sound was coming from all directions. When he looked up, the restaurant and everything in it seemed to be spinning, dissolving into swirls of color that whipped about him as if he were in the middle of a massive centrifuge.

He tried to reach across the table and upend the glass—anything to stop the noise—but now his hand refused to move as well. The ring encircling his pinkie pulsed in time with the frequency from the glass, attracting it somehow until the resonation insinuated itself inside him, poking and probing until it uncovered something he didn't have a word for, something buried deep, then began drawing it out, up to the surface.

He opened his mouth to scream, and what could have been champagne gushed in, filling his mouth, effervescing up the back of his throat and into his nose. He coughed, long and deep, the effort forcing moisture into his eyes, smearing his vision with what seemed to be black ink.

When it cleared, the restaurant—everything—had vanished.

He found himself standing in the middle of a shallow pool surrounded by forest. A kangaroo that had been drinking at the edge looked up, startled, and bounded back into the surrounding bush.

Milt shook his head and splashed out, his clothes heavy with mud —shoes and socks saturated. Oddly, he didn't feel upset or disoriented, and when he looked around he found he could zoom his perspective out or in, so he could either see himself—as if he were watching a movie—or retract back inside his body to use his "own" eyes. Idly he flipped the zoom back and forth as if turning a dial and noted curiously that he was not attached to either. It was as if some objective part of him had disengaged and was simply observing. Curiously, this didn't cause him any anxiety.

The body didn't seem to need him either. It moved of its own accord, the eyes red-rimmed and wide, barely blinking, the lower lip hanging as if in permanent pout, or as if that set of facial muscles had been paralyzed by stroke. Come to think of it, he looked to be in some sort of trance, as if something was drawing him forward, guiding him around obstacles in a zombie-like shamble toward an as yet unknown destination. He still had access to his full range of senses but only if he focused on them; if he wanted to smell something, he needed to place his attention inside his nose.

It was night and very dark, the light from the full moon penetrating through gaps in the old-growth canopy. The forest was alive with nocturnal sounds but every now and again the low resonance from the champagne flute intruded, intermittent, like the buzz of an annoying mosquito; drifting in and out as if signaling the way back so he knew this was some sort of hallucination.

Milt's body finally paused in front of a mound covered with a large branch. He drifted back into the body, feeling himself grip the branch and drag it aside, revealing a polished stone slab set atop what looked like a box made from the same material, but its sides were rough. The chisel marks were still visible. He fell to his knees beside it, the sharp pieces of rock digging into him. Something had been carved into the upper polished surface. Using his fingers to trace the deeply chiseled grooves, he realized they were symbols, not words. His body stood, fingers hooking under the slab's edge where it protruded from the rougher lower section. Milt turned his attention to the effort as he felt the strain move through him, pushing into his tensioned legs, the strength flowing up across his broad back and down through his arms until they trembled with the effort.

It refused to budge. He paused, puffing. Fumbling in his pocket, his fingers closed around a small torch. Flicking it on, he held the torch at shoulder height, angling the narrow beam down at a forty-five degree angle to shine across the top, lighting the glyphs and sigils carved into it. All but one—midway down the slab. He changed the angle of the torch. That recess remained dark, as if resisting the light. Milt reached out, dipping his fingers into the black, half-spherical shape. Tracing the rough surface inside, he heard a loud click. The slab trembled, then popped up before rolling to one side on well-oiled tracks.

Curious, he moved forward and shone the torch inside. The same trick of the light appeared to be happening with this larger space. The light pooled against a deeper blackness, like spilt milk on polished black marble. Milt felt his arm move, easing through the gap. He mentally followed it into the blackness, acutely aware of the brush of fabric against his fingertips and then the unmistakable shape of a body. A woman, it felt like. Her forearms had been laid across her chest, one hand atop the other as if protecting something. Milt's hand eased the lower arm free and drew it out. The dead flesh, while maintaining the cold, waxy feel he knew so well, had remained strangely supple, as if the woman had died only recently.

Her arm was now draped diagonally across the stone slab. One of Milt's hands held it in place while the other reached inside his coat. Milt's attention followed. Something long and hard was strapped tight against the side of his torso. It had the same feel as a shoulder holster only much longer, cinched all the way to the hip. His fingers closed around a cold metal tube, a handle of some kind; finger grooves had been molded into it, and his own stubby digits seemed to be a perfect fit for them. When he tugged it free, he realized it was a long-handled axe topped with back-to-back blades.

Made entirely from shiny metal, its finely ground axe heads caught the moonlight as it swung up and then down in a savage arc, severing the dead woman's hand. It jumped from the slab and into the scree at the base of the mound as if it had been reanimated. Milt drew his awareness back, watching as the axe was resheathed, the hand retrieved and examined. The ring was on the fourth finger.

Strange, I didn't see that before, but it's definitely "the" ring. He watched as the zombie that was him stuffed the hand with the ring finger intact into the side pocket of his suit jacket, then rolled back the slab lid until it clicked into place. The hand was nothing like the decayed specimen he'd found in his meat crisper, yet it had to be the same one. How many amputated hands were there?

The moonlight faded, and he felt himself being drawn back, away from the forest. Once more the colors spun around him, but this time they moved toward a central point, like water swirling down a plug hole, spinning and spinning and....

He opened his eyes. He was back in the restaurant looking down at Aggie's glass, the wine still swirling within it. His eyes followed her finger as it continued to run the rim. Black streaks, like oily tendrils, snaked through the bubbles until the wine turned to frothy ink. The crystal flute, trembling with the prolonged vibration, finally shattered with a sharp crack. Foaming black wine spread across the table, staining the pristine linen.

Milt slumped against the high-backed chair as if something tethering him had been cut. When he looked up, it was as if nothing had changed; even the black stain on the tablecloth had been sopped up by one of the waiters, and a fresh starched napkin had been placed over the top.

Physically, he felt like he did when he ran up the twenty-five floors to his apartment instead of catching the lift: heart hammering, shirt: wet and clingy.

Aggie smiled from across the table and said gently, 'Welcome back. How do you feel?'

'What the hell was that?' he managed, shaking his head, mind awash with jumbled images as it tried to make sense out of nonsense.

'Milt?' she tried again.

Finally he looked up. 'Was that really me? Did it actually happen?'

She nodded.

Milt sighed, feeling the tension bunch between his shoulder blades again. 'But why would I...? And where did that axe come from —' His mouth dropped open. 'Jesus. Don't tell me I'm the Hacker— the one in the paper? That bloody axe looked like—'

'Stop. I need you to listen to me. If you want to blame anyone, try me. I used you to find Angelique's burial mound and then suppressed your memory of it. I'm a psychologist and used some, well, unconventional means to achieve it. Now you have those memories back but they may not appear real, more like a memory of having been to a movie.'

Milt was too drained to feel anything but confused. 'But why? I still don't see what any of this... this has to do with me?'

'I needed to locate Angelique's ring. It may seem odd to you, but you were the only one who could do that for me.'

The waiter returned, carrying their meals and a fresh glass.

She waited until he left before continuing. 'The ring on your finger is already bonded to Angelique's daughter, and unless you help me to locate her, then even more innocent people will die. Milt, are you listening?'

He felt stunned. The base of his head was throbbing. He badly wanted to leave but even the thought of trying to stand was beyond him at this point. He stared dully at Aggie's plate as she deftly sliced, then methodically peeled back the pastry package to reveal vegetables floating in a creamy sauce. It was like being back in the dream, like he was an observer and not really a participant—unless he chose to be—and right now he didn't.

'Milt,' she said sharply, and his head snapped up. 'Concentrate, otherwise you'll drift back. Say something to me. Anything.'

He tried to herd his thoughts toward a sentence, but when the words finally turned up they were slippery, lining up in the wrong order. 'Me... why?' he finally managed.

'You asked that already. Try something else. Come on, this is important.'

She picked up the tumbler of water beside her plate and dashed the liquid into his face.

'What the fuck—' He spluttered, using the large napkin to mop the water from his eyes and face.

'Good, you're back. My apologies. How do you feel? Has the throbbing stopped?'

It had, but he wasn't going to give her that satisfaction.

'You should eat something,' she said as if nothing had happened, spearing a carrot with her fork and wagging it at him. 'It will help ground you.' The carrot disappeared into her mouth.

Carefully Milt retrieved a knife and fork from the cutlery pile by his elbow and began cutting up his meat while he assembled his thoughts. He could feel her watching from across the table, measuring the precise movement of his serrated knife, the determined way he chewed through his meat. You could learn a lot from watching the way a person ate. Milt had done it himself many times. He operated in the same dogged manner that he attacked his steak, sawing at it piece by tiny piece until it was all gone. At this point, he didn't mind her knowing it.

He waved over an anxious-looking waiter and ordered a glass of red wine, just nodding when the waiter babbled something unintelligible in French. He'd had enough of champagne, the woman, and this place, but she had answers to his black-spot questions and he wanted them. Badly.

'Are you angry yet?' she asked.

He glanced up briefly, then back to his meal. 'I'm working on it.'

'Good. That's good. The anger will help center you.'

The red arrived; the color was deep, and its flavor when he tasted it was layered and surprisingly complex. Not unlike the woman opposite. Finishing the last of his steak, he allowed the cutlery to clatter untidily onto the plate and wiped his lips clean with the napkin and dropped it into the remains of the brown sauce.

He leaned forward as if about to share a secret. 'I want some answers and then I'm going to get up and leave. Do you understand me? And I don't want to know about magic rings and out-of-body experiences. Are we clear?'

She smiled broadly. 'Excellent. That's exactly what I had in mind. What do you want to know?'

'I'm still waiting for the answer of why I'm the one with the bushy tail in this foxhunt of yours.'

She pursed her lips and looked thoughtful. 'I told you. You're are the only one who could locate Angelique's tomb and remove the ring.'

Milt held up his hand. 'Right, let's just stop there at that one. Why would I have anything to do with that, much less be the *only one* who could do it?'

'The ring is genetically sentient. That means it has an awareness of the wearer and can identify the next in line. It has been passed from mother to daughter for many centuries.'

'In case you hadn't noticed, I am not a mother, nor anyone's daughter, so why is it perched here on my finger?'

She tapped the side of her nose conspiratorially. 'Ah, but you are the father, so you do have a genetic linkage—slim, I know, but it was all I had to work with.'

Milt burst out laughing. 'The father? Of that woman? Come on, she was as old as I—'

'Not her. Her daughter. Your daughter, Milt.'

A coldness crept up through him. When he finally spoke, his voice was low, carrying with it a subtle threat. 'My daughter is dead.

She was killed in a freak car accident along with my seven-year-old granddaughter, so I warn you, don't try peddling your psychobabble bullshit onto me because it won't work twice, do you hear me? Now tell me the truth or my next call will be to a doctor I know to get this ring surgically removed.'

'I understand that, Milt, but it's true. You do have another daughter. Surely with all the women you have known in your life, you must concede that it could be possible? A daughter you didn't know about? Her birth name was Jessica—if that helps.'

Milt tried to get up and found he still couldn't.

She saw him straining. 'It's posthypnotic. Don't worry, I'll release it shortly. For now, I need you to try to relax and listen.' She looked at her watch and made a face. 'Oh my, time does get on, doesn't it? We'll have to leave soon. Here's the, what might you call it, oh yes, the "fast and dirty version." Whether you like it or not, you are Jessica's father. That ring there guided you to Angelique's tomb because Jess has disappeared and it recognized your share of Jess's genetics. You will be its keeper while it helps you find Jess.'

'Or what, it'll drop off like it did its last owner?'

'That ring—and Jessica—are integral to the survival of a great many innocent people. Isn't that enough?'

'How?'

She sighed, speaking slowly as she picked over her words. 'This planet operates on a very delicate balance; its ability to continue to provide enough oxygen, food, and water is tenuous. That balance is maintained through an ancient series of complex calculations recorded on what are known as the Elemental Scrolls.'

'The elemental what?' Milt asked.

'Scrolls.' Aggie stretched the word out. 'They need to be reactivated every hundred years, and the current cycle is almost up. That ring on your finger is the only way we have of locating them.'

'How?'

'Jessica, Angelique's daughter, is—or will be when you and I find her—the new Messenger of the Scrolls.'

Milt sat back in the chair, his lips stretching into a smile.

'Sounds like you could do with a dose of your own psychobabble bullshit.'

Aggie pressed on. 'The scrolls are the climate's safety valve, Milt. If they are not reactivated, then every life form on the planet will be affected. Now are you getting it? Or has the dramatic increase in the number of natural disasters and cataclysmic weather events just floated on by you unnoticed?'

'Oh, I get it all right. I get it that you're a little—out there. Now, I don't know how you managed to spin my head out just now, or why this ring ended up on my finger, but if you think I'm going to buy a story like that, then you've picked the wrong ex-copper.'

Aggie's eyes narrowed, her gaze intense. He could feel it boring through his defenses like a powerful light, seeking something out. He felt a deep urge to squirm but resisted. Finally she sat back, flicking a strand of hair back from her forehead.

'You're right; it is a lot to swallow. The fact that it's true is inconsequential if you don't believe it. All right, try this instead—just remember I went the easy route first. Do you recall that axe you used to amputate Angelique's hand? It's a particularly unusual design, ancient, and there were only two of them ever made. In fact, they are a pair—identical. I have the one you used—and the Hacker, as you and the popular press are calling him—has the other. My axe has your fingerprints on it, and the bodies of the poor, unfortunate murdered women have the gashes from the blade of the other. They will match exactly in those clever tests they do. As an "ex-copper," I'm assuming you're aware of where this is heading.'

'Blackmail.'

'I call it doing whatever it takes to save the planet.'

'You expect me to believe this pile of steaming crap?'

'I don't expect you to do anything except what I ask of you. Use the ring to find the girl—take the risk that I'm telling the truth about the axes.' Aggie glanced at the slim watch on her wrist and made a face. 'We have no more time. I have to go. I don't expect your answer just yet. There's some more work you need to do. This was just an initial meeting. I've heard you call them a "bum sniffer.""

How the heck does she know I say that?

Something released, and the chair didn't seem stuck to his backside any longer. Pushing down, he lurched to his feet, using the table to steady himself.

Her mouth was still moving but he could no longer hear what she was saying. She seemed to be getting fainter. The pressure at the back of his head returned quickly, scuttling across the top of his scalp, trailing a dense blackness behind it. Milt had to lean heavily on the table to avoid falling. A hissing sound, like a TV tuned to a dead station, filled his head. He could see the flames from the fireplace flickering through the outline of Aggie's body, her mouth curled with what could have been sympathy. Numbness clawed its way up his arms, claiming them centimeter by centimeter. He felt himself tilting to the side, then falling, but was unable to prevent it.

THEY RELEASED him from the emergency ward with a pat on the back and a fistful of meds. He had no memory of what had happened after the restaurant, but he must have made his way outside. He'd been found unconscious on the sidewalk.

His phone was still in the car back at the restaurant. He called a taxi from the public phone on the ground floor of the hospital and went outside to wait.

It was a typical midwinter Melbourne morning, the sky hidden behind gray clouds, a southerly wind leaching the weak sun of any warmth. Milt wondered, not for the first time, why he remained in Melbourne.

He felt something in his jacket pocket and pulled it out. Cigarettes. He looked at the half-empty pack incredulously; a plastic lighter was tucked inside. On impulse he took out a cigarette and lit up, sucking deeply, surprised and pleased at the familiar grip of smoke in his lungs. It may not be good for him, but it sure as hell still tasted great. The hand holding the lighter was shaking; he balled the fingers into a fist and shoved it deep into his jacket pocket.

The cab arrived. He took a final drag and tossed the butt onto the cement, grinding it beneath the sole of his shoe. He wore English shoes these days. Lobbs. Thick soles. Expensive and sturdy. Molded for comfort. He could have done with them on the force. He climbed into the cab.

'Moncrief Restaurant,' he said, buckling himself in.

'Where was that, mate?'

Milt sighed. Tugging the tattered card from the inside pocket of his jacket, he handed it to the driver. The man looked at it, his brow crinkling.

'You sure this is right, mate?'

'I was there last night. I need to collect my car. It's parked out the back.'

'Nah, that can't be right,' the cabbie said, shaking his head. 'That place burned to the ground forty-odd years back.'

THREE

Milt splashed single malt into a tumbler and took it out onto the wide balcony. He hadn't believed the cabbie, of course, and had told him to drive to the restaurant, or where the restaurant should've been. Then pretended to ignore the man's pointed look as he drove off.

He'd walked slowly through the grounds of the five townhouses that were now there. Down near the back boundary he found a lichen-covered plaque with the names of those who'd perished in the fire listed in raised metal letters. He made a note of the date and called another cab to take him to the library, where he searched the newspaper archives. The story about the restaurant fire was there. How much more proof did he need? He'd even found his car safe in the secure parking lot beneath his apartment, apparently unused for days.

Yet part of him, most of him, still resisted. To do otherwise was like leaving the door into himself slightly ajar. It risked letting out that bit over which he had no control, and that scared him. A lot.

His glass was empty, and he went back inside for a refill. He couldn't remember when he'd started liking single malt. Queensland, maybe. He wasn't a purist; he drank it with ice. In Brisbane's heat, what else would you do? Maybe the expensive Scotch was just one of the things that he thought he should do, like this apartment, the car, and English shoes. Part of an image he kept trying to form that, no matter what he did, kept moving and shifting until he had no real likeness of himself anymore, who he really was, only a sniff of what he wasn't.

Carlie would have helped—if she was still alive. Granddaughters did that. She and her mother, Janis, had always been his anchor against the storms.

What was all that crap about another daughter? What was her name? Jessica?

It was possible, he conceded. There had been a lot of women— but a child? And as for those wah-wah scrolls Wilmott was on about.... He snorted.

There was the question of the axe though. He could still feel it in his hands, perfectly balanced, as if it were part of him. Was she right —if "she" existed—were there really two axes, or was this all just his shaken-not-stirred psyche trying to justify the unthinkable?

Could I be the Hacker and this was just some psychological construct?

Shrugging the thought away, he took his fresh drink outside and eased himself into one of the expensive patio chairs that a former girl-friend with a self-confessed taste for interior design had suggested he buy. Lime splice, she'd called the color. It creaked every time he moved his large frame. Milt hated it, but the rest of the place had turned out all right, so he'd said nothing. Just paid for the chairs and promised himself he'd get another lounger. One day.

Across Melbourne it was "light-night time." That's what Carlie used to call the city lights spread around his twenty-fifth level perch. Light night. Loony night, more like it, and from the way things were breaking he was in the front row, ready to howl with the best of them. Maybe mental instability was one of those things that you never quite got over. It kept returning, like shingles or migraines—hit the right trigger and back it bounced, ready to take another chunk out of your life. The blackouts were the worst. He wondered again if there even was such a person as Aggie Wilmott.

He pulled back and cast around for something more solid. He still had the ring and the hand—they were real.

His mobile trilled. *Thank Christ for diversions.* He dug it out of his trouser pocket.

'Milton.'

'It's Hopkins.'

'What did you come up with?'

'I'm well, thanks. The kids are fine too.'

'You don't have any kids, and if you did, you'd probably bill me for their health report, you miserly bastard.'

Hopkins chuckled, then coughed wetly. Milt could almost smell the cigarette smoke drifting through the phone.

'You don't sound so great. I thought you gave the smokes up.' Milt reached for his own. One left, ah well. He lit up.

'I do, in between clients. You're paying for this week's cartons.'

'Maybe. Tell me what you turned up first.'

He heard Hopkins flipping the pages of his notepad.

'She's dead.'

Shit!

'When?'

'Coming up for three months. When did you say you saw her?'

'Last night.'

'How'd she look? Kinda pale?' Hopkins laughed cautiously. 'Aggie Wilmott. Traffic accident coming down a mountain. Seems she hit a car and then a semi came round a bend and cleaned them both up. She was sixty-five. You were a bit off there, Milt. The photo should be coming through now. Check it out.'

Milt hauled himself to his feet and went inside, waiting impatiently while the faxed photo built itself up line by line. Hopkins hadn't moved past fax technology, but then he wasn't a real private detective, he was just someone Milt trusted off a very short list.

Hopkins and he went way back. Milt wedged the phone between his shoulder and ear and tugged the last of the page free.

'Holy shit, it's her,' Milt whispered.

'What was that?' Hopkins sounded anxious. Now that all the snakes were out of the bag, both of them were wondering whether Milt had finally lost it. Milt coughed and ground the cigarette into the ashtray. That would be the last. He was quitting again —right now.

'I said, did you find any connection between her and Angelique Watkins?'

'Nothin'. And I looked from the nursery all the way to the bedroom. If they ever knew each other, it was from a distance. Maybe they had one of those, you know, int-er-netty things,' Hopkins finished hopefully.

Yeah, or we could all have had dinner together in a restaurant that didn't exist.

He tossed down the rest of the drink. The ice hit his teeth. He opened his mouth and crunched it into bits.

'Anything else?'

'Well, there was one queer thing.'

Only one?

'What was that?'

'Well, I said that her car was basically hit twice, once with the car and then with the semi.'

'So?'

'*So* her body was found two hundred meters from where what was left of her four-wheel drive ended up. I saw the photos; there's no way she could have gotten out and crawled that far.'

'Could she have been thrown clear?'

Hopkins wheezed wetly; Milt could almost see the old man shaking his head. 'That's what the official version says but I did some time in Traffic. Believe me, nothing was going to get out of that mess. My guess is she went over first without the car—or was pushed.'

'Pushed?'

'Yeah. Remember the other car? The one she hit. It was a Beamer. Empty. No driver, no bodies ever recovered, toasted or otherwise. My guess is whoever was in that pushed her.'

'Who owned it?'

'Registered to one of those shelf companies that pulls up its tent pegs overnight. No real people. Police are officially still looking, but you know how it is.'

Milt did; the crime machine didn't stop but there were always too many for too few. With nothing obvious to go on, they'd just assume the car was hot or used for drug hauling and the driver had run from the scene.

'What about the truckie?'

'Dead.'

'What?'

'Died at the scene. Heart attack. He had a history. Must have been a shock for him.'

'Death normally is,' Milt said dryly. 'So assuming she was pushed, any thoughts on motive?'

'She wasn't rich, if that's what you mean. Comfortable, maybe. No drug or crime connections. Husband and daughter both deceased. Only living relative is a granddaughter, and this is where it gets really... weird.'

Milt heard Hopkins pause, suck in another lungful, and slowly exhale as if he was reluctant to go on.

'Yeah, what? I'm not paying you by the hour, you know.'

'It's Wallace, Milt. The old lady's granddaughter is Wallace. I got her address here someplace.... Milt? Are you there, mate?'

FOUR

Brisbane:

Wallace replaced the handset, her hand hovering uncertainly over the phone as if it might ring again.

'Hope and fear in equal measure,' as Gran used to... as Gran might yet say, and Wallace felt the butterflies in her stomach stir and flutter.

She tightened the towel around her midriff and retraced her own wet footprints across the polished hardwood, up the stairs, and back into the ensuite. She'd had to run to answer it, picking up just as the phone stopped ringing. It had been exactly the same last night, but then she'd been cutting up vegetables for a stir fry, the old house quiet and cozy-creaky against a rising wind outside. The only sounds: a faint lilting Blues melody wafting in from the adjoining lounge room and the steady chop of the knife against the wooden cutting board. When the raucous ringing had begun, she'd jumped, cutting her finger, instinctively looking at the space on the wall where the old phone used to hang. Sucking at the blood, she'd followed the insistent "briiing" to the old linen press midway down the hall. Inside, behind the spare sheets, she found the clunky push-button handset inside an old shoebox. She couldn't remember putting it there when she'd renovated, but that didn't mean anything, not in this house.

Wary, she'd carried the phone back to the kitchen. The only thing that kept running through her mind was that it still had the same ring tone as when it was up on the wall. Yet, what would she expect? A harp ensemble? An angelic chorus? Gran may be into theatrics, but she'd never wasted energy on peripherals. This was just Gran trying to get through.

From where, and, for that matter, to what? Wallace knew that Gran's ghost wouldn't be at the other end of the phone, which would have been weird enough. No, this was Gran's little "I'm here, darlin', wake up." It meant *come and get me*. It meant Wallace was going to have to try and lift the damn veil on her own.

A coldness seeped through the soles of her bare feet and spread up her legs, arcing into her spine. When it reached her shoulders, she shivered.

The summoning ceremony was simple enough, but she'd only performed it once before and that had been at her initiation thirty years ago. She smiled to herself; "odd" had certainly been the right word for it. She'd just turned eighteen and the only entity she'd managed to connect with was an earth-bound shade that had been fixated on turning off the gas in her tiny Annerley flat. It turned out that the woman had inadvertently blown herself up trying to make a pot of tea just before the war.

That ceremony had divided Wallace's life into two distinct parts. One, the everyday cause and effect of the "normal" world. The other, just as real but with different rules. Gran had liked to call them ice and steam; both were made from water but their qualities were totally different. Wallace's challenge had always been how to straddle both sides without compromising one or the other, and as a result she never quite managed either. When she'd shared these fears with Gran, all she said was "the universe loves to serve those with the gratitude to appreciate." She loved pithy sayings a little too much.

It was all right for Gran, she'd always seen things as black and white, but for Wallace, that just delineated the boundaries. The real work was done somewhere in the grey. That's where she lived—what her ex used to call her "mumbo jumbo bullshit."

Wallace sighed, tugged off the towel, and hung it over the rack. Catching sight of herself in the full-length mirror, she paused, turning to one side, pivoting on the ball of her foot. Larger bits of her still poked out despite the diet; she jiggled the stubborn pouch around her midriff and turned to the other side, moving her hands to her hips. Her boobs were still good though, not that anyone was ever in her bedroom these days to check them out. She sighed again and stepped under the warm stream of water the phone call had interrupted.

ONE OF THE indicators of trance state was the loss of linear time awareness. Wallace realized she'd inadvertently tripped over the edge when the shower went cold. Muttering a curse, she turned off the water and shrugged into her fluffy bathrobe and hurriedly pulled a brush through the knots in her wet hair. Thanks to Gran, she was now officially late. Though did lateness still count when you were on suspension?

The appointment with the psych would run much the same as it had up to now, with both of them working toward a plausible consensus that ultimately was aimed at getting her back to work.

All Wallace had to do was mindfully step over and around those annoyingly persistent truth slippages that, if related and recorded, would move her case diagnosis almost magically from "stress-induced incident" to a no-way-back "unstable with delusional hallucinations."

She picked up the hair dryer, glancing at her watch. There was no time now even if she went wet and wild. She'd have to cancel, call in sick, anything in fact except share the real reason for her lateness. Cinching that thought tightly behind the bathrobe belt, she went in search of her phone, finding it where she'd left it on the bench beside the old plastic handset in the kitchen. She tapped the psych's number onto the screen, waiting as the number rang, once, twice, her eyes restless finding their way back to the old phone, imagining how she would explain that.

"...well, I have this phone in the linen cupboard and it keeps ringing. I'm pretty sure it's my dead grandmother..."

'Oh, hi, sorry. It's Wallace. I've got an appointment in half an hour that I'm not going to be able to....'

Wallace paused. Moving the phone away from her ear, she cocked her head, listening. A tiny scratching sound was coming from behind her, near the back door. She turned to look, stepping closer.

'...hello? Wallace? Did you want to make another time?'

'Sorry, I'll ring you later—when I'm feeling better.' She cut off the call. There definitely was someone—or something—outside.

Surely not even the dumbest thief would attempt a daylight entry to a detective's house.

Would they?

What about a dark Other?

She hadn't kept up Gran's wards on the windows and doors and doubted whether they'd still be strong enough to prevent anything seriously sinister from getting inside if it really wanted to. An image of the last encounter she'd had with a hostile Other flashed into her head. It was a good thing Gran had been around that day, otherwise it wouldn't have been pretty. The thought wasn't a premonition though —she'd learned to tell the difference between fear-induced images and those provided by her notoriously unreliable second sight.

Double shit.

She hated all this grayness, hating herself even more for what it did to her. *I'm a detective, goddammit. Handle it.* She slid out one of the kitchen drawers and laid it on the floor before reaching deep inside the cavity and slipping one of her private "sparies" from where it was taped to the wall. Close up, the .32 would make a decent-sized hole in anything with matter mass. While it wouldn't make any sort of dent in an Other, just holding it made her feel more secure. Silently, she moved closer to the back door.

Someone was working the lock. Entities wouldn't bother with that. She exhaled, grateful that this was something solid. Taking the gun in one hand, she carefully reached forward, clicked open the lock, and flung the door back in one fluid movement, the barrel levelling with the kneeling man's head.

'Back off and put your hands in the air. Now!'

He was big—huge, really, even kneeling. When he lifted his head, her eyes widened. She shifted the gun to her left hand and slapped him hard across the face with the right.

'What the *hell* do you think you're doing here? If you've come to apologize, you're about two years and three sluts too late.'

'Hello, Lacey.' Milt rubbed the reddening place on his bristly cheek.

'Wallace to you, and I told you, Milt, to never, ever come near me again. How dare you try to break in to *my* house.'

'Your house? Since when? You couldn't even afford that dump down the Valley the last time—'

'It was Gran's. She left it to me when she died—not that it's any of your business. No, don't get up and don't try to distract me. I want to know what you're doing here.'

'Can I get up?'

'No! Oh, all right. Do you know I could have killed you just now? Shit, I should have.'

Milt pushed himself to his feet. He looked older, shaggier, more like the bear he'd been nicknamed after, only now his fur was ratty in places and unkempt. Wallace stifled an old reflex to smooth it down.

'You'd better come in. I don't want the neighbors getting too interested.'

'Why aren't you at work? Are you still on the force?'

'Why don't you answer my question first—before you have to leave? You're pretty good at that, I seem to recall.'

Milt shrugged and lumbered inside, looking around the kitchen, nodding.

'Nice. Your grandmother had great taste. What was her name again? Aggie?'

Wallace crossed her arms. 'Subtle as ever. I know that look. We worked together, remember? That's your I'm-just-dumb-as-dogshit-all-innocent look. Tell me what you're really doing here.'

Straddling one of the wooden stools beside the kitchen bench, he shrugged. 'I dunno how to put this, Lacey, but I think I ran into her the other night. At dinner.'

'Gran?'

He nodded.

'Milt, I just told you she's dead.'

'Yeah. I found that out for myself when I went digging for her address afterward. Kinda strange coincidence, don't you think, Lacey? You and her—and me.'

Wallace's head was awash. *What is Gran up to?*

'I told you not to call me that, and yes, it's strange and it would be a coincidence—if anything you said was true, which I doubt. Now, I have some things I have to do, so I'm going to ask you very nicely to leave. If you don't, then remember, I still have this gun.'

Milt stood, squaring his body to face her while he slowly and deliberately reached into his jacket pocket.

Wallace took a step back, spreading her weight evenly across both feet as she brought the gun up once more. 'I'm warning you, Milt, I will shoot if you attempt to produce a weapon.'

Milt glanced at her from under his bushy eyebrows and withdrew his hand. Between the first two fingers he held a battered card that he flicked onto the bench. 'I found this in the meat drawer of my fridge—beneath a pretty ugly-looking left hand. This ring used to belong to it.'

He held up his hand.

'What ring?' she said, managing to quash the quaver before it came out. Her mouth was dry.

'What do you mean, what ring? This one. Can't you see it?' Milt pushed his hand closer, pointing at the pinky of his left hand.

She said nothing. The dryness had morphed into a rising lump at the back of her throat. She tried to swallow.

It couldn't be.

She continued to stare at his hand as if she'd never seen one before. In a way, she hadn't. His nails looked like they belonged to someone else, all round-shaped and buffed. She remembered them as bitten-down stumps. Maybe he'd changed in other ways? There was no ring.

'No,' she said finally. 'What does it look like?'

'Are you blind, Lacey?' He made a grab for her hand and molded her fingers around his little finger. 'If you can't see it, you have to be able to feel it. Tell me.'

'No, you tell me. It's important. Tell me what it looks like,' she said, feeling only his hot sausage finger wrapped in hers.

He released her hand suddenly. When he spoke, he overenunci-ated each word as if she were a recalcitrant child. 'All right. It's big. Thick. Gold. And there's this ugly lump of grayish-looking polished rock in the middle. Satisfied?'

Wallace groped behind her, finding one of the kitchen stools, and slumped onto it, the gun forgotten, her arm hanging limply at her side.

'What was the name of this woman? The one you say you got the ring from.'

'Angelique, I think your granny called her. She was dead at the time. I think I cut her hand off to get it. You know. The one in the meat drawer.'

Wallace felt the blood drain from her face. Suddenly the gun felt like a huge weight. She placed it gently onto the kitchen bench.

'What else did she say?'

'What else?' Milt laughed, the sound bitter with disbelief. 'Most people would still be chewing to swallow that lot down.'

'I'm a fast eater. I asked you what else.'

Milt snorted and shook his head. 'There's a kid, apparently. Her name's Jessica. I'm supposed to be the father. This Angelique lady was her mum.'

Wallace mouthed "father," then laughed, the sound harsh and brittle. Old memories of Angelique and the mystery man who sired the child rose like stale air bubbles bursting to the surface, ripe with new understanding.

Bloody Gran. The whole thing was always a setup.

'Lacey?' He reached out a tentative hand to touch her shoulder. 'Are you all right?'

She jerked away. 'Yes. I'm... I'm just putting a few things together that I should have realized... a long time ago.'

'Don't tell me this is making sense to you, because it sure as hell isn't to me?'

'Maybe,' she said, her throat tight. 'It's all part of an old legend. Gran was obsessed with it right up to her death.' Wallace cleared her throat and stood, feeling equally confined by Milt's hovering bulk and Gran's betrayal.

Wallace didn't know whether she was more upset with Gran for leaving her out of whatever had really been going on all these years, or angry at Milt for just turning up after two years and trying to dump his crap on her—again, as if nothing had happened. Mostly she just felt used.

She walked around Milt to the sink and turned on the tap, splashing water over her face. Milt handed her a tea towel, and she dabbed at her cheeks before continuing.

'The ring you claim to be wearing is the key. Gran used to tell me the only time it can be seen by anyone other than the wearer is when the hand is separated from the body. Did she tell you any of this?'

'The only thing that stuck in my head is the axe I was supposed to have used to get it. Apparently it's a perfect match for the one this Hacker character is using. And it has my prints all over it.'

'Which hand was it?'

He looked confused.

'In your fridge,' she said, her voice rising in frustration.

'Left. What difference does that make?'

'All the Hacker's corpses have had their left hand amputated,' she said.

'That hasn't been in the papers.'

'No.'

'So how do you know that? It's a Vic case, isn't it?'

'Technically. I happen to know there have been Hacker victims in every state. Fifteen so far.'

'Fifteen? No way. That would have created the biggest media gorge—'

'The rest have been made to look like accidents—traffic, industrial, residential, you name it. In each case, the victim just happened to have at least one limb lopped. Always the left, sometimes both.'

Milt made a *phaat* sound with his lips. 'That could be a coincidence. The others were homicides, these could be—'

'No. I knew the women. All of them. They belonged to a group I'm in.'

'Ah, the mysterious group,' he said, nodding. 'Your dead grandmother told me about it. Have you mentioned this to the police, by any chance?'

'I tried. It didn't work out so well because I couldn't tell them…. You may not remember, but I've got a rep for the weird and weirder. The mumbo jumbo—'

'—bullshit.' He nodded. Suddenly he looked like old Milt. Wallace glanced away. 'So you didn't tell them about the ring?' he prompted holding up his left hand.

'The magic ring that will lead them to the chosen one?' Wallace felt a bitter laugh bubbling up and choked it back. 'No, even I'm not quite that stupid.'

'It's material, Wallace. You've got to tell them. What is this group, anyway?'

She met his gaze, forcing it to stay against her desire to look anywhere else as the answer to his question slipped and slid around at the back of her throat. 'They were all members of our coven.'

'Coven?' he said, mouth open, then barked a single *hah*. 'So you're saying you're a—'

'I think the word you're trying hard not to say is witch. Yep. Guilty. Reluctant fifth generation. And you're right, the information is material, but no, I can't tell them. Period. For lots of reasons around oaths but mainly because the second thing they'd do after sacking me is to demand a list of the coven members.'

'So?'

'I don't have it. There was only one copy. I went looking for it through Gran's things when I started hearing about the amputations, but it's gone.'

'But if this is true, you have to at least warn the rest—'

'Don't you think I've been doing that?' she shouted. 'Everyone knows, but there's only so much you can do to stay safe. Accidents aren't always avoidable even with the sort of insight and gifts we have.'

'I'm guessing you have a personal listing in this spooky app too?'

She nodded. 'It's a lineage list. Everyone who has the blood is on it. So is Angelique's daughter.'

'So you're on a short wick to the future, and this Jessica, whoever she is, could realistically already be dead.'

'That would be Jessica—your daughter.'

'Look, I'm on turbo catch up here and news of a long-lost daughter is part of that, so give it a rest, will ya? And no, like a lot of other things about this whole thing, I don't remember who this Angelique woman was.'

'She was pretty.'

'Not the last time I saw her.' He paused, looking at Wallace shrewdly. 'Look, this is all fine and dandy, but I really need to find your gran. She's the only one who knows where that axe with my prints is. What are you staring at?'

She looked away; a wariness had swept over her. It had all

happened so fast she'd forgotten about the axe, about Milt's state of mind the last time she'd seen him.

Finally, he said, 'We're dancing around the main issue here, aren't we, Lacey? First rule rules, remember?'

She knew exactly what he was talking about. They'd been partners before lovers, and the first rule was: the simplest explanation is almost always what happened. The more complicated, the less plausible. She lifted her chin.

'You mean that if you walk, look, and quack like a nutter then you probably really are the Hacker and not a frog with a magic ring on an as yet unnamed quest.'

'Pretty much.'

'I hadn't ruled it out.'

'Good. Because what I haven't shared is that when I went over the dates and times of the attacks on all the girls in Melbourne after I had that "experience" with your granny, not only do I not have alibis for them, I can't remember what I was doing then either. Blackouts. They've been happening a lot.'

They stared at each other, the gap between them widening with each second. Finally he shrugged. 'Either way, I'm stuffed, because even if the duplicate axe story is true and not some self-justification from my subconscious, who would believe it? I mean, my prints will be all over the damned thing.'

She reached across and picked up the dog-eared business card he'd tossed onto the bench earlier. 'The handwriting on this seems to be yours.'

'No kidding, and yes, I've added that to my very long list of "I don't remembers." I'll tell you this, though: if everything I think happened did, then it all leads back to Aggie. I know she's supposed to be your grandmother, Lacey, but I swear to God I wish she wasn't dead so I could have the pleasure of throttling her myself. That way I could at least do the time for something I actually remembered.'

'Right here, right now, you'd have to stand in line.'

What the hell is Gran up to?

There had to be some substance to what Milt was saying; he knew too much to be operating solo. *Where else would he have learned about the ring and Angelique if not from Gran?*

As if in response, the old push-button phone on the bench began to ring.

FIVE

Wallace filled the kettle and placed it on a gas ring to boil before carefully spooning a variety of herbs into Gran's old china teapot. She'd told Milt to go up to her study to wait. There was nothing he could do, and she needed to think for a bit. Milt seemed to take up so much space, both physically and, to her surprise, emotionally that it was an actual relief when he left the room. She'd forgotten the first and underestimated the second.

There had been no voice on the other end of the phone when she'd answered it, of course. That would have been too much to hope for, but nevertheless she could sense Gran's presence, waiting. Even impatient, as if she were willing Wallace to conduct the summoning.

What if I stuff it up again? What if I don't do it at all? Is that even an option?

Not if more people were going to be killed.

Particularly as I'm likely to be one of them.

Her hand paused above the tray, the cup suspended, forgotten as the slithery questions she'd been trying to avoid intruded again.

Could Milt really be the Hacker? Has he deteriorated that much?

The truth was, she didn't really know. Her intuition and rational police head had been at war over that one since he showed up and started reeling out his crazy tale.

If only it all didn't hook up to Gran so tightly....

The kettle whistled, and she sighed, pouring steamy water into the pot. Immediately the stainless steel and tiled kitchen filled with the ancient, fragrant smell. Wallace closed her eyes and inhaled, allowing the smell to transport her back to Gran's old kitchen—before the recent renos. Seeing its huge green-and-cream combustion stove and polished butter-colored floorboards, the strong flour-dusted hands and hugs and good things cooking. Gran's kitchen, the safest place Wallace had ever known.

Was that all a lie too?

She carried the tray upstairs, her steps heavy. When she entered, the study was empty, but the adjoining door to her bedroom was open. She set the tray down on the table and walked over. Milt was lying on her bed, pillows bunched behind him, boots on, ankles crossed. He looked up when she appeared in the doorway; one of her old spell exercise books was open in his lap.

'I told you to go to the study. This is my private space,' she said, resentment coiled in her gut.

'Sorry, there's nowhere in there to sit. In here either,' he said. 'Don't you believe in chairs?'

'I prefer the floor. Do you want to take your shoes off my bed?'

He swung his legs off and shuffled into a seated position on the edge of the bed. She walked in and looked around. Nothing else seemed disturbed. When she looked back, he was studying her curiously, head to one side.

'The tea is in the other room,' she said.

He stood and walked past her. Wallace waited until he'd gone and briskly brushed out the creases Milt had made on the coverlet, bending to square the heels on a pair of shoes under the bed so the backs just nudged the perfect hanging line of Gran's patchwork quilt.

A breeze blew up, and she went over to the window to capture one of the billowing muslin curtains beside the bed. Milt was upsetting her.

She gathered the curtains and tucked them behind the heavy emerald drapes, leaving the long casement window open for cross-flow ventilation. When the energy started to build, the study would become hot. *If* the energy built. Her ineptitude was creeping in on the back of her uncertainty about Milt. He was making her angry and nervous at the same time.

'I'm going into the bathroom to change,' she said from the study door. Milt was sitting on the floor, his back against one of the walls, the old spell books beside him.

He looked up. 'Not too much, I hope. I was just starting to get used to you again.'

'Your jokes haven't improved, and you're also encroaching on my perimeter. Back off,' she said, starting to close the connecting door before pausing to add, 'A lot of things have changed, Milt. For good.'

She shut the door and turned the lock with a decisive click.

Inside the bathroom, she closed the door and hung her navy suit on the back of the door to let the steam ease the creases out. It was last season's, but it still hung well. Quality, even on sale, always would. Another Grannyism.

Naked, she raised her arms in front of the mirror and stretched to prepare her body. While she'd only just showered, the ritual demanded she be cleansed immediately prior. Her thoughts drifted back to Milt, and she felt a flush of blood, surprised to realize she was acutely aware of him in the other room, remembering him sitting on her bed. Shaking the feeling away, she showered quickly, then took the flowing ceremonial robe from the cupboard and slipped it over her head, making a brief but futile attempt to finger comb her damp curls back to bounce before reentering the study.

Milt was standing next to the casement window, staring out, absently sipping tea. He turned at the sound of the door.

'It's a bit earthy for my taste,' he said, holding the dainty cup up in his big paw. 'What's in it? Nice dress, by the way.'

'Worms and snails and puppy dog tails,' she quipped, annoyed that he'd helped himself. Like lying on her bed. He took things—and people—for granted. Some things didn't and wouldn't change—ever—and maybe they weren't supposed to. She needed to remember that as well.

'Figures,' he said. 'What's next?'

'You're being remarkably relaxed about this. The Milt I used to know would be totally intolerant by now. What was it you used to say you avoided? Ah yes, "anything left of rational."'

'I guess there have been a few "left" turns since then. Besides, the only other possible alternative is a lot less attractive. At least to me.'

'And me, or I'm trying to.'

His dark eyes softened. 'I know that, thanks, Lacey. It means a lot.'

'Save that until we see whether this works.'

'You really aren't confident about it, are you? Are you still being that hard on yourself?'

Suddenly her careful composure split apart. 'Look, I'm already seeing a psych, all right? I really don't need any more interpersonal growth advice—especially from someone as screwed up as you.'

'A psych? You? No way.'

'Sit! There!' She pointed back at a spot on the floor. She noted her extended finger had a minor tremor and curled it into her palm.

Milt eased himself down to the floor, extending his legs out in front. She busied her fingers lighting a candle and incense atop a small altar tucked in the far corner surrounded by bookcases. Chanting a blessing, she felt her calm returning as she trailed fragrant incense smoke through an intricate pattern.

'Before you ask, I'm strengthening the existing wards. Protection, if you like.'

'From what?'

'You don't want to know.' She poured more tea into both cups and handed him one.

'Drink. It's supposed to settle you, make you less resistant.'

'To what?'

'Mumbo jumbo BS, what else.'

Milt tossed off his tea and immediately made gagging noises, his expression disgusted. 'Jesus, did I say earthy? Make that six foot under with a half twist and pike.'

Ignoring him, Wallace cradled her own small cup and absorbed the residual warmth into her palms, then touched the bowl to her forehead, heart, and lips, mentally dedicating it the way Gran had taught her.

The last time you tried this, nothing happened, remember? What makes you think—

She tipped back her head and drained the tea in two determined gulps, drowning the harping voice of her mother. The herbs had steeped and were now very bitter. She clenched her abdomen against the spasm. When it came, she shuddered, a muscle memory from when she was twelve now absorbed as part of the ritual. Gran always said ritual was the most important thing. It quietened the mind.

Her pulse slowed with her breath, the flow beginning as always in her toes, moving up through her feet to her legs and torso, dissolving discomfort as it went, preparing her for what might come.

She set the cup back on the tray and sat opposite, drawing her legs into lotus, taking care to tuck the robe around her legs. When she spoke, her voice was tight, still constricted by the herbs. 'I need you to repeat the words as I say them using the same tones I do, got it? It's a simple call and response chant but you have to say it exactly as I do, otherwise this isn't going to work.'

Never has before.

'You mean *sing?*' he said, as if she'd asked him to stand naked in Queen Street with his hand out.

'I mean just do it, all right? This is going to be hard enough to pull off with only the two of us here, without you lobbing smartass comments from the sidelines—or trying to second-guess me.'

'Fine, fine, let's get on with it,' he said, flapping his hand, then quieter, 'Freaking bullshit.'

'Ah, there he is: Milt the septic skeptic. I was beginning to wonder for a while there.'

Wallace cleared her throat, closed her eyes, and began the incantation, her voice gradually adopting a deep and resonant tone. Milt responded well enough, and Wallace felt the first tingle of energy dance lightly between her eyebrows. Encouraged, she brought in the second line, waiting a beat for his response. Again, a small flush of sensation; this time across the back of her neck. Wallace upped the tempo. The energy in the air around her shifted, beginning to layer and build. Sweat beaded her brow and top lip. She ignored it, focusing instead on the tingling space between her eyebrows. Beside her, Milt struggled to keep up. The words came faster, the rhythms more complex.

Almost there. Am I really doing this?

Wallace allowed her voice to dip on the last line, damping down the final word altogether. Milt followed suit. She could feel the energy spiraling through her, seeking an outlet. Her whole body vibrated, tuning into the frequency of the charged air. Hastily she brought an image of Gran to mind, mentally projecting it against the inside of her skull like a full-screen movie. Milt was wheezing.

I can't do this. It's too hard.

A feeling of lightness crept into her left foot and made its way cautiously toward her ankle, pausing there like a suspicious but curious dog sniffing and snuffling its way slowly up the inside of her body, exploring and filling every space before moving on.

It's happening.

The expansiveness reached her chest. Breathing became easier. She wondered whether Milt could feel it too, or was it only her?

Will we both go through the veil?

Wallace realized with a start that if this worked, she had no idea how they would get back, and for one desperate moment panic threatened to overwhelm her. She tried to slough it off the way Gran had shown her, but as always the anxiety was like black sticky mud; no matter how hard she scraped, some remained. She wavered, teetering at the edge. Her mother's mocking, drunken words flailed her, eroding resolve like fine, wind-driven sand.

You may be a little bitch, Wallace, but you're no fuckin' witch.

Wallace tightened her focus, zeroing back in, gathering and coaxing the retreating lightness, opening herself against the overwhelming urge to cower and close down.

It's coming back.

Almost there.

Wallace wasn't sure how the transition happened, but she felt the shift—one moment she was "there" and in the next "where?" as the energy burst around her in a brilliant blaze. When it cleared, she saw Gran on a log beside a small stream. Birdsong filled the air; the air thick and heavy with promise. It was illusion, of course, a "chat room" for Gran—a space where the consciousness of the dead and the living could meet. She and Milt, their bodies anyway, were still in her study.

Remembering Milt, Wallace looked over her shoulder. He was a few paces behind her, his image hazy, as if he were standing behind several sheets of bubbled glass.

'Don't worry about him, he's still transitioning,' Aggie called. 'He'll be along directly.' Aggie patted the log beside her. 'Come on over, love, let's use what time we have.'

Wallace approached slowly, feeling the anger return as Gran went on as if nothing had happened. She eased herself down. The log felt warm, the sun almost directly overhead, yet within her heart she felt increasingly cold, as if something precious had been broken and now could not be put back together.

Gran smiled.

'You lied,' Wallace said, the words falling out of their own accord, stripped of emotion.

'Dear, I'm sorry I—'

Wallace turned toward Aggie. 'About what, Gran?' Wallace felt fire beneath the ice. 'You're my grandmother—*Gran*—first, second, and last. He—' She pointed at the outline of Milt off to the side. '—He used to be the man I loved. Yet, from what he was telling me he also just *happens* to be the father of your new fucking chosen one, Jessica. How's that for a coincidence?'

'Yes, that was rather unfortunate, I agree. Fate does as it must though, child.'

'Fate? Oh, don't try and flick that one back to the keeper. You put that slut in his way. Why can't you just admit it?'

'All right, if that's what's going to make you happy. It's all my fault. Blame me for everything bad in your life and all its disappointments. Does that make you feel any better? I can't change it, Lacey. It's done and I can't undo it. I'm dead and you're not; I don't see what you're complaining about.' She paused, staring off at a small stand of trees in the distance before continuing. 'I won't try and justify it to you. You know me well enough to know my reasons. I'd hoped that might be enough.'

'Enough? Enough for what?' Tears prickled Wallace's eyes. She'd be damned if she'd let them show. Especially now. Aggie reached over to touch her, but Wallace jerked away.

'You not only lied to me, but you broke your "sacred" Wiccan Code about non-interference, and you just say you're sorry? What did you always tell me about unsanctioned action and consequence?'

'This wasn't unsanctioned, dear. We all have our parts to play. I couldn't tell you everything, otherwise the outcome would have been compromised. You know that.'

'Compromised? Oh no, we wouldn't want to do that, would we? Better to "compromise" the only relationship that's meant something to me in my entire life.'

'Darling, Milt is—'

'Not him, damn it. Me. And you!'

Aggie closed her eyes. Wallace could see her words thumping deep into the old woman's chest like poisoned darts. She accepted them all, rejecting none. Wallace felt the rage drain from her until she was left with an afterflow of calm compassion and grudging acceptance. The Way was all, as always. Gran had dedicated her life to it and raised a granddaughter at the same time. She touched Aggie lightly on the shoulder. 'I'm sorry. I do know.'

They hugged. Closer now.

'I always thought the father of the Messenger was chosen by the coven. I can't imagine anyone preselecting Milt as the father of, well, anyone really,' Wallace said.

'We didn't. A suitable male was selected from our group, and Angelique rejected him. She ran away before any of us knew what she was about and used the ring to remain undetected until it was too late. Milt just happened to be in the way. Classic wrong man, wrong place, wrong time.'

'That sounds like Milt. So why is he still involved?'

'He's the father of the Messenger—'

'Meaning Jessica.'

'Yes, yes, all right, Jessica,' Aggie said, her voice impatient. 'The natural father is always the protector of the Messenger after she comes of age. She was always going to be our best hope, given Angelique's reluctance to accept her own destiny.'

'How did you get him to cooperate?' Wallace was genuinely curious now. Milt thought of himself as strong-willed. Wallace just called it set-in-stone stubborn.

Aggie paused, looking down at her hands. Finally she said, 'When Milt had the trouble with that last case, he was sent for psychological assessment. What you don't know is that I arranged for him to be transferred to my practice. I was his psychologist,' she said, nodding vaguely toward where Milt was still appearing. 'During his treatment, I planted a sleeper spell in his subconscious, sort of like a posthypnotic code, that I could activate later if needed. He has no memory of any of that, of course, or me. I recommended he be stood down and placed on a pension. What he thinks happened is he was offered a package to take early retirement and received a significant payout, then sold his story. Sort of like stress leave.'

'What?'

'The coven paid for it all, of course. Along with his police pension, it provides a comfortable living for him—until the time when I might need him to protect Jessica.'

'So what about Milt and me?' Wallace felt a sharp tug at her abdomen. 'I felt that, Gran.'

Aggie's lips firmed, another clue she was hiding something.

'Gran? Tell me.' Her voice tight as realization blossomed and expanded throughout her chest.

Gran nodded. 'All right. I did arrange for your affair to end as well. I had to. There was no future in it for either of you. I tried to tell you that, if you recall. Besides, Jessica was about to come of age, and Milt needed to be in Melbourne for that. It wouldn't have worked if he wasn't receptive—relationally empty.'

Wallace's stomach churned. 'Relationally empty? What about me, Gran? Did you ever once think what I might like in any of this? Oh, God, poor Milt. He's so confused, and all this time I thought—'

'It was all for the best, love.'

'Gran! I loved him,' Wallace shouted, fists clenched, pounding her thighs. 'Don't you get that?'

Aggie picked at a splinter of wood, worrying it away from the log. She studied it for a moment before flicking it away. The thin sliver of wood caught on the light breeze and hung in the air as if it too was waiting to hear what Aggie might say.

'Yes, Wallace. I did *and do* get that. Causing you pain has never given me any pleasure, believe me, but sacrifices for a greater good are necessary. I'm not sure *you* get that.'

Wallace felt the energy leak from her, and she had to concentrate on holding her consciousness there and not collapsing back into the haven of her body waiting with Milt's back at the house.

Aggie draped her arm around Wallace, who shrugged it away, but Aggie persisted. 'I know it's hard, love, but try and get past your emotions—just for a bit—and take a quick peek through the bigger window. For me, please. The lives of a huge number of our people depend on us. Thanks to Milt, we now have the ring, but there's still so much to do, so much you still don't know.'

Wallace closed her eyes, fingers clenching into fists at her side. *How does Gran always do this to me, and why am I the one who always ends up feeling guilty?*

'All right.' The words snagged in her throat. 'For now. But just know, I don't forgive you.'

'I wouldn't expect you to, love. I'm sorry it had to be that way.'

Wallace pointed at Milt's rapidly clearing image. 'Why did you send him to me, anyway? What's he got to do with this, other than being the bastard father?'

'I didn't *send* him. He was supposed to stay in Melbourne. He found out your address himself. As it happens, the two of you may be more effective in locating Jessica, anyway. Milt probably told you the details.'

Wallace nodded. 'How did Angelique die? I'm assuming it wasn't the same as the others.'

Gran shook her head. 'Poor Angie's life never sailed straight. She decided to be proactive and kill herself just after the murders began. She knew what they were looking for.'

'You were murdered too?' Wallace asked, her throat tightening.

'Of course. They needed the Book of Names, and I had the only copy. With the book, all they had to do was start at the top and work their way down. Eventually they would find the Messenger and the ring. One of the Sisters had to have it. Angelique, unwittingly, outsmarted them by entombing herself somewhere in the Dandenongs. That's why I had to get Milt involved. Apart from Jess, he's the only genetic link that could synch to the ring.'

As if on cue, Milt stumbled through the last of the opaque shield and fell to his knees, chin to his chest, breath shallow and labored. Both women rushed over, each taking one of his arms, and helped him to where they'd been sitting, settling him on the grass with his back against the log.

'Is he all right?' Wallace asked.

'Tranced. He'll be out for a bit. The passage affects everyone differently. Remember your first time through the veil?' Aggie smiled.

Wallace ignored the invitation to bond, recognizing it as one of the many ways Gran manipulated others. No more. She sat back down, using Milt's sagging bulk as a barrier, obliging Gran to sit on the other side.

Finally Wallace said, 'Okay, let's say I understand why you used Milt. I still don't see what I can do.'

'You're alive, and I'm not. I told you, he'll need some help once he finds Jessica.'

'And you assume I'll be the one to do it? After everything that happened....'

'No. For everything that is bound to happen.'

'Oh Gran, not those damned Scrolls again.'

'Yes again. Still. Why do you think I was murdered? Why all of our number are being progressively annihilated?'

'Just because there are two crazies who believe in an old legend doesn't make it true.'

'What if it is true? Have you thought of that?' Aggie snapped.

'What bullshit.'

Both women looked down. Milt was scratching his head.

'Milt, are you all right?' Wallace asked.

'No. And neither are you if you think this guy will stop. Serial killers don't stop; they can't. If anything, the frequency and severity of the murders will increase. It's like an addiction, and like any addiction, the payoff decreases with time.'

'Exactly,' Aggie said, 'and that's why we have to do everything we can to find Jessica and protect her until it's time to activate the Scrolls.'

'Oh, can you forget the damned Scrolls, Gran? Our people are dying one by one. That has to be our first priority,' Wallace said, her voice prickly.

'What if I told you Dragos was behind all this?' Aggie said.

'What?' Wallace spluttered. 'Dragos? He's bound in the seventh realm. How could he possibly be doing this?'

'The seventh what?' Milt asked, looking up at Wallace.

She waved her hand. 'It's a sort of prison. Very high security. No one has—or could—escape from there,' Wallace said, looking meaningfully at Aggie.

'I call it a waiting room for Purgatory,' Aggie added. 'Plus it's the only way to contain a demon.'

Wallace threw her hands in the air.

'A what?' Milt asked, laughing.

'Demon, and before you say anything, yes, they exist—and Dragos is a powerful one. While the Sisterhood has bound him, somehow he's found a way to animate a mortal surrogate to do his work here.'

'You mean a lackey who does murder on the side? The devil made me do it doesn't make an original defense strategy,' Milt ventured, voice heavy with sarcasm.

Gran didn't seem to notice. She smiled and patted Milt's hand as if he were a schoolboy who had unexpectedly answered a complex question. 'Yes, think of it as a form of demonic possession, but on a long leash.'

'But why?' Wallace asked.

'The energy. With each killing, Dragos sucks up the deceased's life force. Remember the victims have all been Sisters of our circle. In death their inherent talent and power is released with a rush, and Dragos has been harvesting it. Eventually he'll have accumulated enough to break through our binding spells altogether.'

'I think I'm on drugs. Wallace, what was in that bloody tea anyway?'

Wallace ignored him, staring at Aggie over the top of his head. 'Do you know who this surrogate is? If you can give me a name, I could dig up enough on him to convince the Hacker's task force commander to take a look. We recovered unidentified DNA from one of the victims.'

'That wasn't in the news either,' Milt said. 'If the task force came down on him, he wouldn't know what hit him.'

'No,' Gran said, 'Dragos has him cloaked too well. I can't locate him even from this side of the veil.'

The thought wormed its way through Wallace's consciousness: *So it could still be Milt.*

'So where did this... Dragos come from?' Milt asked.

'Some people get magic and power mixed up. One works for the greater good while the other inflates the ego. Power used in this way can be intoxicating, incredibly so. Some years back, one of our Sisters was led down the left-hand path and summoned a demon for her own selfish ends—Dragos, it turned out to be. It took many years—and lives—to bind him. I now believe Dragos will be the contender.'

'Contender for what?' Milt asked.

Aggie sighed. 'I suppose you have a right to know. Every hundred years there are always two contenders for the Scrolls: one represents the interests of the light, the other the dark. Last century, our sisters managed to win and activated the Scrolls. At other times, dark times, we have come close to losing, and the world has suffered. This time, with a demon as the contender, the results could be catastrophic for everyone.'

Wallace sighed, feeling her anger and frustration leak away. 'So what do you suggest?'

Aggie shrugged. 'Dragos is becoming too strong, even for us. Jessica has no training. That should have started when she was twelve, but Angelique refused to release her. Just after I went to see her for the last time, Angelique upped and disappeared, taking Jess with her. Once we find her, we need to buy some time, and the only thing I can think of is to go back and stop Dragos from getting hold of the Book of Names in the first place. Before he's this strong. Before the killings even start.'

'Go back? What, you mean in time?' Wallace scoffed. 'How? I haven't found that handy hint listed in the Herbal Handbook.'

'Please don't be obtuse, Wallace. There is a way. The Yesterday, Today, and Tomorrow portal. But first you'll need to find Jess and bind the ring. We can then start over and fast cook her with as much magic and lore as we can cram in before the Scrolls have to be reset. Hopefully once time catches up with itself and you all end up back here, she'll be strong enough to go through the necessary challenges and tests to access the Scrolls.'

Wallace closed her eyes and shook her head. 'Gran, that time portal is a myth. No one has ever seen it, much less used it.'

'Since when have the Sisters needed proof? Faith is what our tradition is bound on, Wallace. Faith. So I ask: where's yours? We can summon the portal using the Messenger's ring. The ancient Sisterhood records are quite clear on this.'

Wallace rolled her eyes. Finally she grunted and raised her hands in surrender. 'All right, all right. Legends and myths aside, let's just *pretend* that we can go back in time. What happens then?'

Aggie beamed. 'Why, you retrieve the book and hide it somewhere safe, as I'd intended. Dragos's surrogate caught up with me before I had time to do it. But first you have to find Jess and get her inducted before her name comes up and the Hacker tracks her down. You need to get started now.'

'Now? But I'm on suspension. I need to try and get back in to the psych tomorrow, otherwise I could be dismissed,' Wallace said.

Aggie's brows narrowed. 'That's your job—what we've been talking about is your *work*. Nothing is more important, Lacey. Nothing. Why do you think I'm still rattling around in limbo land and haven't moved on? Because I enjoy it? It's damn hard work staying put, like trying to swim against the current, but do you hear me complaining?'

'Okay, okay. I get it.'

'I should think so. Now remember what the records also tell us about the portal; time accelerates when you travel back through it. It's described as being like an elastic band. It stretches but snaps back in a hurry. Other reports say time moves like energy, in downward spirals. If you attempt to go against the flow, it will tug you back down—fast, like a whirlpool. Either way, it means days pass more quickly, and not evenly. Think chunks. One day you could wake up and find a whole week has gone by, so it's imperative you don't allow Jessica to miss the time nexus of when the Scrolls have to be activated. And that's the other thing: when you go back, don't try and save me. Changing fate, especially someone's life expectancy, alters—other things. Just focus on getting the book, any way you can.'

Aggie looked over at the space where Wallace and Milt had emerged from, her eyes narrowing. 'You need to go back now. The connection is weakening.'

Milt and Wallace stood up and started walking back.

'Oh, and Wallace?'

They both turned.

'Remember your name is in that book as well. Be careful.'

SIX

Milt felt his body swaying, suspended and unanchored. Half-awake, his mind chased snippets of dreams like a dog after cats down alleyways they knew far better than he.

He forced himself to wake, physically moving his body to do so. The swaying increased.

Am I still asleep?

Reaching out to steady himself, he found, then gripped, the sides of something.

Rope?

He lifted his head.

I'm in a bloody hammock.

Levering himself up, he balanced on the edge, legs swinging, looking at but not seeing the huge backyard. Instead, strange images, pretending to be memory, flipped like cards through his head. He found only crazy stuff: dead people talking of demons and ritual killings.

He'd come to Brisbane looking for answers—straight answers—but all he'd found so far was chaos.

'Wallace!' he shouted.

Too loud.

'Wallace!' he yelled, louder.

A door opened and slammed. Bare feet slapped on timber.

'I'm here, Milt. How are you feeling?' Wallace squatted in front of him, her gray eyes searching his.

'Where am I? What the hell happened?'

'Ssh, it's all right. We're back at my house, out on the back deck. See, there's my garden.' She pointed, and his eyes followed. Shortened shadows had created cool shady spaces. It looked to be early afternoon. He felt his heart rate slow. He turned back to her.

'I had these dreams; they seemed so real.'

'I know. I know.' She raised her hand and stroked his brow with cool fingers. It felt good. 'You've been asleep for about two hours. It was a pretty rough trip back.'

'Back?' He started upright. 'You mean this bullshit flipping through my head is actually true?'

'I'm not sure about that, Milt, but if you mean did we both see Gran, then yes, we did. She told us some things. Do you remember any of that?'

He nodded, eyebrows bunching. 'Crazy demon stuff?'

'Let's just focus on the practical for the moment. She also gave us a clue as to how to stop the murders.'

'Find this Jessica, my long-lost heir?'

'Right, and give her the ring.'

He looked down; the ugly ring was still there. That at least was tangible, but then he remembered that only he and Aggie could actually see it—and she was dead.

'And the rest?'

'Remember what we used to say about asking questions that you'd rather not know the answers to?'

He nodded.

'So let's just focus on what we can do, and one of those things is keeping my number from coming up in this game of murder bingo. We can take the rest as it comes. Are you in?'

JESS PAUSED IN THE DOORWAY, peering into the darkness of the flat beyond, her hand still on the key in the lock. Slowly she drew it out and groped for the light switch, the wall surfaces still too unfamiliar to know instinctively where it was.

Finally finding it, she snapped the switch down.

Nothing.

No answering splash of welcoming light. She flicked it again, up and down, making only futile clicking noises. Stopping, she craned forward, her ears straining the darkness for sound, sorting the known from not: the dull hum of the fridge—straight down the hall to the left. A tap, dripping steadily, kitchen again—and behind that the intermittent quiet slap of the pull-down blind against its aluminum window frame.

I'm sure I locked all the windows before I went out.

Prickles of cold swept up her legs. The white noise threatened to rise, but she clamped down on it savagely.

Did I lock them?

Frantically she ransacked her memory, finding only hurry and rush before she'd left the flat earlier that day, still hopeful of making the first of the job interviews on time.

Leave or stay?

Decide now.

The next light switch was in the hallway, just before the archway through to the kitchen. Ten steps, no more.

Leave or stay?

If she left, it would be with her fear. Perfectly packaged and shrink-wrapped for traveling. Running.

She'd already run from Melbourne to Brisbane after the phone call. Run from her apartment, the stage, and even her name to a room by the week and a new prepaid SIM card.

'Hello?' she called hopefully, hoping Tracey, the girl she'd rented the spare room from, had returned early. No answering sound came back, and she wondered whether that was good or not. Perhaps the steady dripping was not coming from a leaky kitchen tap, but Tracey's blood plopping onto the pitted '90s floor tiles in the kitchen.

'Tracey?'

Another splashy drip.

Inhaling deeply, Jess snibbed the front door's lock to keep it open and took one step, then another, the fingers of her left hand trailing the wall.

She kicked off her shoes, sliding them to the far side of the hall. It would be easier to run if she was barefoot. Behind her the front door creaked loudly. She spun; the framed rectangle of light remained unchanged. The door creaked again, and she could just make out a light tremble of its shape on its hinges. Tracey liked to wedge the door open to draw air through the small flat from the front windows. Jess was aware now of a cool breath of breeze against her face.

She exhaled and took two more quick steps—halfway—another two, her hand reached forward, stretching, sliding over the wall.

Click.

Light filled the hallway, chasing her fears back to their dark corners to wait.

'HOLD STILL, MILT.'

'I will if you'll tell me what you're going to do with that frigging knife.'

Wallace sighed and leaned her buttocks against the side of the dining table. 'You asked me how, remember? Well, this is it. I need to make a small nick in the pad of your right thumb, just enough to draw blood.'

'That's it?'

'The painful part, anyway. The rest you leave up to me.'

Milt grunted and held his thumb out, turning his head away. Wallace grinned and made two small, intersecting incisions across his thumb pad. Blood oozed out and trickled down.

'All right, now put your other hand in the bowl.'

'The other hand?'

'Yes, that's the one with the ring, isn't it? I mean, I can't see it, so—'

Milt held up his left hand, palm facing her. 'Yeah, yeah.' He slid it into the waiting water. 'Now what?'

'Quiet.'

Wallace mumbled some words that he couldn't make out, her free hand making shapes around the rim of the bowl.

'Milt, I need you to focus on the ring. Can you see it?'

'Of course I can bloody see it. We've just been through this, Lacey.'

'All right, then really stare at it. I'm going to charge the water with your blood.'

She held his thumb above the bowl, allowing the blood to plop in.

'Good, just a few more. When the drops hit the surface of the water, they create ripples, concentric rings that will get bigger as they move toward the rim of the bowl. I want you to imagine these traveling across the bowl, constantly growing larger. Then imagine the rings moving out past the bowl through the air, traveling right across the city, across the state, covering all the area of the land right across the continent. Can you do that?'

'Yeah, sure, I think so. What then?'

'We wait.'

Wallace raised his hand higher, positioning the wound over the center of the bowl, and squeezed, releasing in turn three drops. He watched them plop into the water, seeing the ripples, imagining them getting bigger. It was hard to concentrate, as the hand under the water was tingling. The ring on his pinky grew tighter, until the finger began to throb.

'Keep concentrating,' Wallace said as he began to fidget. 'Think of the ripples as energy. They've absorbed the genetic code in your blood. If this works, they'll keep on going until they locate a match.'

'Cuts down on the red tape. If this works, you should put it up for the department. Quicker than tracking perps the hard way.'

'Yeah, a real quick way out the door too. Now shut up for second; something is happening. There, did you feel it?'

'What?'

'A sort of flicker, or wash back, like it's hit something.'

All Milt could feel was the increasing tightness around his little finger. He shook his head. Wallace closed her eyes.

'Yes, it's definitely a strike. It's come much sooner than I expected. I think she could even be here in Brisbane.'

'You sound surprised. Does that mean you knew where she was before?'

Wallace opened her eyes and looked at him, 'Yes, of course. She was in Melbourne. I thought Gran told you that.'

'Your gran told me a lot of things. Mostly none of them make a whole lot of sense.'

'Funny, you and Jess both being in Melbourne at the same time,' she added, her voice trailing off.

'You mean along with the other five million people who live there, or do you mean her, me, and the axe?'

Wallace said nothing but was unable to hold his gaze.

'Oh, look, I really don't give a shit. I mean, here I am with one hand in a dish with a ring only I and special dead people can see. Ghosts who not only walk but speak and screw with my head and you—a witch with confidence issues. Make that call to the psych ward, Lacey, or maybe arrest me first. You may as well get the glory of bringing me in before the court checks me into nuthouse central, I don't care.'

'I'm sorry, Milt. I know this is tough. Gran is on your side, that's one thing.'

'I'm not counting on her testimony, Lacey, and—just quietly—neither of us can actually prove she's whispering her BS from the sidelines. Remember that. This could be just as much in your head as mine. So don't rule that one out either. Shared tripping on your super-special tea leaves. It happens.'

Wallace released his hand. 'Innocent until proven, remember that one, Milt? Now, shut up for a minute. I need to try and plot Jessica's location.'

Taking what looked like a highlighter pen, Wallace drew a large circle around the perimeter of the bowl. Immediately the water shimmered, then, where his wrist met the water, the surface changed to silver, as reflective as a mirror, spreading to all sides of the bowl. He went to remove his hand, and Wallace checked it.

'Stay there. We need the ring to remain in the water. Now watch the witch.'

Slowly a street map built itself on the surface of the water. Milt could read some of the street names even though they were in unfamiliar old-fashioned script.

'Our fonts haven't kept up,' Wallace said, peering over his shoulder and making notes on a pad. 'There.' She pointed with the highlighter pen at a red dot that had appeared midway down one of the streets. With great care, she marked out a smaller circle in the air above the red dot, and immediately the image resolved to a close-up showing the street number and then an image of an apartment building.

'Come on, dry your hand. Let's get over there.'

'And do what? Say what? This looks like an apartment block. We don't even know which flat she's in.'

'Have you got a better plan? If you have, roll it out now. Otherwise let's move.'

THE RIDE over to Jessica's apartment was silent and tense. She shouldn't be bringing Milt along at all. There was no doubt he was unstable at best—at worst he could still be the perp. Not a great spread.

He sat beside her, saying nothing, sensing everything. He'd always had trust issues. Over the time they were together she'd watched him use his own iron-hard reasoning and faith in himself to get over them. Take that template away, and only chaos remained. Milt didn't do that well.

Betrayal was his cross. According to him, he'd been nailed to it by his ex-wife when he found her playing up with his former partner in the force. He'd ditched both. Wallace had quickly followed, his partner in crime as well as bed. She'd betrayed both—in Milt's mind —when she hadn't stood behind him when they came after him. It had been his final case; the force had not only let him down, they'd cast him out. He'd accused her of being like "the rest of them"—that nameless, faceless horde of Milt's Enemies. Yet, the only one who'd ever betrayed Milt, paradoxically, was Milt. Talk about needing psychs.

So what the heck is Gran really up to, getting him involved? Getting me involved with him, more to the point.

She pulled up across the road from Jessica's unit block. Wallace glanced over at Milt. His shields were still up.

'What now?' he asked, arms crossed, staring straight ahead.

'We wait. See who comes out.'

'Wait?' The corners of his mouth turned down.

'Or you could trigger the fire alarm? Get them all out and running, how about that?' Wallace snapped, unsure why she was making this harder.

Milt grunted and opened the car door.

'Milt? Where are you going? You're not—'

'Coffee.' He nodded toward a café twenty meters ahead. 'Want some?'

. . .

WALLACE SIPPED HER CAPPUCCINO, staring out through the windscreen. It tasted burnt. She flirted briefly with the idea of taking Milt's lead and returning it before deciding she needed the hit more than the taste.

If police work could be distilled into one word, it would be waiting. Forget everything else: if you didn't have patience, couldn't sit comfortably within yourself for hours at a time, then you were in the wrong job. Crims were the same. The successful ones had mastered the art of waiting. It was the nervous, edgy types who always got caught.

She remembered Milt hated it.

Slurping another gulp of the coffee, she repressed the reflex shudder.

The passenger door opened. 'I don't know why you bother drinking it,' Milt said, sliding back in beside her, a new, freshly frothed cup in his hand. The seat groaned as he settled himself, and the small space in the front of her car was overflowing with him.

She shuffled as far away as she could. 'I've got an addictive thread. I told you that. I find it hard to give things up.'

Milt snorted. 'Yeah, like grudges.'

Wallace hunkered against the door, sinking deeper into her own self-reflective pool. Old lovers knew where all your buttons were. They had a way of wheedling the vulnerabilities out of you and then serving them up later in carefully prepared strips, each with its own stinging barb that snagged in your throat like a fish bone hidden in mashed potato.

All right. I may have overreacted earlier but seeing him again after all this time came as a shock. It was like the past and the present were overlaid, their edges blurry and indistinct. It threw me.

'Why aren't you working, anyway? Where's your partner?' he asked, breaking the latest silence.

'He's laid up. Hospital. He tripped on a set of steps and shot himself in the ankle.'

'You're kidding.'

'Yeah, I am. I shot him. By mistake. We're not talking.'

'Is that why you're on gardening leave with the psych?'

'You got it.' She drank again and made a face. 'Euch, this coffee really sucks. Since when did you become a coffee snob anyhow? Time was you'd be grateful for two spoons of Nescafe and a slurp of condensed milk, Mr. double-shot cap.'

'Things change.'

'Things may. People don't,' she added pointedly.

'Did anyone come out?' He used the back of his hand to wipe foam from his mouth as if erasing the former conversation.

'No.'

Her phone chirped. She answered.

'Carruthers.... Yes. Yes, all right. I'll be there as soon as I can.'

She clicked off and turned to Milt. 'I have to go. I missed my psych visit and the boss wants to see me about it. I'll need to take the car, so you'll have to move over to the café. You should get a better view of the flats from there anyway, and you can brush up on your barista techniques. I shouldn't be too long.'

JESS HAD SLEPT POORLY and at 2:00 a.m. had taken one of Tracey's sedatives. It'd been a mistake, causing her to miss the morning entirely and sleep well into the afternoon. As a result, her rhythm was out. She rarely took drugs, her body didn't seem to be able to handle them, but sleep was the one thing she couldn't afford to go into hock for. If she did, the white noise would start, and if sleep still eluded her, wild hallucinations and unknown voices would run rampant like movies in her head until she was unsure which reel was real.

Rubbing her cheeks, she made a quick stop in the bathroom and then padded through to the kitchen, switching on the kettle and glancing at the clock on the wall. 3:00 p.m. Today was a washout. Still, she had enough money for another couple of months if she watched her spending. The good news was, she could snag an early night tonight and be fresh to look for more jobs tomorrow. Cash gigs, she reminded herself, unless she was willing to use her real name. Even busking was out without her guitar.

The thought of the guitar brought back a memory of his voice on the phone. That fleeting touch. She shuddered and shook the feeling away, dragging herself back into the world of practicalities.

Maybe in a couple of weeks she could resurface, try again with local auditions. They were always looking for new faces in ads. Maybe she was just being overcautious about not applying straight away.

The kettle whistled, and she poured steaming water into a mug, plopping in a peppermint tea bag. Anyway, Tracey would be home tomorrow, and she'd offered to intro her to some peeps in the trade who might be able to help.

Blowing and sipping at the hot tea, she took it through to the lounge room, tucked one leg beneath her, and settled herself on the ragged plaid of the two-seater.

Am I overreacting to what happened in Melbourne?

She'd seen other actors lose themselves in the role of their own lives, injecting drama where there was none, injecting traits from characters they'd played until there was no semblance left of who they truly were, their only true skill an innate ability to instigate constant conflict and drama. Her gaze fell on the small crystal globe on the coffee table. In hindsight, Martin, her ex-everything, was one of those. She reached over and picked up the glass sphere, weighing it in her palm. As always it felt dense; clouded with emotional energy.

Could the stalker be Martin? He was big enough.

She hadn't brought much with her, so when Tracey had spotted the globe on the coffee table, she thought it was significant. The scene replayed in her mind, Tracey asking, 'Did someone special give you that?'

Jess: "My ex. I keep it to remind me how some things look solid and transparent, but when you them get up close, everything gets distorted and turned upside down until you realize what you see can't ever be trusted."

It was a line from a play she'd been in once, and she realized it fitted Martin closer than those Lycra tights he so loved.

But no. Above all else, Martin was a coward. He wasn't capable and wouldn't have the money to pay someone else, because everything he earned, he spent on himself. Who, then?

The scene from that alley flashed up. The feeling of the man reaching out for her. A red man dressed in black; the solid *thunk* of the guitar case connecting with the side of his head. The red blood running almost immediately after.

Is that why I think of him as red?

The answer flashed back: no. It was his energy.

I should have gone to the police instead of running.

Mum had hated the police, and some of that mistrust must have stuck, because Jess hadn't called them. Even with the Hacker stories, Jess was still too scared to come forward, believing if she said nothing, remained anonymous—even from the police—the stalker couldn't find her. There was nothing definite she could tell them anyway—a red man dressed in black? What did that mean in centimeters and kilos? She'd rung Mum's ancient Nokia but, as usual, it wasn't working. Besides, she was pretty sure Mum might have passed into the light. The second beat inside her chest that had always been there and was strongest when Mum was in the room had stopped suddenly a few weeks ago.

She remembered holding her breath when it happened, waiting for it to resume—but it hadn't. Mum had said it would happen like that one day. She knew things like that. After a time, a tear had snaked down her cheek, memories tumbling into the void, but that had been all. It was only later that she realized Mum was running from something. As Jess grew up, they'd been constantly be on the move, "following the sun," she would say whenever it was time to pack up. "We're following the sun, Jess, off to a new adventure. Pack up."

For Jess, there was always another school, another bedroom with bare, stained walls to cover with posters and pretend that the last clutch of friends she'd left behind would look her up or at least keep in touch. Way before social media. Looking around the sparsely furnished flat now, Jess felt her gut tighten as she realized she was doing the very same thing, only this time she was hoping no one would find or remember her. Her mind drifted back to the phone call in Melbourne and that horrible voice.

"I've got your guitar."

Her name and phone number had been inside the guitar case. Stupid, stupid, stupid.

MILT HAD MOVED from coffee to an early dinner, or Linner, as the café menu described it. He hated that trendy crap but ordered fish with the fancy trims anyway. Four o'clock. Wallace had been gone an hour. Her boss must be giving her an earful. He'd tried ringing a couple of times but she wouldn't pick up, and he didn't bother leaving a message. She knew where he was.

Besides, no one had come in or gone out of the building. It was a small, narrow block, dark brick, five floors, with two flats to a floor, flanked by similar-sized buildings on either side. No lift and no roof level. The fire stairs came out in the underground car park. All entries and exits came through the front, so the girl was either out or holed up inside one of them. His latent cop instinct told him she was in there.

Unconsciously he twisted the ring on his little finger. It still felt tight, as if it sensed its rightful owner just across the road and was straining to get loose.

Rightful owner? Where is this crap coming from?

The fish arrived with a flourish, and he attacked it. Wallace arrived soon after.

'Thanks for waiting dinner,' she said, sliding into the chair opposite. She reached across and helped herself to some of his chips.

'Like waiting to be offered some of my very special Linner?'

'Linner?'

He waved his fork, dismissing it. 'What happened?'

'Bad girl. It's all just for the case sheet, to prove he's painting my discharge by the numbers. Canceling on the psych at the last minute is not considered to be a good indicator.'

'Indicator?'

'His word. Anyway, I'm officially on gardening leave for two months. The psych report to date isn't encouraging, apparently.'

'Anything you're not telling me?'

'Not more than that useless ex-partner of mine hasn't already said. The stories he must have told the boss to bring this off.'

'Like?'

'Witchy stuff. When I thought he wasn't looking. Forget it, it's fixable but at least it'll give me some focus space for this. Has anyone come out?'

Milt shook his head and tumbled the cutlery onto his empty plate, pushing back from the table. 'Nope, but I've been working while I was eating.' He smothered a burp and pointed over at the brown brick building. 'There are two flats to a floor, I checked that. The block faces west, see the way the sun is hitting those front windows? That means there's some serious heat and glare going into the ones with their curtains and blinds open. What do you see?'

Wallace narrowed her eyes. 'Four flats have their curtains open, which probably means the occupants left before the sun came down that far.'

'Correct. That would be flats ten, eight, six, and four. Another two, I'm thinking it's three and one, have blinds but only the nets are drawn. My bet is they're empty too.'

'Leaving four possibles.'

'Exactly. Now, I also noticed about half an hour ago the drapes in number one were drawn by an old man.'

'That doesn't mean she's not in there with him. She's likely sharing with someone. There's no record of a lease in her name, I already checked that.'

'No, but I'm betting it's unlikely she'd choose a man to share with.' He paused. 'There's something else. I have no idea what she looks like.'

'The ring does.'

'The ring... knows?'

'Yes, Gran said it will start to vibrate as soon as you see her. Come on.' Wallace stood. 'We can check out two flats each. I'll start at the bottom and work up, you come from the top and move down. That way if she's there or decides to run, we won't miss her.'

'I don't have a badge,' he said.

'When did that ever stop you?'

THE STAIRS WERE WOOD, the varnish scuffed and worn through along with many of the protective brass strips that lined the edge of each riser. Milt paused outside a door with a picture of a red-and-yellow flower pasted underneath a tarnished brass number seven. Nine had been a bust; the old woman wouldn't even open the door, just looked at him through the peephole and yelled out to him to go away until he could show her his "warranty." People definitely watched too many ads between their TV police dramas.

He gave the door of number seven two quick raps, loud and decisive. Down a level, he heard Wallace doing the same.

She must have finished with the old guy in two already. He smiled, knowing she'd be mentally cursing him for being right. Muffled voices drifted up the stairs. He could make out Wallace's tone, but couldn't hear what she was saying. He knocked again, leaning his ear toward the door. Someone was inside, he could hear the faint rattle of a security chain and a Yale lock clunking home. The door opened a crack.

'What do you want?'

It was a woman's voice, and she sounded about the right age.

'Police. Open up.'

The door quivered as if it might close. The ring on his pinky quivered and began vibrating wildly. It was her. Milt shoved the toe of his heavy boot into the small gap.

'Take your foot out.'

'I need you to open the door.'

'Show me your identification. I have a knife.' The door opened to the limit of the chain, and behind it he could make out an eye, blue, surrounded by a lot of brown hair. There was no sign of a knife.

Sighing, he took out his wallet and flipped it open, holding it off to the far side before snapping it closed. He brought his head into her line of vision, and she screamed, the door slamming repeatedly against his foot.

'Open the door!' Milt ordered.

Wallace came pounding up the stairs. 'What is it? What's going on?'

'Shit! It's her, this bloody ring is going ape shit, but she's trying to pulverize my foot. Do you still carry that spare piece, Wallace? Get it in her face.'

Wallace reached behind her and pulled a small pistol from her waistband holster. Cocking it, she leveled it at the face in the crack. 'Stop screaming and move back from the door. We're not here to harm you.'

The door ceased its frenzied bashing against Milt's foot. He pulled it out and limped off to the side.

'Now listen to me in there. My name is Detective Carruthers— Wallace Carruthers. What's the problem? Approach the door and tell me, quietly. No one is going to hurt you,' she repeated quieter, lowering the gun.

'Has he gone?' the girl asked.

Wallace darted a glance over to where Milt was standing on the other side of the small landing.

'Yes. He's gone. Why?'

'He tried to kill me.'

Wallace tried not to laugh. 'What? I didn't see a weapon.'

'Not now, before. In Melbourne.' There was a long pause. 'He's the red man, I mean that Hacker guy they're looking for.'

SEVEN

Wallace swiveled on the ball of her foot to face Milt, bringing the gun up. She motioned downward with the barrel. Milt put his hands up and eased himself down to kneel on the floor.

'You don't say,' she said over her shoulder, not taking her eyes off Milt. 'When was that?'

'A few days ago. I moved up here straight afterward.'

'And you're certain this man is the same one who attacked you? You'd be prepared to make a statement to that effect?'

'Yes... no. I don't want any more trouble.'

'It's a little too late for that. Shut and lock the door, I need to call this in.'

The door closed, and she took two steps toward Milt, the gun extended and steady in her hands.

'Like to comment before I put the cuffs on? Hands on head, you know the drill.'

'Wallace, I—'

'What? Can't remember? That's convenient, but I'm not sure it'll be enough to convince a jury. I should have listened to my intuition. I knew it.'

Milt looked up. 'Wallace, do me a favor. Before you take me in, is there some way you can ask your gran about this?'

Wallace's head was swimming. She was unsure. Now she had a witness to Milt's insanity. A primary witness, and yet....

Keeping the gun trained on him with one hand, she retrieved a pair of handcuffs with the other and tossed them onto the floor in front of him. 'Put them on.'

Milt reached for the cuffs.

'No, not in front. Put your hands behind you and lock down. That's it, now stay on your knees and shuffle over here—good—turn around.' Wallace reached down and tested the locking mechanism. It was tight.

Slowly she backed over toward the door, gun still trained, and kicked at the base of the door with her foot. 'Jess? Open up. I've got the man restrained. You're in no danger but I need to use your phone. Mine is broken.'

Nothing happened.

'Jess, I know you're scared, but I'm a friend of your mother, all right? Angelique and I were in the same group. Do you know what I'm talking about?'

She flashed a fierce look at Milt, who was still kneeling but starting to squirm. She remembered he had a bad knee.

On the other side of the door, she heard the slow slide of the security chain inside its housing and then the heavy *thunk* of the lock. The door opened slowly.

'Do you really know Mum? Is she all right?'

Wallace frowned and slowly shook her head. Jess's eyes filmed, and she looked down before nodding as if she'd expected the answer and opened the door fully, standing well back as Wallace motioned Milt to get up and move inside.

'The phone is over there.' Jess pointed to a mobile on the coffee table. 'I'll get it.' She rushed over.

'Jess.'

The girl halted midstride.

'Before you do, I want to check something.'

She turned slowly, her face white and pinched. 'What?' Her eyes flicked uncertainly to Milt and back again.

'Milt, hold your hands out behind you so we can see them. Jess, what can you see on the little finger of his left hand?'

Jess turned her head like a small, quizzical bird. 'He's wearing a ring. Mum had one just like it.'

Wallace focused her second sight, trying to make out something, anything on Milt's hand.

'It is the same ring. Jess, did you by any chance ever meet my grandmother, Aggie Wilmott?'

'Yes. A couple of times. I remember there was a big row, just after my twelfth birthday. Mum sent me outside but I heard some of it. Your grandmother is sort of in charge, isn't she?'

'She was.'

'She's dead too?' Jess asked, her voice quiet.

Wallace nodded. 'Do you know what the ring means? What it's for?'

Jess shook her head. 'All I know is Mum was always tugging at it, trying to take it off. Did he kill Mum for it?'

'No. At least I don't think so. That's why I need your help. Can you go over and try and take the ring off his finger? Don't worry, he can't hurt you. Milt, make a fist with your left hand but extend the little finger so Jess can get at the ring.'

'It's stuck fast, Wallace, I told you that.'

'Just do it. Jess. Go ahead.'

She reminded Wallace of a small animal, coiled and unpredictable, as she approached Milt's back. But there was something underlying that, a strength suggesting danger if cornered. Maybe that's how she'd escaped in Melbourne. Whoever had attacked her. She hoped it wasn't Milt, but everything pointed to it.

She glanced over at him. Through the tufts of his mussed his hair she could make out scar tissue above his ear, as if he'd been hit with something heavy.

'That's it, Jess, now try and slip it off.'

Keeping her distance from Milt, she reached out, and using only her index finger and thumb she gently glided something along Milt's finger.

'Got it. It came off easily.'

She scurried back to Wallace's side and held out her palm. In the middle of it was a chunky gold ring.

'Wow.' Wallace said. 'It really is there.'

'I told ya,' Milt said.

'You said the stone was gray. This is red, and look at those gold flashes. It's like it's lit up from the inside.'

'It never looked like that for me,' Milt said.

'Jess. This ring belongs to you. It's your birthright. You know that, don't you?'

She shrugged. 'I heard Mum talking about it sometimes when she was high. Mum liked to talk to herself then. I remember she said something like it would end with her. It was like she was frightened or something. Whenever I asked what she meant by it, she'd get mad. I learned not to say anything. You know how it is.'

'All I know is that ring is supposed to be very powerful, Jess. It has been passed from mother to daughter right down your female line, and now you're the only one who can tap into it. What I'm hoping is that you'll help us—me—use the ring to see what really happened that night back in Melbourne when you were attacked. It's important. Will you do that?'

Jess looked at Wallace, fear racing across her face as her blue-green eyes switched between Wallace and Milt and back again, images that Wallace could only guess at.

'Why?' she asked finally.

'Gran seems to think that Milt isn't the one who has been stalking you.'

'But I saw him.'

'I know.'

. . .

WALLACE HAD Jess sit at a small glass table, taking up a position on the other side so they faced each other.

'What about him?' Jess indicated Milt, who was perched uncomfortably on the edge of the two-seater.

'He's not going anywhere, are you, Milt?'

He grunted and tried to adjust his hands. 'Just hurry up, will ya? These things are pulling my arms out of their sockets.'

Wallace placed her hand palm up on the table. 'Put your hand on mine. No, palm up. That's it. Now, with your other hand, place the ring in the middle of your open hand and make a fist around it.'

'What are you going to do?' Jess asked, her voice small. Wallace could only imagine what sort of images the energy from the ring was triggering inside Jess's head.

'Probably nothing, but if I can remember how this is supposed to work, we might be able to get a projection of what happened that night using the ring to boost the signal. At worst, nothing will happen. Otherwise, it will be like watching a movie. Now, close your eyes and allow your mind to drift.'

Wallace led Jess through a muscle relaxation technique, trying to hose down the girl's anxiety. Magic, particularly visual magic, and stress negated each other. After a time, Jess's breathing slowed, and the muscles around her jaw and the corners of her eyes softened. Wallace spoke softly, using a hypnotic technique Gran had taught her where conflicting words and phrases that made no real sense confused the conscious mind, making it more susceptible to suggestion. From there she might be able to access Jess's subconscious, and if she was lucky tap into the ring's power to provide some perspective on what happened. She could feel Gran's presence; occasionally it poked at her, trying to get Wallace's attention. After a few moments, Wallace sighed and consciously reached for it and felt a quiver of response immediately. At least Gran would know what to do with this.

Wallace tested Jessica's other arm for trance response; it flopped heavily onto the table. Good.

'Now, Jess, I want to take you back to that night in Melbourne when you were attacked. You are perfectly safe, do you understand me?'

'Yes.'

'Tell me where you are. What can you see?'

'I'm in an alley. I took a short cut home from busking in a café. I'm scared.

I think someone's following me.' Fear tightened her voice.

'You're perfectly safe.' Wallace floundered, then felt something shift in her head. Gran. A rich flow of confidence melted through her.

'Jess, bring your awareness to the ring in your hand. Can you feel it? It's there to protect you. Draw in its light. Allow the colors to surround you in that alley. Imagine it forming an impenetrable barrier. Nothing can hurt you inside its protective glow. Do you feel it?'

Jessica smiled, nodding.

The space around the table darkened, as if a dimmer switch had been turned.

Yet at the table the colors intensified, the light from the ring pulsing through the gaps between Jess's fingers. Gradually, the colors radiating from her hand formed a 3D picture that hovered above the table.

'Think of this as like a movie. It's a replay of what happened that night drawn from your memory. It may seem very real. Just allow whatever happened to emerge, Jess,' Wallace muttered, intent on watching the images layer up. She could see Jess, running, guitar case bouncing against her leg. At the moment it was in slow motion. Someone appeared to be chasing her. She could see his outline, black and big, highlighted in red.

It was Milt.

He looked like a determined front rower in a rugby game about to make an unlikely tackle. Something was odd, though, because rather than focusing on catching her, he kept looking back over his shoulder.

Jess lost her footing in a puddle. Milt was gaining. He reached out, touched her, and she appeared to scream, then spun around, hitting him hard on the side of his head with the guitar case, following with a foot to his groin. *Ouch.* He doubled over. Even though he was in pain, he was still looking behind him.

'Freeze the motion there,' she snapped, leaning forward, staring into the picture above the table, past Milt, tracking the direction he was looking. To the left near the side of the alley there was something else, inside a deeper patch of black, deep in shadow. Normally it would have been invisible but as she strained to see, she thought she could detect a telltale faint ripple.

'Advance motion: frame by frame,' she called, taking a firmer grip of Jess's hand, feeling Gran's influence steadying her focus.

The image slowed, clicking forward frame by frame like still photographs. The ripple advanced marginally, with each frame changing ever so slightly.

She moved her index finger into one of the frames, pointing at the darker mass.

'Enhance and resolve here, dissolve any visual enchantment,' she said, not knowing whether it would work.

The view expanded, light pouring into the dark mass from her finger. The blackness sloughed away, and there it was. A face. Horribly scarred. She recognized some of the raised shapes on the bare skin of his skull as ancient sigils of protection and dark power. The man wore anger and dark-side energy like a cloak. In one hand he held a double-headed silver axe.

'Enhance threat intent to Jess with yellow, both subjects,' she said finally. In a flash, the scarred man was illuminated yellow, while Milt's curled, pained body on the ground maintained its dull red outline. There had been no threat toward Jess from Milt.

The man kicked Milt cruelly in the ribs and picked up the guitar case.

'Jess,' Wallace said quietly, still staring at the picture, 'I don't think Milt was there to hurt you. I think his job was to protect you. From that.'

She pointed at the scarred man's image. The final still had captured half of his face, caught in a random splash of ambient light. The one eye she could make out was completely black from iris to cornea.

EIGHT

The scarred man stepped over the weathered body and strode purposefully into the old man's bathroom, climbing onto the edge of the bath and then hoisting himself up through the open inspection cover in the ceiling.

Shea had been trained to wait.

Silent. Alert. Invisible. Deadly.

SAID.

His mantra for waiting.

When he was younger, he'd sprayed SAID onto disused walls, perversely pleased that only he knew what it meant. Once, he'd stolen several cans of metallic blue paint and sprayed the letters a meter high onto a cinder block wall that backed onto the train line. Then he'd caught the train just to watch the reaction of other passengers when they saw it. Most didn't even look up from their morning papers, but for those who did, a confused expression would drift across their faces, creating a tiny wrinkle of unpredictability in the washed-out fabric of their day.

He rubbed at his face, feeling the curlicue of scars beneath his fingertips. His face and head were well practiced at making them.

Some peoples' attention flowed over and past him, as it did with cripples or unwashed idiots who shouted at nothing in the middle of the street, while to others he stood out as someone to be avoided.

There wasn't much room in the crawlspace, but his height belied an agility that flowed out and into whatever space he happened to be in. The jungle had taught him how to do that. The jungle had taught him many things.

Shea located the hole he'd previously made in the fire wall that separated the two apartments. Easing away the covering, he slipped through. He was in her space now. He lay across the rafters and closed his eyes, melding with the darkness. This was the most dangerous time. It was imperative to remain motionless until the tiny ripples of energy dissipated and settled. Dragos had warned him that the girl was extremely sensitive. Most people didn't appreciate how much the small things mattered. How little things compounded. How patience really worked. What it was like to become the tree that you were hiding in until the insects and snakes that crawled and slithered across your grease-painted body did not differentiate one surface from the other.

After a while, he eased himself onto all fours and crawled along the rafters, squeezing past dusty pipes and clusters of loosely bound, brittle wires. The building was old, its innards in need of attention, but like most of the bodies that inhabited it, maintenance was limited only to the parts that could be seen.

He located her apartment's inspection cover and cracked the opening to peer through the narrow slit into the bathroom below. In the army, they'd tested his night vision and found it to be almost perfect. Eyes like a cat, they'd said. Except now he found it hard to go out during the day without the darkest shades. He'd spent too much time in the night; his pupils found it hard to shrink back.

The bathroom below was empty. He removed the cover and eased into the hole, holding himself suspended until his feet touched the vanity. He balanced, then kicked away and dropped lightly to the floor.

The apartment layout mirrored that of the one he'd come from next door. The furnishings were cheap, barely functional. His mouth turned down with disgust as his plastic-gloved fingers trailed over a louvered cupboard door, its melamine sides bulging with absorbed moisture.

Easing open the bathroom door, he peered through the crack into the lounge room. The big man from the alley was sprawled across a two-seater. He wouldn't wake. None of them would. Not if he was careful. The sleeping enchantment Dragos had provided him with was powerful.

According to Dragos, recovering the ring was more important than continuing with the deaths. The scarred man had been momentarily disappointed at that. He'd enjoyed the tracking, stalking, and ultimate rush of power as each of the women had died. But there would be more later. Dragos had promised. Besides, there was still tonight—maybe he would wake them up.

The bedroom door was shut. He gripped the doorknob. It turned easily. Noiselessly.

In the bed were the two women. Dragos had warned him about the big one. She was the more dangerous. He would dispatch her first. He drew out the long silver axe strapped in the holster at his side. The moonlight streaming through the window caught the honed edge, reflecting onto the ceiling. The scars across the top of his scalp pulsed, blood coursing through his system, charging it. This was the time he felt the most powerful.

He approached the bed, moving with the curious feline flow he'd learned in Cambodia, part martial art, part dance. The younger one was asleep, curled into a soft pose, one hand tucked beneath her right cheek. Her breathing was irregular, eyelids aquiver with darting dreams as if something behind them was trying to get out. He stood watching her for some time, enjoying the dualistic tug of lust and discipline. He could take her while she slept, rape her with the blood still spurting from her slashed throat, use its juice like scarlet paint to celebrate—the SAID sprawled in running letters on the wall behind the bed. He felt the warning buzz in his head. If he ignored it, Dragos would cause him pain. He used to call Dragos the Voice at first. He'd been given knowledge, advice, money and ultimately power. After that, Dragos had declared himself and the spirit bonding was made.

He froze. The unmistakable jiggle had started inside his head. Dragos was nudging him to remain focused.

He took another step, keeping to the edges of his hardened feet, perfectly balanced and noiseless.

The girl stirred and said something in her sleep, lips moving in response, then her breathing settled once more. Stepping around a pile of discarded clothing on the floor, his nostrils twitched at the stench of perspiration absorbed within the fabric. All his senses were heightened. Standing beside the big woman, he raised the axe, feeling his muscles flex and stretch as it glided up, then down, using both gravity and strength to guide the head of the axe down into the delicious gap between her chin and collarbone.

The axe thunked deeply into the pillow and the mattress below, the blade burying itself in a mass of springs.

The bed was empty save a scattering of erratic energy spirals from a broken illusion spell.

NINE

Milt yawned and stretched, the hammock groaning beneath his weight. He looked at his watch—almost three. He could get used to this. It beat the heck out of the splice green outdoor setting back at his apartment in Melbourne.

Wallace would be back soon; clothes shopping had never been Wallace's thing. They'd left Jess's tiny flat last night in a mad rush, and there'd been no time to pack. God only knew why; more messages from beyond, no doubt. He was just pleased it was over and Jess—whoever's daughter she was—was safe.

He yawned again.

Levering himself up and onto the edge of the hammock, he sat there swinging, looking out at the huge backyard. It was mostly veggies and herbs set out in concentric circles around the gnarly trunks of huge trees. The whole effect was peaceful. He'd always imagined himself to be a city boy but sitting out here, it felt like he was at home in the country, or maybe how the country used to be. Maybe there were parts to Wallace, like this garden, that he'd never bothered exploring. It was too late now. Way too late for anything like that, especially now that she'd gone weird officially. *What the hell had the last few days been about?*

Even leaving Jessica's flat had been a drama, something about "them" being able to trace the energy from the ring so Wallace had to spin some sort of illusion so it would look like the three of them were sleeping there. He hadn't really believed it until he'd turned around as they were about to leave and seen an image of himself sprawled like an oversized dog across the plaid two-seater in the lounge room. More weird shit. He had no idea how any of it worked, but then he also couldn't figure out how Jess had managed to just slip the ring off his finger so easily after everything he'd tried had failed. Then there was that business at the table in her flat. It had been too dark to see much of what happened, but it must have been significant, because afterwards Wallace had just taken off the cuffs and said it was over.

Over.

Just like their relationship. Back when he'd done everything he could to get rid of her while still knowing that she was the only real person in his life.

He remembered the exact moment it'd ended. She'd come up to his apartment; he may even have invited her. It was all pretty hazy. The one thing he could remember for sure was the look on her face as she came through the door, seeing her tenuous smile droop, then fall away utterly as she realized what was happening. He'd been standing in the middle of the floor, pants pooled around his ankles while a skinny Valley girl in a blonde wig blew him, her cheeks moving in and out, back and forth, like a pump working a dry well.

Wallace had simply backed out the door and closed it quietly behind her.

Why had he even done that? He couldn't remember even meeting the blonde woman. She had just been there.

Christ, what am I doing in her house now?

Too much had happened, yet nothing had actually changed.

He should leave. There was no real reason to stay. Not now. They'd found the girl. She had the damned ring, so he'd lived up to his part of the bargain. He should now just back off and disappear. As for the prospect of having a fully hatched daughter, well, let them believe what they wanted. Wallace had told him she would get the incriminating axe back from Aggie, and he believed her.

The killings might stop now that Wallace had a mug shot to work with. Ugly bugger. He wouldn't be hard to track down with features like that; guaranteed he'd have a sheet. All that rubbish about demons. Perps were perps.

Once they snagged him, Wallace could wheel Jess out and she could make a positive ID. Bye bye, Scarface.

Wallace had said that his blackouts should ease off now that Aggie had what she wanted. Bloody Aggie. He'd forgotten what life the other side of normal felt like.

Right now, he'd settle for not having to dig up any more dead bodies.

Jesus. I can still smell that stench.

His skin crawled with the thought of it, and he considered taking a bath.

In Wallace's house? Inside her most private space? No way.

I should leave. Now, before they get back. Get a hotel or, better still, cab it to the airport and just fly home.

Eating, talking dead grandmothers, a surprise live daughter, and an ex-lover were all a bit too much in one week. It was all nuts. He was nuts—that's what really scared him.

He slipped on his shoes. He'd only arrived with hand luggage: a change of clothes and toiletries. Maybe he should leave a note? He couldn't just waltz into Wallace's life after all this time and then just disappear.

Couldn't I?

Why the hell not?

It'll just get awkward otherwise.

He entered the house, pausing in the vestibule at the front door, his hand tight around the handle of his leather overnighter. Every instinct was telling him to leave, get out—right now. Even his feet felt hot and itchy. So why couldn't he make himself move? It was like his shoes were glued to the hallway floor. He considered just stepping out of them, leaving them stuck there forever to the polished wood like one of those always-been-there's in old houses. He hoped the girls were all right. Maybe he should have gone with them....

Outside he heard the rolling crunch of gravel on the drive. He still couldn't move his feet.

Car doors slammed. Quiet but urgent conversation filtered in, the words as yet indistinct. Footsteps, clunky, their sound hollow against the four broad wooden steps leading up to the front verandah. He could see the outline of Wallace and Jess through the stained glass panels on either side of the front door and almost felt the key sliding comfortably into the front door lock.

When Wallace came through the door, she said, 'Oh, there you are.' Looking down at the bag in his hand, 'Leaving? Again?'

'I was thinking about it. Something stopped me. I can't explain what.'

Wallace seemed amused by that and tried to suppress a smile. 'I thought you might be tempted.' The two women exchanged a grin. Jess set down a large suitcase beside the door. It was faded and old, made from fabric with cardboard reinforcing that bulged behind the handle when picked up. It was a bag made for bursting, ready to spew and strew dirty underwear across the nearest airport baggage carousel.

'What's that piece of junk? I thought you went out to get some new clothes for her?' he said.

Wallace set down her keys on a small table near the stairs. 'We did. At the op shop. Pre-loved clothes have a blurring effect on vibrational energy. It makes it harder for bad guys to get a trace on, get it? They even threw in the suitcase for free.'

'Yeah, right,' he murmured, 'of course. Any sign of... trouble?'

'Not a flicker,' Wallace said, 'though Jess has some news to share.'

'Oh really?' Tentatively he tried moving his feet. His shoes were no longer stuck.

Craaaazy.

Cautious, he ambled over and shut the door, turning the deadlock.

'Yes.' Jess picked up the conversational thread. 'Milt. I want to apologize.' She smiled up at him, touching him lightly on the forearm. 'And to say thanks, you know, for everything. Wallace told me that you'd been trying to protect me and that you and Mum....'

He felt his face flush. 'Yeah, well, I feel kinda bad, you know, I really didn't know....' The words stopped coming, and his voice trailed off. Light spilled through the leadlight panels, highlighting her profile. Her nose was a little like his, smaller maybe, but the same sort of shape—before his had been broken. Maybe.

'So what happened, with the ring?' he asked, switching subjects.

'I'm wearing it,' she said, flashing a smile and holding up her hand as if she'd recently become engaged. He could no longer see the ring.

'I'll have to take your word for it. So you're buying into this whole story then? Time travel, save the world, etcetera. Wallace told you about all that?'

Jess shrugged and looked away. 'Wallace said getting this Book of Names...?' She crinkled her nose enquiringly at Wallace, who nodded. '—is the only way this creep would ever stop stalking me. As for how that happens,' she shrugged, 'that all sounds pretty weird and far-fetched.'

'You can say that twice,' he muttered.

'But that's just the thing. Weird has been my life to date, so I've learned not to write anything off. The other thing is... I kind of feel like this is where I'm supposed to be right now. I haven't had that feeling for quite a while. Maybe never.'

'So how do we make this happen, Wallace?' Milt asked.

'I'm hoping Gran will pop by and tell us all.'

'That would be Gran the *dead* grandmother,' he said pointedly to Jess.

'I'll make us some tea, and maybe we'll find out. Why don't you give Jess a hand with her bag so she can get unpacked? Milt, the room at the end of the hall upstairs is made up too, if you want to stay tonight.' Wallace patted Jessica's hand as she passed. 'I'll meet you both out the back in ten minutes with the tea.'

Jess started to climb the stairs. Milt paused, considering whether he should still leave. Somehow it didn't seem quite so important now. He followed Jess up the stairs, automatically noting the creak on the tired timber of the third riser.

'Do you remember my mother?' Jess asked over her shoulder.

'I don't know.' He silently kicked himself, remembering the strangely preserved features of the woman in the stone casket. 'Sorry, I didn't mean it like that.'

'No, it's all right. I understand. Mum was always a bit of a free spirit. Our name back then was Watkins.' Jess watched his face and then continued. 'Mum had this long blonde hair. I remember it was full of curls in the pictures I saw and just went everywhere, with greener eyes than mine and pretty pink lips. She used to wear these free-flowing pretty dresses.'

Milt trawled his memory and failed. Then he flicked back through the mental files—the cases. He tended to remember people that way. Ones he wasn't close to at any rate, which, when he thought about it, was most. An image of a hippy chick with a smart mouth appeared, blown out on too much weed, waving her hands in the air like some witch doctor. She'd been up from Nimbin or some other hippy joint. He'd been in uniform at the time and remembered letting her off a vagrancy and mild possession charge. In the end he'd felt sorry for her and put her up for a couple of nights in his small flat. A half a bottle of tequila later, they'd ended up in bed together. Things had become complicated after that, he recalled. One day she just packed up and left, leaving a note on the table and a promise to pay him back the fifty bucks she'd filched from his wallet. He remembered the only thing he'd felt at the time was a vague sort of relief.

'Yeah. I do remember her. She was beautiful. We could know for sure, you know, if we got a test done.'

Jess's smile faded.

Another clanger. Good one, Milt. I should have left when I had the chance.

'This must be my room,' she said, stopping in front of one of the paneled doors in the hallway. Milt set the suitcase down beside her. He felt her looking at him.

'I don't know what I should call you... I mean....'

He felt a lump rising at the back of his throat, coughed to clear it. 'Milt works for me,' he managed and continued on down the hall.

DOWNSTAIRS, Wallace boiled the kettle and took several jars off the top shelf, adding a pinch of the dried herbs to an aromatic tea brewing in a large ceramic pot. Gran had always used this one when "company" came.

She carried the tray onto the veranda and down into the garden, setting it on a round wooden table. The tabletop was two meters across and had been cut from the base of a Ceremony Tree in Tasmania that had fallen in a massive storm. Their Wiccan tradition was drawn from a nature-based heritage. Trees were considered storehouses of wisdom. This one was imbued with years of sacred ritual and energy. Gran had shipped the slab to Brisbane. She'd then sanded it back herself before spending several days carving an extensive pattern of symbols around its perimeter to stop the captured flow from leaching away. After that, she'd branded sacred runes near the center to keep the energies from stagnating. Once they were established and the wood was ready, she'd applied many coats of lacquer to the surface until it shone.

Wallace sipped the summoning tea, allowing herself to sink into the ritual. Calling Gran over to this side of the divide would be a lot easier now she'd established the link by crossing over herself, not to mention having to drag Milt with her—a sea anchor if ever there was one. She closed her eyes and commenced the chant, mouthing it silently.

The energy around her shivered as the summoning transmitted. Now all she had to do was wait and see if Gran was in range.

'Some table,' Milt said from the steps.

Wallace started.

'Sorry, did I disturb you?'

He knows he did. This table has more sensitivity than he's ever shown.

Wallace pulled herself up and smiled resignedly at her own resentment. 'It's all right. I was just relaxing. It's been a long day.'

He sat down opposite.

He'd changed into jeans and a faded long-sleeved shirt. Wallace noticed there was a dullness to his aura. He wasn't looking after himself.

'I wanted to have a quiet chat. I thought it best to do it before Jess came down.' He rubbed his unshaven chin.

'What about, exactly?' she said, irritated.

He shrugged and looked down at his hands, picking at a nail. 'I was remembering earlier how we, you know ended. It was just before then that I started having these blackouts—'

'Too much alcohol does that, I hear,' Wallace snapped.

He grimaced and snorted. 'Yeah, well, there was a fair share of that back then. Not now though,' he added belatedly, as if this might somehow make a difference. She said nothing, so he plowed on.

'I mean, it all just seems a bit coincidental that back then every-thing tumbled out the way it did. It's pretty obvious from where I sit that your granny was pulling everyone's strings.'

'So you're saying it's really Gran's fault that you had no pants on when I came up to your flat that night? Gran, the she-devil, made you do it, is that it?' Heat pulsed through her. She wasn't sure whether she was more angry at him, Gran, or the plain unfairness of everything.

'No, well, not exactly, though that part is a bit blurry too....' He let the words trail off, then cleared his throat. 'I guess it's all water under the bridge now. Any luck with the happy snap of the perp?' he asked, trying a different subject.

Wallace shrugged, happy to go there. 'I couldn't lift it from the imaging in Jess's flat. I don't know why. Sometimes the two technologies don't mix; they can be like oil and water.'

'I was afraid of that.'

She shrugged. 'I was thinking of trying an identikit but couldn't figure out how I could say I'd seen him.'

'Here, maybe you can use this. I did it from memory. It's not as good as a photo, but I think it's a better likeness than you'd get from an identikit.'

Milt took a sheet of paper from the top pocket of his shirt and handed it to her. When she unfolded it, her eyes widened; the pencil sketch was so clear, the menace radiated from the inked tattoos and malevolent eyes.

'Milt, this is... this is him.' She glanced up. 'Did you draw it? Where did you learn to do this?'

'Art classes.' He glanced down at his feet, something he always used to do when he had to reveal something of himself. 'I had a full breakdown after Carlie and Janis's funeral. Art Therapy seemed to be the only thing that would cut through.'

'Carlie and Janis are dead? Oh, no. Milt, I didn't know, what happened?'

'Car accident. For some reason, neither of them was wearing a belt. Head-on. Anyway, I took it—bad.' He grimaced, his gaze moving down again, distant. 'Real bad.' He looked up, squaring his shoulders, and exhaled. 'Anyway, one day I woke up and found myself in rehab, white coats, the lot. I was lucky; it could have been a lot worse. There's not much memory around any of that either. They tried the usual: CBT and medication, lots of it. Art therapy was a last resort. Somehow that seemed to take me someplace, like stepping into a different space. Somewhere clean, clear; it's hard to describe. In the end, it even helped lower some of those barriers you were always complaining about, let some pretty ugly stuff out. Anyway, when they discharged me, I continued on with it, took a few lessons. The teacher said I had a natural talent, how about that?' He chuckled, face brightening. 'I've even sold a few, watercolors mainly. A mate of mine with a gallery down the Great Ocean Road is even talking about a showing.'

'Milt, that's wonderful. I had no idea,' Wallace said, then tapped the page. 'This will be so helpful. I'll go and email it off now, then send it to— Aargh!'

Wallace dropped the paper and sucked at her scorched fingers, the cruel face crinkling with the heat. It seemed to be mocking her through the flames as it drifted to the ground. Milt hurried over and stamped out the remains of the fire.

'What did you do that for?' he asked, squatting down and sifting through the blackened ash with a stubby index finger.

'I didn't. But someone did.' Wallace's eyes narrowed as she drew on her inner sense and scanned the garden. Spontaneous combustion meant two things: the perp knew where they were, and he was close. Very close. That particular spell only worked within line of sight.

'He's already here. I thought we'd be safe here for a while, but Gran might have been right all along. Can you go inside and check on Jess? Hurry.'

Milt hesitated for a moment, looking from the burned paper to Wallace, then sprinted back to the house, calling out for Jess. Wallace turned away, registering Milt's heavy clumps up the broad steps to the verandah followed by the slam of the back door.

Wallace closed her eyes, trying to center, hoping the summoning tea had had time to work. It was hard to focus knowing the Hacker was out there, perhaps watching her, but the summoning had to be done out here as it required some privacy. Wallace touched her fingertips to the polished surface of the table, drawing on the stored energy of the Sisterhood. She repeated the chant mentally, then mouthed it quietly before singing it in her normal voice.

Gradually, she felt a tugging at her abdomen. She made the connection and countered the draw down of her energy as Gran plugged in. Wallace broadened her stance, laying the palms of both hands on the table. Her skin tingled where it touched.

Wallace felt her heart rate elevate. She drew in several deep breaths and leaned heavily against the table, arms vibrating. *I'm definitely out of condition.*

The feeling passed. When she opened her eyes, Gran was sitting in the chair opposite, her form shimmery and opaque. She felt another enquiring tug at her solar plexus, and Gran raised her eyebrow from across the table. She needed more energy to manifest fully. Wallace nodded, preparing herself as more of her energy leaked away. 'He's here,' she grunted, her voice roughened with the effort.

'It was inevitable,' Aggie said, eyes narrowing as they skirted the perimeter. 'I get a feeling he's high up. I'm sure pretty sure he can see us.' Gran's voice trailed off as her eyes tracked the vantage points that could look down on the house and yard. Finally, she pointed. 'There. Can you see? Near the top of that old ghost gum in the Atkinses' yard? I told them to lop that monster down years ago. It's dangerous. Now especially,' she added dryly.

Wallace could see nothing. The tree Gran was pointing at was at least two hundred meters away. The Atkinses had sold up last month, and the new owners hadn't moved in yet, so the house was empty. Made sense.

'We better get inside. Gran, can you throttle back on the suction? I'm feeling a little weak.'

'Sorry, love.'

Immediately Wallace felt the drain on her lessen. She straightened and looked back toward the ghost gum.

'How long do we have before the perimeter is breached?' she asked.

'I'm not sure. The wards around the house have decayed since you've been here. They need strengthening.'

Wallace's face flushed hot as she recalled her earlier blasé disregard in maintaining the house's protective wards.

'Don't go and start beating yourself up now. I don't have the time, and you don't have the energy. Come on, we can sort something out from inside, but we need to hurry. Tell me as we move, where's Jess up to? Have you told her about going back to get the Book of Names?'

Wallace bustled after her. 'Yes. She thought it sounded exciting, though I'm not sure she actually believed me.'

Gran grunted. 'And what about becoming the Messenger for the Elemental Scrolls?'

'I told her as much as I knew,' Wallace said diplomatically. 'I'm not sure what she made of it all. Quite frankly, I'm not sure I do either.'

'But there's no one else who can do it. You told her that, didn't you? Made plain what's at stake?'

'You can't force her into it, Gran. If there was to have been a Messenger, surely it should have been Angelique, not Jess. It's not fair to expect her to be your damned Messenger just because her mother refused.'

'Don't speak to me about Angelique. She was *weak* and undeserving of her destiny. I should have taken Jess when she reached her bleeding—by force, if necessary—and had her initiated. She's strong underneath. I can sense it. With the right training... well, that's no never mind now. Even if she does agree, she may not be sufficiently prepared.'

'Prepared for what?' Wallace said, trying to keep up. Gran had dropped all pretense of walking and was now floating freely across the lawn.

'The Scrolls are protected,' Aggie called back over her shoulder. 'The Messenger's destiny is to become the next Leader of the Sisters. That requires a natural level of talent plus the discipline gained through training to use it. Otherwise it could be extremely dangerous. Now, with Dragos as the other contender, it will almost certainly be deadly.'

'I don't see how Jess could pass up on that opportunity then,' Wallace mumbled, thumping up the back steps behind Gran and into the kitchen. Flinging the door shut, she fumbled with the lock.

'Turn the deadlock twice, all the way to the left, then once to the right,' Gran said from behind her. 'That'll activate a supplementary ward I laid in for a rainy-day emergency. I guess this would be it. They're looped to self-refresh, so the wards should still be fully charged. It'll buy us some time anyway.'

Wallace did as she was told, feeling the deadlock clunk home solidly. Soon after there was a loud secondary click, followed by a low-pitched thrum that vibrated and spread throughout the bones of the house. Wallace could feel it humming through the floorboards beneath her feet.

When she turned around, Milt was standing in the archway leading from the lounge room, mouth open, staring at Gran. Jess looked small beside him, as if she might tuck herself safely beneath his armpit.

'You again,' he said. 'Are you bloody well haunting me?'

'Psshat, Milt,' Aggie said, her gaze swiveling automatically to Jessica, 'if I wanted to haunt you, believe me, you'd know about it.'

Opening her arms wide, she strode over and placed her hands on the young woman's shoulders. 'And you must be little Jess; not so little now, of course. You've grown into a lovely young woman. Do you remember me? Aggie? You must have only been about eleven or twelve the last time we met.'

'Yes, I think so. You also visited Mum a few times before that.'

'That's right.' She gathered Jess in a massive hug. Wallace recognized it as the "mother hug," designed to drain away any stranger suspicion. When she was released, Jess would feel as if she'd known Gran forever.

Outside, something bumped against the side of the house.

'What was that?' Jess cried.

Milt moved to the window and peered out through the café curtains.

Aggie raised her nose and sniffed the air, the tip of her tongue poking out, pink and brief.

'He's here. Testing the strength of the wards, I wager. Dragos will need to channel a lot of juice to break through those. He's probably not that happy either that I've managed to stick around.'

'Do you think he knows Jess has the ring?' Wallace asked.

'Of course. Dragos does, at any rate.'

'I don't really get why Dragos is interested in who gets to activate the Scrolls. What's it to him whether the climate is balanced or not?'

'He's not but there's a fifth Elemental Scroll: the Akashic. It controls the doorway between his world and ours. He needs the ring and a Cipher to access it. Once he has those, it will open the portal between the two worlds.'

'And for those who don't know what the hell you're talking about...,' Milt said.

Aggie turned to face him, one majestic eyebrow arched in challenge. 'Demonic invasion. When that portal between worlds—dimensions, really—is opened, susceptible humans will be subjugated by their own greed. They'll become puppets to the demons' superior will. They won't even know it's happening until it's too late and the climate becomes extreme. Things will quickly go from bad to terrible, so we're playing for massive stakes here. You may as well know that up front, Milt. This is not just about you and an axe with your fingerprints all over it. The fate of millions will be decided on the decisions we make from here on. I know this is hard for you but what can I say, it's true.'

Milt stared at her for a moment, then took another look through the gap in the kitchen curtains. He let the curtain drop back and turned to face them. 'I'm not sure if I just don't want to know about any of that stuff, or I simply don't believe you. All I know for certain is that there's a bad guy outside who wants us all dead. In the face of that, the "why" doesn't really matter all that much to me right now.' He shot a look at Wallace. 'We should probably have called this in by now, Lacey. We need some backup here, pronto.'

She shook her head. 'I tried. The landline is out; my mobile too.

Have you got a signal?'

Milt tugged a phone from his trouser pocket. The screen was blank. 'No, it looks like the battery has been sucked dry. Funny, 'cause I just charged it.'

'Mine's dead too,' Jess said.

'Dragos,' Aggie said, as if this explained everything.

Another scraping noise; this time from the front of the house. The low thrum through the floor and walls increased in response.

'The wards are holding. Come through to the lounge,' Aggie said, bustling them into the adjoining room. She paused, hovering beside a low coffee table in the center of the room. 'Milt, I don't have enough strength in this form, can you drag this table out of the way? That's it, now everyone help to get this mat rolled up. There's a witch hole beneath it. Hurry.'

Milt knelt down between Jess and Wallace and began rolling the edges of the large mat. 'What sort of hole did she say?' Milt muttered to Wallace.

'Witch. It's like a bolt-hole, or a modern-day safe room,' Wallace said. 'Remember witches were persecuted in the past—they needed somewhere to hide if the guys in the black hats and flaming torches turned up unexpectedly in the middle of the night.'

'The trapdoor is on a pressure release,' Aggie continued. 'Jess, love, get up and put your feet in this spot.' Aggie pointed at two of the polished floorboards. 'Now swivel inwards on the balls of your feet— as if you're pigeon toed. That's it.'

Something clicked beneath the floor, and a section about a meter square popped up just above the surface of the rest of the floor.

'Now slide the top aside—'

Aggie was interrupted by another screech from above, much louder than the others. They all looked up at the ceiling, waiting for the thrumming to kick in again. It did so but sluggishly, like an old car starting up on a cold morning.

'Hurry, the wards are weakening.'

Wallace used her foot to push the trapdoor aside, revealing a short flight of steps leading down into a black space below. The sudden movement brought back the light- headed feeling, and she staggered. Aggie caught her elbow, steadying her.

'Are you all right, Wallace?'

'I feel like I've been sucked dry of everything but the husk I came in,' she whispered.

'Here, let me pull back a little more. I'm still draining you too much.'

Wallace felt the link at her abdomen release and drop away. Immediately energy and renewed strength flowed through her.

'Thanks,' Wallace said, watching as Gran's shape gradually became less defined and more translucent.

'Come on,' Aggie said, her indistinct form floating down the steps. Wallace bundled Jess, then Milt before her. A light sconce set into the wall beside the steps flickered on, illuminating an area below, about four meters square. The others were clustered together at the bottom of the stairs, looking up as another screech slammed against the house. The strained thrumming stopped abruptly.

'He's broken the wards,' Aggie said quietly.

In the deep silence that followed, a sound like a window sliding open was just discernible.

'And is now inside,' Wallace added.

'Quick, Wallace Pull the trapdoor shut.' Aggie shouted. 'There are fresh wards embedded in the trapdoor that will activate once it's locked down. That should give us enough time.'

Wallace reached across and gripped the trapdoor. She heard a familiar creak from the direction of the main stairs. Third riser. He was coming down, being cautious.

She pulled the trapdoor shut and raced down the steps, slamming into Milt, who held on to her.

'There's not a lot of space down here,' he mumbled, releasing her.

'If everything goes well, we won't be here that long. Now, everyone form a circle and join hands,' Aggie said. 'Lacey love, I'll need your help again.'

Wallace felt the inquisitive tug at her navel once more and nodded her assent as Gran plugged in. It was almost worth the energy drain to feel her hand, warm and dry, against hers once more. For all the angst that had been flowing between them, Gran was still Gran.

With the circle complete, energy began to flow around it, traveling from one to the next, faster and faster, the pressure building, a vortex forming in the middle, pulling them inwards.

'Stand firm. Lean back,' Aggie said. 'Keep the space in the middle clear. I'm tapping into the ceremony tree's energy; it will connect us to the Sisters.'

Wallace found the pull of the vortex hard to resist, and she tightened her grip on Aggie's hand. The air in the center was thickening; wispy strands of mist settled around them as the warmer air cooled and its energy was drawn into the middle.

Overhead, they heard a light padding against the floorboards, like an eager toddler stumbling into a room.

'Footsteps,' Jess whispered, eyes wide, looking up.

'Barefoot, from the sound of it,' Aggie added.

They jumped when something heavy slammed into the floor above.

'Ignore it. The new wards will hold,' Aggie said.

Wallace drew in a deep breath, wanting to believe, remembering how quickly the others had buckled. Opposite, Jessica seemed unaware of what was happening. She stared straight ahead, as if she couldn't absorb enough of whatever she was seeing. She appeared to be mesmerized.

Gran's voice popped into Wallace's head. *I'm fast cooking her with what she needs to know about the Scrolls and her role. You'll be pleased to know I'm not going to force her into it but by the end she'll know everything, including what's at stake for her personally. It's risky, but we don't have time for anything fancier.'*

Wallace nodded. Gran resumed speaking out loud.

'I'll need your help, Lacey, but you're too tense. Your resistance is dragging on me. Try and let go of it.'

Another booming crash filled the small room, and she jumped.

'Trust the wards. Trust they'll hold. I told you, I need you relaxed. I can't do this on my own.'

Wallace breathed deeper, letting the tension gradually bleed off. Immediately she was overwhelmed by colors and sounds pulsing from Jess's ring, traveling around the circle before spiraling up into the center and pouring back over them.

The light from it was palpable, flowing like multicolored ink. Wallace could feel it trickling down her face like warm syrup, almost taste its layers as it ran past her mouth and in through her skin, seeming to indelibly stain it with brilliant color. Yet when she glimpsed Jess or Gran through the brilliance, the colors simply ran off them, pooling in psychedelic puddles. They were adrift amidst a storm of light. Milt looked to be in some kind of shock.

Gradually it abated. Aggie muttered a series of incantations, then released her hands from the circle and made a parting motion.

Jess blinked, eyes returning to normal, and she shook herself like a small dog after a nap.

'What the heck was that?' Milt asked.

'The floor show, and the good news is there's no cover charge,' Aggie said, her voice flat but brightening as she turned to face Jess. 'How are you, sweetie?'

'Fine. I think. My head feels a little funny, as if it's eaten too much. That sounds strange, doesn't it?'

Aggie winked at Wallace as she patted the young girl's shoulder. 'I get it. Don't worry. It will pass.'

The crashing from above increased, becoming incessant. Something floated down and landed lightly on Wallace's head. She reached up and picked it off. It was a tiny splinter of wood. She glanced up, and from the light near the stairs could just make out a glinting arc of sharp steel poking through the underfloor above. With a shriek of protesting timber, it was wrenched free and moments later reappeared in almost the same place. Another small sliver of wood fell.

'He has the axe. The Hacker's axe,' she shouted, recognizing the shape of the distinctive curved blade as it bit into and through the wood.

'The two axes have their own power,' Aggie called back. 'An ordinary axe blade would shatter before it cut through those wards.' Gran turned to the other two. 'Milt, Jess. See what I'm doing with my hands? You do the same. We're using the energy we've just channeled in from the Sisters to build the portal. Imagine parting very fine curtains. Keep it up, repeat that action. Wallace, don't worry about that man or his axe. Keep your focus here. I need you to balance out our energies as we do this.'

Wallace refocused, and as she watched, something started forming from the pool of energy in the middle of the circle, building itself up from the floor, layer by layer. Every parting movement of their hands adding another.

Wallace felt as if she were being pulled in three directions at once. It was difficult to stay upright as the energy of the others tugged at her.

'Almost there. Steady, Wallace, steady.' Aggie's voice was loud in the confined space. 'And stop.'

Wallace staggered with the release, almost falling into what had formed. It appeared to be stripes of shimmering vertical light of all colors, secured at the top by a wooden beam

'Milt, take hold of Wallace,' Aggie snapped. 'If she slips into that, there's no telling where she'll end up.'

Wallace felt Milt's arm snake around her waist, pulling her tight beside him. It felt good—familiar and safe. Simultaneously, she felt Gran dissolve some of the link at her navel, and once again strength flooded back through her.

'Everyone take a step back,' Aggie said, her voice sounding hoarse. 'This is the portal of Yesterday, Today, and Tomorrow.'

'It's beautiful,' Jess said. 'Will it work?'

Aggie's shape floated around the panel, her strangely luminous translucence reflecting the light from the stripes.

Above, the crashing notched up a pace, as if the monster could sense what was happening.

Aggie had to shout to be heard. 'We need to set the date, but first … ah, there it is. Jess, can you fit the stone of your ring into that little notch right at the top? That's it. The ring is the key to this portal. That means when you go through, you'll need to be last, Jess. The portal will close once it senses the ring has passed through.'

Jess reached up, fitting the ring into where Aggie was pointing. It clicked in, releasing a square panel from the wooden beam under which was a row of small levers.

'All right, now carefully remove your hand and flick all those down, Jess.'

Another crash. Milt shouldered away a section of planking that had fallen from above. Light from the living room stabbed into the dim space through the irregular gashes in the floor. Through one larger hole, Wallace could make out what looked like a bare ankle and a section of muscular, tattooed leg.

'Ignore him,' Aggie shouted above the now incessant smash of the axe.

'How could anyone swing an axe so fast?' Wallace said, still looking up.

'No one normal, that's for sure,' Milt mumbled.

After Jess had flipped all the switches down, an image of a giant hourglass appeared in the air beside them. It too seemed to be made from light, the sides covered with strange numerals.

'The numbers are in three sections, representing the day, month, and year. Jess, what can you see on your side?'

'Days. Pretty sure they must be days. Two columns, one 0-3, the other 0-10.'

'What have you got, Milt?'

Milt peered closely at the illuminated image. 'Years, I think. It's written in some old-fashioned script that makes it hard to—'

'Good, that means Wallace has the months on her side. Now listen up, to set the date, simply lightly touch whatever section you have in front of you. Now this is important. Keep your fingers on the hourglass until all three sides have been activated. This has to be exact.'

A final massive crash, louder than the rest, slammed against the floor above. They all looked up, Wallace holding her breath, praying the subfloor would hold. It creaked, appeared to stabilize, then with a sickening crack it slowly collapsed, raining chunks of splintered wood down over them. Milt shouldered Wallace out of the way as the Hacker, with a maniacal scream, leaped into the small space.

Picking up one of the broken planks, Milt swung it against the Hacker's head. It splintered, and he laughed, revealing his sharpened canines. His entire head was covered in tattoos and raised scars.

Bunching his fists, Milt managed two solid hits to the man's head. Wallace heard bone crack but couldn't tell whose it was. The Hacker swayed, shaking his head, using the shaft of the axe like a staff to parry another flurry of punches from Milt, finally recovering enough to spear the butt end of the handle deep into Milt's unprotected midriff. Air spilled from him like a punctured balloon, and Milt sank to his knees, head down as if he were praying. Wallace could tell the Hacker's next blow would be across the back of Milt's unprotected neck. She rushed in.

Attacking from the Hacker's blind side, she kicked just as he was swinging the shaft, his dead, black eyes fixed on the back of Milt's head. Her foot connected with the Hacker's unprotected outer knee. He screamed with outrage, sending his swing wild as he struggled to maintain his balance. Wallace heard tendons snap as he toppled sideways. She hurried over to help Milt.

Aggie was shouting. 'Set the date: March fourteenth. Wallace! Jess! Set the date. I can't do it for you. I have no substance in my fingers.'

Jess carefully positioned her fingers over the illuminated day section and then stretched her other arm around the hourglass to reach the months. She found the notation representing March. Wallace ignored Gran's shouting as she dragged Milt to his feet and shuffled him away from immediate danger. The Hacker was trying to stand, using the axe as a support.

'I've done the day and the month, we just need the year,' Jess called out. 'I can't get to it without letting go of the other two.'

'Wallace, leave Milt and come over here. You have to activate the year.'

Milt was still groggy and barely able to support his weight. If she let him go, he would fall. Setting her feet wide and bending her knees, she wrestled him to the front of her. She could hear the Hacker's grunts and curses against the pain as he struggled to his feet, then she heard him moving forward, one leg dragging.

'Hurry, Wallace,' Aggie shouted.

Balancing Milt against her front, Wallace reached up, trying to work out the setup of the numerals for the year. Milt had been right; they were written in a script she didn't recognize. Her hand hovered over the glowing rows of numbers, uncertain, the adrenaline coursing through her system making it hard to think. There were four columns, each showing ten vertical numbers written in a cross between old Roman and something else she didn't recognize.

Using her little finger, she touched what she hoped was two, then with a full bridge stretch managed to reach the zero at the bottom of the next column with her thumb.

Now for the right hand—

'Wallace! Behind you. Look out—'

She made a jab for the next two and zero just as the Hacker's tattooed, muscled arm snaked around her throat. Wallace arched back, causing Milt to cannon off her, lurching him through the panels of vertical lights. There was a flash, and he disappeared.

'Jess,' Aggie yelled. 'Go after him. Now.'

Jess stepped through the light panels from the other side and was swallowed by the brilliant splash of light, taking the Yesterday, Today, and Tomorrow stripesl with her.

TEN

Milt groaned. Every muscle in his body burned. He'd been dreaming of his grandfather's farm, the rich smell of soil still with him. He opened his eyes—the lids had a gritty, end-of-shift feel. He hadn't been imagining the smell either—he was sprawled on his stomach in the dirt. Squinting at his watch to try and see the time, he realized that it had stopped, the face was completely broken.

All he knew was that it was night. Overhead, the full moon backlit layered clouds, but at ground level it only created more shadows. *How long have I been out?*

Pushing himself to his feet, he instantly recognized the distinctive gabled silhouette of Wallace's house against the moonlit sky. His head and body throbbed with pain. Sketchy memories of being confined in that hole, the Hacker, Wallace flinging about, all flitted around like startled birds around spilled crumbs.

How the hell did I end up out here? We were inside a moment ago.

Someone groaned, and he turned, expecting to see the scarred man. The outer edge of his hands moved up defensively.

Was that only moments ago?

When the moon broke through again, he recognized Jess. She

was lying a little way off. He knelt beside her and gently rolled her onto her back. The smell of crushed plants wafted up. They were in what once might have been a veggie patch; a lot of it was dead, and what had happened to all those old trees that Wallace had in the backyard?

'Ooh, my head,' Jessica said, attempting to sit up.

'Easy. Take it easy.' He patted her arm clumsily.

'Freeze! I have a weapon.'

A harsh white light spilled over them. Milt spun around, shielding his eyes, but could see no one, only hear the voice behind the intense light.

'Milt? Jesus, is that you?'

'Lacey? I thought—'

'And Jessica?' Wallace barely choked the name out. 'Thank God. Oh, thank God you made it. I've been waiting for so long, but there was no telling—'

'Turn that bloody light or whatever it is off,' Milt snapped.

Immediately the light softened.

'It's a Mag lens. They came out about ten years ago.' Then, more tenuously, '2030 or thereabouts.'

'What are you on, Wallace? Are you drunk? Why are we out here? What happened to the Hacker and your bloody granny?'

'I'll explain later. Come on. The Wardens will be here soon.' Wallace looked up at the sky.

'We didn't go back, did we?' Jessica asked, her voice small, eyes huge.

'No, Jess, unfortunately not. We're in what you would might call your future—but my present.'

'What are you two on about?' Milt said, his head still groggy, frustration straining his voice. In the distance, he heard a familiar wailing of sirens.

Wallace grabbed Milt's arm, shaking it. 'Will you hurry, Milt? It's them. They're tracking your time hop. Come on.'

Milt's mind felt like it was dredging each thought. It was hard to keep up.

'What do you mean "time hop," Wallace?' he stumbled toward where Wallace and Jess were standing in front of a huge stump.

'*Come on, I'm not kidding!* Give me a hand with this, will you?' Wallace bent down to grip one side of the stump. Milt, still bemused, picked up on Wallace's urgency and hurried over. They heaved up together. It resisted for a moment, then with a deep groan the top portion lifted, turning on two heavily tarnished hinges invisible from the outside. Wallace shone the light down, revealing a series of rammed earth steps inside.

'Get in. Were you always this slow, Milt? I'll come back and get you after they've gone.'

She thrust the light into his hand and pushed him forward, bustling Jess into the hole after him. The siren was louder, coming closer.

Who are the Wardens and why are we hiding from them—under a bloody stump? Where's the Hacker, anyway?

The diffused light extended as far as the first few steps, the darkness seeming to absorb it past that point. Jessica made her way down, fingers trailing the earthen walls for support. Flash card scenes of Wallace, Aggie, and Jessica in freeze-frame strips freewheeled through his mind. He shook his head, trying to clear it, to make sense of—something, anything. He turned the knob on the lamp in his hand and it blazed, lighting up the whole stairwell.

As he passed the seventh step, the hinged cover thumped down above them, sealing them in. Silence bore down, its pressure increasing the deeper they went. The feeling reminded Milt of a SCUBA diving course he'd taken once when he was younger; the pressure against his eardrums was the same. It had been the first time he'd come nose-to-nose with his claustrophobia. Up until then, failure had been something that happened to other people. The best he'd been able to do since then was attempt to keep it hidden.

He focused on his other senses, allowing the musty smell to fill his nostrils to distract him from the feeling that the walls were closing in. His fingers reached out to touch the earthen walls as if to hold them apart. They were dry and crumbly, hung together by the vast root network of the dead tree above.

'I can see the bottom,' Jessica called back over her shoulder. Milt craned his head, eager for a larger space. And air, lots of air. The light spilled across an open area, revealing two well-stuffed lounge chairs, similar to the old square ones his grandparents used to have on their farm. He wondered how anyone had managed to get them down the narrow stairway. Jessica flopped into one of them, her feet not quite reaching the intricately woven mat that covered the dirt floor.

'Some cubbyhouse,' Milt mumbled, looking around, grateful that the excavated hole beneath the tree was generous in both height and breadth. A light ripple of air against his sweat-wet back reassured him that there was ventilation. He exhaled, then allowed his chest to fill from the bottom up just like they'd told him and felt his heartbeat gradually settle.

A bookcase with glass fronts was on one wall. He wandered over and shone the light in. The books inside looked old, their hard covers split, many of the titles along the spines all but worn off with use. He managed to make out a couple.

Ancient Herbs, Modern Remedies.

Necromancy.

More of Wallace's mumbo jumbo. He paced the perimeter of the room. On the side opposite the steps there was a freestanding bench with a cooktop and a jug of water. Above it were several shelves stacked with vials, bottles, and sealed earthenware containers.

He came back and sat opposite Jessica, feeling agitated. 'So, what do you make of all this?'

She shrugged. 'You're asking me? Everything is all jumbled up. I do remember Wallace in the hole trying to set the year, but the scarred man grabbed her. Maybe that caused her to hit the wrong combination when you fell through. I followed right after. Wallace must have been trapped. And what about Aggie, where is she?'

'You believe we're actually in the *future?*'

Jessica kicked off her sneakers and tucked her feet beneath her, grinning. 'Milt, we're twenty meters underground while topside there are things called Wardens wanting to do God knows what to us. It's either the future or another planet. You choose.'

Milt folded his arms and said stiffly, 'We could be dreaming.'

'Mine or yours?' Jess asked, smiling, reaching for a red shawl folded on a small table beside her, then sighed and settled deeper into the chair. She spread the shawl over herself and closed her eyes before adding, 'Besides, if we're not in the future, when did Wallace's hair go white between yesterday and now?'

HE AWOKE to the sound of clinking cups.

Wallace stood at a bench in the kitchen area, her back to him. She was wearing a one-piece navy-colored uniform, elasticized at the waist.

Jessica was right. Wallace's hair was white.

'New outfit?'

She turned on her heel. 'Oh, you're awake. Tea?'

'Any coffee?'

'No. Not what you'd call good coffee anyway, Mr. Barista.' Her voice sounded wistful. Older. 'Even I won't drink it.'

'What is this place?'

'My new witch hole. The old one got busted up, remember?'

'Barely. Jess reckons we're in the future. Are we?'

'Your future—my present. I had half the coordinates for 2020 set, but when I was grabbed from behind the Hacker must have jerked my hand and I hit the wrong year.'

'So what's it now?' Milt asked.

'2040.'

Milt whistled.

'It all happened so fast. I knew you'd come out on March fourteenth, I just didn't know which year. I was hoping I'd still be alive when you did. God only knows what happened to Gran,' she added, her voice wistful. 'She just winked out not long after you guys disappeared. I guess she just couldn't hold on any longer.'

'Don't take this the wrong way, Lacey, but she was dead.'

Wallace stared at him. 'I could never decide whether you were just insensitive or practical, Milt.' She waved her hand. 'But in any case, this time you're right.'

'So how did you get away? From that Hacker creep,' Jess asked, stirring in her chair, her voice still thick with sleep.

Wallace sighed. 'It seems like such a long while ago now. All I remember was a feeling of being choked—he had his arm around my throat—but when Milt went through the portal, he, or probably Dragos, must have realized what was happening. The Hacker pushed me aside and tried to follow. I managed to get another kick in as he went past and connected with the axe handle—he was using it as a crutch. Anyway, it went one way and he went the other. I picked up the axe and just swung it at him. I was so angry.'

Wallace bent down and leaned against the back of Milt's chair. 'It hit him here.' She touched the side of his neck, just above the shoulder, and traced a line across his throat. 'Took his head clean off.'

'That must have been one damn sharp blade,' Milt said.

'It's enchanted. I thought I mentioned that.' She rested her hand on his shoulder. He looked down, seeing the liver spots on her skin, and she hastily drew it away as if his gaze had burned her.

Milt hauled himself up and walked around to face her. She took several steps back, head turning away, looking anywhere but at him. He reached out and cupped her chin, gently raising it so that she was forced to face him. There were lines around her eyes and mouth that hadn't been there yesterday. *His* yesterday, he acknowledged begrudgingly.

'You're still beautiful, Lacey. Despite everything.' He lightly tapped the end of her nose with the index finger of his other hand, grinned, then released her chin and wandered over toward the kitchenette. 'That doesn't change the fact that this whole thing sucks.'

He helped himself to water and turned back to face them, leaning back against the kitchen bench. 'So what's next?'

'Getting you safely back, of course.'

'Back, as in back to where we were, or like way back to where we were supposed to be headed?' Jess asked.

'The last one. The Elemental Scrolls weren't reset, and the world's weather and everything in it has gone to shite since.'

'At least that must mean the fifth gate wasn't opened,' Jess broke in.

Wallace smiled. 'That's something, at least. But we haven't had any real rain here for almost ten years.'

'So you're having a super long drought. That doesn't mean it has anything to do with some magical bits of paper,' Milt said, his jaw jutting.

Wallace sighed, shoulders slumped. 'I thought the same before, but when I take you back topside, you'll see what I mean. No other explanation quite makes sense.'

'Well, Jess is here now, why can't we just go and reset them?'

'It doesn't work like that. The Elemental Scrolls are only accessible at certain defined time intervals. You've heard of things lining up? Well, the next window when that happens won't be for another eighty years. By then it will be too late. The deserts are swallowing up huge chunks of arable land each year. Water is already more valuable than gold. In another ten years, there won't be anything worth saving, much less waiting another seventy for.'

'Unless we go back,' Jess chimed in.

Milt looked unconvinced. 'But if things are so bad, why not just use this time machine thing to go straight to the time period for the Scrolls? If the Hacker is dead, no one else is going to be murdered.'

'That's the other wrinkle Gran failed to spend much time mentioning. To get at the Scrolls, we need a Cipher. It's part of the test that the Messengers have to go through to prove themselves.

That's what the six-year initiation would have prepared you for, Jess. To develop your natural talent. Gran did what she called "fast cooking" with you back in the house, but I'm not sure whether any of it did much good.'

Jess cocked her head as if inspecting something inside it. 'I sort of know what you're talking about, Wallace. It's like déjà vu. Does that mean whatever it was took?'

'You're asking the wrong witch, kid. I'm just one of the spear carriers in this opera.'

Milt interrupted. 'So a Cipher as well as the ring is needed to access these Scrolls?'

'Yes. The ring will open the way, but the Cipher contains the codewords. All Jess has to do is touch the Cipher with the ring and they will upload automatically.'

'Upload?' Milt asked, his voice testy. 'Isn't this supposed to be an ancient thing? I would have thought parchments and quills would have been more the go.'

'The Sisters were early adapters. Does it matter, Milt? Magic is just science without the long, technical explanation.'

'Then Dragos will be after the Cipher as well as the ring?' Jess said, relieving the tension.

'I'm afraid so. Yes. Sorry, Milt, I'm a bit on edge.'

He shrugged, then grinned. 'It's been a big day so far.'

She smiled back shyly before continuing. 'Here's what I've been able to find out from the old Sisterhood records. The five Scrolls are all interdependent, which means one leads on to the other and they have to be activated in that order. The Aquarian is the first. It controls the water supply. That was the first to go. The food supply, or earth element, is directly linked to that. It's called the Cornucopian Scroll. That's number two. As the plants die, then so does the availability of the viable oxygen mix. That's what's unraveling at the moment—the Aether Scroll—but before the world chokes to death, the final element, Piras—fire—will kick in and burn off what's left.'

'And the fifth, this demon gate,' Jess asked.

'Yes. The Akashic Scroll—it means space, as in infinity. That's what Dragos was after. If the first four scrolls are not activated, then a new life form that is not reliant on the same environmental and food sources is able to be introduced, opening the way for the Fifth Scroll. Life goes on. Just in another form.'

'But I have the ring. Surely they can't retrieve the Scrolls unless....' Jess's voice trailed off.

Wallace nodded, feeling Jess reach to her psychically and absorb the deeper meaning. 'Now you're getting it.'

Milt looked from one woman to the other. 'You two might know what you're talking about, but I'm in the middle here, treading water. What do you mean?'

'Where Dragos is being held, he's not restricted by a linear time-line. It's like being outside and looking in; he has a sort of overview. The remaining Sisters and I have managed to keep him restrained up to now, but over the past few months he's been getting stronger again. We don't know how. As a consequence, he could, theoretically, manipulate his surrogate in the past—before I kill him. '

'What she means,' Jess chipped in, 'is if he manages to find and kill an earlier version of me—or Mum—they can still get the ring and the Cipher.'

Wallace nodded.

'I can't believe I'm saying this, but what happens to the "her" that's here?' Milt asked.

'If Angelique dies before Jess is born, then the form she has now will probably just fade out. If they kill Jess's earlier self, my guess is she will die of some sudden cause here. That's why it's so important to do what we have to quickly and get you back before the Book of Names was ever stolen.'

'This all sounds like a science fiction yarn,' Milt started, then grinned. 'I guess it really is.'

'Whatever. Right now it's reality, Milt, so you may as well get used to the rules. It'll make it easier for everyone.'

'All right, all right, I get it. But let's say everything you've said is kosher. Why not just whistle up that magic light time machine of yours and we'll get moving,' Milt said, glancing up at her. 'All of us.'

'Again, it's not quite that simple. We need energy to do that. A lot of it. Gran was able to tap into the Sisterhood last time. Trouble is, now most of the Sisters are dead. I do have a plan that might work though, but it will be tricky. When you came through last night, it created a huge energetic displacement that registered on the Wardens' sensors as an explosion. Fortunately, they could only trace it back to this general area. That's why it was important to get you underground. The residue is still on you though and will be for several hours yet.'

'I assume these Wardens are some sort of police force.'

'More like a cross between the Stazi and Star Trek Klingons. Anyway, I figure we may stand a chance of slipping through the surveillance security, as you two don't have Patriot Implants—they're like a microchip beneath the skin that everyone needs one to access basic water and food.'

'Rationing?' Milt asked.

'Afraid so. It's the only way to manage the low supply of basics. Unfortunately, many people didn't like that, so Australia turned into a right wing police state to keep order. Most countries did. There was a lot of war over water and food, with stronger countries invading others. Fortunately, or not, Australia didn't have a great water supply to start with, so we were pretty much left to starve to death from the start.'

Wallace glanced at a readout on her uniform sleeve. 'I've got to get to work now, but I'll be back as soon as I can. Try and get some sleep. Your bodies have been through a huge shock, so they need to rest. I've left some sandwiches and water on the bench, and there's a bucket behind the blanket near the ventilator if you *really* need to go. The Wardens will have withdrawn surveillance by the time I get back, so you should be able to come up then. If you get into trouble, use this.' She lobbed something over to Milt, who caught it reflexively. It was a polished but irregularly shaped rock. 'It's like a beeper but absorbs and sends the emotion of the user. I'll be able to tell what the problem is without you saying a word. Just hold it and think of me. It's also untraceable. Old Wiccan technology,' she added, winking at Jessica.

'So what's with that WASP thing written on the back of your uniform?' Milt asked as she turned to leave.

'A fancy name for the Water Board.' She laughed grimly to herself before turning to face Milt. 'Everything is about water here. Crazy, heh, for something we used to take for granted? But without it, society doesn't last more than a few days and then all hell breaks loose. A lot of senior police and detectives were transferred over to WASP following the Water Riots of 2027. That's when the Wardens became responsible for enforcement. I'm what's called an extractor.'

'What's that?' he called after her.

Her reply was faint, trailing behind her as she ascended the steps. 'That's another one of those questions you really don't want to know an answer to.'

MILT DRIFTED in and out of a light sleep. He finally gave up and lumbered over to the bookcase. One appeared to be a journal written by Aggie. It talked about Earth Mothers and Nature and also referred to their quest to prepare the Messenger to activate the Elemental Scrolls before disaster befell the earth.

Too late for that one.

I always thought Wallace was on the out-there frequency, but this? How could you know someone and not really know them at all? How was it possible? He snorted. If they really were in the future, then any damn thing was possible.

Jess stirred, stretching her arms and legs, uncurling from the chair like a cat and peering up the stairs.

'I wish Wallace had left us a clock. We don't even know if it's day or night up there,' Milt grumbled.

'What happens if she doesn't come back? Have you thought of that?' Jess asked.

'Now you're starting to sound like me. Watch it, or you may discover depression is hereditary.'

'Ha ha. Wow, I'm parched. Did I hear Wallace mention tea before?'

She walked over to the bench and lit the gas ring, searching through the cupboards for cups.

'Hey, look at this,' she said over her shoulder.

Milt turned. The close-stacked shelves were crammed.

'What is that?'

Jess pulled one out. 'Looks like ration packs—and small bags of water.' She tossed him one. It was tight, vacuum packed, but clearly water. He cracked it open and took a sip. 'Tastes okay. But I'll stick with the tea.'

Jess tore open one of the food packs and smelled it, then brought a small portion to her mouth. 'Hey, the food isn't too bad, want some?'

'Sure. I'll try anything once.'

She closed the cupboards and returned with a food tray and two steaming mugs.

'The tea tastes a little brackish,' he said, making a face, 'but I guess it must have been down here a while. Wallace must have been hoarding.'

Jess took a careful sip. 'No, that's the taste of the tea, I recognize it. Mum used to make it when I was small. It's medicinal. Don't ask me what it does.'

'What else do you remember about back then?' Milt continued in a quiet voice.

She shrugged and flicked her hair back over her shoulder. 'Not much. Mum was a little wild. You probably don't remember,' she finished, her voice tight.

'No, I do. I was thinking about that—her—back at the house.' He paused. 'I know what it's like to lose a child, you know. My daughter

—my other one, Janis—was killed in a head-on a few years back. Her and her little girl. Her name was Carlie.'

'What happened?'

'Carlie was in the back seat. There wasn't much left of either of them once the truck hit them. It was just a dumb accident—no one's fault. But I needed someone to blame, so after a really bad night, I went after the other driver. Tracked him to a bar down at the ratty end of Queen Street. We were both pretty drunk, and I ended up taking him outside into an alley that ran beside the pub. He went down with the first punch. I remember bending down and telling him very plainly and distinctly who I was and why I was going to beat the living crap out of him. After that he just lay there in the middle of that filthy alley, taking my kicks as if he deserved each and every one of them. It was like kicking a carcass. After a while I stopped and found myself on my knees beside him, panting and wailing like a rabid dog.'

'What happened?'

Milt shrugged. 'I called triple-zero and ended up going to the hospital with him. He never pressed charges. He was beating himself up way more than I ever could. That's what I mean about not blaming others—or yourself—about what happens. It took me a long time to learn that. It sounds like you had a shaky start too.'

Jess shrugged. 'I guess.' She paused. 'Living with Mum was like being in the front car of a roller coaster ride that never stopped. It only slowed and leveled out just enough to fool you into thinking things would be okay now before taking off again.'

'Sounds like she was scared. Worried for you too,' Milt said softly.

Jess nodded, eyes down, fingers pulling at the threads in the rug.

'I would have come to you—if I'd known. Sooner, I mean,' he added.

Jess snorted, still looking at her hands. 'I used to dream about that. The archetypal father coming to save me and Mum. I used to make up stories. He was rich but already had a family, but one day he'd realize what he was missing out on and come and get us. Or, at one stage, I imagined he might be a spy, or a thief. Looking back, it seemed to depend on the book I was reading at the time. After a while I stopped hoping and grew to resent, no, hate him for not being there. But it's easy to hate someone you've never met. Harder to realize it really wasn't my fault that he'd abandoned us.'

'I guess you tried the birth record? Was my name on it?'

'No father's details recorded,' she recited. 'Mum refused to discuss anything about it, of course. She went off on a screaming tangent every time I brought it up. In the end, I truly don't think she knew either. Things were always hazy for her at the best of times. I think we were both grateful when I moved out and went to live in Melbourne.'

'I'm sorry,' Milt said. 'I wish I'd known.'

'Me too.'

They paused in the thickening silence until Jess cleared her throat and asked, 'So what do you make of all this magical stuff?'

Milt brightened. 'Beats me. From where I sit, it's up to you. Are you planning to do what these women seem to want?'

Jess looked at him, her gaze steady, almost defiant. 'I don't know. Mum didn't model responsibility well, and if there's one thing I've discovered, fear and magic can be a lethal combination. Mum was the most fearful person I've ever met. In her way, she tried to protect me from what she feared the most. Facing up to things.'

Moisture formed at the corners of Jess's eyes, and she sniffed.

Milt dug through his pockets and brought out a folded checked handkerchief. He held it out to her at arm's length, unsure what else to do.

Jess's mouth lifted into a tired smile as she reached forward and took it, dabbing at her cheeks.

'Thanks. It's been a—'

He dismissed it with a wave. 'Forget it. Wild rides like this are always easier if you're not on your own.'

THEY SETTLED INTO A COMFORTABLE SILENCE.

Milt's little admission had ambushed Jess, caught her unprepared —"with her emotional underpants down," as Mum used to say. Yet he was right, it was too late to be the dad she'd never had. The dad she'd railed and cursed and cried about not having in fits of "unfair," of having to be Mum's mother when all she'd craved was someone to look after her, just once. It wasn't that Mum didn't care, but it was from a different space.

Outer space, mostly.

Jess smiled as she remembered mum ditzying off somewhere with the fairies. Now that the ring was on her finger, she could understand —well, a little better, anyway. The ring did things. Jess was resisting its influence, but she could feel it there nonetheless. No use telling Milt, of course, he wouldn't understand, and why should he? She smiled indulgently over at him sprawled across the lounge, head back, mouth open, snoring lightly.

She heard a scratching noise coming down the stairway and started forward, head cocked, listening. There it went again. *What is that?*

'MILT. MILT, WAKE UP.'

He grunted. Jess was shaking his shoulder.

'Listen,' she whispered.

'What is it?'

Jess shook her head. Milt bounded to his feet and took a couple of steps toward the stairs. It sounded like someone scraping something against the stump hatch. He pressed his index finger to his lips and motioned for her to hide behind one of the chairs. Dimming the torch, he started up the steps.

Near the top, the scraping noise became louder. It sounded like an animal scratching about. It echoed down through the hollow stump. Three steps from the top, Milt doused the light completely and crouched, pressing his back into the side of the wall, waiting.

A crack of light appeared as the hatch lifted revealing a shaft of blue sky. It widened as he watched. Placing the torch on the step, he positioned his hands against the underside of the stump and pushed. The lid flipped back, throwing whoever was above off-balance. Milt clambered out of the passage, grappling the intruder to the ground and drove a fist into his side. It crumpled, offering no resistance. Rolling away, he saw that it wasn't a man at all but rather some sort of machine made to look vaguely human with a tunic and artificial hair. It lay on its back, tentacled arms waving, heavy-duty wheels spinning. Gradually its dials dimmed and went out.

'Jess, come on up,' he called down into the hole. 'Whatever this is, it's found us. We need to get out. Where the hell is Wallace?'

'Use that thing she gave you,' Jessica said, emerging from the hole.

He nodded and dug into his trouser pocket, dragging out the device. He wrapped his fingers around it, visualizing Wallace's face, thinking at the same time that he must be as mad as the rest of them if he thought this would make her appear. The rock became warm, then hot. He held it tighter. Gradually it cooled.

'I guess that's it.'

'What is that?' Jessica said, pointing at the machine on the ground.

'I'm not sure, but it sure as hell isn't Santa.' Milt closed the hatch and looked around. 'Let's get inside the house until Wallace arrives. I hope she hasn't changed the locks.'

'Shouldn't we wait down where she left us? What if—'

Milt held up his hand as if he was stopping traffic, speaking over his shoulder as he walked on. 'Don't even go there, all right, Jess? Right now, I can't figure out whether I'm certifiably nuts, or if this is just another station stop on my delusion train.'

He turned to her. 'You're the one with the special powers. You should be able to tell me.'

'I was afraid you'd say something like that.'

'See, your premonitions are already working. Come on, let's get inside.'

'IT'S A TRACKING DRONE.' Wallace let the curtains on the kitchen window drop back. 'They'll know it's disabled, but that won't matter. The damn things break down so often, no one takes much notice when one bleeps out. We shouldn't stick around, though.'

Wallace had appeared soon after they'd entered the house.

'What now?'

'Why don't we make a start? I've got some spare WASP uniforms under the stairs. They're in your sizes, or how I remembered you both twenty years ago.'

Jessica took a set of navy-colored coveralls from Wallace and held it up against her.

'What about IDs—what did you call them?' Milt said, pulling the uniform over the top of his other clothes.

'Patriot Implants. PIs. They're in the top pocket of your uniform, Milt. They took me a while to get, but then it turned out I had a few years. As I said, everyone has PIs now; they're coded to an individual's DNA and embedded in their forearm. PIs carry a person's details and are used for everything: communication, banking, and security. They've made detective work essentially irrelevant. If anyone tries to do anything illegal, it's immediately trackable. It hasn't stopped crime, but it does cut out the middleman. On the bright side, they're also used for shopping.'

'What, like money?'

'Yep, it works in the same way a debit card used to—but now you just use your forearm. A scanner automatically makes the debit from your account. Cash became obsolete soon after. That decimated the drug business overnight, along with the black economy. Until they figured a way around it.'

Milt stood in front of the hall mirror, squaring the uniform over his shoulders. 'Let me guess. Water is the new black market currency, right?'

Wallace laughed. 'That's what I always liked about you, Milt. You're a dirty crim at heart.'

His reflection grinned back at her. She reached into the top pocket of his jacket and pulled out two small discs, handing one to each of them. They looked to be about the size of an old five-cent piece and half as thick. Turning it slowly between his finger and thumb, he held it up to the light. It flickered with ripple of color.

'What do I do with this?'

Wallace held out a small tumbler of water. 'Hold it against the inside of your forearm. Now watch.'

She dribbled several drops over it. Nothing happened for a moment, then the small disc trembled. The water dried up, as if it had been sucked inside. Wallace tipped the glass a little more, and again the water seemed to evaporate when it hit the disc.

Milt felt the disc grip. There was no other word for it. Gingerly, he removed the finger that had been holding it in place. It stayed put. More water.

'Now watch,' Wallace whispered.

When the final stream of water hit the disc, it dissolved like soluble aspirin, and Milt felt something being drawn in through the outer layer of his skin.

'What the hell! It's inside me,' he said, scratching at the tingling spot with his fingernail.

'Don't worry, it won't hurt. You always were a damned sook. The discs are minute particles bonded together with a water-soluble base. Imagine them as tiny grains, each imprinted like a computer chip, so small they can permeate the skin. Most of them will remain just where they are, exchanging data. Others travel in the bloodstream to the brain and central nervous system. They'll lodge there eventually, accessing the tiny currents from the neural pathways for their power source. They're also interactive with the healthcare system, so they can tell remotely what's going on inside your mind and body.'

'That's amazing,' Jess said as Wallace took her glass over and repeated the process.

'Amazing spelled bloody scary,' Milt said, scratching at the reddened skin on his forearm. 'But you said these are dummy ones?'

'No, Milt. I said they were from the black market. The only difference is yours contain false IDs.'

'Won't someone be suspicious if these signals suddenly start sending?'

'Yes, but they're also designed to uplink data covering the intervening period. As long as no one picks that initial burst going in, you'll be okay. The chances of that happening are millions to one, given the amount of data exchange that goes on every second. Once I get you registered, I'll pair you both up to my roster.'

She led them outside to a van with blacked-out bubble windows. It looked like a cross between a Winnebago and a hearse.

'Get in. I had to use the jet jump on this dinosaur to get here. I was way across town when I got your signal.'

Milt looked for the front cabin door. There wasn't one. Wallace slid the side entry open and motioned them inside. There was no area for the driver either.

'Before you ask, everything is automated. I just key in the destination address on this monitor. A central traffic computer controls all vehicles. If your PI isn't cleared for the keyed quadrant, you don't get through—period.'

'What do you mean, quadrant?' Jess asked.

'Oh sorry, another "innovation." There are four main areas or quadrants within the city, high security down to general access. It's supposed to reduce traffic congestion, but it just segregates the "better thans" from the rest of us.'

'And we are...?' Milt asked, still scratching at his forearm.

'Extractors. We have limited emergency access to all quadrants and permanency in Q2, here. One up from the general workers. Hold out your arms in front of you, I'm going to try and connect your PIs now.'

She touched a small screen on the wall of the van. A beam of red light shone from the padded roof and then divided itself into three, each tracking directly to where the PIs had disappeared. In a few moments, the red light reformed into one beam and retracted back.

They waited for several seconds before the light in the roof turned green.

'We're in. It's accepted the Trojans,' Wallace said, the relief evident in her voice.

'You didn't know whether they'd work or not, did you?' Milt said quietly.

'They were supposed to be quality, but I couldn't test them. If the beam reader senses more bodies than valid PIs, it sends an alert straight to the Wardens.'

Milt felt a vibration beneath his feet, and the van began moving. He fell back onto a bench seat.

'What is this thing anyway? It looks like something Dracula might drive.'

'It's an EV—sorry, extraction van,' Wallace said, 'all solar powered, except for the emergency jet jump. I'm only supposed to use that to bypass the traffic jams that aren't supposed to exist anymore.'

'And Extractors use a van for...?'

Wallace avoided his eyes and stared out the window. 'We extract the water from recently deceased cadavers.'

ELEVEN

The van pulled up outside a dilapidated-looking high-rise. Milt slid the van door open, climbed out, and stretched. He recognized the building. It'd been new the last time he'd seen it.

'I left the Extraction Unit upstairs when I got your call,' Wallace said. 'I told the woman I needed some help with her husband. He's pretty big, he may not even fit through the chute.'

She paused and placed a hand against Jessica's shoulder as she made to follow. 'Jess, honey, can you wait down here with the EV? Someone needs to, it's regulations. We shouldn't be long, and quite frankly, this isn't always pretty.'

Jessica looked relieved. Milt managed a smile and followed Wallace through the cracked glass entry doors into the foyer. They waited by the one working elevator.

'I can't believe any of this,' he said. 'They use dead bodies for water? What sort of world is this?'

'Dry. The Water Index is the one Futures stock on the Exchange that's guaranteed to keep going up; the only question is by how much. The human body is mostly water, and thousands of people die every day. What would you expect to happen? If we get to them fast, we can usually recover up to 60 percent of their body weight.'

'Are you listening to yourself, Wallace?' Milt said.

She spun to face him. 'Yes, Milt. Yes, I am. I've been listening and watching all of this unfold for the past twenty years, remember? This is about race survival, and things get pretty damn ugly when that happens, so instead of galloping your white horse all over my bare moral patches, help me fix it by working toward getting those Scrolls reset, all right?'

He took a breath and nodded. 'Okay. Sorry. You're right.'

A tired smile tugged at the corners of Wallace's mouth. It looked familiar within her unfamiliar lines. She tousled his hair. 'It's not fair. I always thought you'd be bald by now.'

The doors of the ancient elevator trembled before rumbling open. Two desiccated teenagers with dead-looking eyes and white bodies beneath skimpy clothes wandered out. Milt looked at Wallace, and she nodded. 'We still have drugs, except now they sell their body fluids to fund them. Most die of dehydration.'

She pressed the button for the twelfth floor.

The elevator slowed, bounced once, then, as if reluctant, the doors rolled open. 'Maintenance seems to be an issue round here,' Milt said.

'It's the same everywhere, except in the upper two quadrants.'

She paused before one of the doors and made a strange motion in the air with her hand; immediately, the same pattern appeared in luminous green, hovering above the wood. Wallace made another sweep with her fingers, and the door swung inward.

Before he could say anything, she entered, pulling him inside. The door clunked shut behind them.

'I spun you a story about the extraction unit downstairs. I didn't want Jess to see this.'

Milt looked around. 'See what? This looks like a stripped-down apartment. What is all this stuff anyway?' He picked up a bag and sniffed at it dubiously.

'A safe zone.' She eased the bag away from him. 'Only a few of the Sisters have survived. Those of us who did warded some safe houses throughout the city. That way we can practice individually, or together, undetected.'

'Practice what?' Milt said picking up a silver chalice from a table in the center of the room. The table looked vaguely like an altar.

'Magic. Don't be old Milt now, I know for a fact you're not stupid. We're fighting a rearguard action here using the only weapons we have. This is one of the places we do it from. Last month, we disabled the Wardens' surveillance net, and for eighteen hours everyone had free water. It sent the Index into freefall. The Wardens blamed it on a computer malfunction.'

He replaced the chalice carefully and looked around. The windows were opaque, as if the glass had been sandblasted. They appeared to shimmer. He touched a finger tentatively to one and felt a faint tremor as if from a mild electric current.

'They're charged. Designed to break up and deflect any surveillance beam,' Wallace said, gathering items from a variety of shelves that ran along one wall.

'You still haven't told me why you didn't want Jess up here.'

Wallace frowned, her gaze sliding away. 'I couldn't take the risk. Jess is a sensitive. Everything she sees could be retrieved and read by the Wardens like a software program. If this doesn't work out and we're caught... well, what she doesn't know, she can't blab.'

'What about me—and you, for that matter?'

'You're normal. I can overwrite your memory. When we leave here, you'll think we actually did an extraction. I can't do that for Jess. As for me, well, all the practitioners who use these places took a vow to do whatever's necessary to protect the safe houses and the network.'

'Suicide? You'd do that?'

She nodded.

'So if you're going to wipe my head, why bother bringing me up here?'

'I needed your grunt. Grab those bags in the corner for me, will you?'

He gripped the necks of the two bags and tried to lift them.

'They're a little heavy. You may have to bring them over one at a time.'

'What the hell is in here?' Milt said, dragging one of the bags along the floor.

Wallace disappeared into the next room and returned wheeling a large gurney. It was as high as his chest and enclosed on both sides by stainless steel. She touched one of the buttons on the console, and the pillow end of the stretcher portion lifted to forty-five degrees.

'This is an extraction unit. The body slides off here into the base. "Amazing Grace" plays, and I read the rites to the grieving family. It's all horribly tacky.'

'What happens then?'

'The bodies are taken to a central processing unit. A centrifugal drive like a gigantic spin dryer then extracts the water. The remaining solids are fired, and the ashes returned to the family.'

'Efficient.'

'So was Auschwitz. Come on, this unit is dry. Help me pack these bags into the bottom. I don't want to leave Jess on her own for too long.'

BACK IN THE VAN, Wallace allowed a soft smile to disguise her unease. Across from her, Milt was sprawled across the bench seat. The mind wash appeared to have taken, as she'd thought. He had no recollection of the safe zone.

Jessica wasn't so easily fooled though. She'd intuited the spell as soon as they'd climbed back into the van; she just didn't have the words or the experiential knowledge to put it together.

'Where are we going?' Jess asked.

'I told you. Quadrant One. It's what we used to call the big end of town. It's the only place that has enough available energy for what we need.'

'That's it?' Jessica interjected. 'We're going in there on impro? No script, no rehearsal?'

'If you mean do we have a plan? The answer is no, not really, because I don't know what we'll find when we get there. I'm working on: we get in and out, preferably in another time zone with real rain. Pretty simple, really.'

'Jess may be right, Wallace. We'll have a better chance if we use some time for a recce at least,' Milt added.

'Something I haven't told you,' Wallace said. 'The longer we wait, the less reliable those Trojan PIs in your arms become. Following the energy discharge you caused last night, the Wardens will eventually run a full check on the database, looking for implants like we just uplinked. I estimate we've got less than twenty-four hours to pull this off, plus we don't know what or where Dragos is and how much time we have before he takes Jess or her mother out in retro. So, Jess, as you put it, there's no time for scripts or rehearsals. We'll have to shoot this in a single take. Or is that mixing my media? Anyway, we can't afford any mistakes. Can you handle it?' She looked meaningfully at Jess.

'Now, now, you two. Remember you're both in the same convent,' Milt muttered.

The two women exchanged a glance, then a smile. The tension in the van drained off. 'That's coven, not convent, Milt,' Wallace said.

'Ah, it's all the same, just different habits.' He smiled and flashed a mischievous look from beneath his bushy brows. A look from before.

WALLACE FELT the tremor just before the soft ping sounded, signaling that the EV had reached the destination coordinates.

Milt and Jess looked at her expectantly. She nodded. 'We're here. Get ready.' They pushed themselves to their feet as the door opened.

'Milt, can you grab the other end of the extraction unit? Jess, maybe if you can take this?'

She handed her a small backpack emblazoned with the WASP logo. Jess peered inside.

'It's a portable verification sensor. We use them to locate the deceased,' Wallace said.

'Isn't it easier to ask for the address?'

Wallace felt a grimace form. 'The body starts deteriorating pretty much straight away. If we relied on the relatives calling the death in, that would be too late. Everyone's PI automatically monitors signs of life, so when those signs disappear, it automatically generates a signal and a WASP team is dispatched. Our KPIs are set against a fifteen-minute retrieval interval. Any longer and the team goes on report.'

'So, what, you just burst in on the family and snatch the body from them?'

'Body snatchers, that's us. It's another reason for doing everything we can to avoid this particular version of the future happening.'

'It's terrible. This place is just horrible,' Jess said, making a face, looking at the barren urban landscape.

'Come on. The quicker we get back to the past, the sooner this all falls to bits.'

Milt took the weight of the extraction unit against his shoulder. He was sweating heavily.

'Whoa. I thought we were going to pick up the body. This feels like one's already been loaded—and a fatty at that.'

Wallace smiled but said nothing. It was crucial that Milt remain oblivious to the memory of the heavy bags they'd loaded into the extraction unit. The hastily run script that wiped his memory could have left trace tags that could easily snag against anything she might inadvertently say.

'Jess. That verification device I mentioned. Can you take it out and turn it on—that button on the side. That's it, now all you need to do is follow the red arrow on the screen. Go ahead, lead the way.'

They followed Jess across the concourse. A tracking drone trundled past, lights flashing as it validated their PI data. Wallace hoped the Trojans would hold. The black market was notoriously unreliable, the running joke being that Trojans came with lifetime guarantees. However, she'd done some favors for the woman who'd supplied these two and was hoping they'd be better than most.

'Who are those guys?' Milt muttered from behind. Wallace glanced up. Two heavily armed men were watching them from either side of a door that opened into the black glass dome where they were headed.

'Wardens. Keep your eyes down and push hard. WASPs get priority. There's usually no problem.'

"Emphasis being "usually,"' Milt picked up.

'Water foraging attacks are on the rise,' Wallace said. 'The higher the Water Index climbs, the more it increases the risk of poaching raids. The energetic disturbance last night has been officially classified as a diversionary tactic to mask an aborted attempt on the city's reservoir. As a result, all Q_1 domes now have Wardens on access points.'

They slid to a stop before the doors while the Wardens' monitors interrogated their PIs. Wallace waited anxiously for the bank of lights to turn green.

'Any luck?' she asked, looking up into the darkened visor of the man nearest her. The Warden said nothing, just waved her through with a gloved hand when the system cleared them, automatically triggering the sliding doors.

Wallace led them to the middle of a marked-out square with two mushroom-shaped domes in one corner. Milt looked at her curiously.

'Delevator,' she said from the corner of her mouth, 'it goes down. The section of floor we're standing on is a pressure plate. It'll lower us. The shaft forms the walls, so keep your hands in your pockets.'

'Why domes? What happened to all the tall buildings in this quadrant?' he asked, looking up at the huge expanse of glass arching above them.

'Water from the air condenses against the curved glass and is recovered. They found it was cheaper and more energy efficient to build down than up. In the early days, they even struck water once or twice while they were digging the holes.'

'How deep do they go?' Jess asked. 'I've got a phobia about being buried alive.'

'Not very. Think of it as more as a vast open cut mine rather than one long single shaft. Five levels at most, but they run for a long way in all directions. Each dome in $Q1$ is interconnected below ground. The water reservoir, called the water table, is at the very bottom. Everything drains down into it through a variety of filters.'

She tugged free a water canteen and uncorked it, offering it to Milt. He glanced at the extraction unit and shook his head. 'No thanks, I know where that's been.'

'Stay here long enough, and I guarantee you'll end up fighting me for it.'

'That's what I'm afraid of.' He licked his upper lip.

One of the raised mushroom-shaped domes on the floor switched to green. Wallace tapped it with her foot. 'Here we go. Hang on.'

Immediately the broken lines marking out the square they were standing on started flashing, and their section of the floor dropped rapidly. Wallace tapped Milt's forearm, pointing up. 'See, another floor piece slides over automatically. No need to wait for this one to return. This one will stack at the bottom of the shaft until the last section beneath the floor is in place, then they'll all return to start over.'

'Nifty.'

'How's that arrow going, Jess?'

Jess tried a tremulous smile. Wallace could see that neither of them were comfortable underground. 'It's pointing to $L5$ and indicating another five hundred meters from there.'

Wallace nodded, already knowing that, but it was important that Jess look the part. Extraction teams always ran to three. She'd been on that planning team years ago and had made sure of that.

The floor hissed, then eased to a stop. Doors branched off from the delevator in all four directions.

'Jess?' Wallace promoted.

She held up the small screen, finally pointing to a door at the back. Milt swung the big gurney around while Wallace hit the release handle. The door rumbled open, sliding into a wall cavity. A corridor stretched ahead of them, the roof arched and smooth, continued unbroken all the way to the floor.

'More collection points?' Milt pointed at the shallow drain that flanked both sides of the broad corridor.

Wallace nodded, automatically checking the time readout on her sleeve. Ten minutes had elapsed. With the EV tracking their progress and feeding the data back, they had to stay under the red retrieval line. Even one minute over would blip them up onto someone's monitor, and they couldn't afford that sort of scrutiny, not for what she had in mind. That would come soon enough. Access archways branched off either side of the major corridor.

'Come on, we're running late. Move it, Milt.'

She heard him mutter a curse as he matched her pace from the back of the gurney, the sound of his boots against the floor loud in the enclosed space.

Jess jogged alongside. 'What's down here, Wallace? And where are all the people?'

'These are living quarters, mainly. Work and rec areas are usually on the upper levels, and that's where most everyone is at this time of day. People try and avoid being further down than they have to, and besides, the upper levels also have ambient beaming—sorry, big screens that project outdoor scenery. It's virtual, but it mimics what reality used to look like. Most people prefer it now to the actual. It helps with the delusion. How far do we have to go now?' She pointed at the screen bobbing in Jess's hand.

'Oops, sorry.' She turned, calling back to Milt. 'I missed the turn. We need to go back and take the archway to the left.'

Milt slowed, spinning the gurney around.

When Milt had edged the gurney into the corridor that Jess was pointing to, Wallace said, 'I'll go ahead. Follow me. Jess, I'll take the validator. You stay with Milt, just in case.'

Wallace trotted ahead, checking off the doorways against the small screen in her hand as she passed. Finally, she paused outside one of them marked L5 Devereux. She used her electronic passkey and authorization code. The door hissed open. Raising the time readout on her sleeve, she spoke into it, waving the other two through with her other hand.

'This is WASP Extraction Unit Three enforcing entry to D1/L5 —Devereux. Making the collection on my mark: three, two, one.' She touched the time readout on her sleeve to the side of the unit, which bleeped in response. 'Powering up.' She crouched down, tapping a numeric readout. 'Registering net body weight at 120kg, and I have manually disengaged the ceremony program as no one but the extraction team is here at the moment.'

The sound of her voice echoed off the thin walls before finally disappearing into the darker areas toward the back. Lowering her sleeve, Wallace slipped a metal bar from the side of the gurney and struck the locking mechanism next to the door until it fell from the wall, effectively jamming the door.

'Okay, we're off the clock with thirty seconds to spare.'

'So where's the body?' Jess asked.

'There isn't one. I faked the callout. This is one of the safe houses I was talking to Milt about.' He looked at her curiously, his eyebrows bunching. She closed her eyes, trying to retrieve the slip. 'Or maybe I meant to,' she added quietly. 'All right, our group has set up some special places that are protected from external monitoring. That means the Wardens can't hear us in here. We call them safe houses.'

'But people do live here,' Jess persisted, pointing to a montage of family 3D photos beaming up from a round device on a small table.

'No. Not anymore. It just looks that way. The official records show the Devereux family, or some of them anyway, as still living here. They used to be part of our group but chose assisted self-exit some time back. In return, they agreed to donate their PIs, which we maintain remotely from the back bedroom. There were five of them, and we're gradually allowing them to die off as we need to access the space. This will make the third of their PIs that we have had to decommission.'

'Self-exit?' Jess mouthed.

'Assisted suicide. It was their choice and much easier to carry out back then.'

Milt was staring at her and was about to say something else when Jess butted in, 'So why are we here? What's in this place that's so special?'

Wallace turned to her, grateful she wouldn't have to spell out that either way, there was no going back.

'Directly above us is the power cabling for the entire Q1 complex. We'll be tapping into that to kickstart this.' She touched a lever at the side of the gurney, and the top section lifted with a release of pressurized air. Two steel struts set into the base of the unit engaged with a click to keep it open.

'Phew, it smells,' Jess said, standing back, her hand moving to her mouth.

'Death. You can never quite get rid of the stench,' Milt said. 'No matter what sort of chemical you use. It always wafts back.'

Wallace reached in and dragged out one of the bags they'd loaded earlier, carefully retrieving a small harp-shaped instrument that had been tucked beneath it. She held it up to the light, minutely examining the fine wire strings.

Milt looked confused for a moment. 'Where's the body we picked up?' Then his face cleared, and he shook his head. 'You did something, didn't you?'

'It was for your own good. Ours, really. I couldn't take the risk we wouldn't be picked up and interrogated. What you didn't know, etcetera.'

Milt snorted, pointing at the instrument in her hand. 'Your death squad thinks of everything, Lacey, even harps. Got any angels and cupids in there as well?'

'If your jokes get any better, I'll hurt my sides throwing up,' Wallace said, slowly using her finger to test the tension in each connection. When she'd finished, she turned to Jess. 'Sweetie, do you think you can squeeze yourself through that inspection panel up there?' She pointed to a small panel in the ceiling.

Jess nodded.

'Great. Milt and I wouldn't have a hope of fitting through there, so I'm hoping your slim shoulders will. Milt, make yourself useful and give her a boost.'

TWELVE

Jess angled her arm, then a shoulder up through the hole.

'It's just big enough,' she called down. 'Wait until I get my head through, Milt. Oooh, there's not much room, I'll have to crawl.' She gripped a pipe and hauled the rest of her up and in, finally rolling onto her stomach.

'Can you see the junction box? Look for something square and red. It should be on the wall to the front of you,' she heard Wallace say.

Jess coughed, squinting into the darkness. 'I see it. What do I do?'

'Take the harp.'

Jess felt something nudge her side. She wriggled one hand back along her body to retrieve it and then shuffled forward, coming onto her elbows and knees. 'Now what?'

Below, she could hear Wallace and Milt talking to each other but was unable to make out what they were saying. The closeness of the crawl space made her feel like she was cocooned, cut off. A ribbon of anxiety stirred in her stomach, like a snake awakened from hibernation. It was hot and seemed airless, the noise of the silence increasing until it was buzzingly loud against her eardrums.

'I can't hear you,' she shouted, the sound bouncing wild and loud in the enclosed space. The white noise had attacked suddenly, probably in response to her rising anxiety, ratcheting finally into a low-pitched whistle. Sweat beaded on her forehead and upper lip before running in rivulets down her face.

'I can't hear you!' The words chased each other madly through the blackness.

Something touched her stomach, and she jumped, knocking her head.

'Jess. It's all right, I'm here.'

Milt. His voice was muffled but it calmed her nevertheless.

'Move forward, you're lying across the opening.'

Jess shuffled further forward, feeling a stir of air across her legs as her trunk cleared the hole. Gray light crept tentatively up from below. She'd been lying over the bloody hole.

Get a grip.

The white noise backed off but didn't completely disappear.

'I'm all right.' She nodded as if to reassure herself. 'What now?'

'Position the harp beneath the junction box, over the cables that are running into it,' Wallace said, her voice pitched low in a stage whisper, as if she were sharing something with the audience.

What is wrong with me?

'I feel funny, like I'm here and someplace else,' she said loudly in the general direction of down.

'It's the harp, Jess. It does that. It's tuning in to your frequency. Try and ignore it. Once you get it near the current, the strength of that signal will override yours.'

Jess grunted and shuffled forward, pushing the harp along in front of her.

'All right, I'm holding it near the wires. And you're right, I feel a bit better.'

'Good, now hold it there and draw your thumb right across the strings, as if you were playing a chord.'

Jess stretched forward, holding the harp in one hand as she used the thumb of the other.

'The strings are too tight; it hardly made any sound. Should I do it again?'

'No. That doesn't matter. Try taking your hand away. See if it floats.'

Jess released her grip hesitantly. She could just make out the harp suspended in front of the cable, its top tipping a little toward the box, the heavy base leaning back the other way like the keel on a yacht under sail.

'Yes. It's staying there. It looks sort of balanced.'

'Good, come on back then.'

Gratefully Jess pushed back on her knees and shins, all the while keeping her eye on the harp. It seemed to be shimmering.

'It's shining.'

'You may need to hurry up a little then, Jess,' Wallace called, an edge to her voice. 'You don't want to be up there for the fireworks.'

Jess managed to get one leg, then the other through the hole. Wallace and Milt held her while she jiggled her trunk and shoulders down through the hole. They set her lightly back onto the floor. Milt replaced the ceiling panel, and they waited.

From above she could hear something vibrating, like the humming of a rising wind across power lines.

'It's starting,' Wallace said. 'Here, give me a hand to get these bags out.' She reached into the extraction unit, tugging at something. Milt moved to help her, and together they dragged out the rest of the sacks, thumping them to the floor. Wallace tugged on the thick drawstring of one of them, opening it.

'Jess, can you spread this material around in a big circle? Make it large enough to go around all of us.'

Jess couldn't lift the bag, so she reached in and took a double handful of what was inside. It felt and smelled like ash from some long-dead fire, but it was unreasonably heavy so it couldn't be. Milt, grunting, dragged another from the extraction unit. He and Wallace helped spread the contents from the opposite direction, just inside the circle Jess was making.

'Wider,' Wallace called around her arm. 'Make it wider and deeper, Jess, like this one.'

From above, the humming sounded like a hive of agitated bees. A hint of burnt meat floated into the air along with a whiff of smoke.

'Is something burning?' Jess asked. 'And why is this stuff so heavy?'

'Dense, not heavy. Its mass has been compacted to save space. Makes it easier to get around and store.'

'More new technology?' Milt snarled. 'It stinks. Literally.'

'No.' Wallace snorted. 'More ancient than new. Finished?'

Jess nodded, dusting her hands against each other. The inner circle was about a meter in circumference. It was tight standing inside, particularly with Milt—he took up so much space. Funny how genes worked, with him now being her brand-new bio dad. How many times had she wished for a dad, any dad, latching on to any of Mum's brief encounters who'd stay around long enough for little girl "real family" dreams and short-armed hugs?

She caught Milt's eye, and a shy smile formed as he tried to hunch himself to give her and Wallace more room.

'You made things a bit squeezy here, Lacey.'

'Don't worry, it's just right for what we need to happen.'

'And what's that?'

'Listen, hear it?' she said, angling an ear toward the ceiling.

The bee sound was escalating to a full-blown buzz.

'What is that?'

'Resonance. The harp is drawing and storing energy. A lot of it. The faster the strings vibrate, the more power they can store. Soon there'll be enough for the first discharge, and it looks like we'll be ready for it. Look.'

Jess followed Wallace's finger as it pointed down. The circles they'd made seemed alive, as if they were teeming with thousands of tiny insects skittering and writhing inside the ash.

'What is that stuff inside there?' Jess asked, squeezing herself away, in toward the center of the cramped space.

'They're dancing.'

'They? You said "they," Lacey. This is getting creepy. What the hell is in that?'

'Don't worry; they're friendly. They won't hurt you. Just stay inside the circles.' Wallace had to shout to be heard over the increasing din from above. Jess covered her ears; it sounded a lot like her own white noise, but way off the scale.

'Get ready,' Wallace yelled, raising her arms suddenly, nearly knocking Jess out of the circle. 'Discharging.'

There was a huge flash from above. To Jess, it seemed like lightning that forked into two separate bolts simultaneously striking the perimeter of both circles. Immediately the ash began to smoke, then, with a soft *phut* like petrol igniting, they burst into two rings of fire. Above the buzz resumed, escalating sharply.

Wallace, her arms still raised, threw her head back. 'Discharging again, stand clear.'

Another flash. The flames leaped to waist height this time. Jess threw herself against Milt, burying her cheek in his massive chest. Heat from the flames radiated against her legs. She could hear singing, a chorus, faint, interspersed with a pulsing barking of an alarm close by.

'We're lighting up the Wardens' security board. Good thing I deactivated the fire-retardant sprinklers,' Wallace said. 'They'll be tracing the energy disturbance right about now, which means we'll have company in next to no time. We should be able to sneak in one more discharge. I hope it's going to be enough. These old girls have been asleep too long. They're sluggish.'

Again the humming built, but much more quickly. 'Get ready. Close your eyes, both of you. This could get messy. I'm having to rush it.'

'Wallace, I—'

Light burst across Jess's closed eyelids. In reflex, they snapped open, and she screamed. The flames were as high as her chest and while still contained within their circles, outside them, lining the walls, were faces—hundreds of them—floating, arranging themselves in tiers that stacked up to and through the ceiling.

Jess stifled another scream.

'Jesus, Lacey. What the hell have you dragged in here?' Milt spluttered, his eyes wide, head swiveling.

Once Jess allowed her fear to subside, she felt a strange sense of calm drape over her; these faces felt familiar somehow.

'It's all right, Milt,' Jess said. 'I know them.' Then wondered at that, caught midway between the recognizable and not quite yet known.

Wallace brought her arms down. She looked exhausted, flashing a tired smile at Jess, eyes flicking momentarily to the apartment's front door as a determined banging began. Someone out there was shouting, but the door was thick, and it was hard to make out what they were saying. The intention though was unmistakable.

'We're ready,' Wallace said.

'For what?' Milt snapped. 'This looks like something out of the exorcist.'

'Not quite, but maybe. These entities are the ancestors of our order. The energy signatures of them, anyway.'

'The what?'

'Milt, you'll just have to coast down this hill, all right? Go with it, just for once. The essences of the Sisters who have passed have been preserved to transform the raw energy we've tapped up there into something I can draw on and direct with my will so we can manifest the Yesterday, Today, and Tomorrow portal.'

With what felt like a wave of understanding, Jess knew what Wallace was talking about. The circles were ashes, generations of these women. Their cremation ashes.

'You with me on this, Jess?'

She nodded, looking with awe out at the translucent images overlaid on each other, still emerging from the circles, floating up, gradually filling the room.

'Good. I need you to help me now. Close your eyes and draw in their energy, allow them in. Imagine it happening. Hurry now. We don't have much time.'

After a moment's hesitation, Jess felt like something was knocking against her chest. She closed her eyes and focused on the area surrounding her heart, imagining huge wooden doors being flung open to reveal a steady flame within. Immediately, what felt like a warm breeze drifted past the doors and into the flame, fanning it until its color changed from a warm yellow to white, flecked with powerful flashes of blue. She felt one of Wallace's arms slip around her waist; glancing over, she saw the other reach out for Milt.

'Now, like last time, make the parting the curtains motion with your hands. You too, Milt. If all goes as I hope, we all should arrive back a few months before we started.'

'Should?'

'There are no certainties, Milt, I thought you would have picked up on that by now. When the portals form, you go through first, then me. Jess, because you have the ring, you need to go last, as the portal is linked to it. If all goes as it should, we'll arrive back in the bodies we had back then but we'll retain the information and knowledge we now have. The guys outside won't be able to follow.'

Jess felt like her smile would outstretch the corners of her mouth. Knowledge was flowing into her core, sending the flame of her spirit soaring.

The commotion against the front door was increasing; huge dents scarred the smooth metal surface, and with each new assault it shivered inside its housing.

'Where is the portal?' Jess called, looking around, hands still making the parting motion. The number of ghostly faces was depleting rapidly, and with it the energy levels wavered.

'We're not there yet. Keep your focus. Milt, you'll have to do more. Do you trust me?'

'Wallace I—'

'Do you?'

'Yes, all right.' His voice was tight but resigned.

'Good. Then imagine yourself opening up, like some giant can opener is running up the side of your body, peeling it apart. Do it quickly.'

Milt scrunched his eyes shut, mouth set in a determined line. Jess felt something flow from inside her, link up with Wallace, and then encircle Milt.

'Keep making the parting motion with your hands, don't stop.'

Suddenly a space opened in front of them and a huge energetic surge exploded into it. Jess could feel Wallace shepherding and shaping it. Slowly the Yesterday, Today, and Tomorrow portal began to form, hazily at first, then with more certainty, but still too slowly.

The door to the room had been holed by the last impact. Jess distinctly heard a shout as the men outside sensed there was only one rush holding it.

Nervously, she glanced behind her.

'Jess!' Wallace shouted. 'Stay focused.'

When she looked back, the light panels were fading in and out as if they were snagged on something the other side of real. The colors too were less defined, their edges blurring, bleeding into each other.

'Come on. Give me more,' Wallace cajoled, shouting at the wavering image, her grip tightening around Jess.

The front door fractured from bottom to top. The men outside cheered. Jess chanced a look, seeing the men. They were trying to climb through, cautious of the raw, jagged tear. The two sides of the broken door hung to either side at a crazy angle, caught inside the guiderails of the frame. There were only seconds remaining.

'Now!' Wallace shouted hastily keying in the date and year co-ordinates. Jess thrust the ring into the recess at the top. The image stabilized.

'Milt, go. Jess, you come straight after me.'

He dived through. Wallace followed. Everything began to

vibrate, the room filling with white as if someone had shaken a massive snow globe, and Jess thought of Martin, but quickly brushed it aside as she felt something against the back of her collar. It may have been fingers.

She didn't look back but just dived through.

THIRTEEN

The siren stirred him. Strange that it would, because he usually found the city sounds, sirens particularly, reassuring. It meant that everything—despite every other thing—was still working.

Milt rolled onto his back, eyes determinedly shut. The sound of the siren wasn't fading off into the distance or getting closer, as it should. Each shrieking pulse remained at the same volume, and this more than anything was pulling him further up, away from the deep sleep he'd been in. Finally, he opened his eyes. Bright, too-early light forced them back into slits.

Damn, I forgot to pull the curtains. Again. No wonder I'm awake. What is that bloody noise, anyway?

Then he remembered. He'd changed the ringtone of his phone.

Tossing the covers aside, he rolled out of bed, bare feet padding across the thick carpet and out into the lounge. The Melbourne skyline spread before him, the sounds of a city stretching awake floating up with the light breeze from the bay.

Must have forgotten to close the sliding doors again.

He followed the sound to the sofa, where it stopped abruptly mid-whoop. The silence without the blaring sound was intense.

Immediately the ringtone began wailing again. The sound was closer now. He traced it to the coffee table and then to beneath a discarded magazine. He didn't recognize the number. After a moment's hesitation, he picked up.

'Yeah,' he grunted.

'Milt? Is that you?'

His mouth opened, unable to speak. Finally, he managed a choked, 'Wallace?' At the mention of her name, something new seemed to clunk into place inside his head, as if a previously unheard soundtrack had been added to his memory file. His head seemed to be afire with it, full of scenes cascading and mashing together until he felt like passing out. With difficulty, he eased himself down onto the sofa. His head felt like an overripe melon perched at the edge of a wobbly table.

'Lacey?' he repeated, softer this time as more memories, (*could they be memories if I can't actually remember some of them happening?*)—fantasies, more like—floated up.

'Are you sitting down?'

'Yes. Now.'

He imagined her at the other end of the phone, biting her bottom lip. 'What do you remember?' she asked.

'What, right now? Crazy stuff.'

'Like?'

'Like... I dunno. Wallace, is that really you? Am I imagining this... fucking... stuff? Am I imagining talking to you?'

She laughed, the relief heavy in her voice. 'No, you're definitely not. So, how soon can you get on a plane up here?'

WALLACE WAS WAITING at the arrival gate when he clomped out of the aerobridge. Seeing him, she waved and took two tentative steps in his direction. He kept charging, swallowing the distance between them with huge strides until he was close enough to scoop her into a massive hug.

'I wasn't going to let myself believe it until I saw you.'

'Milt.' She laughed, tapping him on the shoulder. 'Put me down.'

'No.' He hugged her closer, lifting her higher, slowly turning in a small circle as he stared up at her face, other passengers flowing past, smiling, on either side.

'This is crazy,' she said.

'I said it first.' He finally eased her down but kept one arm draped around her shoulder as if she might escape if he did not.

He looked around. 'Where's Jess? I thought she'd be here with you?'

'She's wherever she was on this day back in the day. I don't know. I guess that would be Melbourne. I hope she remembers enough to contact us. Her phone number seems to have changed. The one I had isn't working.'

'Any chance that this Dragos may have gotten to her or Angelique already?'

'I hope not.'

They joined the steady flow of passengers toward the exit.

'I looked up the date on my phone after I hung up,' Milt said. 'I seem to be a few months ahead of where I left off the first time I was here. I gotta tell you, Lacey, this is damn spooky stuff.'

'Today is the date when the Book of Names was originally stolen from Gran.

She seemed to think Dragos hadn't fully taken over the body of the man he's using when she was killed. His face wasn't scarred like it was when we saw it. He looked normal, she said. More desperate and sad, if anything. He won't look like the guy we saw until well after the killings start.'

'So how is Dragos getting him to do this stuff now then? Is he just a voice in the crackpot's head?'

'Sort of, but more likely Dragos is projecting a presence, a representation, so the perp thinks he sees Dragos in some form or another. Possibly an animal or a symbol of power. It could be anything, really.'

They emerged from the elevator and entered the airport carpark.

Wallace paused, looking both ways, then with a sigh clicked the remote in her hand. A small white car three rows over beeped and blinked.

'Some things never change,' Milt muttered and smiled.

They drove down the ramp and out onto the road.

Milt reached over and patted her upper thigh. 'You're amazing, Lacey. Remind me never to pick a fight with you.'

'If you don't move that hand right now, you might get that reminder sooner than you wanted.'

He chuckled, but left his hand where it was, turning in his seat as a sign flashed by.

'Hey, this isn't the way to your place. That sign points to the Sunshine Coast.'

Wallace gripped the hand on her thigh and lifted it off, dumping it on his side of the armrest.

'I know, and we need to get there before three. Well before.'

'What happens at three?'

'Gran dies.'

'Maybe you should have called her mobile first and let her know?'

'Gran doesn't use them. I never know—knew—where she was. And besides, she didn't want to be saved, remember? Just get the book, she said.'

'How do you feel about that?' Milt asked, genuinely curious.

Wallace didn't answer for a few moments. 'Ask me when I get there. I don't know. I know what she's saying and understand the reason behind it, but for me, it sounds like allowing someone you love to die. I don't know if I can just stand by and watch that happen.'

THEY DROVE for the next hour and a half, stopping only once for a quick coffee.

'How is it?' she asked before taking a sip through the tasting hole at the top of the cardboard cup.

'Better.'

'Than what?'

'The next time we have coffee—I think it's in about four months from now when we're staking out Jess's flat. Or won't we have to do that now?'

'Not now. Things change.'

'Ah, see, that's what I just don't get with all this future stuff. We're here now, and yet I can remember stuff that hasn't even happened yet—'

'—and may never.'

'Maybe, but logically that doesn't make any sense. If it never happens, how can I remember it?'

'If it doesn't, maybe you won't. Right now, you only have an idea of what could happen. There are any number of variations that could affect that.'

'Like?'

'Think back, what were you doing on this date—the last time? Any idea?'

'When I was in Melbourne before?'

'I don't know. You were there, I wasn't. Were you in Melbourne three months before you came to Brisbane?'

'Yeah. It was just before those blackouts started again.'

'Which was....'

'About when your Gran died.'

'Good. So what would you have been doing today if you weren't here?'

'I'd planned on.... I went to the races. Flemington.'

'The races? That's a new one. You were never a betting man.'

'I'm not, but I had a red-hot tip.'

'So you won?'

'No, I lost a bundle. That's why I remember the date so well.'

'So being here now, you're already ahead, financially at least. That's one change.'

Milt moved his head so he could see the clock on the dash. 'As of about ten minutes ago, yes, I am ahead. I called a bookie I know before I left and put a grand on the real winner who won on that day. Twenty to one.'

'What? So you just won twenty thousand dollars?' Wallace said.

'Thereabouts.' He grinned. 'Only problem is, I can't remember another damn horse that ran after it. I was so grumpy with losing.'

'What else happened, or would have happened?'

Milt reddened. 'There might have been a woman.'

The car swerved. Wallace corrected quickly. 'A woman,' she repeated, nodding to herself.

'It's not like that.'

'That's not the way I remember "it," Milt. With you it's always like that.'

'Oh, Lacey, let's not go there again. That was one time, and your Gran was behind most of it. Besides, it was a long ago.'

'We haven't traveled that far back in time, Milt. Not now, not ever. What was—is—this woman's name?'

'Janice, Rosemary, something like that. How the hell should I know? I haven't even met her yet, have I? This is getting crazy again.' He looked out the side window. The countryside rushing by made him feel car sick; or maybe it was what was rushing through his life. He felt like he was unable to stop, much less exert any control over it. The damn thing seemed to have taken on a life of its own, and it felt like he was trailing after it.

'So she was a pickup?' Wallace persisted.

'Sort of,' he said, shuffling uncomfortably in the seat, suddenly feeling far too big for the small car.

'Oh,' Wallace said, clicking in, 'don't tell me you've resorted to having to pay for it.' She laughed. 'Janice,' she cackled, 'or *Rosemary*? Give me a break, Milt. I've known enough girls in the game to know they don't use names like that. What was it?'

'Lacey,' he said, stretching out her name.

'Detective Curruthers to you, buddy. Hey—that's right.' She grinned, changing the subject. 'I still am a detective. Yip yah! Three months ago, I wasn't on suspension with a pending psych review.

That happened just after Gran died. I knew I went back to work way too soon. Poor Gran, it was a huge shock when she went. Still will be, I bet. God, I wonder if I'm on duty today? I should have checked. Hell, what if they suspend me now for not turning up, can they do that?'

'Lacey?'

'Still, I have no choice. We have to be up at the accident site in time to get the book.'

'And maybe save your Gran?' Milt added, anxious to keep the conversational thread moving away from Janice or whatever the hell her name was.

'No, she's right. We can't avoid pivotal events like death. It's only the bits we order up on the side that are optional. Like, what was her name again, Maisie?'

'Jesus, Lacey.'

Wallace laughed. 'Oh, don't go and get all bent out of shape, Milt. I was just pulling your chain. I don't give a damn what you do. Did. Might do. Oh, whatever. Point is, I don't have any claim on you.' After a pause, she added wistfully, 'I don't think I ever did.'

'That's not true.'

'Whatever. My point is: everything changes, Milt. Us just being here knowing what we do and knowing what we're about to do will change things even more. Like the proverbial butterfly flapping: one thing changes and it affects lots of others. Soon whatever does happen will override what we think is going to, and then what will be real? You tell me.'

'All I know for sure is that I need to stop and take a leak.'

'Aha. In the present moment lies the truth. Milt needs to take a pee. How very Zen of you. Well, you'll just have to hang on, buddy. There's no time. Now that's funny, get it?'

Milt fumed, crossed his arms, then his legs, and stared out the window again.

. . .

'WHY ARE YOU SLOWING DOWN?' he asked, snapping awake. He must have dozed off. They had branched off onto the Bruce Highway and it had broadened to several lanes. Up ahead, all of them were jammed.

'Must be an accident,' Wallace said.

The line of red lights in front stretched as far as he could see. The traffic was at a standstill. In the distance, Milt could hear sirens, definitely coming closer this time, from behind.

'What time is it?'

'Two,' she said, bringing the car to a complete stop.

'How far do we have to go?'

'Another fifty k's, give or take.'

'It'll be tight if we're going to get there by three.'

'What do you want me to do, whistle up a couple of jump-jet broomsticks?'

'Would you mind?' he said, grinning, 'I've always been meaning to get me one of those.'

She smiled back. 'One thing about you, Milt Davis, you could always make a girl laugh, even at times—*especially* at times like this.'

'So, seriously, I mean there must be something you can do. Isn't there some sort of hocus pocus traffic clearing spell in your bag of tricks?'

'If only. You're not the only one who would have cleaned up at the races by now if it were that easy. It doesn't quite work like that. I can handle weather predictions, fertility, lost jewelry, and the occasional house cleansing—with compliant ghosts—but anything else requires a certain amount of help, even willingness, from the universe —Nature. We have to work within her laws.'

'Laws? I would have thought you'd had enough of that already... Detective.'

The dimples at the corners of her mouth deepened. Milt recognized it as what happened when she tried to stop herself from smiling.

'It does, doesn't it? I hadn't picked up on it quite that way before.'

'So what do we need to do, you know, to make something happen "within the laws?"'

Wallace sighed. 'Basically, it's all about channeling and then directing energy. You've seen enough of that to get the idea. We—our group—use artefacts to make that easier. But it all takes time.'

'Just what we don't have. What about the other side? This Dragos character sounds like he has all the time he needs, hanging out in his own brand of Purgatory. Could he have done something with the traffic here to delay us from reaching Aggie in time? You said he doesn't have much of a hold on the scarred man yet, but could he do something like this from over there, wherever that is?'

She pursed her lips as if she were drinking options in through a straw. 'It's possible.' She nodded, releasing her lips. 'Yes. If, as Gran said, he's aware of us and what we're trying to do, he could have managed something like this to delay us.'

'How?'

'Oh, I don't know, interfered with what one of the drivers in a car up ahead thought he was seeing, maybe making him swerve, and then bingo-bango-bingle.'

'How would he do that?' Milt persisted. 'Interfere, I mean.'

'Remote suggestion. It's easier if you already know the person and are tuned to their individual thought frequency. Someone like Dragos would only need to synch in and project a thought of, say, another car coming directly at him for an accident to happen.'

'When there wasn't anything coming at all?'

'That's why a strong will helps keep the barriers up.' She adjusted the rearview mirror. 'Here come the ambos. I better try and move over to make room.'

'No. Better still. Where's your lights switch? We need to get the police strobes going,' he said, searching the dash.

'What?'

'Your police lights. Not that you'd ever want to try and pursue anything in this heap of crap. You'd never have a hope of catching them.'

'Here.' She flipped a switch and the small panels above the dash and at the rear window blinked on. The blue flashers reflected off the white car in front.

'Okay, genius, what good is that going to do? No one is going to move for us. They can't.'

'No, but they will for the ambo. When it goes past, slip into its wake. Once we get near the front of this mess, we can pull the lights. Promise.' He grinned.

The ambulance was getting closer. The cars behind—and in front —were already nudging their way to either side, making way. Wallace opened her window, removed the badge wallet from her bag, and held it up outside the car. When the ambulance glided past, she gunned the engine and slid in tight behind it before the other cars could close ranks.

'That's it,' Milt said, staring down drivers in other cars as they passed. 'Don't these people have any respect for the law? I swear that big guy back there was going to jump out and have a bite of me. I must be losing my gruff police exterior.'

'Could be all the time travel you're doing. I hear it creates additional estrogen.'

'Har-de-har. There! I can see the accident scene. It's not far now. Better to keep these lights going. I just caught a glimpse of some others. Must be traffic guys, they got here quick. This may take some talking through. Get ready.'

'God, Milt. If I was in any doubt how to get myself suspended, I should have known all I had to do was to spend the day with you.'

They pulled around the ambulance when it stopped, slowing as they moved up to the uniforms blocking the road. Ahead, a semi lay across the road, the neck between prime mover and trailer body broken by a jackknife. Colored chunks from up to three cars lay strewn to either side. Wallace flashed her badge and mumbled something about an urgent case up the mountains that they had to get to. The uniform finally waved them through with a warning to be careful. Wallace weaved her way through the mess. As they passed, Milt caught sight of a truck driver sitting at the side of the road, clutching his chest while another man, probably from one of the stationary cars, signaled the newly arrived ambo officers to hurry. No one was trying to help those still inside the mangled sedans, or what was left of them. From what Milt could see, there would be little point. More sirens were approaching, this time from the other direction.

Something about the semi and the truck driver sitting by the road tugged at his memory. It had been when he'd been speaking to Hopkins. He turned to Wallace.

'Wasn't there a semi involved with your Gran's accident up on the mountain? Something about a driver with a heart condition.'

Wallace looked over at him, her expression strained. 'Yes. He ran into both cars and died at the scene. How did you know?'

'I think he may have just got cheated out of an hour. Better get cracking, Detective Curruthers, I have a feeling the future has already changed.'

'What do you mean?'

'I mean do you remember an accident happening on this road last time? It would have blocked the road for hours.'

'No. And I drove up here as soon as I got the news about Gran. The Bruce Highway was clear at the time.'

'Then I get the feeling that three servings of sides you were talking about just got moved around back there—all of them sitting in wrecked cars.' He paused, then added, 'Trouble is, to three families they're not sides, they're pivotal events. I'm getting to hate this guy, or demon, or whatever he is. I never thought I'd say this, but I hope Aggie is all right.'

FOURTEEN

Cars crash.

Cars crash every day.

Accidents happen and people die.

Shea eased his foot off the accelerator, changing down a gear, easing back. Ahead, the old woman's taillights flashed briefly, then again for longer. She'd braked a shade too late entering the hairpin.

He was pretty sure she hadn't seen him yet; her driving still had the same loose, casual feel; the lines into and through the bends were either sloppily wide or tight in, as if she were distracted.

Once she realized he was following, panic would bleed into her rudimentary driving skills and she would make more serious mistakes. Mistakes that would burn precious seconds from her life. Accidental death—not murder.

'Whatever you call it, Mr. Shea, it's the Fire Dance.'

Shea started, his gaze snapping over to the passenger seat. Nestled in the angle where the leather back met the seat, Dragos crouched like a small, deformed bird, his long talons sunk deep into the soft leather.

'Hell, Dragos! I wish you wouldn't just appear like that.'

The gargoyle swiveled its head slowly, the scrape of stone moving against itself loud inside the car's hushed cabin.

'I either appear or I do not, Mr. Shea. How it happens is really quite irrelevant for you. Do you know that you have a habit of slathering convenience over fact? The woman in the car will die, and you will be the cause of it. Whatever sauce you apply as to its cause will not change the dish, only the ease of swallowing it.'

'I told you. I don't kill. Not anymore.'

'Oh, come now, Mr. Shea, the Fire Dance has already begun. You are the predator, she the prey; strangers, yet already intimately connected. Don't tell me you don't recognize it? You were special forces—what is it called, SAS? You can't really get finicky about killing, can you?' Dragos said, his tone patronizing.

'That's why I was at the top of that building. I'd had enough.'

'Then why didn't you jump?' Dragos said silkily.

'Maybe because one of the freaking gargoyles started speaking to me. Promising me peace.'

'And other things. Don't forget those. I recall you had concerns about money. This is a nice car, isn't it? You weren't driving one of these before you met me. I showed you how to get more money than you'd ever seen.'

'But I told you I wouldn't kill. That was the deal.'

'Was it? Perhaps that was what you thought you were agreeing to. No, I'm afraid both you and the witch in front are now both dancing to my music. The Fire Dance concerto, I'll call it.' He allowed the last words space to linger before stretching what passed for his lips to expose long, sandstone fangs.

Shea clamped his molars together, swallowed a retort, and accelerated through the hairpin and out the other side, his eyes automatically tracking down the road, seeking the other car.

It was gone.

'What the hell?'

'I warned you. She's tricky,' Dragos said, his carved wings grinding with annoyance.

Shea slowed the car to an idling creep. Empty—all the way to the next bend.

'Shit!' Shea slapped the wheel. 'Where did she go? There's a rock wall on one side and a sheer drop on the other. There's nowhere she could have pulled in.'

He leaned forward, as if he might have missed something, his mind rapidly factoring distance, speed, and times. Finally, he shook his head. 'There's no way she could have even made it around the next bend in that time.'

'Stop the car,' Dragos snapped, sniffing the air.

'Are you crazy? I just told you there's no room to pull over. If anything comes around that bend, they'll plow straight into us.'

Dragos snarled, and immediately pain seared into Shea's abdomen. The agony was familiar, like being punched in the gut with a meat hook. Each time was a little worse. He was being trained like a dog, and as far as Dragos was concerned, Shea was still in puppy school.

Tensing his abdominal muscles, Shea stopped the car. The pain leaked away in gulps, like black water down a choked drain.

'Thank you,' Dragos said. 'Now be so kind as to turn the car so that it blocks both lanes. Keep my side facing the road coming up the mountain.'

Seething, Shea swung the wheel to the right, then reversed, straightening the black BMW so that it straddled the road. Dragos shuffled toward the passenger door and pecked the switch to lower the window. It whirred, the electric sound ratcheting up the tense silence. When the window had fully retracted, Dragos hopped from the seat to perch unsteadily in the open space, the sound from his sharpened claw tips slipping against the doorframe. Dragos's head swiveled back and forth as if he were scanning the road below.

'She is still there,' he whispered over his shoulder, 'in the other lane. Her car is facing us. Ready to drive back up this way, no doubt anticipating that we would have passed her as we gave chase.'

'Where?' Shea said, craning toward the open passenger window, squinting.

'Place your fingertips against my back,' Dragos said.

Shea hesitated, his hand hovering over the carved wings.

'Hurry.'

Shea's fingers grazed the gargoyle's back, and he shuddered. The weathered sandstone was cold—almost icy. As he continued to stare, he thought he saw a shape resolve further down the road. Not a shape exactly, more like a heat shimmer.

'Do you see it, Mr. Shea? The car's engine is still hot. It is facing us. My senses are receptive to infrared. Mark it well, as when you remove your hand it will disappear once more. She is trapped. The only way open to her now is down. If she tries to open her car door and run, it will break the cloaking seal she has created, and the car will become visible. You must block her exit down the mountain. She will try and turn next. Go.'

'Me? Block her exit? I've got a better idea. Why don't you go do that, and I'll wait here?'

'We all have our purpose, Mr. Shea, and yours is to serve me.'

A ribbon of pain dribbled into his abdomen, more a reminder than warning. Shea gripped the door handle.

Good dog.

He opened the door and slipped out. Bending low, he loped across the road, keeping close to the rock face on his left, fingers trailing to count off each guidepost. The one closest to the car had a broken diamond of reflector plastic. When he reached it, he stopped. If the car hadn't moved, it should now be directly opposite.

He strode across the road, hands in front, groping for the outline of the 4WD, feeling both scared and vaguely foolish. He could see nothing except the dim outline of the safety rail on the opposite side.

How is it she can make her damn car invisible anyway? He snorted. *The same way stone gargoyles get to talk?*

He stepped over the double lines in the middle of the road and sniffed.

Diesel fumes. It had to be the Prado.

Silent running?

How can she damp down the sound and visuals? How about touch?

The questions dropped unchallenged into the bulging "impossible" file he'd opened when Dragos entered his life. Or was it his death? Shea was never completely certain he hadn't managed to make the jump off the building before the gargoyle had spoken that first time.

'Projections. They are cheap illusions. Dissembling matter, now that is a real skill.' Dragos's words dripped like acid into his head, yet Shea knew if he looked, the bird would not be there. It was becoming harder to keep the voice out of his head. It was almost as if it was eager to take him over somehow.

He focused on the task, and his hands jarred against something solid, fingertips registering the smooth shape of the four-wheel drive moving slowly backwards.

Shea unsheathed his hunting knife running for the apex of the bend below, mentally plotting the line she'd have to take to reverse into it. Left hand outstretched and moving in a scanning arc before him, he cocked his knife arm and waited, poised like a dancer awaiting his entrance cue. Was this Dragos's Fire Dance? Whatever.

Nothing happened.

A waft of diesel swirled around him. The breeze was flowing down the mountain, carrying the smell toward him.

Shit! She's going forward instead!

He sprinted back the way he'd come, long powerful legs driving him toward the beached Beamer. She was going to try to ram her way past. Or drive over it.

With meters to go, the familiar hollow *phud* of a car being hit at speed rolled back over him. He saw his BMW lurch as if pulled back on massive strings, its facing doors buckling, side glass shattering, roof caving. Shea still couldn't see the Prado but estimated from the wreckage where the midpoint of the four-wheel drive would have to be and ran toward it. His hand struck glass, then, sliding down, a door —rear—then still further to the tire. He brought his knife hand back and drove the strong blade into the sidewall. It was hard to puncture a tire this way and it took several attempts until it finally exploded with a gratifying bang. He sprang back but held onto the side of the roof rack as the Prado reversed, lifting his legs clear of the road.

The woman was going to make another run at the BMW, and this time, tire or no tire, she would manage to push the Beamer aside far enough to squeeze past. There would be no question of pursuit.

A hopeful image of a pulverized stone bird crushed inside the car flashed into his head, but he knew Dragos was no more inside the gargoyle than any of the other forms he'd seen him take in the past month.

He felt the Prado pause, imagining the woman inside desperately dragging the transmission selector from R to D. He lowered his legs back to the asphalt and released his grip on the roof rack. The Prado jerked forward, sluggish, a combination of the steep incline and the bare, tractionless scream from the bare wheel rim. It gave him enough time to get the knife into the front tire as well. He anticipated the Prado's slew to the right and leaped aside, tumbling expertly to spread the impact before bouncing to his feet near the rock face. When he turned, what looked like a crack in the air had appeared, then widened to reveal a woman's leg and shoe. The Prado's door was opening, and whatever had been hiding it from view was breaking down.

The woman emerged fully. She was old.

What's with Dragos? She's just a harmless old biddy.

She scrambled around, shot him a quick glance, and ran away from the wreckage, making a diagonal toward the sheer drop at the side of the road. Shea could see blood running down her left leg. From the way she was shuffling, he could tell the wound must be deep; the blood was pooling and sloshy in her shoe.

'*Get her!*' Dragos's voice burst into his head. '*You must get her.*'

Shea ran.

She was at the rail, her right leg already over, but she was having trouble with the damaged left.

'*She has the book,*' Dragos screamed inside his head. '*Get it.*'

Shea was still three meters away. The old girl had managed to use her free hand to drag the left leg up onto the top of the safety cable. He dived, catching the foot, hugging it to his chest like a loose ball in a scrum.

'Let me go,' she screamed, alternately pleading and hitting him with the book. It was heavy; the sharp corners cut into his head and arms. 'You don't understand what you're doing. I can't let you—'

Her voice wasn't young, but she was strong. He grunted and hung on, tasting the metallic salt of blood dribbling into his mouth from the gashes in his scalp.

He hauled back on her leg, using his weight to counter her desperation to get over the rail.

'*Get the book!*' Dragos screamed again.

Shea looked up. For a book, it was damned big as it swung toward his head. He pulled back, missing the worst, but it still managed to score a glancing blow to the side of his skull. He couldn't hold her and get the book as well. One of them would have to go over the edge.

'*Forget her. All I need is that book.*' Dragos's voice was deep inside him now, reverberating through his cells, jimmying them apart, loosening his will.

'I told you; I won't—do—that,' he said through clenched teeth, fighting for every word. He tried to tense his legs against the safety rail, readying them to drive himself backward and pull her with him, but his limbs wouldn't obey. It felt like parts of him had been disconnected, the circuits rerouting.

Dragos.

From above, he heard a car horn blasting in short, urgent beeps.

Just what I need, a bloody bystander.

. . .

'THERE SHE IS!' Milt shouted, pointing. Wallace accelerated out of the bend and the full view opened up. 'Christ, look out for those cars, the road is blocked halfway down.'

Wallace jammed her foot hard on the brake, swerving away from the wreckage in the middle of the road. The little car began to slide, its rear tracking out. Wallace turned into it, but the grade was too steep.

'You're going to broadside. Turn away.'

Wallace's car slammed into the guardrail. The safety cable bulged but held. They continued to slide down the hill toward the struggling pair. The man released his grip on Aggie and leaped up, snatching the book from her hands.

Milt heard Aggie scream as she overbalanced and toppled over, fingers clutching the air as if they might claw the book back.

Wallace's car finally slid to a stop. 'Is Gran all right? Can you see her?' Wallace shouted, struggling to open her door. 'God, I can't get out, the door is jammed against the rock wall. Milt! Can you see her?'

'No,' Milt shouldered his door open and slid out. He hobbled over to where Shea was sprawled facedown on the road. Aggie had gone over the edge. He'd seen it; thankfully Wallace hadn't.

Shea gathered himself up, the bulky book hugged tightly to his chest. They surveyed each other. *It's the same guy—but without all the scars. Well, most of them anyway. He looks halfway human now.*

They circled each other slowly.

'Remember me?' Milt asked, more to engage him.

'Should I?' The man's voice was cold, wary, but definitely not the same guttural tone it had been the last time. No axe either, which was a relief, just a long knife.

'He's not in you yet, is he?' Milt said.

'What?' The other man looked confused, the knife blade catching the light as it moved. Milt licked his lips. He didn't do knife fights all that well; he was too big and slow. He hoped it wouldn't be a fatal combination.

'I mean Dragos,' Milt added. The other man's eyes widened.

Bingo.

'He's not inside you yet. I can tell. But he will be. Do you know what happens then? You, whoever the hell you are, disappear. He takes over your levers. Your face and head become scarred. You'll be ugly man. What's your name anyway?'

'Shea,' the man feinted to the right. Milt countered, cursing himself for not thinking to bring a weapon, preferably one with bullets.

'Shea what?' he said, stalling.

'No "what," just Shea.'

'Well, just Shea, do you know what's going on here? Dragos is some sort of demon. I know that sounds nuts, but the longer this goes on, the more he'll take you over. He'll possess you. I've seen it.' Milt felt stupid even saying the words.

'Your mouth is moving, but all I can smell is horseshit,' Shea said, but his tone was saying otherwise.

'It'll happen. I know. From the very first murder, it will start. I can see by your eyes you know that too, don't you.'

The man charged. Milt threw himself to one side, sucking in his gut like an oversized bullfighter after a big lunch. He did manage to land a glancing elbow to the guy's back as he went past.

Milt knew Shea was only testing him out, seeing what he had, and so far, the scoreboard above Milt's head was flashing "no real threat." When the guy charged the next time it would be for real, and Milt would likely be slit and slippery—in several places.

Shea dropped the book. It fell to the road with a loud thump. He used his foot like a hooker in a scrum to scoop it behind him.

'We're police, you know,' Milt said. 'Detectives with Queensland Police. Know what you'll get for killing police officers? I get the feeling you're no stranger to the judicial system, so maybe you do.'

'Yeah, I know exactly what I'll get. Instant relief.'

'In that case, you'll know the drill. Drop the knife and raise your hands,' Wallace snapped. Milt turned his head, Wallace was standing off to one side, feet in a wide stance, a double-handed grip around her gun.

'Hoo-ray,' Milt breathed.

Shea showed no emotion. Milt could see him mentally vectoring the distance and angles. Wallace had been smart; instead of joining Milt and risk Shea rushing them as a single target, she stood back and apart.

After a moment's hesitation, the knife clattered to the road.

'Now step over to the car, keep your hands up. Milt, cuff him.'

She lobbed the handcuffs over. He caught them and slapped one bracelet around Shea's wrist and the other to the door handle of the wrecked BMW.

When he'd finished, Wallace lowered the gun and went over to pick up the book. Milt joined her. It was bulky and bound with rusting iron strips riveted to the cover.

'What is this made of? Wood?' Milt asked, rapping his knuckles on book's cover.

'Yes. It's a box made to look like a book. For protection, the real one is inside.' 'Haven't your lot thought of digitizing?'

'This isn't a regular book, Milt.' She paused, then said in a tight voice. 'Gran went over the edge, didn't she?'

Milt nodded, placing his arm around Wallace's shoulder. She sniffed. 'Well, it's not as if it was going to be a surprise. Come on, I have to call this mess in.'

SINCE WALLACE'S CALL, a long shadow had gradually crept across the road. It had now reached the far edge of the bitumen and was biting into the nature strip. The sun was already behind the mountain and was on its way down. In the distance, Milt could see the long stretch of sandy beaches of the Sunshine Coast, still enjoying full sun.

'It's been a while since you called for backup. What's the usual response time up this way?'

'It depends. Maybe the highway is still blocked,' Wallace said, glancing over to check the prisoner was still securely cuffed to the door handle of her car. From this side, it appeared relatively undamaged.

'Even so,' Milt said, looking up as if measuring the daylight, 'doesn't it strike you as odd that no other cars have come down or up this road in all the time we've been here? Isn't this the main road to and from somewhere?'

'Maleny,' she replied grudgingly. 'Yeah, you're right. I was thinking the same thing.'

He pulled out his phone, tapping it. 'You got a signal? Maybe you can ring and check on them.'

'No. It must be fringe here. I've had no bars since that initial call.'

'What was Aggie doing coming all the way up here on her own, anyway?'

'She was trying to hide the Book of Names. There's a place up here we use for sanctuary. I'm guessing she was going to leave it there. It's the only really secure place I know of.'

'So she knew Dragos was coming after it?'

'I guess,' Wallace said, her tone unsure.

'For a witch, you don't seem to have that many answers.'

'No, but you still have what it takes to qualify as a fully-fledged pain in the backside.'

Milt chuckled, watching the shadow stretch past the safety rail and over the edge.

'I'm going up to take a look,' he said, standing.

'What at?'

'Maybe I can see the cavalry coming from around the other side of the bend. Or get a decent phone signal at least. Besides, I want to pee, this time in private.'

He started the climb back up the road to the blind turn. While it wasn't far, he was puffing by the time he reached it.

I didn't think I was that unfit.

The air seemed to be denser here too, making it hard to breathe. It gave him an uneasy feeling.

Rounding the turn, he stopped. Thick fog blanketed the road and the mountain. He couldn't tell where the road stopped and the drop off into the valley began. It was the thickest fog he'd ever seen. Cautiously, he stretched his hand into the mist. It felt cold, and when he drew the hand out again it was saturated, the water dripping onto the hot surface of the road. He unzipped his fly and relieved himself and then hurried back down the road and flopped beside Wallace.

'We're cut off,' he whispered. 'There's some sort of wet fog stuff blocking the road.'

'Dragos?'

'Has to be. Does it look like a foggy day to you? We have to get out of here. I don't want to be here after the sun goes down.'

'Scared of the dark?'

'Only what might come out of it.'

'And what about him?'

'He can stay there. I'm betting once we move on, this weird fog will too. The uniform guys can pick him up.'

'You mean continue on—up to Maleny?'

'What choice do we have? We're blocked in by the fog that way.'

'How? We can't walk, it's too far.'

'Your car only seems to have damage on one side. Let's see if we can't move some of that mangled mess out of the way and squeeze through with your car.'

They managed to make some room between the rock wall and the remains of the BMW and then Milt clambered over the central console of Wallace's car, flopping heavily into the driver side. It was tight. The driver door was staved in from the impact, but if he leaned in a bit he could just about fit.

He tried the ignition. The motor coughed, thought about it, and then caught. He waved Wallace over, and they scrunched through the narrow gap they'd made,and then eased the little car up the slope, stopping at the top.

'It's happening on this side too,' Milt said, pointing at the hairpin bend curving out and around the mountain. The same thick fog blanketed the road and the way into the turn, making it impossible to see.

'Wow, that's thick. I see what you mean. So, do we go through it?' she asked.

'We can't drive through it, that's for sure. It's impossible to see inside that soup. We'd end up over the edge.' Milt unbuckled his belt, pulling it free of his trousers.

'Why are you taking off your pants?'

'Don't get too excited, it's only the belt. Get out, we're going to walk out of here.' He followed her out of the car. 'Now find somewhere on your clothing to slip my belt through and then thread it back under one of the belt loops at the back of my pants.'

'Finally, we're getting hitched.'

'Buckle up, Lacey. The belt will keep us from getting separated in the fog.'

Milt started forward, easing into the thick mist. The dense, cloying feeling was the same as before, like breathing through water.

'My God, I've only taken two steps and already I'm soaked. Even the road is running with the stuff. What is it? I can barely breathe.'

'Mostly water, I hope. How's that book gonna hold up in all this?'

'The box is warded against all the elements.'

'Water... proof... guarantee, hey?' Milt huffed each word out with an effort. His heart felt too heavy, as if the blood was pooling there and not pumping through his system. Even the belt connecting him to Wallace seemed to be dragging at him. Each step was a shambling effort, breath wheezing.

'Whoa.' His foot drove deep into a pothole filled with water. He stumbled and went down, dragging Wallace with him. They rolled back down the road, rushing surface water hurrying them on. Milt threw out his arms, trying to stop himself tumbling over the edge. His hand hit the back of a post and he made a desperate grab for it.

Missed, then found another. He held on as the belt, heavy with Wallace's weight, jerked tight, nearly pulling him loose.

'Milt? Aaah, my head. What happened?'

'Pothole, big one. I lost my balance. You okay?'

'Think so. But I dropped the book when we fell. What're we going to do? I don't even know what side of the road we're on now. God knows where the edge is. I can't even see my fingers in this stuff.' Her voice sounded flat, deadened by the strange fog. Through the belt's connection, Milt could feel her shivering.

'I'm hanging on to a guide post, if that's any help.'

'There were guide posts on both sides of the road.'

'Try reaching out. Can you feel the edge of the road where the bitumen ends?' Milt asked.

'Yes.'

'All right, let's work our way back up the slope. Hands and knees. Keep track of the road's edge. That'll be our guide out of here. Come on, this stuff can't go on for much farther. We're sure to stumble onto the book; the road's not that wide.'

The rough surface cut into Milt's knees. They had always been his weakness.

'You okay?' he asked over his shoulder.

'Yes. The good news is, I won't need to worry about a knee or palm dermabrasion any time soon.'

'You know, Lacey, we were only a few meters into the fog when I hit that pothole. By rights, we should have rolled straight out of this in the tumble. And up ahead I don't see an end to this cloud stuff. If I didn't know better, I'd say we're going round in circles.'

'How can that be? We're working our way up one edge of the road. It must be going somewhere.'

'You're asking me that? I'm the resident skeptic here, remember? It's just that I get the feeling we're in Dragos's personal brand of limbo here. Like planes stacked in holding patterns at an airport, circling. On hold until he catches up.'

'That's very encouraging,' Wallace said, sneezing. 'I'm soaked, can't even see the road an arm away from my nose, and am too scared to move far in case I roll over the edge of a cliff. On top of that, I managed to lose the bloody Book of Names within an hour of getting it and I can't even seem to get a proper breath.'

'Seems like you managed a few puffs there. Better off saving them. Negative thoughts like that will drag you down faster than anything else.'

'All I keep thinking is I should have left you in Melbourne. Just sent you to look after Jess. I hope she's all right. Gran said, "Change as little as possible, Wallace." But oh, not me. I was so damned anxious to see you again, I couldn't wait to change every bloody thing.'

'You were?'

'What?' she said, sniffing.

'Anxious to see me again.'

'Oh, Milt, forget it. I'm just scared. You know I always talk too much when that happens. Remember that time—'

'Sssh.'

'Well there's no need to be—'

'Wallace please—be quiet.... Do you hear it?' he added in a whisper.

After a breath, 'Yes. Yes, I can. It's like something is being dragged along the road, something metal.'

'Maybe something like the door from a wrecked BMW?'

FIFTEEN

'Jess, have you heard a word I've been saying?'

'Martin?'

Jess shook her head, looking around.

This is my old apartment in Melbourne, before the attack. What am I doing here? Did all that really happen?

'Yes. It's Martin. Your lover,' he said, drama dripping.

Why is he here?

'I'm sorry, Martin, what's the date?'

'The date?' He did one of his "I'm pacing because I'm frustrated things" before turning to face her again. When he spoke, his lips and mouth moved with exaggerated articulation. Sunlight streamed from behind him, highlighting miniscule droplets of spittle—"passion drops," he called them. Martin always thought he was on stage.

'I'm trying to have a deep and *authentic* conversation with you about our *future together* and you're asking me what's the fucking *date?*'

'It's all right. I remember.'

The delicious smell of Indian food floated up from the Singh's apartment one floor down, and she realized she was hungry.

Licking her lips, she sat at the table. They'd already played this performance out three months ago, before the attack that had sent her running off to Brisbane. This particular scene of her life she'd woken into was the one leading up to Martin moving out. Last time it was a pathetic tragedy; this time it would be different. Jess combed her fingers through her hair, startled at its thickness and length. Of course, it was before she'd had it cut.

'Look, Martin. I can't do this right now. Why don't I make this easy for both of us? Just take your things and go. Now. No hard feelings. What's her name, the understudy in that second-rate production you're in?'

'Sonia?' he replied warily, his voice notching up to that grating whine that happened whenever the spotlight shifted.

'Of course, Sonia the redheaded Siren with acne, how could I have forgotten? Why keep her hanging? Tell her she can have you now, before this gets really nasty. Which it will, believe me.'

'What are you saying?' he said, hands moving to his thin hips.

How did I ever think they were sexy?

'What am I saying?' she parroted. 'All right, let's make this so simple, even someone like you can understand. Pack up and piss off. Clear enough?'

The blood drained from Martin's face. This felt so much better than collapsing into a weep-heap.

What had I been thinking?

His bottom lip quivered, and he flounced from the room. Idly, she wondered whether Martin was really gay and played out his denial through serial hetero conquests.

I really need to speak to Wallace but I never got her number. Milt either. How weird. Not even thinking to get the phone number of my long-lost father. Somehow, between all the crazy stuff that happened, it didn't seem relevant. Maybe they'll ring me? I hope they're all right.

But then she remembered she'd changed her number after the attack in the alley. *I do have Wallace's address. That's something. After I get rid of Martin, I'll go straight to the airport.*

She stood and went through to the kitchen to make tea. Green tea would ground her and create enough floor space for Martin to just leave without having to confront her on the way out. Down the hall, she could hear him throwing things—hopefully in the direction of suitcases. He'd use hers, of course; like many "pedestrian items that drag me down," he didn't have any of his own.

Picking up the kettle, she reached over and turned on the tap, pausing just short of the stream of water from the tap, staring down at the hand holding the kettle. Setting the kettle down on the bench, she brought both hands up in front of her face.

The ring was gone.

SIXTEEN

"How close do you think he is?' Wallace whispered.

'Too hard to tell in this fog, it distorts sound.' Milt's voice was husky, as if there were something stuck at the back of his throat. 'Any ideas? I'm fresh out.'

'There may be a way, but for it to work we need to find the book.'

'That book is as slippery as an armful of eels.'

'Let's just look. It has to be on the other side or near the middle of the road. It can't have traveled far. I'll start moving across.'

Milt felt a sideways tug on the belt at his waist as Wallace crawled across the road. He followed, moving cautiously, the uneven, hard surface further abrading his knees.

'All right, I'm on the other side,' Wallace said quietly. 'That would make you roughly in the middle. Let's start crawling back up the slope. If we keep our arms wide, we'll have more chance of stumbling onto it. God knows we won't be able to see it.'

Milt inched forward. Before each forward shuffle, he swept his arm through an arc in front of him, fingers trailing lightly across the asphalt.

'Anything?' Wallace asked.

'You'll be the first to know.'

Behind them, the sound of the scraping metal seemed louder, more insistent. Milt wondered why Shea or Dragos, or whoever it was, didn't just clear the mist. Maybe he couldn't, or—more likely—maybe he didn't have to?

'Got it,' Wallace announced.

Milt heard the clunk of something wooden and hard hit the ground. He reached out in that direction, his fingers brushing against the worn wood grain of the box. It was heavily scored with patterns, their shape reminding him of what had been carved into the tabletop in Aggie's garden. At the center he could feel some crystals; he remembered vaguely from when he'd seen it earlier that the central one had been a purpley color, surrounded on four sides by smaller pink stones that had been set into a deep circular groove. The box gave off a slight buzz, as if it had a current flowing through it.

'Okay, that's it.' Wallace's voice wafted over to him as a wash of golden light illuminated the mist. Milt could make out what could be lettering writing itself onto the mist, then a face.

Beside him, Wallace began crooning in a low voice. Other images appeared; they too were blurred, the mist too thick to see the details.

'Who the hell are they?' he said.

Wallace stopped her chant. 'I should have thought of this before. They're Sisters in the coven. The ones you can see are sort of online, available if you like. I'm going to use the book to see if they can send us some juice to clear this fog.'

More images lit up. The sound of the dragging metal door was now very close. Maybe all Wallace had done with the light was make them easier to see.

'Whatever you're doing, Lacey, can you fast track it? He's closing in.'

Wallace sang louder. Suddenly a beam of golden light speared down, parting the mist. Late afternoon sunlight filled the hole in the fog, lighting the area around them. The golden light seemed to pool on the road and then began to lift, raising the mist like a solid white blob. Soon there was a one-meter clear gap between the road and the mist. Sticking to the ground, Milt could see Shea on all fours less than five meters away. He saw them at the same time.

So he didn't know exactly where we were after all. Odd.

'Come on. Let's go,' Wallace said.

'One minute.' Getting up, Milt undid the belt connecting him to Wallace, and keeping his head below the mist, ran at Shea. The other man saw him coming and tried to swerve, but the heavy door chained to his wrist made it difficult. Milt's shoulder drove into Shea's side, and they both went down onto the door, their combined weight sending it grinding across the asphalt. Shea recovered first and was about to drive his free hand into the side of Milt's face—

'Don't even think about it,' Wallace said, kneeling on one knee, the gun extended, the book open beside her. The golden light still shone strong from the page. 'Milt, why don't you go start the car up, and I'll keep Shea company for a bit.'

Milt grunted and eased himself up. Everything hurt. He was definitely too old for this, even if he was three months younger than yesterday. Behind him, he heard Wallace order Shea to lie facedown on the road.

Milt clambered over the gear stick back into the driver seat and started the engine. When he drove over to Wallace, she transferred the gun to the other hand, flipped the book closed, scooped it up, and carefully climbed in.

Shea seemed to be oblivious to them.

Milt accelerated, and the little car moved off in a series of jerky bursts, the mist hovering just above the car's roof like thick, low cloud.

'It's not shifting,' Milt said, leaning forward to peer up through the windscreen. 'The car is just centimeters below that fog, but there's not even a flutter.'

'Who cares? We're out of it now,' Wallace said, raising her hand to point. 'See, up ahead, it just stops. The road from there on is clear.'

Milt changed down a gear. The motor was really struggling.

'She sounds sick, but there was no real damage to the front end.'

'I think it's the water, or whatever it is in the mist. Remember how hard it was to breathe? Maybe it'll be better from here on.'

They cleared the mist and moved into the late afternoon. Milt felt the pressure lift.

'Wow, I'm pleased to be out of that. So what happened back there, with the book and all?'

'Think of it as last century's version of interactivity. The book contains not only the names of all our members, but also something to hook onto their essence.'

She picked up the book from beside her feet and opened it. The golden light filled the car.

'Each entry has either a lock of their hair or nail clippings, something where all our personal information is held and can be accessed —what today we'd call a full profile. Everything about them. That's how Dragos was able to identify and get to those he killed previously. The book has all their personal details.'

'And that helped us how back there?'

She flipped to the next page and tapped one of the entries. 'See this one, it's glowing brighter than the others?'

Milt glanced over and nodded.

'That means she's tuned in, performing a ceremony or something where she's in what we call the shared zone. Like she's online, available for contact. I simply activated the links of everyone online and asked for their energetic help. They gave it instantly.'

'Like a triple-zero call for witches.'

Wallace smiled. 'Something like that. Anyway, it worked.'

'And you still have the book.'

'Yes, I do. I still feel bad about not helping Gran, even though she told me not to.'

'Yeah, I'm not sure I'd be up for it. Knowing the when and where someone I loved was going to fall off the perch.' He shook his head. 'Big call. But at least we did something to change things today. Everyone in that book is now safe. Jess included.'

SHEA STIRRED, gradually coming to his knees one at a time, and then pushed himself upright, his upper body encased within the stifling fog. He felt old. Tired, as if he'd already gone ten rounds with a heavyweight in what should have been a welter competition. His right wrist dragged, tugging the arm down where it was still attached to the BMW's door. He gave it two sharp shakes and the handcuff released, rattling onto the road.

Collect it. Collect it now.

'Yes, yes, I know,' he muttered in response to Dragos's voice inside his head.

He removed a vellum pouch from the inside pocket of his jacket and undid the leather thong securing the top. Holding the neck open, he repeated the words Dragos whispered to him. The mist moved in response, as if it were listening and deciding. After a moment, the bag trembled as the mist flowed in, carrying with it every entry it had absorbed from the Book of Names, plus the recent memories of Milt and Wallace.

Shea trailed his index finger in the flow near the neck of the bag. Images of women he'd never seen flowed past him like a breeze through a screen door, and he smiled.

This Jess lady seemed to be very interesting, and for the first time he wasn't sure whether the thought came from him or Dragos.

SEVENTEEN

'Do you know where you're going, Wallace?' Milt asked, the space between his eyebrows closing to a deep crease as he strained to see past the bouncing cone of light made by the car's headlights.

'I don't, but it does,' she said, tapping the box on her lap.

'Oh, that's all right then. As long as the old wooden box knows.'

'Not the box, idiot, the book—it knows. Thanks, by the way, for remembering to pick up its box.'

'We try to please,' Milt mumbled, swerving to avoid another large pothole in the grown-over dirt road. They'd been following it for the past hour, the tracks becoming fainter the further in they drove. Outside, it was one of those country nights that made Milt wish he'd never left the city: no moon, with heavy cloud covering the stars, and every few minutes an ominous rumble of thunder that was getting progressively louder.

Milt slowed even further. The track had wound them through and around a succession of large trees until finally spilling them out onto a narrow ridge. Fifty meters ahead it appeared to run close to the edge of a cliff. As they approached, the full force of the wind gusting up the valley buffeted the small car, rocking it.

'The track is a bit too close to the edge. I can't imagine anyone building it that way. Looks like there's been a lot of erosion.'

'I've only been here a couple of times before and that was in daylight. This looks much scarier,' Wallace said, craning forward in her seat. 'Should we chance it do you think?'

Milt's lips firmed. 'There's no room to turn around. With the storm coming, I don't like our chances of staying here, we're fully exposed. I guess we have to push on.'

The car rocked again as a huge crack of thunder burst above them. The rain followed immediately.

'Great, just what I ordered,' Milt said. 'I don't suppose that book wants to get involved, turn night into day, rain into sun, anything?'

'Sorry, it doesn't do weather.'

'Figures. Have I told you I hate this car? These dicky windscreen wipers particularly; they're just stirring the water around.'

He inched forward. The amount of water hitting the windscreen reminded him of going through an automated carwash, coupled with the glare from the headlights that refracted back through the deluge he could barely see.

'Careful.'

'Oh, right, thanks, I hadn't thought of that. Good point.'

The potholes had already filled and now the storm was working on loosening up the top layer of soil, the wheels helping to mush it into slushy mud.

'Careful, Milt,' Wallace repeated. Milt took a breath and exhaled loudly, trying to shift the tension bunching around his shoulders. In front he caught a glimpse of an eroded section that sloped away toward the drop off. Water gushing from a weathered natural gutter directed it in a torrent straight over the edge. He could feel the car wheels sliding with the force of it.

'I'm going to go for it. The longer we wait, the slipperier it will get. Game?'

'No, but I'm really pleased you are. Go on then. Hurry. Something doesn't feel right about this.'

'No kidding, said the skeptic to the psychic,' he said, shifting into second gear and accelerating smoothly. The engine roared, front wheels spinning, losing then finding traction intermittently. He could feel the back end sliding sideways.

Shit.

Milt corrected, went back to first, and slowly eased out the clutch, applying only enough power to keep the front wheels turning. Now that they were side-on, the upwind from the valley below was keeping them from sliding. Finally, the tires found rock beneath the mud and they slithered past the ridge, following the water-filled track into the forest on the other side.

'Whew. Good driving. Well, the good news is, we're close—I think.'

'Great.'

The track recommenced its weaving between the monstrous trees, the thick, leafy canopy above protecting them from the worst of the weather that howled through the branches like a rabid dog denied its kill.

'There.' Wallace pointed. A thin beam of light speared from the tip of her finger into the night, finally striking what looked like one of those red reflector plates on a roadside guidepost. It was nailed to what he now realized was a small wooden cottage set back between two enormous tree trunks. It would have been invisible without Wallace's weird light beam.

'Your lot are right into the tree thing, aren't you?' he said, pulling up alongside.

Wallace was already striding toward a flimsy-looking weathered door by the time he managed to hoist his legs over the gear stick and clamber out the passenger side.

When he reached her, she had the door open and was busy lighting a gas camping lamp on a small table.

'What is this place?' Milt said, wrinkling his nose. 'It smells like it hasn't been used for years. If this was the safe house that Aggie was going to leave her priceless book in, someone should have had a quiet word to her about security.'

He picked up an old book lying on the wooden table in the center of the room, flipping it open. 'And mold prevention,' he added, dropping the book and dusting his hands off against one another. The cottage was basically one room. Snugged into one corner was a single bed, its base strung with the same rusting mesh he'd had on his as a kid, a thin kapok mattress on its side, rested against the wall. On the opposite wall, a camp kitchen had been set up on rickety-looking tables. No plumbing, only a galvanized tub surrounded by a couple of chipped plates and mismatched cutlery. The only attractive feature was a hand-hewn stone fireplace set into the wall opposite the front door.

Milt rooted around in the wood bin next to the hearth.

'No wood, and the rain will have soaked all the wood outside by now. Did she keep any under shelter out the back, do you know?'

Wallace had pulled aside a rotting mat and was fiddling with something on the floor. She mumbled what he thought might have been a "not sure," so he shouldered open the back door. Its warped timbers screeched in protest before opening out onto a porch a step or two off the ground. Above, the roof had been holed in several places.

There was no outside wood bin but he did manage to kick out some of the uprights that supported the rotten railing and gather them into a jagged pile beneath his arm.

Turning back to the door, he said, 'It's too wild to try going back down that track tonight—'

He paused, mouth open. Inside, the squalor had been transformed. The narrow cot had somehow turned into a double bed with plumped pillows and a colorful bed covering. Opposite, a galley kitchen gleamed, its surfaces picking up the subtle beige and pink from the smooth surface of the flagstone floor.

Wallace was propped up on a three-seater lounge positioned directly in front of the blazing fire.

'What the hell happened here?' He dumped the rotting palings on the hearth beside the overflowing wood bin.

'Magic, what else?' she said, her eyes twinkling. She moved her legs aside to give him room to sit down, then replaced them across his lap. 'This,' she continued, her hands taking in the room, 'was always here—except the fire, I just lit that—we just couldn't see it. Gran used a strong enchantment to make it look derelict. That's why it's such a great place to hide stuff.'

'But how?'

'Think of it as taking two steps sideways. We entered one space, I changed the frequency, and now we see what is really there. Clever, hey?'

'That's one word for it,' Milt said, looking around. 'And Aggie did all this?'

'It was her retreat place. No one would bother with it the way we originally saw it, would they?'

'You got that right. Well, it's a lot more comfortable this way, but there's still only one bed,' he said, eyebrows wriggling as he gently laid his hand along Wallace's leg.

'And a couch.' She laughed, batting it away with her bare foot.

'Ouch.'

'Hungry?'

'Starving. Don't tell me there's food as well?'

'Let's see.' Wallace levered herself off the lounge and padded over to the kitchen, opening up the small freezer tucked into one corner.

'Gran was a vegetarian, but I remember sneaking a couple of steaks into the bottom shelf when I came up with her last. Oh yeah, here they are.'

Milt went over to give her a hand. Outside he could hear the hum of a generator which would power the plumbing and the appliances. 'So you've only been here a couple of times?' Milt asked, opening a tin of mushrooms for the sauce.

'Yeah. Wow, it seems like a long while ago and yet not—one part of me feels like it's almost like yesterday—all at the same time. It's funny, you know, coming back to this time when Gran was alive, seeing her again, and before I could do or say anything to her she's gone again, straight away. It's hard to—'

Wallace's shoulders heaved, and two fat tears rolled down her cheeks. She turned away, hand to her mouth, something Milt knew she always did when she was overwhelmed. He'd seen her do the same thing that night she'd walked out of his life. Carefully he placed an arm around her shoulders and gathered her to him, gently patting her back. She finally allowed her head to rest against his chest.

'Sorry,' she said quietly.

'So am I.'

'SO HOW WAS IT?' she asked, pushing back from the small table and taking her glass of red wine over to the lounge.

'Fantastic. The food was good too,' he said, stretching and sighing contentedly before following her to the settee.

'Don't get too comfortable over there, Lacey. That's my bed, remember.'

'Yes, I do remember, Milt. A lot of things.' She patted the seat beside her.

He lowered himself down and she turned to face him, placing one hand on his knee. The light from the fire softened the lines of her face. Milt remembered seeing her older, different, but above all she remained Lacey. He reached out a hand and laid it softly on her shoulder, feeling it relax beneath his fingers. Wallace's gaze drifted away, like a schoolgirl waiting for her first kiss. Milt felt himself leaning toward her, getting closer, when she suddenly pushed him aside and jumped to her feet.

'Jesus, Lacey, what the—'

'Look!' she shouted, running over to the Book of Names. She'd left it open earlier when she'd been fiddling with the code, or what-ever it was that dispelled the illusion of the hovel. Grumbling, Milt pushed himself up and followed. Where before all the handwritten names had shone with a golden glow, some had now turned black.

'What does it mean?' he asked.

'They're dead,' Wallace said, her voice hushed, fingers running across the dark entries as if this might somehow revive them. As she spoke, another name winked out, its essence a lock of golden hair attached beside it singeing and then falling away.

'It's starting again. Dragos is killing us, only this time much more quickly. We need to get back to the city—now. We have to warn them.'

'Can't you use that thing?' Milt asked. 'Hook up a conference psych-up or whatever you do?'

'No, it doesn't work like that. Maybe the ones online, but not for something as complicated as this. No, we have to get back into phone range. Come on.'

Milt started clearing the table.

'Leave all that. Milt, I know this is hard for you to understand without any real evidence, but believe me, right now women are being killed. Some of them are my friends. Something we've done today has somehow exposed them. Despite everything, Dragos has managed to extract their details from the book. I don't know how, and right now it doesn't really matter. What does is getting out of here and ringing them—one by one.'

'Got it. I'll drive—you call.'

Milt picked up his jacket from the back of the lounge and strode toward the door.

'Wait,' she called, 'you'll need this.'

When Milt turned, Wallace was swiveling one of the rocks set into the impressive fireplace. Something clicked, and a section of the mortared stones swung open. Wallace reached inside and with a tug drew something out, using both hands to extend it toward him.

It was the double-headed silver axe.

'I didn't think this would be necessary, but Dragos will get stronger with each new death. This is the only weapon that can stop his vessel.'

'Shea?'

'He won't be that much longer.'

'He's using the other one of these then?'

She nodded. 'The exact same. They were forged by a sorcerer centuries ago from one piece and then shaped separately, representing duality—good and evil. They look like axes but are primarily superconductors of subtle energy.'

'And you want me to have it, because?'

'Gran must have told you. You are the Protector, Jess's protector. It's up to you to keep her safe, and right now she's going to be in terrible danger. We have to find her.'

FORTUNATELY, the rain had eased and the track was navigable on the drive back to the highway and then on to Brisbane. Milt finally turned into Wallace's driveway just as the clock on the dash neared 3:00 a.m. He was exhausted. Wallace had started on the phone calls as soon as she had a strong enough signal. Despite that, another three names had winked out. The long silver axe was laid out on the back seat like some silent executioner waiting for a prospect.

He rubbed his gritty eyes. His hand still smelled of woodsmoke. Wallace wasn't moving. The smashed-in door on the driver side of this car was really starting to irritate him. Maybe he was just frustrated. He shook the memory of what might have been back at the cabin away. His time with Wallace was full of might-have-beens and if-onlys; if there was any such thing as fate, then it was working overtime to keep them apart.

'You going to get out?' he asked, irritation roughening his voice.

Wallace was squinting, as if she were trying to make something out through the windscreen. She touched the sleeve of his jacket. 'Is that someone?' she asked quietly, pointing to a dark shape huddled in the cane chair beside the front door.

'Could be. Don't take this the wrong way, but I really hope it's not your dead grandmother. Hop on out and I'll take a look.'

'Big man. I'm the one with the gun here, remember?'

'Yeah, but I've got the magic axe,' he said, reaching into the back seat and closing his hand around the handle. It was curious how it felt so right, as if it had molded itself to the shape of his fingers. Disquietingly, it also felt vaguely familiar, as if he'd held it before. In the future. Well, it would all start to catch up soon enough.

Wallace opened the door as quietly as she could and made her way up the path. The gravel driveway crunched beneath her feet. Milt struggled out and followed. If it *was* someone on the verandah, they were a sound sleeper—or one of the rising toll of dead witches.

The bundle stirred, its head lifting, lending definition to the rest of the body.

'Jess? Is that you?' Wallace asked, then ran up onto the wooden verandah. 'We've been so worried.'

Milt's chest tightened as the figure in the chair stood and with a little cry threw herself at Wallace.

'I didn't know where you were. I decided just to wait,' he heard her say. She caught sight of Milt around Wallace's shoulder. 'Milt! Oh, it's so good to see you—both of you.'

He grinned back; she did sound pleased to see him. Really pleased. He was more surprised, though, at the curious mix of relief and joy that had welled in him at the sight of her. Trotting up the broad steps to the verandah, he encircled them both in one-armed hug, tucking the axe behind him with the other. After a time, Wallace wriggled free, opened the door and hustled them inside, peppering Jess with questions.

'Better let her catch her breath, Lacey,' Milt said, securing the deadlock, thinking that maybe this was all too easy after what Wallace and he had just been through.

What if Dragos had already gotten to Jess?

He turned and with a forced smile said, 'Jess, you must be all in. Why don't you go up and freshen up? Come on down when you're ready and we can all catch up over some of Wallace's horrible tea?'

Jess gave him a curious glance, then nodded. She bounced up the stairs, disappearing down the hall toward the bathroom.

When he turned, Wallace's eyebrows were raised and her arms crossed over her chest. Never a promising sign. He held up his hand, palm out. 'Look, I know. This is your house and your bag of worms, but before you go off at me again, think just for one minute.'

'About?'

'Jess. How do we know it's really her?'

'You mean she could be—'

'One of Dragos's illusions or creations or whatever the heck he does to them.'

'But why? He has the Book of Names. What possible use could there be for that?'

'The means to stop the real Jess, wherever she might be. Perhaps simply to gain our trust, find out what we know. It just seems odd that we come home and find her here waiting on your doorstep as if nothing has happened just hours after all your people start dying on our watch.'

'I can answer that. Some of it anyway.'

They both spun toward the voice. Jess was halfway down the stairs, hands gripping the banister as she faced them, her knuckles white.

'I ended up back in my old Melbourne flat halfway through a stand-up barney I remember having once before with Martin, my ex. When I finally managed to get rid of him, I realized I needed to let you know I was okay but didn't have your phone numbers, so I did the next best thing and jumped on a plane.' She glanced down at Milt's hand. 'What are you doing with that axe, Milt?'

'You've seen it before?' he asked, still wary.

'Yes, I told you when you and Wallace came to my place here in Brisbane. You also had it that night the scarred man chased me. I thought you were the Hacker, remember, but you saved me.'

Milt and Wallace exchanged a glance. Milt nodded, relaxing the fingers that had been tightening around the axe handle. Only the real Jess would know that.

'Let's go have that tea now,' Wallace said. 'We obviously have a lot to talk about and not a great deal of time.'

They followed Wallace through the hall into the kitchen, filling Jess in on what had happened that afternoon and evening.

'This looks different,' Jess said, looking around the old wooden cupboards lining the walls.

'I haven't had the renovations done yet. You saw it after they'd been finished,' Wallace said. 'The builder is booked in for a couple of weeks.'

'The "after and before" look, hey? Makes a change to the traditional way.' Milt pulled out one of the old kitchen chairs and flopped down at the table. 'I still don't know how Dragos managed to get all those contacts from the book.'

'It doesn't matter,' Wallace said. 'He did, and because he managed it we have to assume he knows much more.'

'Like?'

'What we've been doing, what Jess is supposed to do.'

'There's something else,' Jess said. 'You may not be able to tell, but the ring, Mum's ring, has gone.'

'Gone? It can't have,' Wallace said.

'When?' Milt asked.

'I noticed it wasn't there just after I—got back.'

'To Melbourne? Milt, have you...?' She glanced down at his hand.

Milt shook his head. 'Before my time. Never thought I'd say that much anymore, but I reckon that means the ring is where it would have been in this time period before I *found* it.'

'If you're right, then Jess's mother would still have it.'

Milt watched Wallace's eyes widen as she mentally processed the linear progression.

'Oh no.'

'What?'

'Jess, what date did your Mum pass?' Milt asked gently, his fingers lightly touching the young woman's arm.

'I don't know. She just disappeared. She must have done it after she heard about Aggie's death. That could make it tomorrow.'

'If Dragos gets to that ring, then all bets are off.'

'You mean Mum is going to die tomorrow?'

'Oh, honey,' Wallace said. 'I know what you're thinking. I just went through the same thing with Gran. We can't change people's destiny if it's their time to die. I'm just coming to realize that with the sisters who have just passed.'

'How do we know that? Milt asked. 'Say we go there now. Get to her in time—with Jess. Maybe she'll make a different decision. We could try.'

'Or maybe Dragos will complete her destiny for her and she won't have to take her own life.'

'No offence, but go crap on your destiny,' Milt said, holding up his phone screen. 'See this. Remember that twenty-to-one outsider I backed? The sure thing I saw win over the favorite at Flemington that I backed last time? Well, this is a text from my bookie reminding him I owe him a thousand bucks because the "sure thing" lost. Not only that, it stepped in the same frigging hole as the horse I backed the first time. Stumbled on the line. Same hole, different horse, same horse's arse punter. This proves there is no destiny, Wallace; the present is variable. Stuff happens that affects other stuff. I just wish it would stop costing me money.'

'Very scientific, even for you, but what about if it was your destiny to lose on that day, regardless of which horse you backed?'

'So you're saying I'm a loser?'

'No. Look, no one really knows how it works. The Sisters believe we have free will up to a point but there are also pivotal moments in life that we can't avoid even if we had the opportunity to choose differently. This may have been one of yours.'

'A frigging horse race is my pivotal moment?'

'If it wasn't, we wouldn't be having this conversation—and it's given me an idea to test it out. Jess, do you have your mum's address?'

EIGHTEEN

Angelique Watkins lived in the Dandenongs, not far from Melbourne. They hired a car at the airport. Milt could hear his bag containing the giant silver axe moving around in the boot with the motion of the car as they wended their way around the curves.

Overhead, gray scudding clouds chased each other in a constant stream before a freshening wind. By the time they hit the foothills, it had turned cold and gusty-bleak, what his daughter used to call a Victorian gray-out.

Welcome home.

'We're close, I think. Here! Stop! I think that's it,' Jess said, a ripple of excitement catching in her voice.

Milt slowed and pulled over, peering where Jess was pointing. The driveway was overgrown, not quite as bad as the track to Aggie's mountain cottage but there were similarities. A plastic barrel had been nailed to a post beside the driveway, a purple 25 drawn on it, surrounded by hand-painted yellow flowers.

'This looks like the right number,' he said. 'I'll park further along, and we can walk back. We don't want to spook her by driving in.

From the looks of the undergrowth, it doesn't look like she gets too many visitors.'

'Mum always was a free spirit. She valued her independence above everything,' Jess said, slamming the door. 'It's weird to think she was dead and now she's not.'

Wallace and Milt followed. Wallace cupped her hand at the side of her mouth to say quietly to Milt, 'This could be tricky. I'm sensing some stuff in Jess about Angelique. Remember, she's already gone through the news of her mum's death and she's already speaking about her in the past tense—this could be hard for her.'

Milt nodded and lengthened his stride to catch Jess up. 'How's it going?' he asked, reaching her.

'Fine.'

'No, really, it's all right to say—'

Jess turned to face him. 'Look, I know what you're trying to say—I overheard Wallace just then—she and you just don't get the whispering thing, do you? And I appreciate it, truly, but it'll be fine.'

'Fine?' Milt repeated, reaching out to grab her arm, preventing her from charging off again. 'I just think we need a plan before we go bursting in on someone who is quite likely to be suicidal. Think about what it might mean for you to see your mum before she dies.' He paused, waiting. Finally Jess crossed her arms, gripping each with its opposite hand, and nodded jerkily.

Milt went on, his voice slow and calm and reasoning. 'Maybe if you ring her first, tell her you're outside and want to come up to the house, something like that.'

Wallace joined them, slipping her arm around Jess's shoulders.

Jess shrugged it off and snorted. 'Like, oh so cas-u-al.' She vamped up her voice. 'Oh Mummy, I've arrived in the middle of nowhere, just passing you know.' She paused, biting her lower lip. 'Yeah, sure, why not?' Jess slipped out her phone and found the number. Milt heard the ring both from the phone next to Jess's ear and distantly from the house.

'Mum? Yeah, it's me. I want to come up and see you,' Jess said. Milt detected the tonal change. She sounded more like a kid now.

'No, I'm here. Outside. Yeah.' A giggle. 'On the road. Okay, er, I have some friends with me. No,' she eyed Milt and Wallace wickedly, 'they're cool. Mostly, anyway. Sure.' She ended the call. 'She was miffed at first, then she sounded pleased, relieved almost.'

'Maybe this is a good thing,' Wallace added as they walked up the drive, ducking branches and side-stepping enormous prickly bushes.

Whichever way this ended, at least Angelique and Jess would get to see each other once more, even if it was just to say goodbye.

The house was tucked into the trees, a light wind tugging at the white smoke from the central firebox chimney. While unloved, the house was doing its level best to look trendy in a strangely sixties way. Fibro roof and walls with mismatched wooden push-out windows containing frosted panes. A rickety-looking deck, covered by a canvas sail saggy with leaves and pooled brownish water looked like a "good idea" afterthought. Somehow though, it still worked with the wooden French doors to give it an indoor/outdoor flavor. Angelique was waiting on the deck for them, her forearm at her brow as if to block bright sun, long hair a mixture of the blonde Milt remembered and long threads of gray whipping back and forth in the wind.

'Hi, Mum,' Jess said, pausing five meters from the deck and giving a half-hearted wave. Milt was reminded of the difference in how she'd greeted Wallace, a relative stranger, the previous night. Yeah, there was definitely a truckload of stuff nesting in that five-meter gulf.

'Who's this? Cops? You hang out with cops now, Jess? Well, they'll be disappointed. I got no stuff here. Nothing! Hear me? I'm clean. So clear off, the lot of ya.'

Wallace approached Angelique slowly. 'Angie? It's me, Wallace. I'm Aggie's granddaughter, do you remember? From the Sisterhood.' She gestured at Milt. 'This is a friend of mine, Milt. He's helping Jess. She's had a few problems lately.'

'Problems?' Angie said, the word a little too slow, the emphasis on the wrong parts. No wonder she "had nothing"—she'd probably tanked herself up with all she had left. Suicide was a hard place to get to, even for the committed.

Milt realized she was staring at him. 'I know you,' she said, swaying slightly, steadying herself against the back of one of the green plastic chairs. It wobbled but held, both bending to support each other.

'I'm Milt. Jess's father.'

'Oh Christ.' Angie bent from the waist and threw up over the railing.

Wallace hurried up the steps, gathering the retching woman's shoulders. 'Let's get her inside. Jess, can you get some water and maybe a cloth?'

Milt held the screen door for them, then helped settle Angie into a chair at an old Formica table. Jess went into the adjoining kitchen, returning with an obviously used glass and a wet tea towel. Wallace dabbed the cloth around Angie's face.

'Sorry. You all gave me a bit of a shock, just turning up like that.'

'How are you, Mum?' Jess asked. Milt recognized the tone of it from his own childhood. It was shorthand for "are you straight, or do I have to be the adult here again?"

'I'm all right,' Angie replied, rallying to sit more upright in the chair. 'I guess I know why you're all here.'

'You do?' Wallace asked. 'Why is that, dear?'

'It's nearly time. For those damned Scrolls, isn't it? If he's Jess's father, then that also makes him the bloody Protector or Enforcer or whatever the hell you lot call it.' She pulled away, stabbing her index finger toward Wallace. 'Well, I won't do it. You hear me? If you and Aggie and all the rest of them want to do this, then do it without me. And neither is she,' Angie said, as if suddenly remembering Jess. 'I tried to keep you away from this, all these years. That's why we kept moving, but they always found us.'

She turned to Jess, her eyes widening. 'They treat this ring like it's the Holy bloody Grail. To me, it's just been a curse. I've spent forty years trying to get the damned thing off, I even thought of chopping off my finger as a way to get rid of it.'

Milt looked away, the memory of her in the stone casket still fresh. The thunking sound of the axe. He tuned back in again.

'...been like a rotting piece of flesh like that giant bloody bird they tied around that sailor's neck, always dragging me around, stopping me from getting my life together. Scrolls, who ever heard such rubbish? Thank God you turned out all right in spite of it all, Jess. I never wanted you to have to be part of this.' She paused, her eyes unfocusing for a moment before she said, 'I'm pleased I got to see you before... before anything happened.'

Wallace knelt down beside Angie's chair, her hand continuing to stroke. 'We don't want you to do anything, Angie. Nothing. You don't have to. Jess has agreed to take that on.'

'What have you done to her? Brainwashing, is that it? I always knew—'

Jess reached across the table. 'No, Mum. I've seen what is going to happen. It's horrible; everything they tried to tell us is true. The future, the whole life of the planet is damned unless we, I, help them.'

'Seen it? How?' Angie pulled her hand away.

Jess closed her eyes, seemingly searching for the best way to describe the impossible to a mind wracked by distrust and hazy delusions. 'That doesn't really matter right now. I've agreed to help the Sisterhood, but I need the ring to do so.'

'Jess, can you see the ring?'

'Yes, it's blinking.'

'It senses you. It's ready to migrate,' Wallace said. 'Angie. Will you help Jess make the transfer?'

Angie sniffed, her lips forming into a thin line. Milt thought she was going to refuse for a moment, until finally she opened her fist and placed the hand palm down on the table.

Milt blinked. The memory returned of the ring tight around his pinky, blinking when Jess was near. He couldn't imagine having to wear it for forty years.

'Take it, Jess,' Wallace said.

'No.' Angie snatched her hand away. 'I wouldn't wish this curse on anyone. Especially not my daughter, and you can't expect me to. I don't care what you've told her.'

'Angie, the ring will gravitate to her whether you want it to or not. It'll just be easier if you make the transfer yourself. Easier on you, and Jess.'

Milt felt sorry for her. It seemed to him that she'd never completely grown up. The whizzy-dizzy hippie he'd known with the flowing blonde hair, wasp-shaped figure, and bare, dainty dancing feet was excusable in youth; but now the feet were just dirty and exposed, clothes stained and faded, her features gaunt as if the drugs had vacuumed up her vitality from the inside, leaving only a parody of what used to be.

'Mum, it's all right, truly. I want to do this.'

Angie stared back, her eyes rimmed with red, damp with unshed tears.

Slowly she replaced her hand on the table, fingers spread. Jess set hers down next to it. The ring blipped into sight as the transition was made.

'How does it know?' Jess asked, holding it up.

'It's gone. I can't see even see it anymore,' Angie said, rubbing the empty space on her finger.

'It's done,' Wallace said.

'Mum, we also need the Cipher. Is it here?'

Angie shook her head.

Milt leaned over and whispered in Angie's ear, 'Is it in the casket?'

She jumped as if he'd pinched her.

'Is it?' he persisted.

She shrugged.

'Take me there. The others don't have to know about what you planned, but Jess needs it. Without it, she could be in danger.'

He shot a warning glance across the table toward Jess, who looked like she was about to say something. It would break the flow.

Finally Angie nodded.

Milt helped her to her feet, following her through the house, out the back door, and into a yard that saw too little sun. The ground was mushy, the soil squelching in places beneath his boots. She wove around some low-hanging branches, and he followed, feeling like a blundering bull elephant following a gazelle through the under-growth. Twenty meters in and he could no longer see the house; the track, if you could call it that, was barely visible. Off to the left, he caught glimpses of the pool of water he'd splashed through in the mental trip he'd gone on in the restaurant with Aggie that first time. It didn't pay to think on that stuff for too long.

Five meters in front, Angie paused and knelt down, almost reverently.

Milt slowed as he approached the casket, the lid off to one side on its castors, ready to receive her.

'Interesting piece of sculpture,' he said, the memories cascading over him like inexpertly shuffled cards.

She glanced up like she'd forgotten why they were here. 'Thanks. I sculpted it myself.'

Milt looked around. Scattered around, he could see chunks of the same rock, the edges too sharp to be naturally made.

'You did it? Here? What, from one rock?'

She nodded, reaching forward into the back of the casket and retrieved a small satchel. She handed it to him.

'This is what you asked for. It's all there. I've never opened it.'

Milt turned the satchel over in his hands. It seemed to be made from some sort of animal skin. It had the feeling of suede. He folded it in half, tucking it into the inside pocket of his jacket.

'Yet you wanted it buried with you?'

'No, I wanted it to remain hidden forever, along with that bloody ring.'

'I can relate to that.' Milt was on the point of telling her his own ring story when he heard something and paused. 'Did you hear that?'

Angie shrugged. 'Birds, animals, it could be anything out here.'

'No, no, it's more like.... Come on, I need to get back to the house.'

Milt left her there and started trotting back the way they'd come, increasing his pace as the sounds became clearer. Voices, people shouting. Calling his name.

NINETEEN

Milt slid to stop at the edge of the bush. Through gaps between vines and branches he could see the back of the house. The shouting had stopped, and an unnatural quiet had descended—even the birds, so raucous before, seemed to be waiting and listening.

Something else didn't seem quite right. He brought to mind an image of the yard and house when he'd left and compared it to what he could see now. It was a trick he'd developed as a detective; mental snapshots, he called them. And there it was.

The back door was now open. He remembered closing it before he'd dived into the bush after Angie. An open door in this situation could mean one of two things: the people inside left in a hurry, or someone from outside had entered quietly.

He followed the bush fringe around the perimeter of the house, placing his feet carefully to avoid snapping noisy branches until he reached the front. No one. The house was too dark to be able to see through the French doors.

This could be nothing. Then he remembered Angie. What was she be doing now? He crouched down, trying for a diagonal view back the way he'd come.

Shit!

Oblivious of everything, she was heading straight up to the back of the house. No choices now. He pushed his way past a bush with long green thorns and ran toward the deck, clearing the steps in one leap, pounding across the weathered boards and bursting through the door. The lounge room and adjoining dining/kitchen were empty, the firelight flickering through the glass in the combustion heater the only movement. There was no sign of a disturbance; the glass and cloth they'd used earlier were still on the table. Angie entered from the back.

'Where are they?'

'The back door was open. Maybe they went to get the car? I'll check. You wait here.'

He seemed to recall that Angie didn't have a high stress threshold and under pressure tended toward panic. If there was trouble, keeping her with him would only complicate things. Logically, the threat should have moved on with Wallace and Jess, so leaving Angie in the house should be safe—for now.

She made a half-hearted protest as he rushed past and out the back door. There were footprints in the marshy ground, leading away from the house into the bush, but in the general direction of the road. Individual imprints were hard to make out as they were partly obliterated by what was obviously a man-sized boot. That probably meant the women's impressions were laid down first and the booted man was following.

Milt's only weapon was the double-bladed axe, and he cursed himself for leaving that in the boot of the car. The front driveway would be the fastest way back to the car. He sprinted, knees protesting at the sudden burst, dodging potholes and branches along the drive until he reached the road, slowing to a stop as he neared where he'd parked the car.

It was gone.

.   .   .

ANGIE'S CAR was a tired Toyota from the early nineties, faded from red to an oxidized matte maroon. The driver door, however, was white, and almost closed properly when he pulled it shut.

'Accident. No insurance. A friend put the new door on for me from the wreckers,' Angie said through the open window. 'And if you want to close the window you have to sort of pull the top of the glass up as you turn the handle to get it to stay there.'

'Got it.' Milt grinned, anxious to be gone. 'Thanks for the car, I'll bring it back as soon as I find them.'

'No worries, I'm not going anywhere—not anymore,' she called after him.

He stopped the car at the end of the drive, unsure which way they would have gone. If they were being chased, Wallace would have chosen the most direct escape route. The road narrowed at this point. There would have been no quick way for her to turn back toward Melbourne. She would probably have continued the way the car was pointing.

He swung the cracked steering wheel to the left and accelerated, the back end fishtailing in loose gravel before finding traction against the asphalt. Holding the car steady with one hand, he tried Wallace's mobile with the other. It went straight to voicemail. *'This is Detective Wallace. I am on annual leave at the moment...'* He clicked off, then saw a missed call on his screen.

Wallace. She'd left a message. He rang his own voicemail and retrieved it.

"Milt, Shea is here. He's standing out front just staring at the house holding one of the axes. His stance looks weird, like he's drugged out, and the scars are back all over his face. I'm taking Jess out the back. If you get this message, meet us at the car. Otherwise, white and one.'

"White and one" was their old code for taking a coffee break at the nearest available place. He smiled, remembering Wallace calling him a coffee snob in the car just a few... well, time was turning out to be a mobile event. It was recently, anyway. So much had happened since. He pushed the old Toyota up to ninety. It responded reluctantly. In front, the road opened up to a short, straight section. There were no other cars in sight. He tried Wallace's number again. It bleeped back. No signal.

Forest continued along both sides of the road. There were no buildings of any kind that he could see, much less coffee shops. Rounding the next bend, he caught sight of a motorbike coming toward him, a red Ducati, its driver in black leather, a tinted visor over his helmet. It passed with a growl. Serious money between two wheels.

It was followed by a green Ford Transit campervan and a farmer's battered ute, with two black-and-white cattle dogs in the tray, testing the wind with their long tongues.

Still no cars on his side of the road.

He was considering turning around and heading back the other way when he spotted a peeling sign ahead advertising Devonshire Teas and a warm fire, 500 meters. He slowed, turning into the drive, sighting a small cottage. No cars outside. The place seemed to be closed.

Milt stopped the car, using his shoulder to help the door when the handle wouldn't quite engage. It clunked open, dropping on its hinges. Climbing out, he examined the scene in front of him. The door to the café was shut; furniture that would normally be arranged on the shaded verandah was stacked neatly inside. The red brick chimney for the promised "warm fire" was smokeless. It didn't look like there would be any "white and ones" here today, but that might not have put Wallace off. Milt made his way along the front to the far side. A narrow drive protected by a drooping chain with a faded "private" sign hanging from it ran along the side of the cottage. The chain was rusty, the driveway overgrown, but Milt could just make out some flattened patches of clover. A car had been down here recently. He stepped over the chain and made his way along the building, hugging the wall, prepping his arms and shoulders for a fight.

The back of the cottage was as deserted as the front: an old-fashioned wooden clothesline, a couple of fruit trees in need of a heavy pruning, and two derelict cars on blocks, the weeds growing beneath and up into the wheel wells. The light rain that had been threatening all afternoon finally became tired of waiting and drifted over him in fine, misty sheets. He swiped it away from his eyes, narrowing them, trying to put himself in Wallace's shoes. The derelict cars were empty, the back door to the café secured by a large padlock.

'Wallace?' he called softly, then tried her phone again. It must be off, as it went straight to voicemail.

He was about to leave when he noticed a gap in the galvanized mesh fence at the back of the yard. It could be wide enough. He strode over to it; wheel tracks had recently flattened the long grass. They led off to the right. Following, Milt finally found their car. Wallace was standing off to one side, the long axe handle leaning against her thigh, the gun from the glovebox pointing straight at him.

'Finally. Where the hell have you been?' she said, lowering the weapon and reholstering it with a shove.

'Me? You're the ones that took off. Where's Jess?'

'In the car. I told her to lie on the back seat.'

'Yeah, some hideout,' Jess said, climbing out. 'Hey Milt.'

He grinned and winked. 'So what happened? I got your message, obviously. What happened to Shea?'

Wallace shrugged. 'He was behind us, I know that, I caught him in the rearview a couple of times. That red Ducati was hard to miss. He must have gone straight past.'

Milt straightened. 'Red Ducati? I passed it, a few klicks back. It was going the other way.'

'Where's Mum?' Jess asked, looking around.

MILT FOUND Angie where he expected. The stone casket was closed when he reached it. He motioned to Wallace, and she put her arm around Jess, preventing her from following.

He slipped his finger into the glyph containing the locking mechanism and waited for the click as the latches disengaged. Sliding it across, he found Angie arranged inside, her left arm severed, the limb placed neatly across her chest. It looked like she'd bled out. He closed the casket again, and looking over at the two women, shook his head.

'BUT I HEARD YOU SHOUTING, calling my name.'

'I don't think so, Milt. We were trying not to draw attention to ourselves while Shea was outside. The last thing I would have done was shout,' Wallace said.

Failing light and the rapidly deteriorating weather had encouraged Milt to follow a Vacancy sign he spotted on the gate of a small cottage-based B&B just outside Emerald, a small village in the Dandenongs.

'I know what I heard,' Milt persisted, blowing on, then loudly slurping at a mug of hot tea.

'And I know what I was doing. That's not to say I wasn't shouting mentally. Hey, you could be becoming sensitized. All that time slipping, back and forth, could have done it. Wow, that would be something. Milt becoming a sensitive, who'd-a-thought it?' Wallace said, chuckling and shaking her head.

'Shouldn't you be checking on Jess?' he asked, voice sullen.

'Oh, she's fine. The ensuite is twice the size of your bedroom and is completely secure. She needs some time on her own to integrate everything that happened this afternoon—and take it from me, one of the best ways to do that is in a hot spa bath.'

They both sipped their tea, allowing the silence to stretch comfortably between them. Outside, rain pattered against the windows, driven by a squally wind, its faint sighing around the eaves making the lounge space with its crackling fire cozy.

'So what now?' Milt asked finally.

'Dinner. It's about half an hour away. The lady of the house told me when she dropped off the tea. It should be tasty, if these biscuits are any guide.'

'You know what I mean,' Milt said, pushing himself to his feet and moving across to the fireplace, stirring the embers with a poker before laying a new log on top. He turned his back to the fire, hands clasped behind him, looking at Wallace. 'I mean what do we do next?'

Wallace sighed and flopped back into her chair. 'I don't know. Thanks to you, Jess has recovered the ring and we now have the Cipher, but none of us can read it.'

'Probably why they're called ciphers,' he quipped.

'Funny guy.'

'I try.'

'Not hard enough.'

Milt felt that one thud home and changed tack. 'I thought all Jess had to do was place the ring on the Cipher and it would upload, or whatever you called it.'

'That's right, but the language it's in must be able to be comprehended by the Messenger. Jess's initiation was incomplete, remember. She doesn't know how to do that. Gran's fast cooking could only cover so much before it would have sent her into overload. Anyway, the good thing is we still have time. The window for the Scrolls isn't due to open for a while.'

'But remember what your Gran said about time moving faster when we move back through it. I can already feel that happening. Did you notice how short the day seemed to be today?' Milt asked.

'I thought that was just winter. Days are naturally shorter then.'

'No, I don't think so. What's more, the effect may escalate. We traveled back a long way, remember.'

'So we may not have as much time as we thought?' Wallace asked.

'No. Is there anyone who can be a bit more specific?'

'I'll call in some of the girls; one of the older ones I know might be able to help. She's the unofficial leader of the Sisterhood until we can call a formal gathering.'

'Assuming Shea doesn't get to her first.'

Wallace puffed out her cheeks. 'You're a cheery bugger to have around—have I ever told you that? Anyway, I've managed to warn everyone. They'll be harder to find now.'

'So where's that leave our mate Dragos? Doesn't he need all those dead bodies to manifest himself?'

'Supposedly, but I don't know what the critical mass is. He may already have enough.'

'He obviously took Angelique out,' Milt said, 'Poor beggar. You may be right, it can't be a numbers game for him, otherwise he'd have gone after you two first. It was almost as if he were leading us away so he could have time to go back on his own.'

'I've been wondering about that too. Whatever way Dragos managed to get the information on the Sisterhood, it seems to be much more comprehensive than it was the last time, when he was trying to find the ring by elimination. Today he knew exactly who had it and where she could be found. It was just fortunate that we made the exchange when we did. That wasn't the case before.'

'Angie still managed to die on the same day and in the same casket. Only the method varied,' Milt said gloomily.

'Well, you're the one who claimed nothing in the future was set in concrete. You and your bloody horses.'

'Are we back to that?' he said, feeling the irritation rise. He felt hot and took a step away from the fire.

'See, I told you. You are getting more sensitive. Especially to criticism,' Wallace snapped back.

'Are you two arguing again?' Jess asked from the stairs, trying to wind a thick towel around her hair.

'Just letting off a little steam. It's been a strange day,' Milt said, pausing before adding in a neutral tone, 'Hasn't it, Lacey?'

Wallace took a big inhale and sighed it out. 'Yes. Yes, it has been one crazy day. One of the many. I'm sorry, Milt.' Wallace sipped more of her tea. 'You know, the even crazier thing is I have to go home tomorrow and arrange Gran's funeral—all over again.'

'I guess I'll have to as well. How do I do that? Mum's already buried herself.' Jess came down the rest of the stairs before folding herself down next to Wallace on the two-seater, laying her head on her shoulder.

'Wallace keeps telling me I'm becoming more sensitive, and if that's so, I got the distinct impression that Angie is where she wanted to be. There's no real need to disturb her, as far as I can see,' Milt said.

'Milt's right. If you like, we could make it a double memorial service with Gran. Though with Shea still on the loose, who knows if anyone will come? Last time the killings hadn't really started when Aggie died.'

There was a knock at the door. Milt walked over and opened it a crack, his boot and shoulder holding it secure while he took a look.

'Ah, dinner is served,' he said, opening the door wide.

'Here we are.' The gray-haired owners carried in two trays, filling the room with wonderfully rich smells.

'We'll set up the table for you,' the woman said, methodically laying out the cutlery and linen napkins. 'It's a good thing you arrived when you did.'

'Yes, the weather has certainly closed in.'

'Not only that,' she said, straightening with an effort, 'we had another fellow ride up just after we'd checked you in. On a motorbike, asking about a room. I had to tell him your little group had just taken our last cottage. I gave him the name of a few other B&Bs close by. Shame, poor fellow, I felt sorry for him. It looked like he'd been in an accident at some stage, scars all over his face.'

Milt closed the door behind them. 'Shea is obviously letting us know that he knows where we are—if he wants us.'

'Mind games?' Jess asked, her nose wrinkling disbelief. 'Really?'

'Sounds like it, plus a bit of caution. He's only one guy after all,' Milt said, sitting down at the table, pulling one of the steaming plates toward him. 'Ah, cottage pie just the way I like it—nice and big.'

'That's where you're wrong, Milt: he's not just one man. Dragos is a demon,' Wallace said.

'Ah, demon schmemon,' he said, waving his fork in the air. 'If he's that all-powerful, why isn't he here slicing us up right now, sucking up more magic power from our dismembered limbs? That makes twice in one day he's let us off.'

'I think he's waiting,' Wallace replied, pushing food around her plate. Milt pretended not to notice. For Wallace to not be hungry meant she was either sick or really worried.

'For what?'

'Well,' she said, putting aside her cutlery along with the pretense of eating, 'we have the axe. It's the only weapon capable of stopping him.'

'That didn't stop him before—when I was in Melbourne,' Jess said. 'Milt had the axe then and he still came after me.'

'No, you're missing something,' Milt said, reaching for Wallace's plate and scraping its remains onto his. 'You're assuming his behavior is consistent. It's not, that's what I was trying to get at before.'

'So you're saying that the one thing we have now that we didn't the first time is the Cipher.'

'That's what it sounds like to me.'

'Even though I don't know how to read it?' Jess interjected.

'He doesn't know that,' Wallace said, weighing her words, index finger wagging as she put it together in her head. 'He'll assume that because the Cipher was created by our group, one of us will be able to read what it says.'

'That would be logical. So then what?' Milt asked.

'You know everything came unstuck when we were inside that fog he created. Somehow it sucked up everything inside the Book of Names after I activated it.'

'You mean when all that gold writing appeared.'

'Yes. Looking back now, I think Dragos planned it that way. Using the book was

always going to be the only way out of that fog; it just took me a while to get there.'

Milt cupped a hand to his ear. 'Is that the "let's beat up Wallace's lousy witch skills" song I'm hearing?'

'I'm just being factual,' she snapped. 'How did he know we'd be here today? Luck? There are hundreds of names in the Book of Names, why pick on Angelique? There was no mention in the book that she was the keeper of the ring.'

'So, he followed us,' Milt persisted.

'Will you stop sounding like a burned-out old dick?'

'Oh, charming,' Milt said, grinning across the table. 'Not in front of the children, dear.'

'Oh, I see where you're going, with this,' Jess said, nodding. 'What if we split up?'

'Unlike father,' Wallace said, indicating first Milt, then Jess, 'like daughter.'

'Split up? How does that help?'

'It means if I show Jess how to maintain the energetic levels as if all three of us were still here, I can go and find us a witch who can read this damn animal skin for us. Shea won't even know I'm gone.'

TWENTY

The rain had stopped about an hour ago, though the woolen rug Wallace had tugged out of the dog's kennel and thrown over her shoulders was still wet. The dog had been out, probably curled up and cozy inside the B&B's main house on what had turned out to be a bitterly cold night.

Wallace adjusted the car heater, moving it to high, and slipped the blanket onto the seat beside her, the smell of wet dog clinging. Surely not even Dragos's remote scenting would have detected her beneath that.

Overhead, the rising wind had tugged holes in the cloud cover and was now busy herding them back toward the coast, Wallace doing her best to chase them. She was betting Dragos wouldn't have expended the additional energy necessary to keep the cottages under surveillance. Controlling a surrogate through pure will was draining even for an entity like Dragos. Once daylight came, he might have Shea drive by, but their cottage was at the back and not visible from the road. Unless he came right into the driveway, it might take him a while to realize the rental car was no longer there. By then, Wallace hoped to be off the Sydney flight and on a train up to the Blue Mountains. With any luck, she'd see Old Mary, get the key to allow Jess to read the Cipher, and be back in time for dinner. She had to be, otherwise her clever plan would start to break down along with the complex energetic pattern she'd woven over Milt and Jess.

Those two were such a strange pairing. Polar opposites, yet still so much alike—sometimes infuriatingly so. Wallace smiled, remembering the bouncing banter across the table earlier in the night. It had been like watching ping pong as the comments slammed from one end and back to the other, Wallace in the middle, like always, watching the net, ready to call the fouls.

They'd even conspired about where they'd been together. "You look good old," had been Milt's major commentary about his foray into the future. It was dispiriting to realize that her future self was the same boring, inflexible rule watcher as she was today. Even more so because Milt seemed to have changed so much.

The longer he was around, the harder it was to remember what he'd really been like before. The time shifts hadn't helped in keeping track—and that was another thing: who was this Milt? A painter? And not bad, if that drawing was anything to go by. He'd not only captured the likeness but also the energy around the man, if man Shea still was.

Old Milt would have cracked by now—the bull would definitely not only have left the china shop, he would have taken the plate glass with him. Which version was more likeable? She'd almost stumbled a couple of times. When he'd put his hand on her leg on the way up the coast, and later, thank God they hadn't had to stay overnight in Gran's cottage—that bed had looked.... She felt her face flush. Well, it had been a while, and they say anything starts to look good after a bit, even old discarded lovers.

A car approaching from the other direction flashed her, and she belatedly dimmed her own headlights. *Focus, Wallace.* She took a deep breath and brought her attention back to the road. If she couldn't change herself, then maybe she could be the change, a catalyst. What had her old science teacher used to say? A catalyst makes change happen, yet within itself stays the same. Not as exciting, or inspiring, but if that was all there was, then it would do. It would have to. Gran's voice piped in from some laid down track, *"We exist to serve, Wallace. That's all. Service is all."*

BEHIND, unseen by Wallace, the car that had just passed swerved, tires screeching, traction control and ABS fighting for stability over the uneven bitumen. The driver slowing, panting, stopping, unsure now whether he'd really seen two red eyes coming toward him out of the dark; the sound of a revving motorbike still reverberating in his ears.

OLD MARY'S HOUSE, like so many of the Sisterhood, was nestled within nature in the mountains. "Lovingly ensconced," Gran used to say. The two women had been very close, both going through their initiation in the same year, even taking rotational turns as leader of the Sisterhood. Both always seemed to know what the other one was thinking or about to say.

Mary, however, had never had children, and that may have embittered her. Wallace recalled the deep lines of disapproval on either side of her mouth. There must have been a "Young Mary" once, her life tree still heavy with hopes and dreams that, over time, she'd been forced to watch fall one by one—some withered and dry, others green and unformed, their nourishment diverted to the overriding greater need of the Sisterhood. Mary was martyred to the cause—and didn't mind who knew it.

Wallace stopped the car in front of the house. The same high gabled slate roof and Tudor windows, the walls a mixture of heavy wooden beams and polished stone. It looked solid, set amongst the trees and sprawling flowerbeds. Climbing ivy thick but neat all along one side combined with the rest to make the house seem as if it too was rooted to the earth.

Stepping from the warmth of the morning sun onto the small shaded porch felt like a difference of ten degrees. Wallace shivered and rapped on the solid door. She remembered Gran bending down right here, whispering that it was made of solid oak—as if this would have been significant to a five-year-old Wallace. Hugging her arms close, Wallace considered waiting out in the sunlight, then, rubbing her arms, knocked again, on the inset leadlight this time. It sounded hollow and fragile compared to the heavy door.

After a time, something clicked near the latch. Wallace recognized the sound of metal clunking home and the door shifted inward, away from the jamb. Then, slowly, as if realizing freedom, it continued to swing inwards, hinges creaking as if unused to the effort.

'Mary?'

Wallace took a step into the small weather room that separated outside and in; a bench with tuck boxes beneath for muddy shoes was set into either side. Wallace slipped out of her low-heeled shoes, leaving them beside the arch leading into the rest of the house.

'Mary? Are you here?'

Her words were sucked into the center of the house and swamped by a deep silence. Odd, because Mary was always here. To Wallace's childhood memory, it was impossible to picture her anywhere else.

'Mary?' *No one. Who had opened the door? Maybe she had it on remote locking?*

Something large, black, and hairy landed next to her bare feet with a soft whumpf. Wallace jumped back, then realized it was Midnight, Mary's cat. It must have been sitting on the bench beside the door. It stared up at her with knowing green eyes.

'Hello, Midnight. You gave me a start.'

The cat flowed to its feet, fluffy tail high. Swaying, it entered the house, pausing at the bottom of the stairs to look back at Wallace as if to ask if she was coming.

Wallace followed. The stairs were polished wood, stained dark, a weary carpet runner fastened to the middle, skirted by brass strips on either side. Even they were polished.

A hall at the top of the stairs led off to the left. Midnight had disappeared.

'Mary, it's Wallace Carruthers... Aggie's granddaughter,' she added, reaching the landing. The dingy hall absorbed the additional identification without a whisper, Wallace's steps the only sound. On either side, tall doors remained firmly closed. Only one at the very end was ajar. Midnight sat outside, idly licking herself. Wallace had the distinct impression the cat was waiting.

Mary's room.

Wallace remembered visiting it as a child: dark with too-tall drawers that for some strange, adult reason they'd called lowboys. She paused outside.

'Mary?' she tried again, index finger lightly touching the highly varnished door. Nothing. A light push, and the door swung in. Midnight slipped through the gap, and in one graceful pounce landed on the high bed, pawing the woman lying there. Old Mary was atop the mattress, her legs draped over one side as if she couldn't decide to get out or in. Wallace gasped and ran across the room.

'Mary, are you all right?'

The old woman opened her eyes. They were blue, faded, and red-rimmed with fatigue.

Slowly, as if it were a great weight, her hand lifted, waving vaguely toward the bedside table.

'What do you need?' Wallace asked, hand hovering midway between a water glass, an overturned dark-brown bottle, and a half-eaten sandwich—ham by the looks, thick with butter, crusts curling. Mary's eyes tracked to the brown bottle and then closed once more, as if this had been too much effort. She must have knocked it over when she had tried to reach for it. Wallace picked up the bottle; there was no lid, and most of the contents had spilled onto the wooden floor. Only a small amount remained in the bottom, Wallace took a tentative sniff and recoiled—the smell was obnoxious, heavy with ancient herbs and stabilizing alcohol. Home brewed—Mary had always been a gifted, energetic herbalist. She poured half of what remained into the glass and, sliding her other arm gently beneath the old woman's shoulders, eased her up. There was no flesh to her; the ribs felt like corrugated iron beneath the full-length flannelette nightdress. Wallace brought the glass to Mary's thin lips. She slurped it eagerly, pink tip of her tongue removing the residue from around her mouth.

'More. A little more, love.'

Wallace poured the remainder of the mixture. Two spots of color about the size of twenty-cent pieces appeared on Mary's cheeks after she'd swallowed the second dose.

'Can I help you lie back down?' Wallace said, more by way of information as she was already gently lifting the withered legs back onto the bed. The nightdress rode up, revealing pale skin and long veins that looked like they'd been drawn on the underside of her skin with blue crayon.

Mary said nothing, sinking back against the fluffy pillows with a sigh, her eyelids fluttering shut for a moment.

Wallace placed the glass back on the embroidered doily atop the night table and looked around. The lowboy was still opposite the bed but didn't look quite as intimidating now that she had grown taller than the drawers. To the left, the same picture she remembered of young women hung above the fireplace; at either end of the marble mantle were long white candles in polished brass holders, and in the middle a cut flower arrangement, from some of the plants Wallace had seen growing in the garden downstairs. They looked fresh, so Old Mary couldn't have been indisposed for long—unless she had home help?

'Sorry, not very hospitable today. The herbs help keep it at bay.'

Wallace turned back, her eyes tracking across Mary's face, looking for signs of violence or what might have happened. The cheeks were sunken, the lines falling deeper in on themselves. She still didn't look well. No use messing about with small talk.

'Mary, I'm going to ring and get you an ambulance. I don't think you should be alone when you're feeling like this, but first, if you can, I need your help. I apologize, I know you're sick, but this is urgent—Sisterhood business. It's almost time to activate the Scrolls, and Jess, Angelique's daughter, is ready to go through with it but she can't read the Cipher. I remember Gran saying once that you kept a copy of the code here. I'm wondering, do you still have it?'

Mary closed her eyes briefly. The lids were overly large, as if her eyes had seen too much and the skin had grown over, trying to protect them.

'Mary? Did you understand what I just said?' Wallace repeated patiently, her fingers on the old woman's forearm. Her skin felt like wax paper.

Mary's thin lips moved, opening and closing a couple of times before she repeated, 'You shouldn't have come here.'

Wallace's mouth firmed. She was half inclined to agree, wondering at the same time whether Mary had suffered a stroke. She cupped her hand gently under Mary's chin so she could look at her eyes.

'Mary, do you know who I am?'

The old woman fussed Wallace's hands away. 'Of course I know who you are, Wallace, what do you think I am, senile?'

'No, I....'

Color returned with a flush to Mary's cheeks, and her eyes now had the directness Wallace remembered, as if the faded blue shades had snapped open and someone inside had turned on the lights. The herbs must be kicking in.

'He followed you here—he's out there now. Surely you must feel it?' The skin at the sides of Mary's eyes creased into easy folds as she focused, staring deeply into Wallace. Then dismissively, perhaps with a soupçon of pity, 'No, I can see that you can't.'

'I don't know what you're talking about, Mary—'

'I know, love. You can't help it,' she said, patting Wallace's hand absently and then using her elbows and hands to shuffle herself up into a seated position. 'The craft isn't really in you, I always said that. Not that Aggie would ever have a bar of it, mind.'

Wallace felt her face flush, old wounds smarting. 'Mary. I really don't have time to stay and chat about—'

Mary's eyes flashed. 'Don't patronize me. You're the reason we're all in this mess in the first place. Do you understand nothing?'

'Me?' Wallace took a step back.

'Yes. You.' Mary took a breath. 'When you called on the Sisters, using the Book of Names.'

'What? From the fog?'

'Is that what you're calling it? It was probably Baymist. Not that it matters now. Whatever happened was Dragos's doing. He set it up so you'd have to use the book and call for help. When you did, he was waiting, ready to suck up the names—and our power. Yes, it would be Baymist, sticky fog—you'd have known that if you'd continued your studies.'

Wallace felt her face flush, remembering how she used to evade going to lessons on Sisterhood lore. A memory of the dusty smell of those ancient tomes with their crackly pages and handwritten script intruded.

'But how?'

Mary closed her eyes briefly again, whether from tiredness or exasperation, Wallace couldn't be sure. 'You young people always want to focus on the peripherals—as if it mattered.' She sighed, then said patiently, 'When you called on us, he automatically linked in to everyone that answered your call, then later he followed those energetic connections back to each and every one of us and started to pump, sucking us dry, little by little.'

'I suspected as much,' Wallace admitted, 'but he hasn't managed to get to you, yet.' She remembered Mary's words about Shea being outside, thinking Mary was possibly delusional. Perhaps the herbal mix was psychotropic?

'Oh girl, can't you see it?' She waved her hand in the air above her head. 'Use what sight the Mother gave you. Even with your limited ability, you should be able to make it out.'

Wallace suppressed her irritation and did as she was asked. Mary and Gran had a lot in common; both could be exasperating—spelled r-u-d-e. Wallace half closed her eyes and created the sensation of physically withdrawing her sense of sight, contracting into herself, and in its place allowed an activation to flutter between her brows, near the middle of her forehead. Once there, she fanned it as she would a delicate flame, consciously allowing it to expand. Mary was right, of course, Wallace was no good at this, but she was damned if she'd admit it—especially to this old crone.

'Do you see them?' Mary snapped, finger pointing above her own head.

Wallace allowed her awareness to open. There did seem to be something hanging there, still very hazy. She relaxed her physical gaze still further and the image took on a sharper focus. They looked like tentacles, red, four—no, five of them, anchored deep into Mary's aura. Another four were truncated and waved in the ether above like snapped vines blowing in the breeze.

'What are they?'

'Dragos's energetic suckers. I managed to snap some before they got hold, but in the end, there were too many. The herbs help, blocking the flow off for a while but that was the last of it. Its effect gets less with every dose anyway.'

'So that's where Dragos is getting his power? That's why he hasn't begun the massacre,' Wallace said to herself. 'He didn't have to. Oh my God, I've been such an idiot.'

'Naïve is all, and maybe a little short-sighted—I mean that in our terms.'

'I'm trying to remember how many sisters responded?'

Mary shrugged. 'A lot. I've had others ring in asking what is going on with them. There have been hundreds so far. We've tried everything to sever them. It's now no longer a matter of how many, it's how long—for all of us. Many have already passed.'

'What can I do?' Wallace asked.

'Keep going, what else. That's why you're here, isn't it? That's why he's downstairs waiting.'

'No way.' Wallace walked over to the window and pulled aside the net curtain. The courtyard was empty except for her car. 'You're saying he followed me here?'

'I told you that already.'

'But I was so careful. I didn't see anyone following me.'

'You didn't use the right kind of sight, as usual. Whoever was exposed to that fog Dragos is linked into knows everything you're doing. He's playing you, Wallace.'

Wallace hurried over to a freestanding mirror in the corner, narrowing her gaze, attempting to see the same tendrils that had attached themselves to Mary.

'Not like that. He doesn't want to suck energy out of you, not yet, just information. He's linked in psychically to you and whoever else was with you in the Baymist.' Mary groaned. 'The herbs are wearing off. Close the curtain and come back here. I don't have much more time.'

Returning to the bed, Wallace was shocked at the change in Mary's features; her face had once again lost its color, the flesh hanging loose and pale. Midnight had settled on Mary's chest, paws fast-kneading the old woman's chest. Mary had one hand on the cat and absently patted the mattress with the other. Wallace sat down carefully, leaning close to the old woman's lips to hear what she was saying. Her breath was sour with the aftertaste of herbs.

'Take care of Midnight—she knows—I can't tell you—he'll hear.' She paused for several moments, then straining, her lips trying to shape unsaid, words she flopped back onto the pillows.

'Mary?'

Wallace could see her trying to speak; the words stuck in her throat.

'What is it Mary, what else are you trying to tell me?'

Wallace wanted to look away. It was like watching death wash up Mary's body in a slow-moving wave, claiming her by centimeters, each muscle progressively twitching, followed immediately by a slow and total release. The wave was now at her pelvis. Mary's eyes didn't waver from Wallace; her thin lips quivered with the effort to speak. It was like watching someone sink gradually into quicksand; the head would be last.

'What can I do?' Wallace repeated, anxiety rising as she watched Mary being consumed.

Grunting, the old woman reached up and gripped Wallace's wrist, tugging her in close, the tired blue eyes widening as if she were seeing something beyond Wallace.

With an effort, Mary pursed her lips, working them as if she had just sucked on a lemon. The sound, when it came, was a whispered hiss. The pale lips were making exaggerated shapes, word shapes.

'He's... on... you now too.'

TWENTY-ONE

The feeling of being a kid in the back seat of the car stole over Jessica.

She shifted uncomfortably as memories rose up like reflux, projecting themselves onto the back of Milt and Wallace's heads, substituting them for her mother and the latest version of "uncle," both arguing loudly from the front seat.

'I don't believe you, Wallace. You're a police detective, and someone you were sitting with died suddenly in what are arguably suspicious circumstances, and you didn't call it in?'

'And say what? Mary had these tentacles attached to her head by a demon called Dragos and they sucked her dry? Yes, I can really see how that would work.'

'You know what I mean. What about the autopsy? God only knows what was in those herbs you said she was downing like shots at happy hour.'

'Milt, leave it, will you? I told you, we can't risk the police closing down the scene before Jess has a chance to get the translation to the Cipher—'

'—because you and I are being bugged by demons, yes, I do

remember that bit,' he said, crossing his arms. 'I knew we should have been wearing our tin foil hats.'

Jess tuned them out. There would be no winner, there never was, just loud, scared voices shouting in the dark, pretending they had answers.

Outside dusk was early, the setting sun casting shadows of the surrounding mountains down the valley. She and Milt had made good time since Wallace had called just before lunch. Luckily Milt had a credit card that covered the taxi fare from the B&B all the way out to Tullamarine and then some. Business class had been all that was available when they'd arrived at the terminal. If it had been left up to her to pay, they'd still be on some road between here and there with their thumbs out. *But then I guess that's what real dads are for— not "uncles" who have trouble just dressing themselves.* Wallace had hired a car and picked them up from the station.

'Here we are.' Wallace's voice intruded. Gravel crunched beneath the tires as they left the bitumen and bumped up a driveway. Leaning forward to peer between Milt and Wallace, she saw an old house with a high gabled roof looming out of the gloom. It looked spooky, but then this was supposed to be a witch's house.

Wallace turned her head towards Jess. 'You okay, love?'

'Sure.'

Liar.

She opened the door. 'You guys coming in?' Jess asked, one foot outside, resting on the gravel.

'We can't,' Wallace said. 'If what Mary said was true and Dragos is tapped into Milt and me, he'll hear and see everything we do. You're the only one who wasn't in the fog. Besides, someone has to ride the boundary and check out the grounds. That's why I brought him.' She jerked her thumb at Milt slouched beside her. 'Just go in. See what you can find.'

'So long as it's not who.' Jess imagined the old woman rising up off the bed like some ghost.

'Just go, I want to be out of here before dark. Milt, come on, you take the back. I bought some torches. Here, Jess, you take one as well, just in case.'

Milt grunted something Jess couldn't make out as she slid out of the station wagon and shut the door. Looking up at the house, she shivered; the air was cold here too. They'd had just enough time to buy new coats and scarves at the airport—Milt again. She'd never felt warm in Melbourne, but then she'd never had a coat like this. She snuggled deeper into it before walking to the heavy wooden door with the separate portcullis. The weather room, Wallace had called it. Funny name. The door opened at her touch, as if anticipating her approach. A light draft floated by, warmer air from inside the house carrying with it a curious smell-mix of beeswax polish, age, and...

Cat?

Jess started as it landed lightly at her feet. Barely visible inside the dark house, its black fur was simply a darker shape within the gloom. The eyes, though, were arresting; they were bright blue, almost luminous, staring straight up and into her.

'Hello there, you gave me a bit of a fright,' Jess said, bending down. The cat stood and wandered off before she could pat it. Pausing at the entrance to the house proper, it paused, looking over its shoulder.

'Oh, I see. All right, I'm coming.'

Inside, the smell of wax, furniture polish, and lavender was stronger; the only sound in an otherwise intense silence the metronomic ticking of a large clock, as if it were the house's solid, steady heartbeat. Jess flicked on a light switch. It was one of the old sort: black and thick, and made a solid clunking click. Two weak bulbs lit up, one near the door and the other in the lounge room. She walked in further. Everything was too neat. Being raised with Angelique, who always seemed to tow chaos behind her wherever she went, Jess had come to value tidiness, however, this place was nailed firmly to the other end of the continuum, veering dangerously toward obsessive. Even the wood in the fireplace looked arranged, with logs all cut to the exact same size. The cat had stopped in front of it and was again looking up at her with those shining bright blue eyes, at once curious, intense, and dismissive.

'What? This place creeps me out. I had a difficult childhood, all right?'

Now I'm not only talking to the cat, I'm treating it like my psych. What the hell am I supposed to be looking for?

As if in answer, the cat wandered over to a bookcase built into the far wall and sat down in front of it. The books looked expensive and old. Some had worn leather covers and what looked like faded gold leaf on the spine. They were arranged by size, a hand-written catalogue attached to the side of each shelf.

How could books look so neat?

The cat seemed to be waiting for her to come over. Jess did, and this time it allowed a quick pat before it stood and placed a paw delicately on one of the books on the bottom shelf. Jess snorted. *Yeah right, the cat told me. Next I'll start thinking like Mum.* An image of the lonely stone box they'd left her in flashed up. *This place is a bit like that, a tomb, just a lot bigger—and neater.*

She crouched down and slid the book out. Something clunked heavily behind her, and when she turned, part of the floor in the lounge room had rolled aside.

'What the heck—'

Jess took a closer look. Stairs led down, just wide enough for one person. It reminded her of the steps beneath Wallace's house. What did she call it—a witch hole, that was it. Except these stairs looked much older, stone, by the looks. Remembering the torch in her coat pocket, she flicked it on and followed the cat down.

There were fourteen steps. When she reached the bottom, something clicked and the floor above her head rumbled shut, cutting off the light. Jess felt an immediate rush of claustrophobia, her world shrinking to the cone of torchlight.

The ring pulsed against her finger, feeling hot and impatient, urging her on like old Mrs. Harris, her wizened fifth grade teacher who used to stand, hands on her hips, foot tapping. Even her big toe would keep time in those ridiculous sandals. 'Well, Jess,' she'd say, 'well, what are you going to do about this mess you're in?'

Damn good question, Mrs. Harris. Damn good question.

Conscious of keeping her breathing slow and deep to ward off the white noise, she methodically swept the torch around the small space. Unlike beneath Wallace's tree, there was no furniture in this area, just rough-hewn walls reinforced with cement pillars and wooden framing, the smell of musty earth strong in her nostrils. The cat made a mewing noise off to the left. Jess brought the torch light down and around until she found it digging determinedly in the dirt.

'Ah, there you are. Well this is very nice and all but... what are you doing there anyway?'

Jess came closer.

'What is that?'

Bending down, Jess reached into the freshly dug hole. Something was in there. It felt like a metal lever. Jess cleared more of the loose dirt away until the lever was completely uncovered. The cat looked at Jess as if to say, 'Well now I've shown you—pull it.'

She did, and one of the wooden reinforcing panels slid aside to reveal a manhole-sized door set into the wall.

'You're one clever cat, you know that? What do we have here?'

Jess had no doubt that whatever she was here to find was on the other side.

As for the curious question of the cat leading her to this point... where did she go anyway...?

Another meow from beside her foot. When she looked down, Midnight was grooming her paws.

Working on the dirt from the digging, no doubt. Maybe obsessive cleaning is contagious. The cat seems to have caught it anyway.

Jess moved to the manhole, hooked her fingers on the underside of the door, and pulled. The door hinged up easily. The hole was just large enough for her to wriggle through. The cat sprang through first with what could have been a triumphant meow. Picking up the torch, Jess followed, angling and scraping her way through to the other side.

She landed in an untidy heap, the trapdoor snapping shut behind her.

Old Mary must have been paranoid about being burned at the stake for her to have put in these precautions—or she had something really valuable to hide.

Jess rolled onto her back and ran the torch beam around the space. She was in a continuation of the passageway, low ceiling, same reinforcing and earthen floor. When she shone the light down farther, she could make out a larger space. Midnight was already swaggering toward it, bushy tail high. Keeping low, Jess followed, trying not to think how fresh air could possibly reach this underground cut-off place.

The larger area opened into a space somewhere between a vast wine cellar and library. Two of the upper walls were entirely devoted to shelves of books, protected behind glass-fronted cupboards, while below hundreds of dark brown bottles of varying shapes were arranged in gradated sizes on more shelves, each painstakingly hand-labeled. In between the books and bottles, two long wooden work-benches had been fitted. An array of measuring equipment for Mary's herbal preparations was laid out ready. Jess took the cap off one large bottle and sniffed at the open neck before wrinkling her nose and backing away, coughing the concentrated smell from her lungs.

Alcohol. For steeping the herbs.

She replaced the stopper and wandered on. A little further, mounted onto the bench, was an electric ignition gas burner, tripod, and some petrie dishes. It reminded her a little of the science labs at one of the high schools she'd attended. There'd been a lot of schools and she couldn't rightly remember which one; besides science hadn't been, and still wasn't, her strength but she remembered the teacher in that particular lab had been kinda cute. He'd called her Miss Jessy.

At the back, set into the narrower wall, was a large stainless steel sink and compact kitchenette. A comfy-looking chair upholstered with red and orange fabric that looked as if it might also covert to a bed was set off to one side.

There was even electric light.

Jess snapped on the wall switch and fluorescents inset above both workbenches flickered on. Unlike the house upstairs, this space had a lived-in feel to it. Jess had the distinct impression Mary must have spent a lot of her time down here.

'Nice setup,' Jess said to herself, nodding.

The cat, curled up in the chair, preened one of its legs.

Jess wandered along one of the benches, occasionally picking something up, not really sure what she was looking for, idly wondering how the other two were going outside. They'd made her leave her phone in the car, lest Dragos or whoever was supposed to be out there hear her if it rang. As if.... She stopped, hand paused over an oversized eye-dropper on the bench.

What was that sound?

The cat too had stopped licking and was staring into the dark space at the opposite end, its back leg still extended. The passageway seemed to continue on past the room. *Probably leads to another exit in the garden where all the herbs are. That would make sense. It also means someone could have found their way in.*

'Hello?' Jess called. 'Wallace? Milt? Is that you?'

No reply. She wished there was some way of calling the words back. Now whoever, or whatever, was coming would know she was in here.

The cat jumped to the floor and onto the bench, its blue eyes shining. Making its way along the bench, it paused in front of one of the concentrated tincture bottles and knocked it over, daintily stepping into the widening brown puddle, then with a low mewling growl rolling from its throat, dropped back to the floor.

From the passageway, Jess could just make out a low whistling sound, as if someone were idly trying to recall a lost tune.

This can't be good.

Looking around, she realized there was nowhere to hide. Behind the armchair was the only possibility, if only it were dark....

She snapped off the lights and sank to her knees, crawling fast in what she thought might have been the general direction of the chair, all semblance of relative proximity and what things were where dissolving with every forward shuffle. The paving stones were cold and hard against her knees.

Ignoring the temptation to use the torch—*just for a quick flash*—her head eventually collided with something hard. Tentative fingers relayed touch data back to her brain, and after a couple of breaths she decided it must be the cupboard in the kitchenette—the upholstered chair should only be a meter or so to the right.

The whistling coming from the passage was louder now, more confident; it was a tune she recognized from her childhood, one her mother used to sing before Jess went to sleep each night. It was supposed to keep away the monsters.

Definitely not good.

A small part of her ardently wished she hadn't turned out the lights.

Her hands found the chair. Trying to quit her huffing, she fumbled her way around to the back and hunkered down. If there'd been sand on the floor, she would have been tempted to bury her head. She could feel her heart thumping, breath coming in shallow gasps that she tried to quieten by inhaling slower, which made her more anxious so the breath rasped louder.

The whistling stopped abruptly, and she held her breath.

He was inside the room. She didn't know how she knew that— she just did. There was a different feel to the air, a displacement and a sense of sharing the air. Uneasily she drew in a ragged breath. Something fluttered past, like the after beat of a distant bat wing.

'Miss Jessy? You in here?'

Jess almost wet herself.

The voice filled the room. It was her old science teacher. Almost, but not quite. *How could that be?*

'Oh, Milt, stop teasing her. Don't listen to him, Jess. Come on out. It's all right.'

Wallace?

It was Wallace's voice—but somehow without Wallace. *Another trick.*

Whoever it was took a step nearer, leather soles grinding the small traces of dirt they'd carried in from the passageway. *The darkness is total. Why isn't he carrying a torch? How can he see?*

The whistling began again, low, but loud in the confined space.

Angelique appeared suddenly in a burst of light. She seemed to be looking directly at Jess and was singing the monster song. *"... saffron wings with gilded spears, guard my Jess from all her fears..."*

Jess bowed her head, hands covering her ears to block it out, her mind reciting over and over *It's all in my head. Mum is dead.*

Finally the apparition, or whatever it was, faded. Angelique's voice along with it.

'That was fun. Kind of. But I really need you to give me that Cipher now. You can't read it anyway.'

A torch clicked on, its beam strong and very white. Jess covered her eyes, the light was so bright, and then it was shining directly at her. She couldn't see a thing.

There was no use pretending anymore.

'I don't have it.'

The voice sighed, long and dramatically. When next it spoke, it was Martin.

'How many times do we have to do this? You always want to make it hard, don't you, Jess? Draw everything out, make me work for *every-freaking-thing*. You make me mine my darkness. It's you, you know, not me that makes me do those things to you.'

'Go away. I don't have it,' Jess sobbed, her throat thick with memories of Dark Martin, as he used to call his alter self. And now she was right back there. She forced herself to focus, huddling away from the strong light, trying to preserve her night sight. She heard him come another step closer. He was halfway down the room now. She had to get away from the torch's spotlight.

An ear-curdling screech, and the light beam jerked into the air.

'Fucking cat.'

It was followed immediately by the sound of fragile glass breaking and something heavier hitting and smashing against the stone flagstones. Then blessed, blessed darkness. It flowed back with an engulfing rush. Slipping off her shoes, Jess scampered out from behind the chair and over to the opposite side of the room. Locating the bench, she grabbed whatever her hands stumbled upon and started throwing it in all directions, hoping to disorient him, moving at the same time back toward the passageway. She imagined the glass-fronted cupboards, large brown tincture and dosage bottles fragmenting and showering the demon man with every thrown missile. He was cursing, fumbling at the wall opposite.

He's trying to find the light switch. Where are Milt and Wallace?

She considered calling for them but dismissed it immediately. They wouldn't be able to hear her, and even if they could, there was no guarantee they'd be able to find the entrance. It would only give away her position.

The cat screeched again. Jess caught a glimpse of two burning blue eyes as they dashed past, toward the back of the room. The cat howled in what could have been triumph as the man cursed again. It must have landed on him; she imagined its sharp claws sinking in, scoring deep red welts down his unprotected skin.

She was at the far end of the bench and had run out of things to throw. If she tried for the narrow passage leading to the outside, he would catch her. The way back to the house was locked, and she had no idea how to open either the manhole or the sliding panel in the lounge room floor.

Think.

She could almost hear them both listening for each other. Jess thought she could make out the quiet sound of his breath and stilled hers even more. He took a step, and broken glass crunched beneath his shoes.

Five meters, eleven o'clock.

One of her "uncles" had been in the air force and used clockface time as directions for where things might be in the house. It used to drive scatty Angelique batty but somehow it had stuck with Jess, particularly in stressed out moments.

Rising onto her toes, she crept across the floor, biting her bottom lip as jagged shards of glass dug into her bare feet. At the other bench, she reached out both arms, then drew them slowly toward each other across the bench. One finally nudged against the large glass container of alcohol. Excited, she slipped off the stopper. It came free with a quiet plop, but the noise was enough. He heard, and following the sound rushed over, barreling into her. They both went down, falling to the floor, her hand still around the neck of the open bottle, dragging it with her. It smashed against the floor, the smell filling the room as the alcohol formed a large pool on the floor, soaking them both as they struggled. He was bigger and much stronger, but something seemed to be wrong with his hands; they kept sliding off before they could get a decent grip on her. It was as if his hands and fingers were refusing basic commands.

The cat.

Just before the lights went out, Jess remembered seeing it walk back and forward through that puddle of tincture from the bottle it had overturned on the bench. Whatever had been in it—and she was betting some kind of paralyzing poison—would have coated the extended claws so that when they scored his hands just before... oh, yes, clever, clever puss.

The incapacity didn't stop him from hitting though. With a grunt, he brought what must have been his elbow in a crossing backwards arc that connected with her temple. Jess's head exploded, pinpoints of light going off inside her brain. He used that moment to consolidate his position, straddling her thighs, hands and wrists anchoring her shoulders with his upper body weight.

'Where is it?' he said, his voice thick as if he'd just come from the dentist after a solid dose of Novocain. Part of Jess that wasn't in pain told her to hang on; whatever had been on the cat's paws was going systemic, spreading throughout his nervous system. She just had to hang on.

'All right,' she yelled, drawing on the raw emotional edge of a part she'd once played about a victim. 'All right.'

She felt the pressure against her shoulders ease slightly. She sensed relief; he knew his body was failing but unlike her didn't know why. She could use that.

'You'll have to let me up. I'll go get it.'

The man shifted his weight from her, one leg at a time; it seemed to be an effort, but she couldn't be sure. *Oh God, I hope I'm not imagining all this Super Cat stuff. The alcohol fumes are making it hard to think straight.*

'Get up. Hands and knees only, or I'll hit you again.'

Jess did as he said. He came around behind her and caught her neck in the crook of his arm.

'Try anything and I'll crush your larynx. Got it?' he said with an effort, overenunciating certain words like a drunk trying to prove he wasn't.

Jess couldn't speak anyway, the pressure against her throat was too much. She could feel his biceps and forearm muscles hard against either side of her neck. That crushingly simple movement of muscle contraction would be one of the last to go.

She did her best to nod, and the pressure lessened slightly.

'Good. Get up. Slowly.'

He followed her, matching her movements to keep her close.

'Where?'

She pointed, then realized that was silly. 'Just to the right, above the bench. I hid it there when I heard you come in,' she lied—as her drama teacher used to say—with conviction.

He dragged her along the edge of the bench.

'Turn on the lights first. You know where the switch is—I saw them go out before.'

Jess tried to stall, move slower, but he pushed.

'They're further down, I think, it's hard to tell in the dark,' she croaked.

He allowed her to lead but molded himself against her back. She could feel his pelvis moving against her buttocks and had a sense that his legs were starting to drag and stiffen.

Clever bastard. He's using me to hold him up. That must have been damned good stuff, Mary. But how did the cat know....

Jess groped the wall with one hand, pretending to fumble for the light switch, using the other to sweep the bench.

It has to be here somewhere.

Then she had it, and without allowing herself too much time to think, raised one foot and then drove it up and back, her heel catching him right in the base of the crotch, crushing his testicles. He grunted, instinctively rolling forward, the grip around her throat loosening. Jess slid down and twisted free, scrambling around behind him.

He swore and tried to catch her, but she was nimble, and he was staggering. It was like a macabre dance with each trying to sense the other in the dark, Jess leading, maneuvering while frantically groping along the bench to locate the gas valve for the Bunsen burner. When she found it, she grabbed a handful of his shirt and pulled him toward her, ducking as she opened the valve to full, flicking the ignition.

A tongue of blue-yellow flame erupted with a roar, greedily devouring the evaporating alcohol fumes, sucking its way back to the saturated clothes of the man, devouring him in whooshing hot licks and slurps.

Jess ran, not looking back, hands covering her ears to block out the tortured screams that followed her along the passageway.

TWENTY-TWO

It was dark, the floor pounded earth, uneven. She stumbled several times, falling once, jarring her wrists. After a while the screams came less often and then finally—blessedly—stopped altogether and she slowed, feeling her way along the wall.

The passageway seemed to go on for a long way. Jess tried to imagine how far and failed. The garden just hadn't seemed that big earlier, she hoped the passage didn't loop back to the same room.

Too many old scary movies.

After a time, she ran into a barrier. It felt like a wooden door, reinforced with roughened steel bands.

An exit?

Excited, she felt all around the edges for a latch or a release catch. There was nothing. She pushed, leaning her shoulder against it and heaving when it failed to budge. Nothing happened.

Not again.

She heard scuttling and then felt something hairy run over the top of her bare foot. Squealing, she jumped back, stifling the full scream, expecting a giant rat with hungry red eyes to leap at her face and start gnawing. Instead she heard an enquiring meow.

Midnight.

Biting her bottom lip to prevent the bubbling relief audibly escaping, she bent down and scooped Midnight up. She began purring immediately. In the confined space it sounded like a motorcycle engine idling.

'Almost there, puss,' she whispered. 'Just one problem to go and we're both outta here. I wish we had some light.'

The torch! She remembered jamming it into her coat pocket earlier, and mercy of mercies it was still there. Pulling it out, she clicked it on.

Hey presto, let there be light. Talk about magic.

Shining it onto the door, then down at the floor, she could see immediately what the problem was. The arced scrape marks in the dirt indicated the door opened in, not out. Which kind of made sense, except there was no door handle to pull on. But there was a knobbed pull-up lever, similar to a childproof pool gate. Jess flipped it up, and a latch inside the door clicked. Like the one inside the house, it released itself from the jamb. *House of hidden locks and doors.*

The door was heavy though, its outer surface overgrown with thick vegetation that resisted her pulling. When she finally had it wide enough, she squeezed through, the bitter night air momentarily stealing breath as her body attempted to reacclimatize to the change in temperature.

Jess staggered away from the door. It felt like she'd been through her front loader's heavy wash and full spin program. Still shots of memory revolved in her head, refusing to connect with one another. That was one thing she admired about Milt. In Milt's world, there were only two traffic lights: green and red. Amber didn't even get a look in. *He could have passed that one on in the gene dump.*

Her throat felt constricted. Dehydrated. She knew the signs; voice care was integral to an actor. She found a hose, traced it back to the tap, and turned it on. The water was freezing but tasted like nectar.

Moving further, the torch revealed that she was in the middle of a massive herb garden, planted out randomly between trees and bushes. There was no sign of the driveway or their car. Looking back, the overgrowth of vegetation across the door would have made the entrance impossible to find, much less stumble across.

So how did that scarred creep find his way?

'Milt,' she called, taking a few steps, tucking the cat inside the flap of her big coat. It curled up into a furry ball. Out here, the torch didn't have as wide a spill as in the narrower passage, and no moon meant it was even harder to see and orient herself. That was odd: no moon, yet the sky was clear. She could have sworn that down in the Dandenongs yesterday the moon was into its third quarter. Maybe as Aggie had warned, time was moving faster.

Her feet were cold too, and now that the numbing panic had worn off, the embedded splinters of glass made it painful to walk.

'Wallace?'

The cat meowed and snuggled closer. Ducking beneath a low branch, she caught a glimpse of light off to the left and hobbled toward it. The natural bush ended suddenly, and then she was on the driveway. She gasped as sharp edges of gravel ground into her bleeding feet. Hugging the edges, she sought out the soft mosses and turf as she made her way up to the house. The lights she'd seen were the ones she'd turned on earlier in the downstairs lounge. The front door to the house was still open. Inside her coat, the cat mewed and struggled, smelling home. Jess pulled the coat tighter. There was no telling how safe the house was just yet and she wasn't going to be chasing this minx if she let her free.

There was still no sign of Milt or Wallace. She paused, unsure. The distant lonely screech of a nocturnal bird was the only sound. If she called out, her voice would just be another bleating into the dark —uncertain whether it would be heard, and if so, by whom.

The car was where they'd left it. Jess allowed the torch to play over the windows. There was a dull glow coming from it. Cautious, she moved closer, lifting the torch so it shone down, maximizing the light spread inside the car. The glow must have been a reflection from the torch or the house. When she looked inside, she gasped.

Milt was sprawled across the front seats, a deep gash on the side of his head. She tried to drag the driver's door open. It was locked.

She knocked at the side window.

'Milt.'

Then ran around to the opposite side. Those doors were locked as well.

Where is Wallace?

Was Milt hit by the guy before he went down into the underground passageway, or are there more of them out here? And where the heck is Wallace? Those two are joined at the hip most of the time.

The same bird screeched again, louder and closer. Scraps from banshee and bunyip stories she'd been told as a child bumped against the more present danger, none of it making any sense and accomplishing nothing other than to ramp up her anxiety. They'd brought her here to get the code for the Cipher, and despite everything she still didn't have it. So far there were just bodies—more term deposits for her personal nightmare bank. She hobbled away from the car and over toward the house. Light spilled through the open door, at once inviting and unknown. Wallace had to be here somewhere.

'Hello?' she called. 'Wallace?' Her voice wavered, catching on the fear.

She nudged the door, and it swung open noiselessly, revealing the polished wooden stairs and living room beyond. Cautiously she entered, her feet leaving bloody prints on the boards. She peeked around the archway leading into the lounge. Empty, though someone had lit the fire and pulled the drapes. That was encouraging. It was unlikely that whoever was crisped up downstairs would have that down as a priority. She could only hope it had been—

'Jess! There you are, I've been looking everywhere.'

She started, spinning around to face—

'Wallace!'

The two women ran to each other, Jess feeling the bigger woman's arms sweep her up into a hug.

'Careful,' Jess said, laughing with relief. 'I've got a cat buried in here. It'll get squished.'

She opened the coat and a black head bobbed out. It looked at Wallace and hissed.

'Midnight? I wondered where she'd gotten to,' Wallace said, backing off a little but keeping her hands firmly planted on Jess's shoulders.

Wallace examined her, eyes squinting in a way Jess recognized as using more than just physical sight. Mum used to do it too. It always made her feel guilty. 'You okay?' Wallace asked after a while.

Jess shrugged and glanced down, Wallace following the gaze. 'Whoa, take a look at those feet. Let's get those seen to first.'

'Wait. What about Milt?' Jess said.

'Milt? What about him? I sent him into the village to get us some food. There's nothing in the cupboards except tins of kitty food. The damn car wouldn't start, so he had to call a cab. That station wagon was all they had left at the rental company—now I know why. He left mumbling something about always being stuck with the cab fare.'

'No. No, I saw him. He's in the car, outside. He looks badly hurt.' She pointed back at the open door.

Wallace shrugged. 'That's funny. Are you sure, because I saw him get in that cab?'

'Yes. I know what I saw. He's hurt out there.'

'Well, let's go see. Why don't you put your arm around me; those feet must be screaming at you.'

Wallace helped her shuffle back outside. When they reached the car, Jess hurried forward, rubbing at the condensation that had formed on the outside of the side window.

The front seat was empty. She felt Wallace come up beside her, and a huge sob welled up from her chest.

'But I saw him.'

'Come on, love, you've had a big night, let's get you back inside.' Wallace's voice seemed to be coming from a long way off.

I saw him!

She wasn't sure whether she'd said the words aloud. She wasn't sure of anything, not now.

What had really happened? Had there been a man? Had a black cat really shown her how to go downstairs?

The white noise rose, howling between her ears. Wallace was in front of her now, mouthing words that Jess couldn't hear. Only the white noise, consuming everything. Distantly she was aware of her knees turning to slush. A blackness slid down from the crown of her head and over her eyes. Only the white noise remained; everything else was shutting down.

WHEN SHE CAME TO, Jess was propped up in one of the over-stuffed chairs in the lounge room, her feet elevated on several fat, frilly cushions. Wallace, glasses balanced at the end of her nose, was using tweezers to pull out shards of glass from Jess's feet.

'Sorry, that one must have hurt. It was a biggie.'

She dropped a jagged sliver of glass into a bowl. It made a small ping. The white noise had stopped. Jess took a cautious breath and finally asked, 'What happened?'

'You passed out. I'm not surprised, you must have been through a lot if these feet are anything to go by.'

'I don't know anymore. It's all a bit of a blur. I was so sure Milt was out there. It's made me doubt everything.'

Wallace shrugged, her face softening. 'One thing that happens when your sensitivity and talent start to open up is you start to see things. Sometimes they're what we hope for, other times we see what we fear might happen—more often it's a mix of both. Severe anxiety and terror are the prime ways to bring it on—at least they were when I was starting out. Gran helped a lot back then.'

'But what about the man, Shea....'

'Dragos's stalker?' Wallace swabbed away some blood from a cut that had reopened. Jess started when the antiseptic bit. 'Oops, sorry again. No, if he was here, he didn't show himself. Maybe Mary wasn't all that lucid when she said what she did, who knows? Anyway, Milt and I searched the grounds thoroughly before he left. I know Shea was supposed to be invisible and all, but that sort of enchantment relies on blocking other peoples' perception so they literally don't see you rather than actually making themselves invisible. Even if Dragos had the talent to pull that off, generating that sort of imagery interference pulls down a lot of juice, so to maintain it even for short bursts is incredibly taxing. Simple fact, Dragos wouldn't have been able to, especially acting remotely through Shea. No, if he was here before, he's certainly not now.'

'That's because he was with me. I saw him. I killed him. Downstairs. At least, I think I did. I don't know anymore.'

'Where do you think you saw him then?' Wallace asked, picking up the tweezers again and examining Jess's feet.

'Down there.' Jess pointed down at the wooden floor. 'In the witch hole.'

Wallace glanced up. 'You found it? I always knew Mary had one.'

'I didn't. The cat, Midnight, did. She did everything. Like you said, she met me when I came inside the house.'

'Midnight? Really? She's a case, isn't she? You've heard of cantankerous—well, Midnight is cat-nakerous.'

As if on cue Midnight sprang onto Jess's lap and began pummeling her legs. Jess could feel the energetic tremor travel through her front paws. Smiling, she stroked the cat's back until it looked up at her.

'Her eyes are green,' Jess said, looking closer.

Wallace made an "uh-huh" noise, intent on extracting a long piece of glass.

'No, I mean Midnight's eyes are green. They were this intense blue color before.'

'Not likely that her eyes would change color, though, is it?'

Wallace's voice remained neutral. Jess knew what she was trying to do: guide her back to the middle of the channel so looking back she could recognize her own imbalance.

Wallace paused, setting down the tweezers, and picked up a roll of bandages. She carefully wrapped Jess's feet. 'Always been green as far as I can recall.'

'Wallace, I know what I saw.'

'You just said you weren't sure. You've been through a lot, Jess, not just tonight but this whole thing. The speeded-up initiation that Gran did. Who knows what after-effects that had?' Wallace secured the bandages with a section of strong elastic tape.

Jess felt a tear form in one corner of her eye. Slowly it filled and rolled out; she could feel its track down her cheek.

Wallace sighed, coming over to squat in front of her, resting a hand on Jess's arm. 'Look, love. Our brain is what we see with, not our eyes. It puts the light impulses together and tries to make sense of them. Problem is, when we start to open up psychically, there's too many bits getting through the normal filters, too much sensory data. It's like having the wrong-sized puzzle pieces in a jigsaw. It doesn't quite fit, so the mind makes bits up, connecting the dots, trying to fill in the gaps and overlaps. I don't doubt what you think you saw. I've been there. I know exactly what you're going through. Just spare yourself the grief and allow some doubt to be in there as well.'

'I know.' Another tear, this time from the opposite eye.

"Balance is the key."

Jess shuddered. Where did that come from? It was a woman's voice. *Now I've got voices in my head as well.*

She almost admitted it to Wallace but held back. That would dissolve any lingering doubts.

I'm so tired.

"Stay alert!"

Jess jumped. The voice was so loud, surely Wallace must have heard it as well. But no, she was just staring, like she had earlier. Jess looked away, running her tongue across her lips.

'Why would I make up that the cat had blue eyes? What difference would that even make?'

Wallace said nothing, just patted Jess's hand. Angry, Jess pulled it away.

'Okay, fine,' she said finally. 'Leave the cat be for a moment. But I know for a fact that there's a dead freak in the cellar. Is he a figment of my too-active imagination as well?'

Wallace squinted in the same way she had outside as she stared deeply into her. 'I don't know, love, but let's go take a look, shall we?'

OF COURSE THE book that triggered the roll-back floor to the witch hole was missing. That had been too much to hope for. Or, if it was there, the mechanism was no longer working. Naturally, when she asked Midnight, the cat just stared at the pile of books strewn across the floor through half-closed lids and yawned. Finally Jess suggested they use the garden entrance. Wallace sighed and followed, insisting Jess put on a pair of Mary's gardening shoes to protect her feet. They were faded lime green Crocs—too floppy, made for bigger, thicker feet, but at least it was less painful to walk.

Jess led the way back down the drive and into the herb garden, pulling frenetically at the wall of vines and shrubs until she revealed the door.

'Looks like it hasn't been used in years,' Wallace said dubiously, shining the torch over the rusting iron bands.

'Just help me push. It'll open. Look, here's the latch, it's the same as the one on the other side.'

'I thought you said you hadn't closed it.'

Jess let that one slide, not wanting to think too much about what might have pushed the door shut. *At least the damned thing is here. At least that much was true. I was starting to think I was going crazy.*

The door creaked open and they stepped through, entering the passage. With the light from the two torches, it was a lot less scary.

'Seems to go back a long way,' Wallace said, her tone dubious, playing the torchlight down the passageway until it fell short of the continuing darkness.

'Come on, it's not that far,' Jess called over her shoulder. Her feet were hurting but she was anxious to have this done. It had moved past the stage of proving anything; it was now a case of keeping her head clear.

They moved along the tunnel in silence, its floor surface sloping down sharply. The reinforced earth walls were oppressive now that she could see them, thick with roots and damp from the gardens above. Finally the slope leveled out and they came to the lab space.

'In there.' Jess said, pausing at the edge, both unwilling and unable to go further. Wallace slipped past her and into the room, the flicker from her torch beam moving quickly, seeking out and dismissing possible threats.

'Clear,' she called.

'What?' Jess said, bursting in, looking immediately at the floor where the charred remains should be. The flagstones were bare; not only that, they weren't even scorched. Not even any broken glass, nor a whiff of spilled alcohol.

'I don't understand,' she said, reaching out for the edge of the bench. Her legs felt weak again.

What is wrong with me?

'No one does, not really,' Wallace replied, her voice kind. 'My advice is just go with it. I don't know what you saw or thought you saw down here, Jess, but it isn't here now. But,' she added, moving across the room, 'on the plus side, we do have lights.' Wallace flicked them on, and the benches lit up. 'And secondly, whichever way you got here, you did manage to find Old Mary's hidey-hole. The Cipher key is sure to be in here somewhere. Let's look around. You take the left side, I'll go right. Look for hidden switches. Mary loved those.'

In the end, Jess discovered it. The box it was hidden in was set into the thick workbench. It popped up when Jess ran her fingers along the underside of the bench just behind a bulk supply of brown dosage bottles.

'I think this might be it,' she said, removing the package and unwrapping the cloth surrounding a small parchment scroll.

Wallace joined her, looking over her shoulder as Jess unrolled it.

'It's just a series of holes. Did the moths get to it, do you think?' she asked, holding it up to the light.

'Looks like it, doesn't it? No, love, I think it's designed that way. I reckon if you place this over that incomprehensible Cipher thing you have it will block out certain letters and reveal others. Hopefully those will be the correct sequence.'

Jess rolled the scroll back up and tucked it into her bra along with the Cipher. It was getting a little crowded down there, but right now it was the most secure place she could think of.

'Hopefully. Come on let's get out of here,' she said, looking down at the flagstones. 'This place gives me the willies.'

Retracing their steps, Wallace closed the garden door and in typical Wallace fashion forged a way through the garden to the driveway.

'Milt should be back by now, shouldn't he?' Jess asked, seeing the car and remembering the earlier vision of him across the front seat. The strange glow that had been around the car before had vanished.

'Oh, he'll be along. Milt has his own timeline. You must have noticed that about him by now.'

'Mmm.' Jess's mind was still on the car. She slowed her pace as she came abreast of it.

Wallace turned at the front door, 'Coming in? It's freezing out there.'

'In a minute. I want to grab my suitcase first, it's in the boot. Do you have the car keys? It's locked.'

Wallace hesitated for a moment, then reached into her pocket and pulled out the remote locking fob. The indicators flashed twice in response. 'See you inside.'

Jess wandered over to the tailgate of the small station wagon and opened it. Their bags were where they'd put them this afternoon when Wallace had met them at the station. That all seemed so long ago. Somehow seeing the luggage grounded her; the bags were part of normal.

On impulse, she unzipped Milt's big suitcase and carefully pulled aside the clothes. The lethal-looking axe was still at the bottom, its sharp blades wrapped in one of his dirty shirts. She eased the shirt free, balling it in her fists, and brought it to her nose. The smell of him swept through her, conjuring the last "memory." Him lying across the front seats.

What is wrong with me? That had seemed so real too.

On impulse, she went round to the front of the car and opened the passenger door, triggering the interior courtesy light. The almost-new smell of the rental car was faint but still detectable, a little like the memory of Milt lying across the seats, bloodied head on the passenger side. She could almost see him. The seats were black leather, so if there'd been stains, "someone" had wiped up.

Maybe this is how paranoia starts? With mysterious someones who act irrationally but with purpose. None of it makes any sense.

The courtesy lights timed out, and the interior darkened. She was about to shut the door and go inside when something in the back caught her eye. A reflection of something flashing onto the side window. Curious, she leaned in, easing herself between the front seats. The reflection disappeared. However, now she could see where it was coming from: the molded plastic amenity holder in the door. A memory flashed up of Milt telling her not to take her phone and then dropping it into the door pocket. It'd landed face up, and the sloping side window must have caught the LED reflection.

The flashing red light meant she had a voicemail message.

She retrieved it. One missed call. Milt. 8:10 p.m.

8:10? That wasn't long after she'd gone into the house. Since then she'd lost track of time, and when she checked the phone readout it was 12:35.

What happened to Milt?

Apprehensive, Jess touched the icon for voicemail. One new message.

"*Jess, it's me. Something's wrong with Wallace. I caught her talking to that scarred character out in the bushes—they saw me and then they both came after me. I ran, made it to the car but forgot she had the bloody keys. Be careful.*'

The call clicked off.

What did he mean "something's wrong with Wallace?"

A guilty glance up toward the house.

What's true anymore?

'Jess, you okay out there?' She jumped, bumping her head against the roof. Looking through the back window, she could see Wallace calling from the front door, the light from the house behind making her appear black.

Jess levered herself back out the front door of the car, waved. 'Coming.'

Shit on toast with a cherry on top. What now?

TWENTY-THREE

'Are you bringing in Milt's bag as well?'

Jess felt her face redden, hoping the gloom would conceal it as she struggled with both bags toward the weather room. 'May as well. That way it'll be ready when he gets back. Have you heard from him yet?'

'No.'

Did her voice sound strained?

'Let me give you a hand?' Wallace reached for Milt's larger suitcase.

Jess turned her body slightly, angling the bag away from Wallace. 'No, I'm fine. Really.' Squeezing past, she set the bags down beside the staircase. 'Maybe I'll ring him. See if he's okay.'

'I'm sure he's fine. He said he was going to contact the local police about poor old Mary—her body is still upstairs, of course. He'll probably wait and come back with them—then there's the undertaker to organize. It all takes time, particularly at night. Why don't I put the kettle on? Maybe I can even have a scratch around in the freezer to see if there's anything edible,' Wallace said.

Jess waited until she heard the clatter of cups and plates from the kitchen before quietly unzipping Milt's suitcase and removing the axe. She rested it, blades down, behind a small potted palm near the archway opening into the lounge room. Exactly why she'd done that was difficult to work out, it just made her feel better to have it close. In a strange way it worked like the shirt, bringing Milt in, so she didn't feel so alone.

Mind awash, Jess went back into the lounge room and settled herself into the armchair. Wallace returned soon after, carrying a tray with two cups, a teapot, and a plate with what looked like toast. She set it down on the dark, wooden coffee table between the two chairs. 'I found some bread. I think it's okay. Only butter for the spread, unless you're really into unspecified tinned fish.'

'Not that desperate—thanks, anyway.'

Am I being paranoid or is there something strange about Wallace? Different? She exhaled slowly. *Only one way to find out.*

As Wallace poured the tea, Jess took out her phone and tapped the contact for Milt's number, adding as she brought the handset to her ear, 'I think I'll ring Milt anyway.'

Watching. Waiting.

Wallace's hand paused midway between cups, her head slowly turning to look at Jess. Their glares locked. The number was connecting, ringing, first in Jess's ear and seconds later from across the room, its tone muffled. The sound coming from inside Wallace's handbag.

Jess stood and walked over to the shoulder bag hooked beside the door. She opened it and looked inside. Milt's phone was flashing at the bottom of the bag, the light reflecting on the keys to the car and the front door. Using both hands she reached in, grabbed the phone in one and palmed the keys behind her thumb with the other. She held up the ringing phone dramatically and walked back to the lounge, dropping it onto the seat beside Wallace as she passed. The hand with the key slid unnoticed into her coat pocket.

'Where is he?' she demanded.

The time for pretense had passed. Jess hung up, and the ringing stopped, making space for a thick silence.

'Outside—in the garden shed.'

'Alive?' Jess found the word hard to say. So much seemed to be hanging off it.

'For now.'

'But why? I don't understand?'

'Don't you? Well, maybe it is time for everyone to fess up.'

Something flickered across Wallace's face, like electrical interference across a monitor. Jess gasped as Wallace's face rearranged itself.

'Wallace?' She could hardly get the word out.

It was an "almost Wallace," as if an artist had tried to make a copy but didn't quite have the talent to pull it off. One corner of the woman's mouth slid up into a sneer. 'Who are you? What's happened to Wallace?' Jess repeated, her mind spinning, not really believing what she was saying.

'Her? Oh, she's around here someplace,' she said smirking, patting her abdomen and the pockets of her slacks. 'She's just taking a break from the captain's chair. Ultimately it all comes down to whoever has the stronger will, and Wallace, well, as that old biddy upstairs said earlier, she never did quite have it.'

'You're in this with Dragos?'

'For someone who's supposed to be so special, you are a little slow —you know that? Use that ring of yours and take a closer look, witch.'

Jess allowed the ring to pulse and narrowed her eyes, looking beyond and between what was immediately in front of her. What appeared to be four tendrils, or suckers, were attached to Wallace's head.

She shook her head, clearing the disturbing image from her sight.

'You're Dragos.'

The demon's smile inside Wallace mouth looked greasy.

'And Milt? What about him?'

Wallace's face smirked. 'You managed to make quite a mess of my man downstairs. I had to scrape him up off the floor while you were out of it up here. They're wired up to each other out in the shed. Your old man is proving to be an excellent battery.'

'Dying,' Jess stated, her voice dull.

'But in a good cause. Now you're getting it. So be a good girl and dig out the Cipher and its code from between your tits and we can work out the "secret" message so we're ready to go get those damned Scrolls. In case you hadn't quite worked it out yet, time's a wastin'. The window to access the Scrolls opens tomorrow.'

'Tomorrow?' Jess said, the question reflexive, wondering whether this was just another of the demon's deceptions.

'Oh, of course, you've been time slipping, haven't you? Well, time is not only moving faster, mortal, it's leap frogging. The nexus is tomorrow. That's why we have to be sharp and on our game. Now give me the ring, the cipher and its code.'

'What if I refuse?' Jess said, backing up one slow step at a time.

'Not an option, little sister. Not an option.'

Wallace's body walked around the oversized lounge suite, keeping pace. For every backward step Jess made, Wallace took one forward.

'Where do you think you're going? The doors are locked. There is nowhere to run to, no one left to help—except me, of course.' She looked down at Wallace's watch. 'Shea should be coming around soon. I know he's looking forward to "meeting" you again.'

Jess was at the archway that separated the lounge from the vestibule. The little potted palm was less than a meter to her left. Balling a fist, she brought it to her mouth, aping fear, hoping it would divert attention from the other arm tucking behind her.

Wallace's nose twitched, nostrils flaring. She was like a cat playing with her food, enjoying the fear dance, feasting on the power. Jess took half a step to the left, and finally felt a delicate palm frond nestle softly against the back of her hand. So close. Dragos was a lunge away. Jess tensioned through the soles of her feet. They were still sore; she wasn't sure whether they'd hold up to what she had in mind, but the alternative was worse. Moving onto the ball of her foot, Jess spun, snatching up the handle of the axe on the exit of the turn, using the toes of her other foot to launch herself toward the stairs, creating space. The movement took Dragos by surprise. Jess faced him from the foot of the stairs, the silver axe drawn back, ready to swing.

Dragos brought Wallace's hands together in a slow clap.

'You know what this is,' Jess said, hefting the axe, trying not to be thrown by the other's nonchalance. 'This is the demon killer. One swipe, you're gone.' Jess firmed her mouth and charged, bringing the axe through in a wide deadly arc. Wallace stepped deftly aside, feet together, flowing like a matador in the ring. The axe blades whistled harmlessly past.

Using the momentum, Jess spun again, arms at full length, increasing the velocity of the swing. Wallace ducked, deftly stepping inside the decaying arc of the axe as it passed over her, and seized its handle, the hardened edge of her other hand coming down painfully on Jess's wrist. The axe clattered to the floor.

Wallace drove herself at Jess, pinning her against the stair railing, their faces centimeters apart.

'Give up?' Dragos said, lips firming into a cruel line as he tried to pin Jess's arms.

The surge of energy Jess had summoned to swing the axe had dissipated, leaving in its wake a deep tiredness, as if a plug had been pulled and everything strong in her was leaking away. It would be so easy to stop struggling; just let him have what he wanted.... *That isn't me! It's him—inside my head.*

Dragos grinned. Wallace's body now had Jess in a bear hug and was squeezing the air from her lungs. *How did Wallace become so strong?*

Fuzzy blackness framed Jess's field of vision. It was difficult to feel her legs; they were no longer strong enough to support her. Jess felt herself sag, sliding down, legs, body deflating like a balloon with a slow leak.

Lying on the floor, looking up, Jess's vision came in and out of focus. Looming over her, Wallace seemed like a colossus.

Dragos removed the Cipher and code from inside Jess's bra with a flourish.

'Now for that ring,' he said, reaching for the axe.

He didn't see the creeping black shape flow up the stairs, nor its startling blue eyes as it leaned out between a banister upright and its adjacent step. With a shrill screech, Midnight launched herself, claws extended, straight toward Wallace's unprotected face.

Wallace screamed, dropping the papers as she tried to disengage the squealing cat. Jess wasted precious seconds watching the claws embed themselves in Wallace's scalp and cheeks, blood already running freely in long streaks down her face. Both the woman and the cat were wailing.

Gathering her scrambled wits, Jess scooped up the Cipher and code, shoving them back inside her bra as she scrambled across the floor to the axe and used it to help herself up. The room's horizon dipped before she found a wobbly balance. Just as Dragos managed to disengage the cat and hurl it away, Jess swung the axe. It lacked both power and direction. Dragos, seeing the silver flash from the corner of his eye, tried to dive toward her, managing to avoid the lethal blades but Wallace's head was not quite low enough to avoid the shaft. It came in hard against her temple. Wallace fell back, dazed, arms spreadeagled, staring up. As she watched, the eyes changed from green to what could only be black. They stared up at her; Jess felt if she looked into them long enough, she'd fall in, the space behind them infinite and terrible.

'Go on, do it. Do you have the guts? You could be rid of this curse forever.' Dragos's voice cut through the stillness, the black eyes challenging. He seemed to be awake inside an unconscious body.

Jess stood over Wallace's sprawled body, axe raised above her head, breath heaving. Only moments before she would have happily beheaded the demon, but now that her hot blood was cooling, she wasn't sure she could. Unconscious, the body now looked more like Wallace again, yet obviously it wasn't, not with that teasing, sickly smile on its mouth and the black eyes daring her to strike.

She considered just leaving and making a run for it in the car, but there was no telling if Wallace's body was strong enough to give chase. Her breathing looked to be regular, and now the facial muscles were twitching.

Biting her bottom lip, Jess raised the axe again, paused, and then with a huge whoosh of air brought it down, deftly shearing through two of the horrible orange tentacles. Dragos screamed, and Wallace's body convulsed as if she'd received defib to her heart, the severed tentacles dancing in the air like cut guy wires.

Jess's stomach quailed, her legs trembling with adrenaline as she forced herself to remain and not run screaming to the door. Two tentacles remained connected. Wallace's body was squirming, recovering, pushing itself up to a sitting position. It seemed to be a struggle.

Jess backed away, the axe dragging down on her arms. Even with the blades resting on the floor, it seemed almost too heavy to hold. The black gaze tracked her, capturing her own until she felt as if she couldn't look away.

Wallace's mouth stretched sideways, revealing teeth and a strange hunger. The two connected tentacles swelled like water pumping through constricted tubes. From a distance, Jess's brain seemed to be silently mouthing that the demon was pulling in more energy through those tubes. It urged her to run, to escape; avoidance had always worked in the past. But Dragos's eyes pinned her, both in place and space. It was as if she were suspended.

The axe dragged on her arms, as if gravity had decided to quadruple its pull on it. She felt her fingers slipping, unsure whether she could maintain the effort. Yet she knew with deep certainty that if the axe fell, she'd never be able to pick it up again. Jess took another step backward and shook her head, trying to clear it.

"Draw up; not down. Draw up."

That voice in her head again. The same woman. Where was it coming from? What did it mean?

Wallace's body was now on its feet; above her head, the two severed tentacles hung lifeless like withered vines, while those still connected bulged even more, pumping in whatever it was that Dragos was drawing down to animate the body.

'Wallace? If you're in there, Wallace, help me, please,' Jess called, desperately resisting the overwhelming urge to release the axe.

Dragos laughed and shuffled a little closer but did not attack.

Why is he hesitating?

She saw him flick a glance down at the axe before taking another step. Jess managed to keep the distance between them by relinquishing more ground. Behind her, she could feel the mass of the wall looming; there would be no further retreat soon.

She'd been unable to drag the axe with her. Stretched forward, arms extended, she was only able to keep hold of the handle. Desperately she tried to pull back on her arms. It was as if the axe blade was embedded in the floor. It wouldn't budge, and its sheer weight was dragging on her shoulders. Sweat beaded on her brow with the effort. It felt as if her shoulders would dislocate.

"Draw up!" A whisper this time, the frustration at Jess's inability to understand evident even within the screaming white noise inside her head.

Was it all going to end like this? Was this it?

For the first time, Jess understood Angelique's lifelong fear; knew it as deeply and intimately as if she were swimming atop it—with no shoreline in sight, no end to its depth below, only cold, gut-wrenching fear that would eventually sneak in to fill and claim her. Jess felt so tired. Tired of trying to prove something, of trying to be different, stronger, more whole. Than what? She wasn't, couldn't hope to be this Messenger. Mum had been right all along. *What a wretched bloody joke this was from the Universe. Humanity, all life, now doomed to a fate I was always incapable of saving them from. Me, the hope for the world. Better choosing next century, honey.*

"Draw up." The voice tried again, weaker now, but more desperate.

Jess was finding it hard to think at all. White noise leaked, threatened to dissolve her thoughts even as they tried to form.

What did "drawing up" mean? Milt was the artist, not her. No, not that sort of drawing. She was fairly sure of that. Oh, this was too hard.

Milt.

Milt was still alive out in the shed. Oddly, she could sense a faint flicker of him, like a waft of a familiar smell on an unexpected breeze. She clung to that, firm, familiar, solid. A rock. So different to Mum. The sensation puffed in again, briefly clearing a small space in her head. Something important was happening; something she had to do.

Looking down, she managed to tighten her fingers around the handle of the axe. They'd almost let go that time. Grimly she held on, focusing on the feel of the handle, the imprint of the shaft against her skin. Tighter. Gradually it became easier. She made the mistake of glancing up into the black eyes opposite and hastily jerked her gaze away before it locked.

Jess managed another step back, her arms and back now extended at full stretch, the wall pushing back from behind. Retreat no more. She could no longer run, her default response to life ended here with the wall. There was nowhere else to go other than here, right now, and suddenly she knew what that meant.

Draw up.

From the floor, from the very depths of this house on this mountain, she felt the deep pulsing power of the Sisterhood, plugged into Nature. She forced in a ragged breath and tugged, pulling on the axe handle. It resisted, and she drew up more. Slowly, slowly it moved as if shifting a great weight, scoring deep, raw lines into the polished wood floor as she dragged it toward her.

Across from her, something had changed; Jess could sense it. Dragos's power was still strong, almost magnetic, but he was also very wary of the axe. That was why he hadn't attacked. She intuited that he couldn't, not while the axe blades were between them and it still pulsed with her energy.

Pulling it closer, she made one last effort and heaved it over and up, the blade clearing the floor with a sticky sucking sound. As it did so, Dragos stumbled back, momentarily unbalanced with the sudden release of energy.

Jess swung the axe up; it felt effortless now. The two orange suckers atop Wallace's head were bulging as Dragos tried to channel in more energy. Jess could feel her own essence pulsing up through the tattered soles of her feet, into her arms, and flowing finally into the axe handle. It was a perfect conductor. She took careful aim and swung it through a wide upward arc. Dragos swerved, but the tentacles, being longer, were a fraction slower to respond, and the axe blade separated their connection to him. Wallace's back arched and then the body crumpled to the floor. Standing over it, breath heaving in her chest, Jess stared down. Slowly the malevolence from the black eyes faded as they lost awareness, the eyelids closing. Part of her longed to decapitate the demon.

I'm not a murderer. No matter how many roles I play, I'll never do that. Not even to that thing.

Using the axe as support, Jess began to hobble toward the door, digging in her coat pocket for the keys. Her steps faltered halfway. *Does Wallace still live somewhere in there? Is some part of her recoverable, like some deeply buried hard drive in a smashed laptop?*

This was the worst part. Not knowing; never knowing. And the only people who did were either dead or on their way there. Doubts slithered in again, sliding through the cracks in her hastily erected resolve.

Right now, there's me—and a cat (and who the heck knows about that)—on the job to save the world. Sounded like a song title or an alien movie she would have once loved to have played the lead in. Sigourney II. Jess imagined herself in a khaki shirt and combat pants and chuckled, recognizing it as the aftereffects of severe stress. If she didn't watch it, she'd start laughing and wouldn't be able to stop.

As if in anticipation, a memory of a future with crazy climates and water that wars would be fought over bubbled up and slid into frame, hosing down the threatening release.

All right, all right, but why me? Why do I have to be the one to do it?

"You are the Messenger now. It's your destiny. No one else can."

That voice again. Jess shook her head, her fingers fumbling uncertainly with the keys. Behind her, Wallace's body groaned. Jess turned, and as if unaware of where her feet directed her, shambled back, the axe handle balanced and ready on her shoulder.

As she approached, Wallace's body convulsed, the back arching once more into some sort of spasm, then collapsed completely against the floor.

Jess stood over her. Wallace's breathing was now regular; the face had resolved back into the familiar. *Has Dragos gone?* The tentacles certainly had. Jess tuned into the ring on her finger to make sure. Not even a sign of where they'd been connected. Tentatively she nudged Wallace with her toes, bringing the foot back quickly.

'Wallace?' Her voice cracked.

Another nudge, stronger this time, using the ball of her foot to shake Wallace's shoulder. She groaned again and then opened her eyes. Jess sighed with relief. They were green, not black.

'Are you all right?' she asked.

Wallace grimaced and rubbed weakly at her face as if checking everything was still in place.

'Yeah, I think so.'

'Do you remember—'

'Unfortunately, yes. I saw it all. Couldn't do a thing about it though. Talk about mind rape.'

Relief flushed through Jess. She bent down and helped Wallace up to a sitting position.

'I know you don't want to hear this, Wallace, but we need to get out of here. Dragos could come back.'

'Oh, there's no doubt of that,' Wallace said, grunting as she pushed herself up. 'We, or rather you, beat him tonight but the real test comes tomorrow.'

'With the Scrolls?'

Wallace nodded, accepting Jess's help to stand up.

Together they walked to the door and out through the weather room.

The night air was cold and tight inside her lungs, but it sloughed away the aftereffects of the adrenaline.

She eased Wallace into the back seat and climbed into the front.

What the heck is that noise?

Flicking on the headlights, she saw Midnight in front of the car, tail sweeping the ground, a sound of grinding glass marbles coming from her throat.

'Come on then, hurry up,' Jess said, hanging out the car door, motioning for the cat to get in. 'In or out, hurry up.'

Midnight stood and walked a couple of paces, then turned and looked back. Her eyes seemed to be that same startling blue they'd been before. Jess wondered whether whatever had happened to her made her interpret eye color differently. Did that mean something?

Midnight was still blocking the way.

'Oh, for goodness sake.' Jess nudged the car forward, hoping Midnight would get the message, then tried to drive around her. As she turned the wheel, the headlights picked up something through the shrubbery, down a narrow track leading off the drive.

The garden shed.

Milt.

A wave of remorse flooded through her.

Milt was down there.

'Wallace, wake up. You have to help me get Milt.' She turned in her seat. Wallace was unconscious, curled into a ball on one side of the back seat.

Swearing, she turned the car onto the narrow track, Midnight bounding ahead. She stopped just outside the shed door and climbed out, the axe dragging behind as if reluctant to accompany her. She left the engine running, lights on, trained on the shed door.

Hefting the axe, she hacked through the weathered wood. It

yielded without a struggle, the door bursting apart to hang at an angle from its remaining rusty hinge.

Some of the headlights' reflected wash spilled through the narrow doorway. Milt was sprawled across a large wheelbarrow, arms and legs hanging over the sides like giant, limp noodles. *I wondered how Wallace had managed to carry the big oaf. Even with the barrow it would have been a struggle.* Maybe that didn't count if you were possessed by a demon?

She turned her mind back to the practical.

Milt was connected by what seemed to be a series of luminous ribbons or tapes to a shape on the long bench running right along the back of the shed. Some of the ribbons were bright with yellow light, others duller. Jess ripped them all away, both bodies spasming as she pulled the final one free. Clumsily she felt for Milt's pulse; it was faint but still there. With no place else to put it, she laid the silver axe along Milt's prone body while she tried to lift the handles of the barrow. Nothing budged. He was too heavy for her.

Midnight jumped up onto Milt's chest and began pummeling it.

'Not now, cat. This is serious,' Jess said, grunting as she bent her legs, pushing through the soles of her feet, taking the strain through her strong thighs. Her damaged feet were sore and incredibly cold. The wheelbarrow lifted a little, and she took a staggered step back, dragging it with her. Puffing, she set it down again. Midnight continued to pummel Milt. The axe seemed to be shining. Jess moved her head to look at it quizzically. *Maybe it's just the reflection from the headlights.*

The burned body on the bench groaned, moving one of its blackened arms. Shea. Jess sobbed, remembering, now knowing everything that she feared had really happened. She managed to drag the wheelbarrow another half meter. She was now almost level with the broken door. In the brighter light, Jess could see Milt's face was drawn and white. Turning to face the car, she gripped the wheelbarrow's handles and lifted, managing to drag it another meter.

Wallace was still passed out in the back seat.

Could Dragos "do" anything remotely? Some sort of disabling spell?

'Jess? Is that you?' Milt croaked.

She turned back. Milt's head was lolling over the back lip of the wheelbarrow. His mouth moved into a weak grin that disappeared almost immediately. 'Thought I recognized the family scent,' he said faintly. The axe was definitely glowing.

There's still a chance.

Renewed, Jess dragged, cursed, and grunted the load along. Popping the station wagon's tailgate, she brought the side of the wheelbarrow tight in against the open cargo area. Fortunately, this was a small car—and low enough so the edge of the loading area was almost level with the lip of the barrow. *With a bit of luck and umph, I should be able to roll him off and in.*

Going around to the side door, she pushed Wallace further to one side and popped the opposite side of the rear seat flat before crawling through to the back of the station wagon. Reaching for Milt's furthest arm, she placed her feet on either side of the tailgate's frame and leaned back, pushing through her feet for extra leverage as she pulled on the arm. Milt grunted. This had to be hurting, but it sure as heck beat being an Eveready battery to the mess inside the shed.

She needed to rock him in. Keeping hold of his arm, she allowed Milt's bulk to slowly drift back toward the barrow, then, knees bent, Jess tensioned through her feet and tugged back. Then repeated the process, building momentum.

An *uuumph.*

Good, wake up Milt.

'Help me, you big lump. God, you're heavy.'

He was on his side. As he rolled back, she pulled hard, and he flopped halfway into the car.

'Come on, Milt, I need you to give me a hand—can you crawl?'

Nothing.

Cursing under her breath, Jess scuttled out and went back around to the barrow. This time she used the handle of the axe as a lever, wedging it between Milt's hips and the base of the barrow. She almost had him in when from inside the shed she heard chanting, the voice powerful and penetrating.

She recognized it. Dragos. He was trying to reanimate Shea.

'Wallace, wake up. Help me,' she shouted over her shoulder, imagining the blackened image of Shea's crisped body seizing her from behind.

Turning back to Milt, Jess redoubled her efforts until he finally tumbled into the rear of the station wagon. Slamming the tailgate shut, she hobbled along the side of the car to the driver door, keeping the axe close. Midnight had curled herself into a ball on the passenger seat.

'Looks like it's unanimous. We're all outta here.'

Midnight yawned, her green eyes closing.

Jess slid the transmission into reverse and had turned in her seat to back down the narrow track to the driveway when something slammed against the hood. She screamed. A blackened hand, white bones stark against the charred flesh, scrabbled against the windscreen. Shea. Or what was left of him.

She floored the accelerator, and the car shot backward. Shea hooked his skeletal fingers around the windscreen wipers, hanging on, his ghoulish face now only inches from hers, leering through a lipless half mouth, teeth grotesquely exposed as if stuck in a maniacal grin. She spun the steering wheel to full lock, and the rear of the station wagon smashed into one of the many trees lining the track. Cursing, Jess dragged the seat belt across and clicked it home. Midnight was all paws and legs on the floor, her yowling adding to the tension.

She didn't even want to think about how Milt was doing in the back. She'd felt his unrestrained body weight slam through the gap into the back of her seat.

No time.

She could hear Shea clambering on the roof. He'd been thrown back over the windscreen with the impact. One of the windscreen wipers had broken off, and Shea was using it to try and spear through the thin metal of the roof. Jess glanced down at the axe wedged between the passenger seat and the door, pleased she hadn't left it behind. She drove forward, alternately accelerating and braking hard, hoping to throw Shea off. A hole ripped through the roof's inner layer, jagged spikes of metal surrounding it. He'd broken through. Jess put the car into drive and came around in a tight turn, wheels spinning in the soft scree and leaf litter, back end fishtailing. The slamming noise stopped; now there was only a disconcerting scramble like claws struggling for purchase.

She jammed both feet onto the large brake pedal, and the car pitched to a halt. Shea kept going right off the front.

There was a bump beneath the offside front and back wheels; the car's suspension bounced and shuddered. Shea was roadkill, and she was pleased. Turning the car out of the drive and onto the road, Jess was aware of the lava-like panic raging in her belly, unsure whether it would erupt. She wasn't used to this level of prolonged stress, the simultaneous feelings of terror like steel bands around her temples while another part of her felt like laughing with relief and never stopping.

TWENTY-FOUR

She drove wildly and fast, unmindful of direction or purpose other than escape, her breath hot and ragged, spreading and fogging against the cold glass of the windscreen. Her surroundings intruded in chunks: oncoming headlights, blaring horns as she hastily swerved back into her own lane, then roadside signs warning of bends and speed restrictions, and finally the inside of her own vehicle and her clammy hands, fingers like claws clamped around the steering wheel.

Jess allowed her breath to deepen, consciously releasing her hands then fingers, one by one, willing them to rub the condensation from the glass before finally flicking on the demister. The fog cleared from the bottom, vanishing upward as if it were lifting the same way as the tension from her body. As it did, cognition returned. *Where can I go?* The very thought of safety now seemed laughable.

All she could hope for was sanctuary, another place to hide where she could perhaps eat and snatch some precious sleep before this whole nightmare started again. What did Wallace call it? Oh yes, the "real test." How could time leapfrog like that?

She didn't know where to go.

Midnight stirred on the seat beside her and stretched long. Yawning, the cat gave herself a couple of half-hearted licks and then hopped onto the top of the seat, plopping over to the back.

'Hey, where are you off to?' Jess said, looking into the rearview mirror. In the splash of light from a passing car's headlights she saw Midnight settle atop Milt's chest, beginning the pawing and purring ritual she'd performed earlier.

'Weird cat,' she muttered, though part of her hoped that whatever Midnight was doing amounted to something magical, rather than simply getting comfortable. She needed Milt—hell, she needed someone. She didn't even know what she was doing here anymore. She turned a corner, and something glinting from the side seat caught her eye.

The axe.

Its head reflected ambient light from the dash. Thank goodness she hadn't beheaded Wallace, not that she hadn't been tempted when those black eyes opened. Possessed or not, in the law's eyes it would've been murder, and not just anyone, a police detective.

Well, your honor, she was really this demon called Dragos that took over Detective Carruthers's body....

In hindsight, this would have just been just another way to take her out of contention for the Scrolls. Dragos would have survived it, she knew that now.

Tiredness crept up the back of her skull, sneaking down through her body like ink dispersing through water. It was becoming harder to concentrate, and several times she had to jerk herself awake as the tires drifted off the bitumen toward the guardrail. Slowing down didn't help. Neither did opening the window and gulping in lungfuls of freezing night air. She needed to find somewhere to pull over and rest, if only for a couple of minutes. Squinting into the furthest reach of her headlights, she spied a turnoff up ahead. Coming closer, she could see it had a mailbox and a long driveway. Jess didn't care; it was 2:00 a.m.

She jolted onto the narrow asphalt drive, dimming the lights to parkers. The asphalt gave out twenty meters further on, becoming packed dirt embedded with rough stones. It continued to wind steeply up the side of a rise; there was no house that she could see, but to play it safe she stopped the car beneath a large tree and flicked off the lights. Her car blocked the road, but right now, she didn't care. There were no lights from further up, so if there was a house it was likely the occupants would be sleeping now. By the time anyone wanted to come down the road, she'd be long gone.

Jess put the seat back into full recline and closed her eyes, allowing herself to drift, becoming part of the nightscape, the only sound Midnight's rough purr and from the top of the driveway a single barked challenge of a dog sensing something had changed but unsure exactly what. Rolling into a more comfortable position, she felt the packages inside her bra shift. She touched the stiff rolled parchment. Her greatest challenge was still to come, and she wondered whether she was ready.

SHE AWOKE TO STRONG LIGHT, bright against her closed lids. Her mouth was gummy and her neck hurt where she'd slept in an awkward position. There was also another sound, something she knew she should recognize but was too groggy to work out. Jess listened harder, the sound fighting through persistent layers of sleep.

Voices.

Hushed.

Just outside.

The events of the evening returned with a clash, like a scenery backdrop thudding into place for the next act. Sitting up with a start, she banged her knee painfully against the steering column. She rubbed away the condensation from the side window with a grimy hand, expecting to see Shea outside. Instead she recognized Milt's broad back. He was leaning against the driver door and seemed to be talking amiably. When she peered around him, she could see a man in a flannel shirt, heavy leather jacket, and jeans; to the front a faded red Jeep, thick plumes of blue exhaust snaking into the cold air behind it.

Jess knocked against the window. Milt jumped away from the door, and she clambered out. The men made way for her on the narrow driveway.

'Oh, Jess, good, you're awake. I was just telling Dave here that our car was running rough last night, and we pulled off to let it cool down. He offered to ring the NRMA for us, but I said we can probably get it going long enough to make it to the next town. It's only five k's.'

Jess found herself nodding, waving fingers airily at the tall man. 'Sorry we blocked you in. Er, are you feeling... better... now, Milt?'

'Just fine, Jess, nothing a little more sleep couldn't cure. Best be getting on though. I didn't want to wake Wallace, she's still sleeping. I assume she's... all right?'

Jess nodded dumbly as the two men shook hands. Milt came around the hood and settled into the passenger seat. Jess looked across at him and he winked.

'He's waiting,' he said, flicking a stubby finger toward Dave.

She reversed back out the drive and onto the road. A thousand questions peppered her head.

'Are you really all right? You look terrible.'

'And good morning to you too. Yes, and what's more, I remember everything. I may have been out to it, but somehow I was still aware of what was happening. It was like being consciously paralyzed. I woke up a few minutes ago with the cat clawing the crap out of my chest and Dave back there tapping on the window.'

'God, I didn't even hear him. I thought it was Shea or Dragos out there for a minute. You know that Wallace is....'

'Yeah, something went wrong with her last night. I figured that out just before she clocked me. How did that happen?'

'Dragos possessed her somehow. I saw these strange-looking tentacle things... never mind. I'm just hoping Wallace is still all right in there somewhere. She seemed herself when I was getting her into the car.'

'Nuts,' Milt muttered. 'Either everyone else is or I am.' He looked out the side window. 'Is she all right, physically?'

Jess paused. 'For a while back there I could have Red-Queened her, you know, "off with her head"—Dragos, that is.'

'I'm pleased you didn't. So you got whatever you needed to read the code thing?'

'It's all here.' She tapped her sternum.

'So where are we headed then?'

'Not sure exactly, but today's the day for the Scrolls.'

'What? I thought we had ages before that.'

'Time flipped or leap frogged. Take a look at the date on my phone if you don't believe me.'

She tapped the slim phone in the center console.

'You're right. This might be the fastest few years of my life. At this rate, I'll be dead before dinnertime.'

'We better save the world by brunch then.'

'Do you know where we're going? What to do?' He saw a sign flash by. 'Blackheath? We didn't get far, did we? Considering so much time has, apparently, flashed by. Dragos is sure to be coming after us —what are we, twenty k's max from Old Mary's place at Leura.'

'Give or take.'

'And the scarred guy, Shea? Is he still alive?'

'He's mobile, pissed, and pretty well burned to a crisp, last time I saw him. I'm not sure how he's still moving. Obviously Dragos is still pulling his strings. This is scary-weird shit, Milt. He was like some sort of barbequed zombie back there. He wouldn't let up after I disconnected you both.'

'Yeah, that's right, I remember we were roomies for a while. It felt like he was sucking the life out of me in that shed.'

'Literally, I think.'

Milt reached over and patted the back of her hand clumsily.

'Thanks for coming for me, Jess. I really can't imagine what you had to go through back there.'

'It's all a bit of a blur,' she lied, gulping back the rising lump. 'I'm only pleased you're here. For a while there it was only me and Midnight leading the charge.'

'There's something strange about that cat, have you noticed?'

Jess smiled. 'Only when she has blue eyes.'

'Blue?' Milt said, turning to look into the back of the car. The cat stared back at him. 'They're green.'

'Yeah, that's what I mean.'

Milt grunted, letting that one slide. 'So you didn't answer me, why aren't we miles from here by now?'

Jess shrugged. 'I'm really not sure. Last night I felt as if I couldn't go another meter without passing out and now, I don't know, but I'm reluctant to leave the mountains. It's as if there's a strength here. I can't explain it. I felt it back at the house too. These mountains are special somehow. There's have a power here that the Sisters can tap into. Thinking of driving down the other side of the range is like jumping out of a perfectly fine boat into the open ocean. I could do it, but why would I?'

'Okay. That doesn't make any sense, but then again nothing has for a while. Where to then? We need to get out of the open.'

Jess shrugged again. 'All I know is we aren't there yet. But I'm pretty sure this is the way. It's a feeling, Milt.'

'Oh, right, one of those, they've been a great help so far,' he said, dragging the axe closer.

'Plus, there's the ring, it seems to think we're on the right track,' she added, waggling her hand in front of him. The stone was blinking from its normal gray to a dull red.

'Oh, that bloody ring. I'm pleased I can't see it.'

They drove for another ten kilometers, slowing as they entered another small village. Hartley. Jess braked, peering closer as they approached a sign. She pointed, stopping the car completely. From behind there was a squeal of brakes and a long hard horn blast before a car swept around them, the driver shooting eye daggers through the side window. Milt gave them the finger.

'Jenolan Caves?' he said reading the sign. 'Are you sure?'

Jess flicked the blinker on to turn left. 'No. But the ring seems to be.' It was flashing more urgently now, its color brighter as well. 'At least there'll be a crowd to lose ourselves in. That's a start.'

'Yeah right. That's what we need right now, a bunch of strangers, any one of whom could be induced to kill.' He wriggled his fingers at the sides of his head. "The demon made me do it, your honor."

'Been there already. We have to trust something, and right now this feeling and the ring are all we've got.' She glanced into the rearview mirror. 'That and a cat with color-shifting eyes.'

THEY LEFT the car in the day visitors' car park and went into the ticket office. Milt made a show of examining the tour times for various caves, his gaze flicking constantly across the faces of the growing number of visitors.

Jess wasn't sure what else to do, so she joined the queue, hoping for some sort of inspiration. The ring had stopped flashing and was now glowing a dull red. She hoped that meant they were getting warmer.

'You'll need this,' Milt said from behind, thrusting some notes into her hand.

She felt like a teenager on her first trip away from home. *Is that what a real life would have been like?* The thought sneaked out before she could contain it, and her eyes watered. She rubbed them with the back of one hand as the queue advanced and it was suddenly her turn. She still didn't know what they were doing here. The certainty she'd felt earlier had evaporated. The man behind the counter was looking at her quizzically. She stepped forward.

'Hi.'

He nodded, waiting expectantly.

'Two please,' she said, trying to smile.

'Eleven o'clock Lucas Cave?'

She nodded.

He slid across two tickets.

Rejoining Milt, she gave him one of them. 'Are you sure?' he hissed.

'No. But he seemed to be.'

'Great,' Milt murmured, following her out. 'What now?'

'Midnight. We need her. There's a carry bag in the car; we can put her in that.'

'You want to take a cat into the cave with us?'

'I keep telling you, *I* don't know, it's just what I *feel* has to happen.' Jess didn't want to tell him about the voice in her head. 'The jury is out as to whether that makes you crazier for taking notice. The ring thinks so too, look.' She held her hand out. The color of the stone had brightened and was now shining with a strong red light.

'If you say so,' Milt said.

They collected the cat and zipped her into the bag, slipping a torch into the side pocket. There was no spitting or protests. Jess took that to be a good sign.

'What about Wallace?' Milt asked, pointing at the slumped body in the back seat.

'She hasn't stirred since I put her in there. I can't see her being of much help, can you? We'll leave the windows partway open and the keys in her pocket. How's that?' Jess said, settling the larger woman more comfortably and closing the door.

She and Milt joined the group for the tour and followed the leader up to the cave mouth. After some instructions she really didn't listen to, they all started down.

They walked through the cave, the natural sights sliding past her as she waited for something to happen. Nearing the end of the underground tour, she paused, allowing the group to flow past her as she pretended to examine a small stream flowing below. Milt stayed beside her, arms perched on the protective fence, managing not to ask anything more after her first impatient shush.

The guide was waiting, wanting to hustle the group on. Reluctantly she moved, Milt following. Fear rose in her chest. She had no idea what she was supposed to do down here, or even if this was where she was supposed to be. Maybe this had been a mistake, and what she was interpreting as guidance was simply her mind making stuff up. No surprises there. Practice makes perfect. She could feel Milt's anxiety and impatience. It seemed to be rolling off him. For someone who didn't show his feelings, he had a way of sharing. Whatever was going to happen—if something was going to happen— it had to be soon.

They were leaving a well-lit cavern, spots illuminating limestone columns that had dripped themselves into being. Milt was fiddling and fussing with the shoulder bag.

'What's up?' she asked.

'It's the bloody cat, it's trying to claw its way out.'

'Maybe it can't breathe? Can you open the zip a bit and let some air in. Poor thing.'

Milt tugged the zip open a little and Midnight thrust her head through, eyes clenched shut, then with a mighty yowl she arched her body against the freely moving zip, forcing it open enough to scramble free. Milt made a wild grab for her, but Midnight was all claws and teeth.

'Shit! Bloody cat,' he said, sucking the side of his hand.

'Midnight,' Jess called. The cat ran into a small roped-off passageway. It was narrow and dark. Jess scrambled under the rope and ran after her. Milt, cursing, followed.

Cries of 'Is that a cat?' 'I thought animals weren't allowed down here,' and 'Are they on drugs?' drifted after them, the anxious voice of the guide cutting through, bouncing off the sharp rocks, unsure whether to follow, his responsibilities divided.

Jess ran, Milt blundering along behind, both following the faint blue light that seemed to be shining from Midnight's eyes.

TWENTY-FIVE

The passageway narrowed, forcing them to turn sideways. Midnight, seeming to sense their slowed pace, waited for them to catch up.

'Can you hear them?' Jess whispered, her breath struggling with effort. She found the torch in her pocket and flicked it on.

'No. I'm not sure whether that's good news or not. If this gets any narrower, I won't be able to fit,' he grunted turning sideways to squeeze between two jagged outcrops.

Midnight, her blue eyes eerily alight, sat waiting for them on the sandy floor. She looked up at Jess expectantly.

'I think this is it,' Jess said, reaching into her bra and pulling out the Cipher and key. 'Here, hold the torch for me. Shine it on this.'

Milt took the torch and directed the pale cone of light onto the Cipher. Carefully she placed the sheet with the irregularly cut holes over it.

'What's that?' he asked, pointing with the beam.

'The cipher and the key. The holes reveal the letters that are supposed to let me read the jumbled letters on the Cipher.' She glanced up at Milt. 'I think it's time. Now hold that light steady.'

'Better hurry, I can hear voices coming.'

Through the cut-out squares, words revealed themselves while others were obscured.

'Look,' Jess said.

'I see it.'

The unblocked words were glowing with a soft blue luminescence that, as they watched, turned yellow and bright, almost dancing off the page.

'Do something. Quick! They're almost here.'

Jess placed the hand wearing the ring atop the glowing words and she felt them flow off the page and into the ring and up through her in a way that both reassured and strengthened her. When she removed her hand, the page was blank. the words forming instead inside her head and strangely behind her tongue. Spontaneously she began to chant them, her voice high and wavery in the confined space.

'Nothing is happening,' Milt said. 'Try it again.' Milt looked back the way they'd come. The voices were getting louder. 'I'll go and try to hold them back.'

'No, stay here. We need to stay together. I'll try and tune in to the pronunciation better this time.'

'Tune in?'

'Just go with it, Milt.'

'Yeah right, where have I heard that before?'

Jess focused. She allowed the words from the Cipher to fill her; the information was inside her, all she had to do was allow it to flow out in the right way. This time when she began the recitation, the word sounds appeared phonetically in her mind before she said them. As they left her mouth, they took form, glowing bright, stretching and lengthening, joining together until they formed a glowing panel.

'Look, the words have arranged themselves into a door,' she said.

'Can you open it?' Milt said over his shoulder. 'I can see torchlight flashes back along the passageway now.'

Reaching out, her fingers tentatively brushed the surface of the door. It felt solid. An ancient latch was set into the center. Gingerly, she lifted it, and the door swung in. A deeper blackness extended beyond.

'Milt.'

Midnight mewed and slipped through the gap.

Jess followed, dragging Milt after her. The door closed behind them, its light and form winking out.

Inside, the blackness was intense.

'Midnight?' Jess whispered. A heavy hand clamped onto her shoulder, and she jumped.

'Relax, it's only me, I didn't want to lose you in here. It's so bloody dark. Where are we?'

'You're asking those questions again, Milt. Midnight has gone.'

'So's the door, in case you hadn't noticed.'

'And I can't hear those men from the cave anymore either,' she said quietly.

'You're both in another dimension. Some call it limbo, the place between,' a woman's voice said, floating out from the dark. Jess recognized it as the one she'd heard in her head earlier.

She felt Milt's hand jump against her shoulder.

'Did you hear that?' she asked.

'Yes, why? Do you know who it is?'

Jess nodded, then realized he couldn't see and patted the back of his hand instead, not wanting to speak and risk not hearing. Something, a shape, was emerging from the dark. Jess sensed more than saw it. She took a step back, running into Milt.

'Do you see that?' she whispered over her shoulder.

'Yeah, I think so.'

Jess knew what he meant. The darkness surrounding them remained absolute but out of it a grayness, a lighter dark, was emerging. It was roughly her height and shape. *A spirit?*

'Who are you?'

The shape made a sound that could have been a chuckle but said nothing.

'Who are you?' Jess repeated, her voice stronger, remembering her mother telling her once that if you could force an entity to give you its name, then you had a greater chance. At what, she'd forgotten to ask, but right now it seemed important.

The spirit seemed to hesitate, then said, 'I was known once as Mary.'

'Old Mary?' Milt said. 'But she's dead.'

'That doesn't seem to matter here, Milt,' Jess said, pointing. 'Look where her eyes would be. They're shining and they're blue. Recognize the shade?'

'Oh right, of course. You mean this really must be Captain Midnight—so who's this? Cat Woman? This is one-hundred-and-ten-proof bullshit if I've ever tasted it.'

'Milt.'

'Ghosts? Is that what we're up to now?'

'Like Aggie?'

Milt grunted. 'I guess it's no stranger than any of the other stuff we've been through,' he conceded.

'You must hurry,' Mary said. 'Time is moving faster for you. Without an anchor, time becomes slippery until it returns to where it started. I will try and equalize it for you.'

Mary's shape glowed brighter. She was definitely lighter, but still had no real substance.

'Follow me,' Mary said after a time, wafting away from them. Jess and Milt stumbled after her, Milt keeping hold of Jess's shoulders. They tripped on unseen rocks embedded in the sandy floor, following the drifting shape in front as best they could.

'Here,' Mary said, 'place your hand against the wall beside you, child.'

Jess did as she was asked and felt something slippery, like a water slick atop thick moss.

'Imagine light,' Mary said.

She felt something tingle against her palms and then grow and glow. The walls beneath her hands illuminated with a soft green light.

Mary's shape was more visible now too, the blueness seeming to permeate her, but still without feature or definition. What might have been an arm pointed up—a wash of blue lit an ancient hourglass hovering over them. Sand was emptying from the upper chamber.

'Time has equalized,' Mary said. 'But you must still act quickly. You must activate the Scrolls before the sand in the hourglass empties.'

'How?' Jess asked.

'First comes the proof. Make a fist with the hand that holds the ring and place its stone there.' The hazy arm pointed at an indentation in the wall. When Jess looked closer, there were three other indentations forming an upward triangle around the central point. A chiseled line linked the three.

'What is it?' Jess asked.

'The triangle that you see there is a locking mechanism. It has three parts. The bottom two points assess your energetic and physical identity to determine that you are a true Messenger. If you are one of the two contenders, the first two locks will open. The upper one measures your ability and training. Pray you have enough of both.'

'What if she doesn't?' Milt asked, his voice raspy and gruff against the silence.

'Then you will go no further. There is no way forward, nor back, from here.'

'You mean we're stuck? Here?'

Mary ignored him and again pointed at the indentation.

'Insert the ring, child, hurry. Others approach.'

'Others?'

'The other contender, Dragos, and his minions. This is a place of between and is where he's been tethered and bound.'

'You said "been"—'

Mary cut him off, her voice slicing across Milt's like a whip crack.

'There is no time for this.' She sighed, her voice becoming resigned. 'If you activate the Scrolls, that will seal the demon gate for another hundred years. His kind will not be able to cross. That is all you need to know.'

'You mean others like him?' Milt persisted.

Mary sighed impatiently. 'If the Akashic Scroll is activated, the one you call Dragos will be bound once more and he will gradually lose his power.'

'Will Wallace be all right?' Milt asked.

'Basically, yes. Perhaps. Possession is never an easy road to return from.'

'Why didn't you say so, then? Go on, stick the ring into that rock, Jess.'

Jess curled her fingers into her palm and inserted the stone into the indentation.

'Nothing's happening,' Jess said, feeling panic swell in her chest. *What if Mum was supposed to be the Messenger after all?*

Slowly, as if with deliberation, the two lower points began to glow a dull red.

'What about the top one?' she asked, turning to look at Mary over her shoulder.

'It has yet to respond,' she said dully.

'How long do we have to wait?' Jess asked, feeling perspiration form on her palm, wondering whether that would somehow help with conductivity. She willed confidence into her hand, glancing at the hourglass above her. The sand flowed steadily. Finally, Mary said, 'Your maternal lineage has been proven. Your training lacks.'

'What language does this woman speak?' Milt asked, his voice frustrated.

'The portal will not open. Her will is not strong enough. The training lacks.'

'What do I have to do?'

'There is no time for what must be done,' Mary said, pointing at the hourglass. 'Your training should have been done over many years. I warned Aggie—'

'Tell me! There must be something.'

Mary sighed again. 'The only way now would be for you to cross over. However, that would almost certainly take too much time and there is no guarantee—'

'Cross over where?' Milt snapped.

'Here is limbo, the in-between. Beyond....' She waved her hand airily down the dark passageway.

'You mean we have to die?' Jess asked.

'Not precisely, but you would have to pass through the veil.'

'And do what?'

'That is not for me to say. What training you have will have to lead you. That is why there is no time. The sands are passing.'

'Just say it, woman,' Milt blustered.

Mary seemed to bristle. Finally she said tightly, 'There is a second way. A key. If you can find it and can bring it back in time, you will be proven. It needs to be inserted here.'

She pointed down at the wall. Where the indentation for the ring had been in the center of the triangle, there was now another hole, horizontal—more a gap—slightly wider in the middle.

Jess knew the hole hadn't been there before.

'How do I cross over?'

Again Mary used what might have been an arm to point behind her.

'Come on, Milt, let's go.'

'Wait. Protector, you may want to take this.'

Mary drifted to one side, revealing the silver axe in its long leather holster leaning against a wall.

'Where the hell did that come from? I left that in the trunk of the car.'

'It is always available to you. It is part of you. You only need will it.'

Milt gripped the handle, hefting the weight.

'Feels comfortable, doesn't it?' Mary said. 'Like an extension of your own arm? Use it truly and it will become so.'

'I'll look forward to that,' he said, then muttered, 'I may just use it on you first.'

He buckled it against the side of his body and then stepped around Jess, leading the way down the passageway. She followed, the green light travelling with them, lighting only the section of the passage where they were.

Rounding a bend, Milt stopped suddenly, and Jess ran into him again. When she peeked around his back, she saw light streaming through an opening at the end. Blue sky, and clouds so close Jess felt she only had to reach out to touch them. Air was also moving through the passage, the jagged edges of what must be a cave mouth capturing chunks of breeze as it passed.

'That must be it. All change for Death Row,' he said, voice croaky, betraying his nervousness. He cleared his throat and tried a smile. 'Got your coppers ready for the ferryman?'

They approached the opening and looked out—then down. Thousands of feet below, a cold, dark snake of a river flowed between rocks. Jess could just make out the flecks of foam against black rocks as it rushed through the chasm. Stretching between their cave and a mountain opposite was a knotted rope bridge, whipping back and forth in the gusting wind.

'Not quite what I imagined,' he said.

'There are many ways to cross the River Styx,' Mary's voice said from behind them.

''Struth, I thought we'd gotten rid of you,' Milt said.

'As you pointed out, Protector, I am dead. The only purpose in delaying my trip to the High Plateau was to assist you and the Messenger. It was not easy to wait,' she added testily. 'Midnight was kind to be so accommodating but she was not the ideal vessel.'

Jess reached out toward the shape. Her hand went straight through, the only sensation a cold quiver, like passing in front of an open freezer. Jess drew back her hand. Mary seemed not to notice.

'We appreciate it. You called it the High Plateau, what's that?'

Jess asked, looking down at the gaps between the rope rungs of the bridge.

'It's where our kind go. You have noticed we tend to cluster on mountaintops? That's where our energy is drawn from. Even in death, it seems we prefer to approach the familiar, so that is what awaits us. Once I cross, I cannot return.'

'How do we get back?' Milt asked.

'Any way you can. Be guided by your intuition. If you have the time. Otherwise you will be trapped there.'

Mary's shape drifted to the mouth of the cave and out, seeming to step from one cloud to another like stones across a river, finally dissolving into the mist obscuring the other side.

'I'm guessing we'll have to take the lower road,' he said, gripping the rough hemp of the bridge.

'I'll go first. I'm lighter. You can be the anchor man,' Jess said, stepping onto the first unsteady rung, hands gripping the thick, rough rope that ran along either side of the bridge.

I won't look down. I also won't tell him I hate heights.

'Did I ever tell you I have a thing about heights?' he said from behind.

More genetic bombshells.

The wind whistled and gusted about her as if it had been waiting. The bridge swayed, rocking without rhythm whenever, whichever way the wind blew.

She took another teetering step, keeping the rope beneath the arches of her feet to better maintain her balance. Between the rungs there was nothing—thousands of feet of nothing.

I won't look down.

She felt the bridge shift and creak. She wondered whether Milt's weight behind her would help stabilize, or tip them both off. Another step. It was like walking a tightrope, but with more slack. The bridge dipped deeply to the middle before climbing again, which meant there was more play and whip when the wind blew.

I won't look down.

Reaching forward with her foot, she found the next rung, waited for the back swing, and eased her weight onto it, steadying herself with her hands. She repeated the move several times more. Her wounded feet protested, but she tried to ignore the pain.

Behind her she could hear Milt's voice, his words snatched away before they had time to reach her. Just as well; they both needed to keep their concentration. She'd almost reached the middle when she felt Milt lose his footing and fall against the side of the bridge, sending her sprawling into the opposite rope. Bouncing, she bent her knees, curling her toes around the ropes to avoid falling over the side. Once she'd steadied herself sufficiently, she chanced a look back. Milt had one leg all the way through the gap between two wide rungs and was trying to pull himself up.

Cautiously, she made her way back, and holding on tightly with one hand reached out with the other. Milt gripped it, his huge hand crushing hers as he used the leverage of her forward position to slide his leg up and through. She watched him reposition his foot on the rung, her gaze inevitably following the trajectory down.

The space beneath her spiraled away. What balance she retained was tugged away by the wind, vertigo rushing in to take its place. She could feel herself teetering, drawn down to the sinuous black line of water thrashing itself to a frenzy far below.

Milt's arm looped around her waist. 'Steady,' he said directly into her ear. 'Look only at the end of the bridge, take the ropes in your hand, that's it, now take a step, find the next rung. I'm with you.'

They reached the middle, Milt somehow staying with her. Their weight in the center seemed to steady the bridge, making it less susceptible to wild movements from the wind. It still swayed, but the swing was more predictable. They paused there, breathing deeply. The next section should be easier; they'd be climbing up. Jess started forward.

The side where they were heading was still shrouded in mist.

Jess felt more secure going up, and they made better time, finally climbing onto firm land.

'So here we are on the other side,' Milt said. 'I always wondered what it would be like. Misty. Typical.'

'Here, look, the mist is only at the edges. It's clear through there.'

Jess waved away the last wisps of cloud and stared out at the landscape spread before her. Mountains surrounded what appeared to be a valley—or plateau, Mary had called it. Everything was green, lush, the colors bright as if someone had turned up the contrast button. The sensation of energy thrumming up from the earth was overwhelming.

'Some place,' Milt said, hands on his hips. 'So what now? I don't see anyone. Do you think anyone lives here?'

'Ha ha. Funny. I'm pleased you didn't pass on your keen sense of humor in your gene pool.'

'Some folks got it, others don't,' he said, squinting into the distance.

The sun seemed overly bright. Jess closed her eyes and tried to tune into the frequency of the place. It was hard. There was so much happening, it was like standing beneath a mobile phone tower with a listening device, trying to detect one particular voice from the thousands that were constantly being relayed.

She shook her head and opened her eyes. 'It's no good—let's move further down, it may be less jumbled there.'

Milt had the grace not to ask what might be jumbling. In truth, she found his jokes reassuring; he was solid in a place where there was no substance, nothing to hang on to, and she knew she wouldn't have made it this far without him.

They walked downhill, crushing long, luscious grass beneath their feet, its sweet scent rising up. Other smells drifted by, flowers, their perfumes brief and intense. Even the air tasted sharp and pure against the back of her throat. She sensed a whispered temptation for her to stay but thrust the thought away sharply.

From the top, Jess had noticed a fast-flowing stream cascading down one side, bisecting their path. Beside it was a large tree. On impulse, Jess changed direction and headed for it.

As they drew closer, the detail of the tree became more distinct. She yelled back to Milt, who had stopped a few paces behind and was squinting off back up the hill, his hand on the hilt of the axe. Jess shivered, remembering its feel in her hands as she stood over Wallace.

'That tree has a feel to it,' she said. 'It's different to the other things here.'

Milt turned and shrugged; something seemed to be bothering him.

She approached the tree. It was huge, its branches so rich and heavy with foliage that they dipped under the weight, providing a pool of cool shade around the base of its wide trunk. She folded her body down onto the lush grass, spreading her arms wide and staring up. The tree canopy seemed to spiral away forever. With a knowledge that escaped her, she knew this was one of the Sisters' Ceremony Trees.

Milt remained at the edge of the shade, his back to her, still looking up the way they'd come.

'What's up?'

He pointed. In the distance there seemed to be figures emerging from the mist at the top of the ridge. Behind them came others—many others. Jess focused her awareness, sending it toward the approaching horde, testing their defenses. She shuddered. Their wards were solid; it was like accelerating a car into a concrete wall.

Milt walked backward slowly, sliding the axe free of its holster, eyes fixed on the figures making their way down the slope.

'Better hurry with whatever you need to do,' he said.

Jess nodded. It could only be Dragos, but it seemed neither of them wanted to actually say his name. What to do? Jess imagined the hole back in the wall of the cavern, remembered its shape and size, and mentally asked for help.

She received no answer. Instead she felt faint; the sun beating down had made her thirsty. Unsteadily, she made it to the stream and dropped to her knees, dipping her hands into the rushing water. It felt incredibly cool and refreshing. The sound was babbly, as if it were chattering to her, the ruffled surface strewn with large black rocks, the water busy as it rushed over and around them.

Succumbing to her thirst, she bent to the water, using her hand as a scoop and brought it to her mouth. The water tasted sweet, almost effervescent. She used both hands to take more, finally holding her breath and dipping her whole head into the water.

"*Stay,*" it gushed.

Her mind became awash with images. Unlike what it had been like higher up the slope, this was one long series, strong and slow. Slowly she withdrew her head, the water dripping from her hair onto her shoulders, but despite its temperature she was not cold.

'Jess, you okay?' she heard from a distance. She waved vaguely back at Milt, the images continuing, vivid against her eyelids, yet at the same time she was still able to see the tree, brook, and the surroundings quite clearly. She now knew what she was looking for.

"*Stay.*"

She ignored the beguiling voice inside her head.

'Jess?' Milt was now beside her, one hand on her shoulder, his face concerned, intermittently keeping watch on the figures coming down the hill and her.

'I'm all right,' Jess said, sliding his hand away as she stood, her head turning, looking for something...

There.

She approached the bush reverently. It was beside the stream at the edge of the tree's shadow where the light dappled. The bush was in bloom; the flowers a deep purple and shaped like a fleur-de-lis. Jess cupped one of the flowers in her hand, gently turning it over with one finger. The opposite side reminded her of a Merlin-like monk in purple robes, the bright yellow stamen where its eyes would be, the arms standing out from the middle portion in a curved replica of arms.

Jess closed her eyes, the flower nestling in her cupped palms. She felt something shift inside her, as if something long, cracked, and broken had finally joined, then sealed. When she opened her eyes, the flower had been replaced by a dagger. It was the same shape and deep purple color, only now much larger. Its engraved blade was slightly raised at the center, making it thicker in the middle, tapering quickly to sharp edges on either side. The blade would be the exact same shape as the hole in the wall, Jess was certain of it.

'Milt, I've got it.'

He looked down at what she was holding, thick eyebrows knitting as they evaluated the dagger. 'Great. It'll come in real handy at a picnic, but for now we still have to make it back through that lot, and I don't think that letter opener is going to cut it—or them,' he said, dipping the axe back in the general direction of the line of people on the slope. They'd paused midway down, knowing they were blocking the only way back. They were too far away to make out the detail on their faces.

'What do we do?' Jess asked.

'You go. I'll keep them entertained.'

Jess laughed. 'Don't be silly, there must be twenty of them.'

'Twenty-two, if you want to get technical. And I didn't say anything about staying here, did I? You may have some screws loose on your mother's side of the family, but mine are all tightened up just fine, thanks. No, I just plan on providing a distraction and then I'll be right on your tail, swinging across that gorge like a fat Tarzan if I have to, don't you worry. I figure you should wait here behind this tree until I get close, then, when they're occupied, skedaddle down that way, follow the band of trees along the stream, and then use those boulders over there to shield yourself as you climb back up the slope. You can get back to the bridge that way. I've been working this all out since I spotted them a while back.'

'No, Milt, you can't.'

Milt gave her a clumsy hug and said into her ear, 'In case I don't get a chance later, I want you to know you're a daughter any father would be proud to boast about... and my only regret is that we never got to know one another better.'

He pushed himself away and turned to walk back up the hill.

'Milt,' she said quietly.

Milt continued to walk.

'Wait.' The words cut through the space between them, and he stopped.

'You hear that?' he asked, turning. 'It sounded like that bloody woman....'

'Aggie?'

'Yeah. Another dead 'un. Well I guess if we're going to find them, this is where they'll be.' Milt took several steps back down the slope. 'Where are you, witch? Show yourself, and it better be good.'

'Over here, on the tree. I see your manners haven't improved, Milt.'

Jess turned to where the voice was coming from. Aggie's face, or what it would look like if it were carved on the trunk of a tree, stared back at them. The lips and eyes were all that moved when she spoke.

'What you see on the hill up there is an illusion. Only the dead and mortals can cross the divide to the High Plateau. Dragos cannot. He is projecting through his animate, Shea, who like you has managed the crossing. His purpose is to delay your return. Now you have opened the gateway, if the first four Elemental Scrolls are not activated in time, the demon gate will open automatically.'

'That's new news,' Jess said.

'And it's all bad,' Milt finished. 'Any other surprises?'

'The wards you feel up there from the men will fail. Dragos has no real power on this side, other than through Shea.'

'What about this?' Jess asked, holding out the dagger.

'You are being tested, Jess. If you'd been initiated properly, your totem animal and Nature Connection would have revealed themselves to you long ago. You would have had time to know their power and explore your own potential through them. As it is, you have had to do it all on the run. The totem has already been an aid to you,' Aggie added.

Totem?

'You mean Midnight?'

'Yes, your totem animal is the cat. Your connection to Nature is that bush, angelsword: the shape of a dagger on one side, on the other a wizard or a monk—some call that side Angel's Word. A fortuitous choice, as both are necessary for what lies ahead. Time is your enemy now. You cannot afford to fail. This is your second and last chance to activate the Scrolls. I must go now, and so should you. Trust your connections, Jess.'

Aggie's face resolved back into the furrowed bark of the tree.

'That was reassuring,' Milt said, looking up at the line of men ranged across the hill. 'They look bloody real to me.'

'I guess they're meant to, otherwise there wouldn't be any point, would there?'

'Well, I still think you should take the route I showed you—'

Jess sighed. 'There's no time, Milt. I can see that damn hourglass, it's floating above your head. I'm going up there with you. One way or the other, we'll find out.'

'But—'

Jess strode off, tucking the dagger into her belt; she narrowed her eyes, focusing her awareness, testing the energy further up the hill. She detected a ripple of anticipation as they watched her approach. Behind her, she could hear Milt puffing as he ran to catch up. Poor Milt, he was doing all this on blind faith; as far as he was concerned, there were twenty-plus big guys waiting to put him down and he was running toward them. She allowed herself a grateful smile, and her heart filled.

'Stay behind me, do that much,' he panted as he trotted ahead, the axe held at his side. Mary had been right, it did look like an extension of him. From behind he looked like a Viking with a bad haircut.

The closer she came to the men, the less sure she was that they were a projection. Their faces were mean, all different, each wearing the same hungry leer for lust and violence that she'd experienced so many times before. Some of them were shouting taunts at Milt, who was less than twenty paces from the first of them. Searching for a distraction, she tried to locate Shea, but he didn't seem to be there.

One of the biggest men rushed at Milt, swinging a club around his head and howling something that seemed to crawl up from his gut. Milt spread his feet, drew back the axe, and waited. The man ducked as Milt brought the axe through, rolling off to one side. Immediately three others surged out of the pack, yowling the same guttural noise; encircling him. The first man slipped seamlessly into the circle to make four. Milt, legs bent, axe poised and cocked, waited.

'They're not real, Milt,' Jess called.

One of the four laughed and spat, the globule landing at her feet.

'That's good, because for a minute there I thought I could smell their stink. No... come to think of it, I still can.'

Jess swallowed and edged a little closer to the four. Milt was right, she too could smell their unwashed bodies, recognized the curious blend of fear and bravado that used to drench her own armpits backstage just before a performance. *Why do they seem so real? Could Aggie have been wrong? How can I doubt what all my senses are telling me?*

"Forget all this. Just stay here with us."

Firming her mouth, Jess's hand closed over the hilt of the angelsword dagger. She felt a ripple of power through her fingers. She held the dagger out in front of her. The four continued to circle Milt; they were stalling for time. Time she didn't have. Waiting until one of the men's backs was toward her, she rushed forward and drove the dagger into his shoulder. She felt the blade slide in, its sharp edge grinding against bone, watched him stiffen, then cry out, trying to turn. Desperately she tried to tug out the blade, but it was embedded up to the hilt. It was wedged, as if the flesh had closed over it and was holding on.

This is real. These men are real.

Jess screamed and jumped back. The dagger remained, sticking out from his oversized shoulder muscles like a handle waiting to be pulled. His eyes locked onto hers and he took a step towards her, his meaty hand cupping his groin as he aped what he planned to do.

Milt was watching, horrified, she could see he was trying to reach her, but the other three cut him off each time, dancing in and out of his guard, feinting and jeering. More of them were coming down the slope now, chanting loudly. They all seemed to have Dragos's voice.

Overhead the hourglass was almost empty, but somehow that seemed almost irrelevant. They couldn't beat these brutes, couldn't make it back to the rock wall anyway. It would be easier to run. Stay here, there was safety further on. She felt that with a certainty she couldn't explain.

There were now more than a dozen men spread out in a huge meandering circle. Almost as many still further up the hill.

What are they waiting for?

She and Milt were back to back inside the circle, moving with them. Milt took a swing at a couple, but they were too fast.

Where was the man she'd stabbed?

She couldn't remember his features, they all seemed to blur. On the ground in front of her, she saw the angelsword dagger, glinting in the sun. There wasn't a trace of blood on it. Swooping on it, Jess snatched it up and brought it over.

'Milt, look. Aggie was right. This is just an elaborate illusion. I stabbed that guy, saw him bleed, look, the knife is clean. They can't really harm us—unless we believe they can. We have to use our will to dispel what we think our senses are telling us. There's nothing really here.'

Milt examined the knife, glanced at the circle of men, and rested the axe head on the ground, handle leaning against his leg. He opened his arms wide.

'Come on then, come and get us—if you can,' he shouted at them. 'Come on!'

The circle slowed, then stopped. None of the men came toward them.

Milt took Jess's arm. 'You're right. They could have swarmed us anytime. It's a ruse; they sure sucked me in. Let's get out of here. We'll walk straight through them, come on.'

He picked up the axe and led the way, still holding her forearm.

Jess hurried to keep up. The circle of men was less than a meter away. They still looked fierce and started yelling, the stench of their breath foul in her nose, closer still. Milt pushed his way through, and Jess followed; it was like walking through a shimmering hologram.

When they'd passed, he turned. 'Just shim sham—bloody realistic though. Who'da thought—'

'Milt,' Jess nudged him. 'Look out.'

Running toward them was who could only be Shea, blackened and burned, swinging the axe-twin of Milt's above his head.

'Uh-oh. This one's real. Stay here.' He ran forward, bringing his own weapon up to parry the killing blow Shea was swinging toward Milt's head. The two axes rang as they clashed. Jess could see the impact jarring through Milt's arms. Shea seemed abnormally strong, and he was very real.

Milt feinted and drove the blunt end of the shiny metal handle against Shea's forehead, forcing him back several paces. Quickly he moved in, using the handle as a club, slamming it against Shea's body twice in quick succession. Jess heard something crack, then all the air whooshed out of Shea's lungs as he doubled over.

Raising the axe above his head, Milt paused too long, and Shea rolled, using the slope to gather speed and spring to his feet near Jess, axe already singing through an arc level with her neck.

Jess screamed and fell to the ground, rolling; she could feel the rush of air as the blade passed just above her. Charging in, Milt managed a clumsy block of the next swing, the clash creating a shower of silver sparks. Shea countered, and Milt lost his grip as Shea's weapon came down on the shaft of Milt's axe. It fell. Jess watched it bounce away as if in slow motion. Shea's lips were long gone—burned away—his mouth in a permanent grimace. It managed to stretch wider, sensing victory.

Jess pushed herself up, and holding her dagger, rushed Shea from the side. Her angle was wrong and while the blade cut, it failed to penetrate deeply, sliding away as it met his ribcage. Shea grunted and batted her away with a bunched fist. She fell at his feet, curling into a ball, hands cupping her head.

There was a thunk—the vibration traveling through her, she waited for the pain, the gush of arterial blood. But nothing came. When she dared look up, Shea was on his knees, Milt's axe hanging from his back as if embedded in a chopping block. Slowly, what used to be Shea toppled forward onto his face.

'Thanks,' she muttered.

'Likewise. Come on, we gotta go.'

The horde of men had vanished. Only Shea remained, dying in the land of the dead.

'What about him?' she asked.

'Too late, in so many ways. Come on.'

They raced up the hill, back to the bridge. The gusting air buffeted them as soon as they reached the ridge. It was colder now; the clouds that previously had hugged the ridge had been sucked into the gorge. Jess was breathing hard; the air cold on its way into her lungs.

'Uh-oh,' Milt said.

'I really hate it when you do that. It always means—oh shit. Is that who I think it is?'

On the opposite side of the abyss, a muscular figure was rapidly sawing the hemp of the handrails. Jess could see the thick woven fibers fraying, whipping wildly in the wind. One side was already severed, hanging limply, flapping at the mercy of the wind.

'He's cutting the bridge. Who is it? I can't make him out?'

'Must be Dragos, the main man.'

'Man?'

'Well, he looks the part. He's certainly sending over mean vibes, I can tell you that. Perps have a way about them that you can sense.'

'Now you fess up to feeling.'

The second rope flapped free. Dragos, hands on his hips, took a breather, daring them to cross.

'He's going to wait until we start coming over and then cut the rest. He's dragging it out, making a show of it.'

'We haven't any time to play games. Remember what Aggie said, this is all a test? Well, what if the biggest test, the thing I had to learn, was faith. Maybe what I've been battling all along was my own fear and insecurity.'

'Meaning?' Milt asked, still preoccupied with staring down Dragos.

'Meaning, what if I believe I really can do this and everything will be okay? Remember what Mary said? "There are many ways to cross the Styx".'

Jess stretched her mouth, drew her lips back and settled the dagger gently between her teeth, then, with a deep inhale, she swan dived straight off the cliff.

TWENTY-SIX

Gone.

Milt yelled, first in surprise, then despair as he watched Jess fall, her clothes fluttering about her like immature, unformed wings. *Could she have really jumped?*

Jess disappeared through the clouds. He waited, expecting to hear something echo back. Only the wind answered.

He glanced across to the other side of what remained of the bridge. Dragos had seen her go as well and seemed equally bemused, but when he caught Milt's eye, he grinned and cut the remaining strands. The bridge slid away, dangling down the cliff face on Milt's side.

Bastard.

Why had she done it?

Slowly, Milt's own perilous position pushed its way through the shock. He was trapped in the dead zone; the only way back was hanging down the opposite rock face like a limp dick.

What had Jess said again? '*It was all a test and she just had to show some faith.*'

That was all very fine and noble, but was it worth jumping off the edge of a mountain for? To prove what? To do what? The only options they'd had were falling—and Dragos almost certainly would have cut the ropes when they were halfway across—waiting, or jumping. She'd chosen the high jump. Now he had to decide. Stay and possibly live here or follow Jess and hope for some sort of salvation net.

If I stayed, would I die? What would be worse? Staying here on my jack for eternity or cutting loose and ending up where I was supposed to go? Obviously, there is somewhere for everyone. At least that question could be ticked off the "who knows" list.

Bloody hell.

Maybe literally.

He chuckled and had to suppress a mad desire to laugh out loud. Not a good sign. He'd never been great on his own for too long, remembering a once-was lover on her way out the door saying that even he couldn't stand his own company. Not entirely true, but pretty damn close. Solitary gave him too much time to think, and after a while without anything to do the white noise would start. Come to think of it, he wasn't all that great for other people to be around either. Except for Lacey. Now even she was beyond his reach, worst case trapped inside her own body.

All his significant others were gone. Carlie... the memory of losing a granddaughter and daughter in the one awful moment was still a wound he'd allowed to fester rather than heal. Then there was Lacey, lost and found, and now Jess. Ah, what the heck. He gripped the axe in both hands, held it straight out in front of him, closed his eyes, and leaned forward, allowing gravity and the weight of the axe to draw him over the edge.

The wind whistled past. It was freezing and exhilarating at the same time.

He forced his eyes to open, seeing the clouds approach, the cold air making his eyes stream. The cloud was so dense it looked like the ground approaching. Beneath that, he had no idea how many hundred meters remained before he hit the wild water, black, flecked with frothy brown where it churned around the outcrops of the shoreline. Was that what he could hear, its gurgling, excited rush? Were they the first fine droplets of spray against his cheeks shooting up from the rapids?

No, it was more likely condensation, his view disappearing for a blink as he passed through the clouds, then, incredibly, he plunged deep into water. *So soon? Nah, way too close.*

He thrashed about, expecting to fight the vicious current, his body tensing for the first impact against a sharp black rock, but the effort just sank him deeper.

The impact had knocked the air from his lungs, and he suppressed an urge to inhale. Instead he slowed his descent by releasing the heavy axe. Slipping off his shoes so he could use his feet more effectively, he kicked, legs scissoring, arms dragging at the water. He could see the surface; that helped. It shimmered with light, which didn't make sense because this water was clear, not black. *Am I imagining this? Have I died and just not realized it?*

His mind screamed for breath. Faster. He bit down onto his tongue in an effort not to take that first, final inhale. Blood pooled in his mouth; he left it there, scared if he swallowed, he might cough. The surface was less than ten meters away; his head was swimming too, only it wasn't toward the surface. Vision clouding; blackening from the edges as the focal area contracted inward. It was either breathe or black out. One part of his mind that was still struggling to clunk on struggled to tell him: five meters. His mouth was now full of blood, he opened it to allow the water to wash it away, and his traitorous lungs gulped at the chance. Water rushed in and down. What little buoyancy he'd had fled, and his ascendency foundered. Desperate, seeing death swimming alongside, and through that knowing life must still flicker within, he somehow managed to kick himself up the final meters to the surface. Lung water spewed from his mouth. Gagging, he managed to draw in one small, ragged breath, which displaced even more water. Coughing to breathe, he leaned his head back, opening his chest, arms wide, floating atop the calm water.

When his breathing had returned to what he could call a relatively normal cycle, he took closer note of his surroundings. While he was definitely midstream in a river, that was as close as the similarity came to the view from the top of the cliff. This place was the polar opposite of what he'd seen—or thought he'd seen—from above, the breadth wide, current slow and languorous with depth, lush rainforest lining either side of the gently sloping banks. Looking up, the cliffs—if they could even be called that now, hilltops more like it—seemed to be within reach. A good "yahoo jump," he'd have called it when he was a kid jumping from a bridge into a river below.

It had been an illusion. All a test. And this must be part of it.

Had Jess known? How could she? But she must have survived, just like him. Where could she have gone?

Treading water, he used his arms to rotate his body, searching both sides of the banks, finally spotting what appeared to be a dark opening in the hill overgrown with plants, but even from here he could see some of them had been pulled aside. What's more, it seemed to be on the side where they'd started. He swam to the bank, clambering over the water-worn rocks in the shallows and onto the coarse river sand. The opening was just above; trampled vegetation led to it through the bush. He followed, his bare city feet protesting at some of the sharp-edged plants. There'd been a time when he could have run over any surface and not felt a thing. Ducking his head, he entered the cave. More sand. Excellent. Small footprints led the way. He followed them until the light gave out, then raising his arms into a T, he trailed first one set of fingers along the wall and then, as the passage narrowed, the other to keep himself in the center. The floor continued to slope upward.

At one point, the fingers on one side lost contact with the wall. Keeping in touch with the other, he shuffled forward, the opposite arm still extended, fingers reaching. Gradually, he became aware of a brush of air against his right cheek. *Not that way*, his mind whispered, remembering the passage down, flashing up an imagined intersection, joining the "where" he'd come from to "where" they'd gone. He turned away from the breeze, and his other hand found the opposite wall. Soon after, he emerged into the cavern. The rock with the lock was still there, but now that whole section of the wall had swung in like a door. Gently, his fingers traced the shape of the hole. He could see how it was the same irregular shape as the dagger's blade, but now instead of being horizontal, the hole ran vertically. The open position. Jess, though, was nowhere to be seen.

He slipped through the gap to the other side of the wall. He wondered whether this was another one of those dimensions they kept talking about. *Forget it, just move.*

The space opened into a larger chamber, rock walls sheer and high, narrowing in toward the top where light filtered in from a small opening, revealing an irregular glimpse of blue sky above. At floor level, the cavern was circular, and carved into the walls were five concave areas. A small candle burned in each, some strongly, others almost guttering out. Milt followed the small footprints in the sandy floor to one of them. The candle here was new and burning strongly. Chiseled into the smooth curved section was one word: Aquarius.

That was the water one, wasn't it?

The footprints continued following the perimeter of the chamber, their direction changing to face the next carved section: Cornucopia. Here too the candle was strong and bright. The same followed for Air in the next, but when he reached Fire, the candle, paradoxically, had burnt right down and was barely alight; old wax thick at the base, clinging to the sides of the ancient candle holder.

Milt crouched down, looking at the footprints. Rather than simply facing the rock as they'd done at the other three, here they were scuffed and, more concerning, there appeared to be another set —broader and longer.

He wondered what a demon's footprint looked like, then realized he was probably still inhabiting the body he had from the last time he was let loose.

At a guess, it seemed Jess had managed to do whatever she'd had to do at the first few, but it looked like Dragos had caught up with her here. He glanced quickly over at the remaining section. That had to be the one that controlled the demon gate; its candle too was almost out.

What now?

'Jess,' he yelled, his voice loud, echoing hollowly in the large, empty space, not caring whether Dragos heard him. All the better if he did, maybe he'd stop whatever atrocity he was doing. *Where the hell is she?*

Grunting, he pushed himself up, noticing as he did so something glinting in the wall. He paused, reaching out to touch it, recognizing the handle of Jess's dagger. It was embedded there, inserted all the way to the hilt in an opening the same as the one outside. Gingerly he gripped the handle, feeling a flicker of energy run through his fingers. On impulse, he applied pressure and tried to rotate the handle first one way—nothing—and then the other. He felt it give slightly, like a reluctant, irregularly used lock, finally clicking when it reached verti-cal. The whole section of wall opened inward, revealing a smaller chamber. In the center was a flat rock upon which rested what looked to be an old parchment. The Scroll? Reluctant to enter without a weapon, Milt eased the dagger free, ready to slam it back in if the door began to shut. Nothing happened. Narrowing his eyes, he peered into the cavern, the ambient light from the larger room leaking in.

'Jess? You in here?' he said, his voice quieter now but still too loud.

'Milt?'

'Where are you?'

'Back here. Oh, thank all that's good that you followed, I was so scared you wouldn't.'

He stepped further inside and looked around behind the door. Dimly he could make out her shape. She appeared to be hanging from the rock wall.

'You know me, I'll yell Geronimo and jump off a cliff after anyone. Are you all right?' He hurried over to her.

'Yes, apart from these chains. What the heck does Geronimo mean anyway?'

'It's a generational thing. For me it means commitment—to the death. Risk everything and go for it,' he said absently, examining the chains.

Jess was attached to the wall by her ankles and wrists, the chains and manacles black and heavy.

'Where is he?' Milt asked, scanning the room.

'Gone. He's waiting for the two remaining candles to go out. I managed to activate three of them, but.... Milt, you have to get me free somehow....'

'Did he have a key?' Milt asked, running his fingers across the manacles. The surface was completely smooth. 'How do they open?'

'I don't know. He attacked me from behind as soon as the wall opened. I must have hit my head when I fell, because when I came to, he was attaching the last of these chains to my ankle. He said something about it being ironic that the ones who bound him in them for life should now learn how to die in them. I think they must be the chains the Sisters used on him.'

'No help. I wish I had that bloody axe. I dropped it in the river.'

'But, you can,' she said, her voice excited. 'Don't you remember? Old Mary said you could access it any time, if it's become part of you. Try, Milt, oh please just try.'

He had a vague recollection of what she was saying, but it butted up hard against his reality. Lately though, that line in the sand seemed to shift any old damn time it chose.

'All right, I'll try. I'm not real good with this stuff though.'

'Maybe I can help,' she said. She paused, gathering her thoughts, then she spoke, her voice low. 'Allow an image of it to form in your mind, let it build. Feel the texture of the handle, its coolness against your skin. Test the sharpness of the blades with the back of your thumb. Recognize the weight. You know it intimately, the perfect balance. Imagine it in your hand, an extension of your arm as if it's always been there and always will be whenever you want it to. Want it to now.'

Milt did his best. Her words helped; he could almost feel it there for a moment, then it was gone as if it had never been.

'Again. Try again. We almost had it.'

This time he sank into the words, allowed the image to form, then really felt the sensation of the axe in his hand, and it was there.

'It worked,' he said, unable to quite believe it himself as he brought it up for her to see.

'Now see if it is truly magic. See if it will cut me free.'

Milt positioned himself beside the wall, raising the axe above his head. The manacles were separated from the wall by a large spike that had been driven into the rock. He swung, angling the head in to meet the point where the wall met the spike. The mighty axe blade sliced straight through.

'I'll be damned.'

'Not if you hurry.'

Milt made short work of the other three. The manacles and chains were still attached, but at least she was free of the wall. Jess hurried over to the rock in the center of the room and gently picked up the Scroll. The candlelight was now so dim she had to take the Scroll outside to read it, the ankle chains dragging in the sand behind her. Milt followed, axe ready in case Dragos was waiting. The chamber was empty, the large footprints leading away down another passage. Milt was tempted to follow them but protecting Jess was the most important thing at the moment.

She angled the parchment to catch the last of the sputtering glow and began to read, her actor's voice strong and powerful, rebounding off the rock walls. With each line, the light became clearer, until with a final flourish the candle seemed to renew, lengthening and burning with a steady light. In the smaller chamber, the whole back wall was afire, its warm brightness sending flickering reds and oranges over the walls.

'What the hell.'

'It's been the same in all the others. The Aquarius one had a huge waterfall all along the back wall after I finished. It was incredible.'

'Come on, one to go. The most important one, remember.'

They hurried back out, Milt using the dagger in the hole to lock the rock wall door, then handed it to Jess.

'Funny how it's all coming together now.'

'As if you were born to it,' he said dryly, following her to the last carved station. They were almost like small altars.

The last candle was sputtering, its flame flaring in a pool of melted wax.

'That can't be good.'

'No, I'd better—' Jess staggered as something hit the side of her head.

'Jess!' Milt caught her before she fell. She was breathing, but out cold. A splatter of blood indicated where the rock had struck. Milt put the axe down and crouched over her, checking for a pulse.

'Such a pity, and after all your good work too.'

Milt spun around, following the direction of the voice.

'What have you done to her?' Milt yelled. Dragos was a little over five meters away, absently tossing a solid-looking ball from one hand to the other.

'A little psychic knock. Nothing serious. Not yet anyhow. She'll make an excellent vessel. This one I've been using is getting a little old and battered. I didn't want to damage her too much that's why I hung her on the wall to wait for me.'

Dragos was taller than Milt, and the body he occupied looked much younger. He stood, positioning himself between her and Dragos, tensioning his legs, bending into a defensive crouch.

'Ah, the reluctant Protector, even to the end,' Dragos said. 'Far too late, of course. But I admire your... dumb persistence.'

'Then admire this, arsehole.' Milt imagined the axe, and immediately it appeared in his hands. Dragos looked mildly surprised.

Milt's circle of focus centered. He allowed the background to fade, now noting every movement of his opponent. With Jess out for the count, all Dragos had to do was keep Milt engaged until the candle went out. The portal would open automatically.

Dragos yawned, then with a blur of movement he threw the other rock he'd been holding straight at Milt. Milt ducked and brought the axe up at the same time. His arms jerked with the impact against the rock, and a high-pitched whine, much like that of a ricocheting bullet, screamed through the cavern, hitting the wall several times before dropping to the ground.

'Missed,' Milt said, trying not to let the shakiness show in his voice, hefting the axe higher.

He chanced a quick glance down at Jess. She was still breathing. The candle flame adjacent to the gate flickered. He thought he could detect a faint rumble.

'My horde grows inpatient. They're waiting. On the other side of the inside gate. Did I tell you that he who manages to open the fifth gate is automatically king of the Akashic realm? And for that matter, of your world too.'

'Not if I've got anything to say about, you won't be.'

'Ready then? This shouldn't take long,' Dragos said, as if he were an instructor and Milt the dimwitted student.

'When I was a cocky constable, my old sergeant told me arrogance would get me killed. It was only a matter of time,' Milt said. 'It nearly did too. I'd say you're way over your arrogance quota, buddy.'

'Everything is only a matter of time mortal; the only question is how much—present company excepted.' Dragos laughed, 'Like young Carlie and your "other" daughter—what was her name? They didn't seem to get quite enough time, did they, Detective?' He made it sound like "Defective." 'A real shame.' Dragos shook his head, his mouth a mocking counterpoint.

Milt felt his blood rise. He recognized the surge of rage and did his best to bank it down. Running at Dragos through a red fog would only lead to a faster death.

'She was ridiculously easy to kill, you know, your "other" daughter,' Dragos said as if in afterthought.

'What did you say?' Milt's voice was choked with the rage in his chest.

'I said I killed her, or rather I had that fool truck driver do it for me.'

'What are you talking about? They had nothing to do with any of this.'

'You were the Protector. I'd hoped that by disabling you early, it would make it easier later.'

Part of Milt realized that Dragos was goading him, lying to make him do something rash. He had a rep in the force for going off like New Year's fireworks over much less. Dragos hadn't known Jess was the Messenger, much less her relationship to him back then. He was goading him. Probing old raw wounds with red-hot needles of guilt. Plucking unresolved emotional gunk straight from his head.

Shunting the rage to one side, he searched for something else to focus on. He had no doubt the banked anger would come in handy, but it had to be directed, not just released blindly.

He forced himself into the calm space he found before any fight, realizing that Dragos wouldn't initiate the attack. He was just as happy to drag it out and wait for the candle to go out. Milt had to be the one to take the initiative.

He brought his axe up, swinging it through a horizontal figure eight, allowing the angle to vary as the momentum of the pattern increased. The air whooshed with the passage of the fine steel. It was a complicated move but strangely he didn't feel the effort; the axe seemed to have a life and lift of its own, seeming to anticipate the trajectory pattern. Dragos took a measured step sideways, bringing his body side on, his own identical axe magically appearing in his hands.

The demon flipped his axe into the air, catching it at the very end of the handle, and began spinning Sufi-like in a circle, large feet pivoting, axe blade quickly becoming a blur at the end of his extended arms. Milt's figure eight tightened, becoming even faster, making the position of his axe blade impossible to see or predict where it would be. All he could make out at the end of his hands was a silvery blur.

When the blades struck, the sound echoed off the rocky wall. Milt's arms shuddered with the impact, the vibration traveling down through his body and out through the soles of his feet. The figure eight pattern somehow continued, helping him to maintain his balance. The impact, however, had made Dragos stumble. Milt moved in, trying to gain advantage before the demon could recover. As his axe came within range, Dragos pivoted and bent his body back at an impossible angle while reversing the direction of his axe swing, a combined movement Milt would have thought impossible unless he'd seen it. Too late, he realized that Dragos's stumble had been a bluff to draw him in.

The blades slammed together again, this time in a showering flurry of silver sparks. Milt was off-balance and he stumbled, the momentum of his huge axe dragging him toward the floor. Dragos advanced, his smile wide, changing his grip on the axe so that it clipped Milt's using a parallel trajectory. It was enough for the combined momentum to send Milt's axe spinning away.

Dragos laughed. 'You were saying something about arrogance?' he said. Milt was on his back, hands and heels scrabbling in the sand as he shoved himself out of range while mentally summoning the axe.

Dragos's eyes widened as he intuited what Milt was trying to do.

'Not this time. You see what you did, you naughty Defective,' Dragos said, pointing up.

Despite himself, his gaze followed. His axe head was buried deep in the rock wall.

'Your axe might be able to sever steel, but these cursed walls are enchanted. Why do you think I was held down here for so long? All a matter of time—as you said—and unfortunately for you, Defective Protector, yours has definitely run out.'

Milt positioned himself in front of Jess. Breath heaving, on all fours, he felt like a baited bear protecting his cub. Jess stirred. He could see she was breathing evenly, her eyelids fluttering. She'd be coming round soon.

Dragos seemed to be enjoying Milt's discomfort. He was like a cat teasing a mouse.

A matter of time.

The candle beside the Akashic gate guttered, making a sucking noise before bravely flickering again. It must only have seconds remaining.

Milt glimpsed something near his left hand, half buried in the sand.

Jess's dagger.

Subtly he shifted his weight, his hand moving over the dagger, pushing it deeper into the sand as his fingers closed around the hilt.

He made a show of trying to imagine the axe again. It vibrated against the wall but remined stuck. Dragos laughed and took a step forward.

Milt tensed his shoulder and leg muscles, waiting for Dragos to raise his foot to take the next step, and then launched himself toward him, driving his shoulder deep into the demon's abdomen, hoping to push him off-balance. It was all hard muscle but he heard a satisfying whoosh as Dragos's lungs emptied. Milt had played front row rugby for years and knew what it took to bring a man down.

A man, but not a demon. Dragos staggered but remained on his feet. In reflex, Milt drove the small blade into Dragos's foot, but it hit bone and glanced away. There was barely a cut when he pulled out the blade. There was pain though. Dragos howled with rage. Purplish stuff was flowing from it.

'Milt?'

Jess.

He turned reflexively. Jess was sitting up, eyes groggy, but seemed okay.

'Milt, look out. Behind you!' She yelled.

Milt threw himself down. He heard the deadly whoosh of air as the axe passed over him. Spitting sand from his mouth, he rolled toward Jess before Dragos could change the angle of the axe for the next strike.

Jess was standing.

'Geronimo! Jess! Geronimo!' he shouted, flipping her the dagger, pointing at the wall. At the same time, he threw himself at Dragos, but this time the demon was ready, the axe already coming down, the blade biting through Milt's arm, severing the hand. He saw it fall onto the sand, flopping there, palm up. Ignoring it, Milt drove himself forward, encircling Dragos's midsection with his arms. There was a warm sharpness on his arm but blissfully no pain. Not yet. He had a few seconds for that to fully register. He hung on grimly to Dragos's midsection and hoped Jess had picked up on the Geronimo thing.

This would be his final scene. His measly life was all he had to offer her. He hoped it had been enough.

Unable to swing the axe, Dragos drove the butt of the axe handle into Milt's upper back repeatedly. Gritting his teeth, Milt held on, determinedly using his bulk like a front row forward in a rugby pack, determinedly driving Dragos back.

Off to the side, he heard Jess chanting, the sound strong and loud in the chamber.

'Noooo.' He felt the demon's frustration course through his body as Jess turned the dagger in the wall, locking down the Akashic portal. The candle flame leapt up, renewed.

Milt's strength, though, was leaking away. His grip loosened, arms sliding down Dragos's legs. The demon howled again, and taking a fistful of hair, tossed Milt against the wall. He felt something crack as he hit. The pain registered, but oddly he didn't really feel it. There was still too much adrenaline in his system.

Dragos limped over to intercept Jess, the axe already cocked at the apex of the backswing, ready to finish her. From the portal, Jess turned to face the snarling demon, the dagger upraised in her hand.

'Run, Jess,' Milt yelled, trying to clamber to his feet. Nothing worked. The best he could do was lean against the wall, arms hanging uselessly at his side, and watch as Dragos thundered toward her. He waited for Jess to dive out of the way, but she didn't move.

'Run.' The sound was barely audible this time. He tried to struggle up but fell to his knees, dimly registering that his trunk and knees were wet yet somehow warm and chillingly cold at the same time. When the axe was almost on her, Jess sprang directly at Dragos, coming in just under the blade's arc, managing to drive the dagger deep into the side of Dragos's neck, dragging the wound open with her weight as she sank to the floor and rolled to the side.

Purple liquid fire poured from the jagged gash in Dragos's neck. He squealed like a stuck pig. Jess scampered away. Dragos tried to give chase but the fire had spread to his clothing. He was burning in his own blood.

Milt fell facedown into the sand.

TWENTY-SEVEN

The sun was setting, radiating red-tinged promises to return, the surrounding mountains already drawing in the night like a shawl around their shoulders. Jess turned from the window, allowing the curtains to fall back, and folded her arms. The chill was already here, ever ready, like 'them,' she supposed, waiting on the other side of the Fifth Gate, frustrated beyond measure but prepared to wait again, a little more. After all, they'd come so close this time.

Was this how Mary had become "old," her youth leached from her by this house, waiting, keeping constant watch in case any had slipped through? Was that to be Jess's own fate now as well? The sisters needed her. What few of them remained had said so, asked her to stay. Be the new leader. What would that be like, to belong? Could she avoid becoming like Aggie or old Mary?

Midnight swaggered in, tail high, and curled up in front of the fire. Jess felt the corners of her mouth tug up and her concern soften. She went over and knelt by the cat, stroking its glossy fur, mind drifting as she stared into the fire.

Dragos was dead. Other than that, she just wasn't sure of

anything. None of them were. They were, after all, simply watchers, waiting.

Midnight started, sitting up suddenly, ears pricked. No raised hackles, so it wasn't a threat, and Jess allowed the stress reaction to bleed away. How long would that take to ease off?

Someone was coming though. Now she could hear the footsteps, hurried and heavy coming down the stairs. The door opened suddenly. It was Wallace, eyes wide and hopeful. 'He's awake.'

Jess bolted past her and up the stairs, pausing at the door at the top.

Milt was still pale, as if the blood he'd lost hadn't been replaced, as if the multiple transfusions hadn't taken and were siphoned off somewhere waiting in reserve. The Sisters' doctor, looked less pessimistic than she had when they'd brought Milt here from their hospital four days ago.

She paused, uncertain, at the door. 'Hey there.'

'Hey yourself,' he managed, though his eyes were shining. She hadn't seen them in over a fortnight. Missed them.

'I thought you were going to sleep the whole month away.'

She felt Wallace hovering behind her and moved further into the room, going over to one of the chairs beside the bed. They'd taken turns on what they had been warned by the Sisters' own specialist could have been a deathwatch. One they'd insisted be held at Old Mary's home, where the healing vibrations were strongest.

Every day he survived had meant a slow improvement. She gripped his hand and felt a light but reassuring squeeze in return. Wallace appeared on the other side of the bed, raising her hand as well but allowing it instead to flutter and finally settle on the heavy padded dressing on his forearm. Jess felt she could read Milt's intention of taking Wallace's hand too, realizing finally that it couldn't happen when he glanced down and saw his bandaged stump.

'Looks like I'll be a bit short on the left-hand jabs now,' he said, shrugging, then winced as the arm moved. 'Shame I didn't throw this one in the freezer. I guess that's what someone clever might call ironic. This whole thing started with a severed left hand.'

'Someone clever would be able to spell it too.' Wallace clucked, settling him back against the thick pillows. 'You're lucky to even be here to see it. You lost so much blood.'

'You don't have to tell me. I'm the one on the wearing this battered old carcass. I can see you made it back all right,' he said, squinting into Wallace's eyes. 'Is it really you?'

'You asked me that last time you came to. What can I say, yes.'

'And to think I haven't even asked you that particular question yet,' he whispered.

Wallace colored.

He turned to Jess. 'What happened?'

'I swore once that I'd never take a human life—but apparently that didn't include evil entities.' She smiled. 'You were threatening to bleed out though, so I used the dagger to channel poor Wallace here a mental bolt to wake her up. I used your belt as a tourniquet until she got there.'

Wallace picked up the story. 'All I could hear was "help—Lucas cave" and "wounded." When I raced up there, luckily an emergency team was already in the cave searching for you. I managed to convince them you'd managed to phone me giving me a description of exactly where you were.'

'Weren't we in some other bloody dimension, or something?'

'We were,' Jess said, 'but that all shifted and changed when Dragos died. The body he was in just burned up to nothing, and the Elemental Scroll portals vanished into plain rock walls along with those axes. Wallace was able to tune in to me and led the rescue team straight there. Your injuries took some explaining. I said you'd fallen onto your knife trying to scale some rocks to find a way out.'

'That sounds a little unlikely,' Milt said.

'I had to use some of Gran's hyper suggestions to bring them around to that way of thinking. It wasn't easy. Then I remembered some of our Sisters were doctors in Sydney, so I called them. They took over your treatment and had you transferred to a specialist facility,' Wallace added.

Raindrops pattered against the large sash window, and Wallace hurried over to shut it. They all listened for a moment, appreciating the sound and what it meant.

'It's still raining, so I guess you did it?' he asked finally, his voice weak, eyes heavy.

'Yes, Milt. We all did.'

'Then thank Christ we won't have to do that for another century or so,' he whispered.

STAR GALLERY

My books pass through the hands of many stars before they're ready for publication. Some are clever, others kind, still more incredibly talented. Here are a few thank you's, in no particular order:

The title
Deb Kelly
Copy editor
Olivia Ventura
Cover art
Claire Smith@Booksmith Design
Promotion and all round enthusiasm
Zali:Bespoke Social Media
Support and encouragement
Fiona McIntosh
Readers
Jason Nahrung, Mark Curtis, Deb Kelly, Russell Cornhill, Helen Stubbs, Deb Kelly, Kathy Stewart, Kirsty Cramer, Sue Reynolds.

ABOUT THE AUTHOR

Jack lives on the Blackall Range in the beautiful Sunshine Coast hinterland

In addition to writing Jack is also a registered Yoga Therapist, loves bushwalking and is due to complete a masters in Gestalt Therapy.

Mine the Darkness is Jack's fourth book.

ALSO BY JACK GARRETY

The Seventh Wave (writing as Paul Garrety)

The Emerald Tablets (writing as paul Garrety)

Last Caravan to Carmelsara

http://jackgarrety.com

Coming Soon:

In the Broken Places (mid 2020)